Jenny Pattrick is a writer and jeweller who lives in Wellington, New Zealand. She has written fiction and commentary for radio and, with her musician husband, Laughton, songs and musical shows for children. This is her first novel, and she has since published a sequel, *Heart of Coal*.

The Denniston Rose

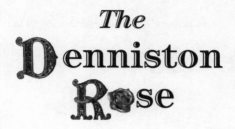

JENNY PATTRICK

National Library of New Zealand Cataloguing-in-Publication Data

Pattrick, Jenny, 1936-
The Denniston rose / Jenny Pattrick.
ISBN 1-86941-561-2
I. Title.
NZ823.2—dc 21

A BLACK SWAN BOOK
published by
Random House New Zealand
18 Poland Road, Glenfield, Auckland, New Zealand
www.randomhouse.co.nz

First published 2003, reprinted 2003 (five times), 2004 (five times),
2005 (twice), 2006

ISBN 1 86941 561 2

Design: Elin Termannsen
Cover design: Matthew Trbuhovic
Cover photographs:
Front: model - Erin Auchterlonie, photographer - Wade Auchterlonie
Front: view of Burnetts Face, 1907, Alexander Turnbull Library, Wellington
        F-8501-1/2-
Back: view from the top of the Denniston Incline Tramway, c 1885-1910, by
        Henry Thomas Lock, Alexander Turnbull Library, Wellington,
        F-35121-1/2-
Printed in Australia by Griffin Press

For Laughton

ACKNOWLEDGEMENTS

I would like to pay tribute to the late Geoff Kitchin, Denniston miner, son, grandson and great-grandson of Denniston miners, who walked me all over the now-deserted plateau where the settlements of Denniston, Burnett's Face and the Camp once thrived. Geoff breathed life into every lone chimney and homeless doorstep; he demonstrated how the rope-road worked and showed me the entrances of long-abandoned mines. His knowledge of early mining methods and his wonderful collection of historical photographs and documents was invaluable.

Also my thanks to Anna Rogers and Ian Watt, whose advice and encouragement kept me going and on track, and to Rachel Scott for the clarity and good sense of her editing.

And, of course, to Harriet Allan and Random House for taking a punt on me.

Denniston is a real coal-mining town, now deserted, on a high, barren plateau above the West Coast of the South Island of New Zealand.

In my story, events on 'the Hill' in the 1880s are as accurate as I could make them. The isolation, the appalling climate, the tyranny of the Denniston Incline (which was the only means of access), the circumstances leading to New Zealand's first miners' strike are all historical facts.

The people on the other hand are pure fiction. I apologise to the descendants of those tough men and women — mine managers, teachers, businessmen and colliers — whose real-life positions my characters have usurped. I hope the imaginary characters have inherited some of the spirit of those true pioneers.

Damn Denniston
Damn the track
Damn the way both there and back
Damn the wind and damn the weather
God damn Denniston altogether.

From J.T. Ward, 'Recollections of a Lifetime on the West Coast of the South Island', *Westport News*, 21/9/1884

CONTENTS

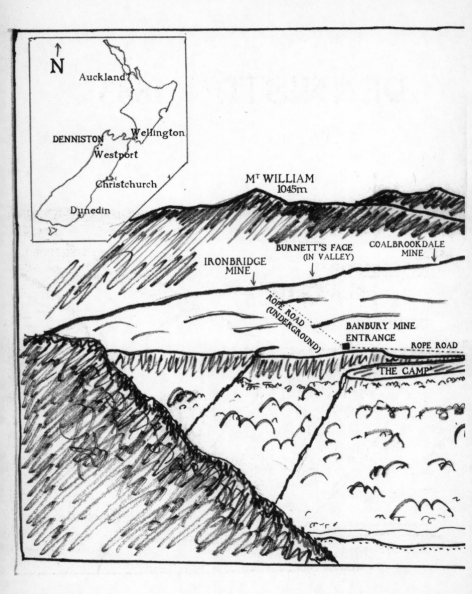

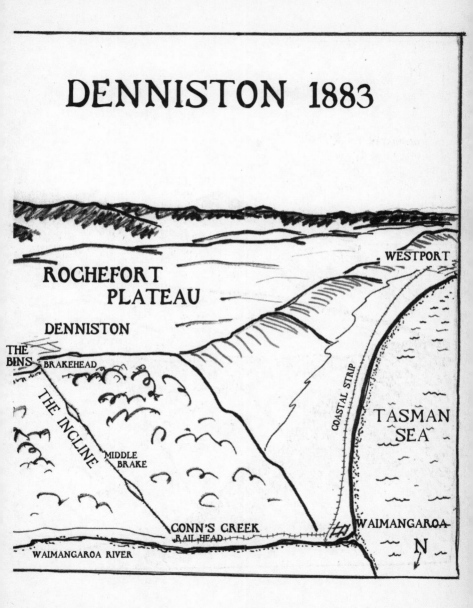

DENNISTON 1883

WESTPORT

ROCHEFORT
PLATEAU

DENNISTON

THE
BINS

BRAKEHEAD

THE INCLINE

MIDDLE
BRAKE

CONN'S CREEK
RAIL HEAD

WAIMANGAROA RIVER

COASTAL STRIP

TASMAN
SEA

WAIMANGAROA

N

Arrivals

Rose

ROSE OF TRALEE and her mother arrived on the Hill at night during a storm. Con the Brake insisted it was the worst storm of '82; possibly even since the mine opened, though that was hotly debated. There were, after all, plenty of good examples to argue over. Like the one in 1880, where the wind, screaming unchecked over that dead plateau, drove hail thirty feet into Banbury mine, sending young Jimmy Cotter, who fancied it was a cave-in, screaming for the entrance. Or those terrible three days — January, was it? — the next year: thirty inches of rain in thirty-six hours and mud up to your knees around the Brake Head. That was the same storm blew one of the new miners' tents, wooden floor and all, off the Camp and down into the gully, taking Tom Garter and Willie Huff with it. You couldn't have a worse storm than that. *And* they closed the Incline that time.

Con the Brake had never been known to concede a point in an argument.

'Well,' he would say, hammering his great fist on the rough plank that served as Red Minifie's bar table, 'they should have closed it the night Rose arrived. Running loaded wagons down the Incline was tricky enough in broad daylight, you know, with no wind. Only that night there was a bloody order to fill, remember, and the Company facing ruin, and naturally those mean bastards put money ahead of men's safety every time. You know it's the truth!'

It's true anyway that the weather was bad that night. A gale-force westerly came straight off the sea, heavy with salt and rain. Down there at sea level, on the narrow band of swampy land, trapped between black mountains and stormy sea, in the tiny settlement of Waimangaroa, unpainted iron on the new Company houses heaved and squealed against nails not yet settled in. The storm roared inland, over the town, over the flat coastal strip, straight up the gully towards the mountains. In the gorge the river rose and ran oily with a mixture of mud and coal-slack. Great ancient beech trees groaned, their slapping branches showering tiny leaves into the shrieking air. At the head of the gully the wind butted, whump! into the black rampart of the escarpment, bent almost vertical and raced on up, two thousand feet up, howling all the way, up to Denniston.

Rose's mother never said why she chose to arrive at night, let alone in that storm. In another town, people would worry away at a mystery like that, gnawing at the hard, bright bone, over teacups and white lace tablecloth. But plenty of people at Denniston had secrets. There was a saying that every living soul on the Hill had been chased up there — by the law or some other fury; that they escaped onto that desolate plateau and then somehow mutated, like a tough breed of goats, into a race that actually enjoyed mist and cold and isolation. The recruited English miners would be an exception perhaps — no secrets there. They were on the Hill to work — to hew coal and get on with it. Con the Brake, himself a walking treasure-chest of secrets, would say that generations underground in the Midlands had mutated the English miners before they arrived.

So no one knew what brought Rose's mother. She must've been desperate, that was obvious, considering who she was coming to join, and the manner of her arrival, but you didn't ask nosy questions on the Hill, and she never offered a reason. Not to folk who might pass on the gossip, anyway. Rose's mother was never one you could have a normal chat with. There was some kind of angry fire burning in that woman, a fire that had been damped down with too much slack. Most of the time she smouldered away in some private world of her own; walked past as if the rest of the world didn't exist. If she decided to speak, the words blazed out — shreds and tatters of speech, not decent sentences you could respond to. A hint of some foreign lingo underlying her words. Also a touch of madness. An embarrassing woman, was the general opinion, with her shouts, snorts of laughter, hands in all directions. Who would know whether she was enjoying herself or in a furious temper? The truth was, Rose's mother was always too difficult, too uncomfortable. Would it have made a difference if one of the other women had befriended her? It's debatable.

Con the Brake, on the other hand, every bit as foreign as Rose's mother, with a past every bit as mysterious, was as open as the sea with his friendships and favours. That night might not have been the best moment to judge, mind you. Being on duty on such a night would strain the good nature of a saint. Never one to hold back in the words department, Con let loose a good flow in at least two languages, shouting and cursing at the blinding rain, the money-grubbing mine manager, the icy-cold iron of the brake controls. Rain and hail blinded the little window of the brake-shed.

He risked leaving, for a moment, the two handles that had become, over the past two years, like extensions of his own arms. Out on the platform he peered down the rails over the edge of the bluff. The lantern, swinging on the tail of the descending loaded wagon, had disappeared into the storm. Somewhere below, the empty wagon was rising in the wild dark, its lantern equally obliterated.

'Shut your mouth!' yells Con the Brake to the hook-man. Con's temper frays to a strand under pressure. 'How can a bod count if you yak?'

The hook-man, in dripping oilskins and dripping moustache, shrugs and turns away. If Con can curse while he counts, you'd think he could pass the time of day too. But no one wants to be responsible for an accident. Better to stay mum. He taps a wooden chock, testing its fit against the wheels of the waiting full wagon, then crouches under its sloping metal side, taking what cover he can from the storm.

Back in the shed, Con counts seconds in some other language. A new-fangled invention, attached to the drum, is supposed to tell him the position of the wagon, but he doesn't trust the thing. A man's experience and judgement is better in a storm like this. His great fists handle the wheels with surprising delicacy. These wheels, smaller than wagon wheels but similar, are mounted, waist high, horizontal to the concrete floor. On each, a knob like a cheerful thumb tucks into Con's paw. He turns one wheel a quarter, the other less. Cold water flows into the pistons, cooling them. Towering behind him, the great winding drum slows, and slows again. Better safe than sorry tonight. The wire rope, snaking round and round the drum, and quivering with the tension of its two burdens — a descending full wagon and an ascending empty one — groans as it gives out more slowly on the Company side, takes up at the same slowing speed on the donkey. This time the empty wagon is being hauled up on the donkey side. That's the north. Why donkey is a mystery. Company you can understand. Nearer to Westport, 'the Cardiff of the South Seas', where the streets are straight, where the manager wears a clean shirt every day and lives with his wife in his comfortable, dry home.

Con the Brake and the hook-man are both peering into the howling darkness. Con hoping to hell he's got the timing right and not slowed the bloody thing too soon, John Gantry Senior, hook-man, waiting to uncouple the empty, hook up the full one, and run the empty on down to the Bins for reloading. Four more full wagons and the shift's over, please God and good luck.

First they see a pale halo of light rising through cloud and rain. The lantern's wagging back and forth in the wind as if signalling a disaster. Con grunts. Timing's right enough. He winds with a will now, and the great brake-drum groans. If the wagon comes over too fast John Gantry could be history and Con out of a job. Con nods grimly — good, good, here she comes nice and sweet over the brow.

Next they see, like some unlikely ghost story, a pale face swimming in and out of the rain and mist. Holy Mary, there's someone coming up in the wagon! A woman by the shape of the hat and the size of her. Not crouching down, taking what cover she might from the sloping metal sides, but upright, straight as a tree and grim. She comes up inside the wagon, clinging to the leading side as if it were a ship's prow, feet apart like a man, leaning her good black coat into the rusty metal. Both arms are stretched wide, hooked over the lip to hold her firm against the steep grade and the storm. A plume of coal-slack, whipped off the descending wagon as it roared down past her, must have caught her full in the face. Now, rain and wind have etched lines in the sooty mask. Her skin is a shifting landscape like moonlight on a dark river.

The woman stares ahead, the one still thing in this buffeting night. That wagon, rising up an impossible slope on a filthy night, is most definitely in her charge.

Metal wheels squeal on wet rails; the wagon comes level and mounts the siding ramp. Even Con the Brake is silenced by the apparition. John Gantry Senior stands in awe. For a single moment the woman turns her head and looks down at Con. He jerks violently as if an electric current has struck up at him through his controls. Then the bell announcing the safe arrival, at Middle Brake, of the full wagon reminds them all that nothing waits for the Company. Even the woman seems to know this. She stands braced while the streaming hook-man knocks out the pin, heaves the great metal hook from its socket and lays it on the ground. He pushes her wagon gently ahead toward the Bins and goes back to the hook. Grunting with the effort — no one's going to tell him he's getting past it — he drags the heavy hook and its four-inch cable over to the full wagon, waiting poised on the edge. First he uncouples the safety rope. Now he rams the hook home and drives in the locking pin. Last, he taps out the chock from under the wheels and gives Con the nod. Bells ring. The great drum groans and turns; the cable leaps up and snaps taut. The wagon moves. Four minutes on the dot seven more ton of bright coal hurtles down, down, to Middle Brake and then on down to Conn's Creek. The Denniston Incline, Engineering Masterpiece, Eighth Wonder of the Modern World: eighteen hundred feet in two near-vertical drops.

With his hands still on the controls, counting still, Con watches over his shoulder. He is shaking. In the wavering light from the Pumphouse lamps he sees the woman reach down into her wagon. She hands out three wet bundles which John places carefully on the mud of the siding. The first is a brown leather suitcase, battered but decent. Then comes a large bundle — linen perhaps — wrapped in tarpaulin and tied with string. The third, also wrapped in tarpaulin, is a child. A small hole cut in the stiff canvas shows a wet face with sharp, interested eyes. String, tied under the child's chin and around the back of her neck, turns the square of tarpaulin into a dark hood and cape.

'Ah Jesus!' Con moans. 'Jesus!'

The mother hands her out like any other parcel. John Gantry Senior takes the child gently as a handful of suds and puts her little boots on the driest patch he can find. She stands by the other luggage, hardly distinguishable in shape and size, but a wonder to Con and the hook-man.

The mother takes John's offered hand; allows herself to be lowered to the ground. She bellows words into the wind and Con can see by the way John shrugs that he hasn't heard. The woman pushes back her streaming hair in a gesture familiar to Con and shouts again. This time John gathers the gist. She's asking for Jimmy Cork's place.

John Gantry Senior looks sharply over to Con the Brake, who stares down the rail, pretending he hasn't heard.

'Jesus save us all,' mutters Con. 'And especially me.'

Later that night, Con, washed and night-gowned, slides his tree-trunk of a body between clean sheets and wakes up the woman, soft and warm as dough, who is the joy of his life and is known on Denniston as Mrs C. Rasmussen, Con the Brake's wife. She explodes.

'What?' she shouts so half the men's quarters can hear. 'You never sent a woman and child over to Jimmy Cork's!'

'What could we do?' mumbles Con into the great welcoming bosom. 'Hook-man try, all right. He say to her it's a bitty late for a visit. Tell her she might stay at Hanrattys' till morning.'

Mrs C. Rasmussen snorts. 'A woman arriving in the middle of the night is not going to have money for boarding houses.'

'Totty would not turn her away.' Con's hands are gentle on his wife, but the picture of that woman still burns. Maybe it wasn't Angel. Surely that woman would never bed up with Jimmy Cork. All that soot and rain — how could he recognise any poor soul? No, no, that bad storm has spooked him, is all.

Mrs Rasmussen groans. 'The child, the child!'

Con's great bleak face, cracked and craggy as fjords in winter, softens into a warmer, rounder landscape. 'The child,' he says and he kneads his woman's — his wife's — lovely flesh, 'The child smiled at us as if she were out on a Sunday picnic. Terror, you wouldn't be surprised. Or tears, you know? All you could see was two eyes and a bitty yellow hair, but that smile — it was like sun coming out, I'm saying it.'

'They went to Jimmy Cork's?' demands Mrs C. Rasmussen, withholding favours till she knows the worst: what chaos might need putting to rights in the morning.

'They did, woman,' mutters Con, hard and ready for her. He is ashamed of his urgency. It won't be her, please Jesus it won't. 'To Jimmy's. Now let be. I'd say they were survivors both. Like we two.'

'Like us,' corrects Mrs C. Rasmussen, but lets be.

Evangeline Strauss
and Jimmy (Cork)

IF ANY ONE moment in those dreadful two days might have dented Lenie Strauss's indomitable will, this would be it — when she took the direction indicated by the hook-man, and floundered her way through rain, mud and goodness knows what stinking else towards some distant tent. A tent, he said! What use was a tent in all this wild weather? If she weren't so cold she might have sat down and wept. In four years — five nearly — Jimmy could surely have done better than a tent. Something had gone wrong, as she'd suspected this past many years. Jimmy was all quick brain and loud mouth — not a grain of good sense to glue him together. If that man had been lying to her he would shortly have his neck wrung like a chicken.

Jimmy had first met Lenie Strauss four years earlier. Then she was known as Angel, but, by her own laughing admission, was a reasonably tarnished member of the heavenly choir. Angel told Jimmy she was born 1852, which was only two years short of the truth. In fact she was twenty-eight, born of German parents at the goldfields of Victoria, Australia. At age sixteen she had married a John Anchorage.

'Nothing else to do,' she would laugh, stamping her fine narrow feet and tossing her petticoats in the saloon called Angel's Palace, which she ran in Hokitika. 'A girl, sixteen, and every man in the goldfields after a piece of her! That John Anchorage was a good man with his fists. Protection I needed bad!'

Two years later Lenie Anchorage travelled with her husband and baby daughter to chilly Orepuki, South of Dunedin, New Zealand, where John's friend James Kirkton promised good gold was to be found in the black iron sands. The colour was there all right, but the baby died, and not a month later John was murdered in an argument over claims.

'So then,' Lenie, who loved recounting her colourful past, would continue, 'time to try my own hand at the colour. Haymaking in the sand is not so hard work, but my luck was only so-so. Then I meet that bastard Simon Lamb. You remember him, Gaffer — you were here then. Up we come, by some hell-hole boat that went down one year later, here to Hokitika in the high old times. Well — more low, truth was. That Simon dumps me flat to follow a duffer. Stupid feller. When he realises his mistake and comes crawling back for a bit of comfort — he feels the flat of my hand, no? By then I have my own saloon. Sitting pretty till some prune-faced lawman does me in. Jealous he was, and did me for spite.'

Here Angel would sigh and toss her mane of dark hair, till all her audience licked their lips, anticipating a taste of her. Some remembered her arrest for prostitution and 'lewd behaviour'. Jailed,

26

with one month hard labour. Out she came and in a month had opened a new 'guest house'. Oh, Angel Lamb had a grand energy for the high time! Arrested again she was, with more hard labour, but no lawman ever tamed her.

By 1878, when Jimmy Cork met her, she was older and, some said, more settled. Her saloon, Angel's Palace on Revell Street, Hokitika, was well patronised. You could always have a good time at Angel's. Jimmy, in particular, came back often for a good time. They were a spirited pair, she with her wild hair and wild ways, he with his knowledge and speechifying. He was not from County Cork as his nickname suggested, but (some said) from London. His fine singing voice and his flow of language earned him the reputation of an Irishman. Jimmy Cork would down you in an argument no matter what the topic, but always with good humour, mind.

'Ah, Angel,' he said one night, tickling her beautiful breasts with his ginger beard, 'Hokitika is done for, my lovely, the colour has been stripped. The golden future is further north, I have it on good authority.'

He promised to send for her shortly when he had found a good stake.

No word for several months. By now, Angel is pregnant. Gossip lays the honour evenly to either Mr Arthur Byatt, the barber, or that giant of a fellow with a shock of blond hair working down at Gibsons Quay, but Angel plumps for Jimmy Cork. She sends him the news. Six months later, after her baby is born, Jimmy writes that he has made a great find, to keep it under her hat, and that he will send for her and the baby shortly. Nothing for six more months. Angel, never one for fidelity, gives up on Jimmy and goes for the big fellow at the wharves. (Arthur Byatt is already married.)

The final confrontation is famous. Angel has already been down to the wharves a couple of times to give Big Snow the news that he is the lucky father. He has promptly sent her away. It seems Big Snow is lately patronising a different saloon, and a paternity suit will definitely not assist his hopes with that other sweet hostess. Angel must have been a bit desperate. She wasn't usually one to barge in on someone else's affair, but then Hokitika, as Jimmy had predicted, was on the down: gold-rushes a thing of the past and the population drifting away. Angel marches a third time down to the wharf, this time with the little girl — golden haired like Big Snow. When he ignores her she lets fly. All kinds of obscenities mouthed by those big red lips; the audience could make out only one word in ten. Bella, Big Snow's 'sweet hostess', heard about it of course, but never made the connection to Rose till many a year later. She and Angel operated rival establishments, and naturally were not on speaking terms. If they had met, down there in Hokitika, matters on the Hill may have ended differently. But then again, perhaps not.

So Angel rages on. Shouts, screams, claws at Big Snow, accuses him of every sin under the sun. Quite a crowd gathers to watch. Big Snow, who has a temper himself, holds back for a while but finally lands a slap on her you can hear right down the Quay. Angel runs at him, catches him wrong-footed and pushes him into the drink.

A great shout of laughter from the crowd. Angel accepts the applause. Then amid growing consternation comes the realisation that Big Snow has not surfaced. Someone jumps in to search among the piles. No sign. The tide is on the run.

The theory is that Big Snow knocked his head on something, sank and was dragged out to sea.

Angel is not forgiven. Big Snow was popular. Before a charge of manslaughter or worse can be laid, Angel and child disappear.

Two years later a Lenie Strauss, with a little daughter, turns up at Addison's Flat, near Westport, haymaking again on the ironsands there and asking after Jimmy Cork.

It's not clear what caused her sudden flight up to Denniston. Obviously she had found out Jimmy's whereabouts, but why the middle of the night? Rose remembers a fight — 'worse than the usual' — over a piece of bread. Another woman was involved, and accusations of theft were laid. It can be assumed that Lenie's temper went over the top again and she struck the woman a blow too severe for even the goldfield community to ignore. Rose remembers her mother hastily throwing things together, and then a dreadful tramp through the rain, her mother shouting at her to keep up. They slept in a barn. At Westport they climbed into an empty coal wagon, and waited to be carried up the gorge towards Denniston. Lenie Strauss had no idea what kind of place she was coming to.

UP at Denniston, in the dark and the freezing rain, Lenie stumbles against a pile of something rotten. Her bundle drops into the mud. Somewhere behind in the dark the child is crying for her to wait. 'Sweet Maria!' screams Lenie into the equally furious air. 'Help me! Some person help!' She beats the bundle with both fists. 'Is some person not here to help?' She tosses her head in rage and her good hat is swept away into the dark. A mass of damp ropy hair lashes at her face, cutting swathes in the mask of coal dust.

For a moment Lenie breaks the tantrum to listen for results. The child has caught up now and is holding tight to her coat. 'Where is the house?' says Rose. 'I'm cold.' But before Lenie can resume her shouting they both hear the bang of a door, and see, against the looming wall of a cliff, that there is a row of huts and, from one, a lantern is advancing.

The owner of the lantern stumbles, curses, stumbles again but keeps coming. When his face appears in a circle of pale light, the child Rose backs off and hides behind her mother. The face is badly scarred — a livid slash from hair-line to chin, and the skin along the jaw and down the neck puckered like lumpy porridge.

The face attempts a grin. 'Well, well, my lucky night! The Lord has sent a visitation upon me! This way, lady, this way; it's snug as a bug in my little hut, and who would want to be out in this bloody mess longer than she needed?' Billy Genesis, one-time jail-bird, presently Company blacksmith and drunk as usual, shakes himself like a dog to shed the rain.

Lenie, a match for any man, drunk or sober, swings her bundle up into his arms. 'Thank you, mister, but it's Jimmy from County Cork I'm after. Please to take me.' This is an order, not a request.

'Jimmy, eh?' says Billy, grinning and nodding, 'Well, now, he's a partner of mine in a manner of speaking; we share most things . . .' (Lenie gives him a look) '. . . but I'll not queer his pitch on his first night.' He roars with laughter and is about to move in the direction of Jimmy's when he notices the child. 'Well, look what is here!' he bellows, and raises a finger to point heavenwards. '"And God Almighty bless thee, and make thee fruitful and multiply thee that thou mayest be a multitude of people." Genesis 28 verse 3.'

He lunges to scoop up the child, but Rose, slippery in her stiff coat, dodges away into the dark.

Lenie glowers. 'Jimmy Cork's!' she shouts. Billy's glazed eyes focus for a moment and begin to spark. This man can be dangerous too. Then he shrugs and moves ahead. The unsteady procession sets off past shacks and tents, then over a narrow track through all kinds of rubbish — iron, timber, coal-slack, welded together with stinking mud.

Rose wants to hold on to her mother's coat but her arms are trapped inside the cape. Soon she sees the dim sweep of a tent roof, sucking and billowing in the wind; a black cliff sheer above it. The tent stands alone — nothing but dark storm on each side. There is a wooden door in the tent and Rose stands in front of it, watching rivers of rain, caught in the lamplight, run over the rough surface and down onto the slab of stone below. Her mother is arguing again, shouting at the man to go away, leave her now, this is private. The man laughs and says he's earned the right to stay and see the fun. Rose faces the door, humming to block the sound, and waits. The flapping tent looks like a dying sea-bird.

Billy Genesis suddenly puts down his lamp, grabs the raging woman in both arms and kisses her full on the mouth. Quickly as the drink will allow, which is not quick enough, he moves back then, away from a flailing slap. 'Wake up, Jimmy!' he shouts, rubbing his livid scar. 'For the Lord has sent a pestilence upon you. "And the Lord sent thunder and hail, and the fire ran along upon the ground, and the Lord rained hail upon the land of Egypt." Exodus 9, 23!' Back he stumbles, laughing and shouting, his lantern making mad patterns in the storm, leaving the two alone in the dark.

Lenie pounds on the door. Rose waits beside her. Her mother knocks again and then pushes the door open. She calls out and steps into the house. Rose stands close behind her mother in the dark, straining to see.

The tent smells. The floor is wet. A man speaks and her mother answers. The man coughs. He coughs again and spits. He knocks something over and it rolls on the floor. Rose hopes he is trying to light a lamp. Her mother steps away into the dark but Rose waits by the door. She holds both hands under her cape to keep them safe.

Then there is a circle of light around a candle. Slowly a man's face with a red beard and then the whole place with everything in it comes out of the dark. Rose stares. There is a cave here! Half of the room is a little cave and half is tent with a wooden floor. At one end of the tent part is a fireplace but the fire is out. Rose stays by the door, and watches. She tells herself this is a story — a real one —

and she is the princess in the cave. The man might turn out to be a wicked stepfather. She watches his face to see what he will do.

'Holy Mary!' says her mother. She drops her bundles and goes to stand over the man. 'What's happened to you?' The man shakes his head back and forth, back and forth. Once he looks up at her and mutters something, then goes back to his shaking. Lenie groans. 'Is every damned person in this hell-hole drunk? If not worse? Ah, Jimmy, Jimmy.'

But her voice is not as angry as usual.

'Come and say hello to your father,' says her mother. Rose bends down to untie her boots because they are muddy and she has been taught to leave them outside, but also because she is afraid of the man. 'You can leave the boots on,' says her mother, so she walks over to the man and stands in front of him. Her mother unties the string around her neck and lifts off the heavy cape and goes to hang it on a nail on the back of the door.

The man looks at her. Rose stares back. The wind hits the tent hard and it rocks. The man's eyes are swimming, and then he puts his head down again and he cries.

'Ah, Jesus,' he says. 'Ah, Jesus.'

Where one arm should be, there is a stump hanging from the shoulder and the skin looks angry. Rose reaches out to touch the skin where the arm ends. It feels soft and hot, like a puppy's skin.

'Hello,' she says, and smiles hard.

'Ah, Jesus,' says Jimmy, without looking up to see the smile.

'At least look at the child to see what you have made!' shouts Lenie. She hangs her own hat and coat on the door, then puts the big bundle on the table and unties it. She spreads the layers of cloth carefully and takes from the middle a cardboard box. She lifts off the lid. Rose wants to see in.

'Don't touch!' says her mother in a sharp voice. 'They're

precious.' The box has eggs in it, each one wrapped in a piece of woollen cloth. One is broken and a sort of chicken is lying mixed up with the egg.

'What is it?' asks Rose, but Lenie just picks up the thing by one thin leg, opens the door and throws it outside.

Opposite the bed is a rough fireplace and chimney made from rusty iron. The chimney has a wooden frame and the canvas walls are attached to this. Rose's mother takes the box over to the fireplace and puts her hand on the stones. Then she puts her hand in the fire itself and stirs the ashes till she's made a nest. She puts the whole box right in the fire. Rose waits for it to burn up but it doesn't. Lenie washes her hands in the bucket in the corner. She takes out a towel from the bundle and dips it in water too, and washes the mud off Rose's legs and off her own legs, then wipes mud from the hem of her good coat hanging on the door.

'Your face is black too,' says Rose. Lenie wipes her face and cries out at the black on the towel. 'What I must look like! Some black savage!' She looks over to Jimmy Cork but all the time he is crying, 'Ah, Jesus, Angel. Ah, Jesus.'

'That's enough of Ah Jesus,' says Rose's mother, and stands in front of him waiting. Jimmy won't look up. 'Ah, Jimmy, Jimmy, I'm too tired for all this,' says Lenie. 'Look at you! The arm! The house! So then. The gold was all words, was it, like your entire life? All a dream? So? All in your head?'

Jimmy frowns. 'Don't be so damned sure, woman. There are complications, that's all, and this is not the moment to go into them.'

'Complications! Complications I have plenty myself without yours.' Lenie suddenly yawns hugely. The yawn turns into yelping cries, like a wounded animal. 'Ah! Ah! Ah! What luck I have!'

Rose thinks her mother might be crying too. She stands on the cold floor and watches while her mother turns away from Jimmy and goes to the bundle again. She takes a blanket from the bundle and another towel. She rolls the towel up and puts it on the platform-bed. 'Pillow,' she announces, and Rose understands that she is to sleep next to this man who is her father. Lenie wraps the child twice around with the blanket, lifts her up like a sausage and tells her to sleep at the bottom of her father's bed. Rose doesn't want to. She sits up for a while, leaning against the tent at the farthest corner of the bed. Where she leans rain comes through, so she sits up straight again. She can't get her hands out to balance and she can feel herself falling towards the man. Rose thinks she might be going to cry too, but doesn't want to make her mother angry. Jimmy stares at her. His eyes are pale and watery, and a drip hangs off his nose.

'What do they call you?' he says.

'Rose.'

'Ah, Rosie, Rosie,' says her father. 'Ah, Jesus,' and he starts to cry again. Rose pulls her head down into the blanket and shuts her eyes. She sings a song to herself about the ride up in the railway wagon and the nice man who lifted her out. She thinks about hot scones in the frying pan which Mr Thrush back at the beach used to make for her, and another nice lady who often talked to her.

The bundled-up grey sausage that is Rose slowly keels over and comes to rest on her father's feet. She is asleep.

Lenie takes off her jacket and shakes out her hair. Jimmy turns his shaggy head to watch her. Lenie's hair is thick and wild, like his, only a darker red. Her body is more solid than he remembers, but splendid still, and her wide red mouth a temptation, even in his present state. Over huge black eyes the eyebrows, thick as a man's and straight as boot-brushes, are fiercely at odds with the tender mouth. Jimmy had forgotten the brooding force of this woman, her power to excite. She makes a move towards the bed and then stops, looks around. Out go the arms, flung wide in exasperation.

'Where? Where?' she almost shouts.

'There is a bucket in the cave. I wasn't expecting company.'

'You are living like a pig, Jimmy Cork, you who used to be a fine man with education and ideas!'

'This place is comfortable enough, by standards up here,' he says, convincing no one.

'Comfortable!' she snorts, her volatile hands speaking for her as she turns and feels her way into the dark indentation of the cave.

He is on fire now, booze and desire mixing in his blood, but there is a stirring also of apprehension. This unpredictable woman will make trouble and he will have little or no control over her. Evangeline Strauss can no more keep a secret than jump over the moon. Words tumble out of her of their own volition. Nevertheless . . . He glances down at the sleeping child. Then with a grin he uses his one good hand to pull out his prick and keep it up until Angel returns.

WHEN Rose wakes there is a greyness to the dark outside that means it's morning. She lies still so as not to wake her mother and the man. She hums a song, but quietly.

'Be quiet and go back to sleep!' says her mother.

Rose lies still, looking up at the canvas. It is black with soot and she can see a drop of water growing where the canvas is nailed to the door frame. She watches as it falls to the floor and another one starts to grow. When her mother is snoring again she swings off the bed and holds the blanket around her while she looks for her clothes. She finds her pinafore and a knitted coat made by a kind lady down at the beach. Her stockings and vest and drawers are already on. She finds her hat and puts that on too, but she's still cold. Every now and then the tent roof rattles as if someone is

35

trying to come in. I don't like this house, thinks Rose. It was much better at the beach.

Opposite the fire is a table and beside the table are some wooden boxes with things in them. She looks to see if any have food in them.

'For goodness sake go outside and play if you can't be quiet!' says her mother. She and the man who is supposed to be her father are lying close together, very still. Rose watches them for a while. When her mother is holding on to a man like that she usually doesn't hear. Still watching them, she tiptoes to her mother's coat and slides her hand into the pocket. The purse is there! Without taking her eyes off her mother she snaps open the lock and feels for a threepence. The cold round feel in her hand is very good.

Now she puts on the canvas cape and ties the string around her neck, but not very well because the sides of the cape get in the way. Then she can't do up her boots because every time she bends down the canvas reaches the floor and the boots are inside under the cape.

'For pity's sake! Crash crash!' says her mother, without looking, 'What's the matter now?'

'I can't do up my boots,' says Rose.

'Take your cape off and do up the boots first, ninny,' says her mother.

Rose sighs and starts all over again.

Outside, she can't see very far. Everything is grey as if she were still under her blanket. The lumpy things they walked past in the night are rocks, not animals. The houses must be there somewhere but the mist is too thick. The mist smells of coal. She runs at one of the rocks and says boo to it in a loud voice, beating at it hard with a stick and laughing at it. In her other hand the threepence is held so tightly it hurts. She jumps along the path like a rabbit but her cape bounces up and down and scratches her neck. Now she can see the long row of huts but doesn't want to go near there today. She walks past a long building and hears snoring. Lots of loud snoring like a pen of pigs. She snores too, then runs away along the path, past other sleeping huts, looking for one that is awake.

Hanrattys

THE HANRATTYS HAD been at Denniston three years when Rose and her mother arrived. Totty Hanratty was out in the lean-to, red in the face from trying to get a good heat under the kerosene tins for her boarders' hot water. Just when she thought the coal was catching nicely, a rogue wind would drive rain in around the corner and the yellow-red glow would spit and fade.

Totty straightened to ease her back for a moment and saw what she thought was one of the stray dogs from the Camp coming up out of the mist in search of breakfast. Another heartbeat and she'd have let fly with a lump of coal. You didn't expect, then, to see a child; there was only her Michael and three or four older ones working round the mines.

But a child it was: over her head a square of wet tarp that fanned out right down to her boots. A rough hole had been cut for her face, and quick blue eyes examined the dismal sight of Dickson Street in the rain. An astonishing sight. The child trotted through the mud as if she owned the place.

Forgetting fire and boarders, Totty Hanratty goes to the fence for a better look. The triangular bundle, about four years old at a guess, zigzags down the lane, looking in windows, until Totty calls her over. The child makes a beeline for her, displaying a smile so sunny it surely must cover something darker on a morning like this. She holds out her hand; a threepenny piece lies on a bloody, muddy palm.

'Can I buy some bread here?' she asks, smiling still.

'Come in quick!' says Totty, frowning to see the caked blood. She holds open the gate and the little one trots in, trusting as a puppy. 'Give me a moment with this fire, then we'll see what we can find.' The child stands under the lean-to, close to the fire which after all has got itself going, as soon as no one was watching, wouldn't you know it.

'The Company Store is the place you want,' says Totty, busy with the shovel and glad to talk to anyone. 'Down by the Bins. But it won't be open yet, sweetheart. If you're hungry you can have a bite with my Michael.'

'Mother and Father will want some too.'

'And who are they?' asks Totty, dying to know.

The child frowns and looks at the fire for a bit. 'They're still asleep.'

'Down at the Camp are they?'

The child looks at Mrs Hanratty in a conversational kind of way, like an adult. 'I don't know the names here yet. Mother and I only came in the night.'

Totty smiles, thinking the child has got her times wrong. No one could have arrived last night. Yet it's strange she hasn't heard. Another child, after all.

'Well, then, so your father has been here for a bit, has he?'

'I suppose so,' says the child doubtfully. Then the smile comes out again as she remembers something. 'He's called Mr James of County Cork.' The name is pronounced with pride.

Totty Hanratty breathes in sharply and can think of nothing to say. She flips two cloths from the nail on the wall, wraps them around the wire handles of a pair of steaming tins, lifts them down, heaves two fresh ones onto the grate in their place, careful not to slop water on the coals.

'Well, come in anyway,' she says finally, but her face is less welcoming.

The weight of the tins wrenches her arms down, drives her boots deeper as she crosses the yard to the back door. The child follows, the hem of her stiff little cape dipping into the mud with each bobbing step.

Totty's stern look melts when she sees the child lay her three-pence carefully on the doorstep where she can see it, and unlace her boots one by one. Michael can't anywhere near do that. The hand is clearly giving pain but the child shakes her head, proud of her skill, when offered help.

In the wash-house Totty cleans the wound, sponging gently with some of her warm water. The thought of this little girl wandering unknown on the Hill is almost more than the mind can take in.

'That's a nasty gash. Does it hurt?'

'No.' Though the smile is stiffer now.

'How did it happen?' Totty suspects Jimmy Cork.

'There was something sharp in the — the thing we came up on. It was too dark to see.' The child winces, but smiles again as soon as she is able, as if to reassure the adult. A strange child. There is something too self-contained, almost manipulative about her. Totty shakes her head to chase off these impressions. I am being silly, she thinks. It's the idea of Jimmy Cork.

In the kitchen, Michael, warm and golden as a fresh scone, is amusing himself banging porridge spoons, like any proper four-year-old. At the sight of the girl in the doorway his mouth drops open. Then he's off his chair and on the floor in front of her, laughing and pointing. It's the first time Michael has seen anyone his own size. The child's face is equally amazed. She reaches out her good hand; offers the threepence. Michael accepts.

Totty wants to keep her.

TOTTY Hanratty, six months pregnant, married only two, had been the second woman to arrive on the Hill. Mrs C. Rasmussen, of course, was the first. When Rose arrived, neither woman had left the bleak plateau in three years.

She was a McGuire, Totty was; a McGuire from Westport. Her father, Mr Rufus McGuire, owned the General Store on Palmerston Street and had shares in the Royal Mail Service to Reefton. He was also a good friend of Mr Bickerton Fisher, who was expected to represent Buller District in Parliament after the next election. Oh yes, McGuires were respected in Westport society; Mrs McGuire saw to that.

Rufus McGuire, red-headed as his name suggested, passed the hair colour along with a wilful disposition down to his elder daughter, Dorothy. Everything about this fiery daughter broke her mother's heart. She was a natural beauty, clever and accomplished, sang like a bird, recited long poems to make a grown man cry, was tall but not a bean-pole, slim enough not to need corsets, and sunny natured. The red hair — aggressive bristles in the father's case — on Totty's head curled softly around her ears and escaped in shining tendrils from the clasp at the nape of her neck. In short, Dorothy

McGuire had all the attributes to make an excellent match, yet spent all her days ensuring she would make a bad one. Totty ran on the beach with young people of any station or no station. She walked out of the house without a chaperone and attended Entertainments with rowdy lads and lasses. She argued with business partners of her father's, and scorned afternoon-tea parties with her mother's friends. Totty loved the bush, would climb hills and stony riverbeds like a man. Worst of all, she spent too much time with Tom Hanratty, a rough carpenter's son and a Catholic.

Totty McGuire paid her first visit to Denniston in daylight, not a cloud in the sky. March 10th 1879 it was — three years before Rose arrived — and about three hundred others were with her. It was not often the mayor announced a public holiday. And who could resist when the Company laid on a free train to take anyone with a fancy for adventure to the opening of the Denniston Incline, the Eighth Wonder of the Engineering World, to be followed by a dance with entertainment down at Waimang?

'You'll ride with us, in the official party, Dorothy,' says Mrs McGuire. 'There is a closed carriage reserved.' Her words are abrupt but the eyes plead.

Totty mutters some excuse and runs down the line to the open wagons with plank seats for the working classes. Tom Hanratty's mates laugh and wink to see his fancy girl's lace petticoats flying, showing pretty buttoned boots and a fair bit of ankle too, but Tom leans down proudly and pulls her up as if she were any decent working-class woman. Totty smiles and bobs to Tom's family, sitting in the open wagon behind, and earns a nod, sour as lemon, from Mrs Hanratty.

'You'd best ride up with your family, Miss McGuire.' Her words are square and nasal, causing heads to turn three wagons away. 'That dress won't survive the journey out here in the open.'

Mrs Hanratty is dressed head to toe in sensible black against the soot and coal dust, as are all the other women in sight. A worn grey blanket stretches across her broad knees and over the skinny legs of the four youngest Hanrattys. Even ten-year-old Meg wears a black kerchief over her curls. Totty stands out like a whore in a nunnery.

She sighs. 'I can't please anyone today.' But Tom's warm arm, steadying her as they chuff and rattle up the coast, tells her different.

At Waimangaroa Junction the train stops to take on more picnickers. Tom stands up and waves both arms. 'Hey, Jacko, it's a holiday, man! Join the picnic!'

Jacko, perched on the roof struts of a skeleton cottage, banging nails in the morning sun, hears nothing but waves his hammer and grins.

'It's his own house he's building,' shouts Tom into Totty's ear. 'I could do the same for us if I work for the Company.' She smiles and nods, though the certainty of family opposition hangs heavy as engine smoke above them both.

The train whoops and turns inland towards the gorge. Ahead, bush-clad foothills rise sharply to the plateau. People shout and point up to the distant gash of the Incline, the Powerhouse chimney rising above it like a preacher's finger invoking the wrath of the Lord. Then the awesome view slides out of sight behind dripping ferny cliffs as the train creaks its way around the tight curves of the gorge. They pass the bridge across to the Wellington Mine and see the first workings for the Koranui Incline. They say there's wonderful coal up at the Koranui, but getting it down is even more of a problem than from the Rochefort Plateau, where they're headed today. No sign of work today, though, on either Wellington or Koranui. The opening of the Incline is an event not to be missed, and even the dour English miners are in holiday mood.

Totty is entranced. On a shining day like this, anything is

possible. She turns to Tom, her smile warm as sunlight.

'Hold still. You've got a smut.' She licks one delicate forefinger and touches the flake of soot on his clean white collar. Attracted to the spit, it comes away with hardly a trace. Totty squashes it like a bed-bug between forefinger and thumb.

Tom laughs at the trick and tries to return the compliment. His solid carpenter's finger approaches a smut on her muslin, but the soft thing collapses and the skirt is smudged. He groans and dabs with his handkerchief. Three more dark shadows appear. Tom looks down at his clumsy hands.

'Ah, Totty, what have I done? Your dress . . .' His face is desperate.

Mrs Hanratty, tight-lipped, hands forward her own shawl but Totty declines the dark cover. She will not succumb to propriety, not today. Standing in the rocking wagon, so everyone can see, she raises her hands to her hair, drags them slowly over her face, her shoulders, down over the neatly corseted bosom and waist, all the way down to the frilled hem. In the wake of her hands black flowers bloom over flesh, over lace, over sprigged yellow muslin. Every eye, even Tom's, is scandalised.

Totty, now spotted like a blackcurrant pudding, sits. She and Tom ride, straight-backed and silent, up the gorge. Other picnickers exclaim over the size and grandeur of the trees, the sparkle on the river below, the coal seam clearly visible in the wall of the gorge (but how could you ever reach it?). Totty blinks, pretending the sun is in her eyes. But when two fat pigeons burst out of the bush, close enough to touch and iridescent as opals, Tom glances sideways in the general stir and winks stoutly at his wilful girl. Totty's giggle is half sob, but the day — and a dynasty — is rescued.

It turns out that the bottom half of the Incline is not yet functioning. Mr Dickson, Company manager, resplendent in top hat, explains to the milling picnickers that he cannot guarantee the safety of the ladies until the lower brake-drum has been inspected. But if the gentlemen would offer a hand to the ladies, they might all make their way safely up over the railway sleepers, up the steep slope of the Incline, to Middle Brake, where brand-new wagons, untouched by coal dust, are ready to haul them up the second, steeper section of the Incline.

Several women and a few men, quoting varicose veins, hearts, delicate shoes or dispositions, decide to picnic at the railhead. Conn's Creek is, after all, very pretty; much more suitable than the high plateau. Mrs Hanratty is one of these. She spreads her rug and sits with other women, dark and formal in the sun, like heavy boulders guarding against the exuberance of the bush.

Others, including Mrs McGuire, feel their duty is to be at their husbands' sides during the opening ceremony. They struggle up over stones and sleepers, but finally quail at the sight of the wagons rising vertically into the sky and out of sight. Middle Brake has a splendid view, anyway; the men and the young ones can manage the ceremony quite well on their own.

But the sight of Totty sends Mrs McGuire into a tightly controlled fit of hysteria.

'Your dress, your dress, Dorothy! How can you ever make your recitation now? Elizabeth will have to do it.'

'Mother, it *is* a coal mine after all . . .'

'And Mrs Leake spending such care on the stitching. Oh, Totty, how can you be so careless?'

'It will wash out, Mother.'

'What will they think? Mr McGuire's daughter . . . You will have to stay down here with me; you have missed your chance of fame. Oh, what a madam! Mr McGuire! Oh, Lord, where has Elizabeth got to, and she's wearing her blue, not at all the right thing. Mr McGuire!'

'He can't hear you, Mother.'

'Well, run and fetch him, this is a crisis, with the programme announced in the paper, and your name in it. Mr McGuire!'

THAT is why Miss Elizabeth McGuire, not her older sister Dorothy as reported, rather nervously recited *Prophetic Lines From Locksleigh Hall*:

> *For I dipped into the future*
> *Far as human eye could see*
> *Saw the Vision of the world*
> *And all the wonders that would be . . .*

as Miss Mary Dickson, daughter of the Company manager, drove the silver-plated spike (two misses and one strike, according to Con the Brake, who counted everything) commemorating the opening of the Denniston Incline. And why Totty was free to walk hand in hand with Tom, away from the Brake Head and the ceremony, away over the humming plateau, a good mile away, to a mossy hollow where they sat and then lay together in the sun, and where, because they were headstrong and in love, and of a mind to make their own future, Totty conceived Michael. On that day Totty developed a taste for a landscape as wilful and contrary as herself, and bred the flavour into her son's bones.

AT the Brake Head Mr Dickson, Company manager, has stayed back for a word with mine manager, Mr Denniston. The rest of the official party has plunged off the edge, teeth clamped to hold in place rocketing stomachs and hearts, until Con the Brake slows them just in time to arrange laughing, hearty faces for the women at Middle Brake, who have laid out bacon and egg pie and corned beef sandwiches and are now busy holding back the children until the men arrive.

Up top, Mr Dickson's wink at two late-comers, wandering back over the plateau, gives way to a frown when he recognises Totty McGuire, whose dress now has a new set of stains.

'It's not the thing, young Tom. Mr McGuire's daughter.'

Tom looks back stoutly but it's Totty who answers. 'Tom wants a job, Mr Dickson. You must need carpenters up here.'

'You're right, we do.'

'We could build accommodations up here. And our own. Maybe a boarding house if you'd help us. And we could run it.'

Mr Denniston, mine manager, a progressive man and well liked by the men, speaks up.

'We could do with some solid accommodation, sir. Tents are no comfort to a man in winter up here. Boarding houses, now,' he laughed and gave Tom a cuff, 'we may not be quite as fancy as that yet.'

Mr Dickson frowns. 'Don't be too sure, Robert. Coal up here is as good as any I've seen in the world. And I know my coal.' He looks out over barren rocks and scrub, but what he sees are the bags of coal, stacked high and waiting for transport, an underground city of roads and crossroads driven through hard coal, an army of miners and miles of rails. He sees money pouring in and an easing of the heavy debt his Company owes. Mr Dickson is an optimist on this fine day. 'I'll wager you a pound to a penny,' he says, 'that we'll have boarding houses, shops, streets — schools even, within the year. Two at most,' he adds, because he is also a mean man who hates to lose a bet.

He turns back to Tom. 'I'd be happy to give you a job, young Tom. I know your dad's work and he's sound. I'll help with the building of the boarding house, too — on a proper financial basis, mind. But this is no place for a woman, Tom, let alone a well-bred one.'

Totty is getting up speed to reply when Con the Brake, never one to hold back in a good debate, joins in with his thick foreign tongue.

'We are bred all sorts up here, sir; she might not be so out-class as you think. Also,' he adds with some pride, 'I am thinking to bring a woman to the Hill. They will come, sir; we must have them.'

Robert Denniston, mine manager, nods. 'We must have them. And will.'

Mr Dickson still shakes his head at the thought of the stir back in Westport, of Mrs McGuire's desolation. But Tom grins widely and offers his hand to the big man who has argued his case. 'Tom Hanratty, carpenter,' he says.

The giant removes one paw from the brake-wheel and shakes briefly. 'Conrad, me,' he answers. 'Known up here Con the Brake. Welcome then.'

Three years later, when Rose and Evangeline Strauss arrived, Hanrattys', on the muddy lane known as Dickson Street, was a fine guest house: six rooms and a basement under, and respectable, all four sides wooden, not like the icy iron sheds most people built. The other landmark home was Con the Brake's great log house, which Rose missed on her first night, for though it was down at the Camp, Con had chosen the highest, driest spot, away from the rattle of the mine and the damp of the cliff. This fine edifice he had built for his beloved Mrs C, from fine West Coast beech logs felled by himself in the gorge and hauled up on the Spinner, a dangerous contraption of ropes and chutes that brought all the timber up from the river below. An outlandish, foreign castle of a place it was, Con's log house, standing among the temporary tents and shacks of the Camp like a whale in a school of dolphins. It was even grander than the home of the new mine manager, Eddie Carmichael, who'd replaced Mr Denniston the previous year.

Hanrattys and Rasmussens: homes and families that would become life-lines to Rose, and dangerous rivals to her mother's ambition. Scobies too, in a way, though they, of course, were different.

Scobies

MR WILLIAM DICKSON, the managing director of the Westport Coal Company, despite his breeding, could develop a good rage if the occasion called for it. One such occasion was when the list of his twenty miners, recruited in England, and now disembarked at Nelson, was laid on the varnished wood of his office desk in Westport by his new mine manager Eddie Carmichael.

'Let them rot in Nelson, then!' he had shouted to Eddie Carmichael. 'I'll not have one of those nippy bastards within twenty miles of a Company mine!'

'We need the men, sir.'

'We'll use the old goldminers, Eddie. They won't make trouble.'

'Aye, and they won't fill our orders neither. They're too slow, sir. And that's only the half of it.'

Mr Dickson had sighed and tapped the paper on his desk.

'Look at it, Eddie. Cast your eye down the list, man. Chapel, every one. I asked for good solid Catholic miners.'

But Eddie, in his best jacket and waistcoat, watch chain properly spanning his stomach, stood his ground. He had come all the way in to Westport to argue with his boss and would not go home without a fight.

'They are trained miners, sir, and they have come half round the world in expectation of a job . . .'

'I wouldn't give them a job, Eddie, if they could hew at double the rate.'

'Which they no doubt can, sir.'

Mr Dickson turned around from the window to eye his blunt manager, who had interrupted him twice now. The man fidgeted, his boots scraping at the polished floor of the Company office. Mr Dickson let the pause develop, then spoke with the full weight of a voice that was known, in Westport, to be a fine baritone.

'I will not be responsible for importing the scourge of unionism into the colony. It will ruin the Company. We simply cannot afford troublemakers. No, Eddie; no Chapel men. That is my last word.'

Eddie looked sideways out the window, more than ready to be somewhere else but as stubborn as his employer.

'We cannot know they will be unionists. I will speak to them . . .'

Mr Dickson brought his soft white hand down slap! on his desk; came around nose to nose with Eddie Carmichael.

'You will do no such thing! A Chapel miner is a union miner; that is common knowledge. Look here — it's in black and white. Their leader, Josiah Scobie, is a lay preacher, for pity's sake! I tell you what, Eddie: Midland collieries back Home are fobbing them off on us! Getting rid of their trouble-makers. I specifically stated no unionists and look what we get! A Chapel preacher!'

He ran a well-manicured finger down the sheet of paper.

'And look at this! Look at all these Scobies. Josiah Scobie, Chapel preacher; six working Scobies; a female Scobie and three Scobie children. They will breed whole armies of new unionists unless they are stopped. No! I will not have them! Now, please, I have other work to attend to.' He held open the door in a manner that somehow propelled Eddie's worker's boots out into the street before he knew what they were doing.

In this way Josiah Scobie, his two brothers, his wife Mary, their six children, and seventeen other men, every one with a miner's ticket, had found themselves stranded in Nelson, their expectation of a better life severely dented.

'Well, you must think of something,' said Mary to her raging husband, 'for the whole family was persuaded by your fine rhetoric to immigrate and you are now responsible for their welfare.'

'It is the Company should be responsible!' stormed Josiah. 'They have brought us here under false pretences!'

'I hear there is work to be had clearing the land, Josiah.'

As indeed there was. For the next six months Scobies' Gang earned a fine reputation in the district. They were small-bodied, mostly, these Midlands men, but wiry as springs and could clear twelve acres a day, cutting all timber and scrub two feet in diameter and down. There's plenty of good farms around Murchison that owe their start to Josiah Scobie and his gang.

But it was not what the men were born to. They missed the coal, the rough jokes down the mine at smoko, the closeness and camaraderie. Banter sounded different out in the open air. Swinging an axe was hard enough work but had none of the precision and excitement of hewing at a good seam a mile underground.

'Wait another week or two,' said Josiah to his men. He leaned on his axe in a new-cleared patch where a stream ran clear over marble pebbles all the colours of the rainbow. Their cutting had disturbed clouds of insects, and cheeky fan-tailed birds swooped and dived through the buzzing feast. On a warm rise Mary and the three youngest were waiting with a picnic lunch.

'Hey, young Brennan!' laughed Josiah, tossing his youngest into the air. 'We can't have you learning soft ways, can we? How can we make a good miner of a lad who's never had coal dust up his nose?'

Mary smiled at her husband. 'Well, now, I think a woman might grow fond of the "soft ways". You could do worse, Josiah, than set up in business here. There is more than enough work.'

The dark man only laughed at his wife's teasing. 'What's this? Daughter and grand-daughter of the best mine managers in the Midlands? You would miss the collier's life as much as any of us. Eh, young Brennan?'

But there was something in the way Mary looked out over the bush, a dreaminess in her movements, that told Josiah he had better get his family settled in a proper mining town before too long. This gentle land was undermining generations of a more gritty tradition.

'Three weeks at most,' he promised his men, 'and we'll be back underground. I hear that the Company's in trouble. They need us, lads, and they'll come crawling.'

The men nodded. News was filtering north that the West Coast coal mines were losing good orders. Coal coming out was of mixed quality — too much stone in it. Output was irregular. Frank Scobie nodded dourly at his brother.

'Aye. You can't expect those fly-by-night Johnnies from the goldfields to know what we learned with our mother's milk. They'll call for us.'

At that very moment, as it happened, a letter from Mr W.H. Dickson, Westport Coal Company, and addressed to Josiah Scobie, was travelling up by Royal Mail Coach. The Company had suffered a bad winter. At Denniston snow and storms had devastated the tiny community. Men were walking off the plateau in droves. Now, behind on orders, almost bankrupt, and with a lucrative shipping contract for steaming coal in the offing, Mr Dickson was desperate. Methodists, unionists: he was forced to hire whoever he could find.

'We are all hired!' said a jubilant Josiah, waving the letter, and our young ones will have work too. Here is the beginning of our new life! Let us thank the good Lord and pack our belongings forth-with!'

THE jubilation is somewhat dampened on arrival at the bottom of the Incline. A grey mist lies over the bush. The wagons appear out of it, descending and ascending eerily. Mary climbs aboard a wagon willingly enough and gives the twins a hand up. She has seen coal wagons before, though never ridden in one. But as the wretched jerking thing rises she loses her balance and tumbles backwards, with the twins, several bundles and the bed-head on top of her. For a moment she fears she will fall out, and screams aloud as the jagged ends of cut branches tear past, a nose-breadth away. The twins, white-faced, grab at her, as much frightened by their capable mother's screams as by the ride itself.

At Middle Brake they come level, and stop. Mary sits in the wagon, pale and trembling. It seems there is yet another climb ahead of her. She realises the twins are whimpering, needing her comfort, but she cannot move. If she even inches one hand upward to brush back her hair she knows she will crack, lose control, jump out of the wagon and walk away downhill on her own two feet. Somewhere below, she supposes, Josiah, young Brennan in his arms, is rising, tumbling and crashing, the older boys and their belongings with him. Somewhere above, her friends and relatives will be standing on the plateau, this new and terrifying home, high in the mist. Mary Scobie feels utterly isolated, in a no-man's-land of rails and machinery and running men. Giant trees loom out of the mist wherever she looks; no sign of streets or houses or the comforting sign of washing hanging to dry. It seems impossible that any kind of civilisation can survive even higher on the Hill, as people below call this place. The light and warmth of Nelson seem a lifetime away.

It is the first time in her life Mary Scobie is not in control of herself and she cannot bear it.

A cheerful fellow is at the back of her wagon, running it over rails, forward, backward, forward again at a changed angle. He's talking to her but Mary stares ahead, rigid, feet collapsed under her, petticoat soaking wet. She has wet herself.

The fellow shouts advice, grins and jumps down. Mary feels another jerk as her wagon is hooked up to the menacing rope, stretching up and out of sight. She whimpers with the twins as the whole nightmare begins again. She is incapable of holding on; is as disembodied as one of her bundles of linen. Up they go, rattling, swaying, bodies and possessions threatening to shake out over the treacherous slope of the back wall of the wagon. The rise is almost vertical. At some point a full wagon careers past, going down, trailing a plume of coal-slack. Damp mist and coal dust cling to them. Mary can't believe she is making these terrible noises.

At last they jerk over the brow and come horizontal. Some giant of a man, peering through the window of his shelter, his hands welded to a brake-wheel, shouts a greeting; another someone jumps on behind and runs them onto a siding. Mary can't move. She is lifted out, scarlet with shame at her wet undergarments, her tears. This is not at all how Mrs Josiah Scobie imagined arriving at her new home.

Frank, her brother-in-law, approaches, then hesitates and looks away. Mary stands, a trembling twin pressed at each side, into her skirts. She is a dark island, surrounded by snaking rails and scattered coal. Wagons and workers weave around her, but there she stands until Josiah Scobie takes her gently by the elbow and walks her step by step down to the Camp, where they will sleep a night or two before moving their possessions to the new Company accommodation further up the plateau.

Within an hour Mary Scobie is shaking out mattresses, spreading blankets, handing bread and dripping to hungry children. She is once more manager of a large household. But her world has been shaken and will never feel quite secure again.

Josiah stamps his feet at the door and smiles to see his wife making order among the bedlam of children and possessions. A chicken runs in with him and everyone laughs to see young Brennan dancing and shooing it out.

'Well, lads,' Josiah says to his sons, 'did you see that coal? Clean as a sailor's whistle. Hard, bright stuff.' His eyes are shining. 'I've been up to see Eddie Carmichael and I'm to start straight in as a deputy. Underviewer soon, like as not. There is a great seam, they say — eight, ten feet high in places — running true, chain after chain. And others just waiting to be opened up. We are sitting on a mountain of good steaming coal! Aye, Mary; we have come to the right place.'

Mary straightens from the beds. She pushes back a damp strand of dark hair.

'Well, I pray the good Lord you are right, Father, for I will not be leaving until they have built a proper road up and I may travel down in a horse and trap.'

The older boys laugh to see their mother so fierce.

'Nay, Mam, it's as nifty as a fair ride. Did you see me tumble?'

'You never held on, Mam! I stayed upright, didn't I, Andy?'

'I'm going down again tomorrow! Who's coming with me?'

Mary rounds on them all. 'Well, you may laugh, but just wait till one of you takes a fall in the mine. How do we get to a doctor?'

'Everything comes and goes on the Incline,' rumbles Josiah. 'We will get the hang of it in time . . .'

Mary grunts. 'Just as well I have seven men to care for. I will need to keep myself busy, stuck up here and no way out.'

'Aye, my dear, it is a challenge, but a worthwhile one. And we may do some good in time. We will organise the men in the end, never fear.'

Josiah Scobie unpacks his Bible, greets the men under his care as they crowd into the hut for the evening prayers.

In the distance, near the Powerhouse, men are singing; a lively song with accordion underlying it. Feet are stamping on wood in time to the music. In another direction, somewhere in the Camp, a man and a woman are shrieking at each other, accusations tearing the air. Mary frowns. Drunk, it sounds like. But any human sound is welcome if it overrides the groan of the wagons on the Incline and the resounding silence of the trees below.

Inside their hut, in the glow of oil lamps, Josiah prays. Twenty or so sturdy heads are bowed with him. Mary holds the twins tightly, as if they are life-lines, and prays too.

Outside, perched on an upturned box, Rose peers in. She sees the bare white necks of the men and their pink ears. She sees a single woman, dark and fierce in her prayer. She does not see young Brennan, who is under blankets, excused prayers because of his age and the tiring journey.

'Grant us, oh Lord,' says Josiah, 'the strength to do Thy work here at Denniston. Give us strong arms for the hewing of coal, and love in our hearts for the condition of our fellow men, believers and unbelievers, united here in this lonely corner of Thy world. In the name of our Lord Jesus Christ, amen.'

'Amen,' echo the men, their voices a roll of thunder against the thin wall where Rose leans. She sees a dark wall of shoulders rising to sing:

> *Lead kindly Light, amid the encircling gloom*
> *Lead Thou me on!*
> *The night is dark and I am far from home:*
> *Lead Thou me on!*
> *Keep Thou my feet; I do not ask to see*
> *The distant scene: one step enough for me.*

In the 'encircling gloom' outside Rose smiles. The mournful plodding tune has, for a moment, drowned the shouts of her parents. She stays there for a while, pressing against the wood as if to absorb the warmth inside. Then the door opens, boots crash out into the night, and Rose, unseen, plods back through the mud to the far corner of the Camp, where, stoic, because it is the life she's used to, she will put herself to bed.

Denniston 1882-83

Evangeline Strauss
/Eva Storm

UP THERE THEY will sit around their mean little coal fires in their mean little houses and swap yarns all night, but you will never find them telling my story. I myself must tell if anyone is to hear. My story is more for a fine log fire blazing on an open beach, a fair tot of moonshine aboard and a handful of free-roving spirits to listen. Think of me, then, telling in this way, my boots to the fire, my back to a log of driftwood, a warm man on each side to block the draught, and two or three fire-lit faces enjoying the tale.

Oh, I made a bad mistake, yes, I admit, coming up to that cold, tight town on the Hill. It was not my place. No. But for the moment there was a need to lie low, understand? And how could I know Jimmy had changed so? Also the gold.

So. Listen. A new name, I thought, would give me a fresh start. Evangeline Strauss is fine enough, but too often used in not so pretty times. That is the name of a sad child, Evangeline Strauss. My two past husbands called me Evie, and both came to bad ends. Angel, that Jimmy called me, was for a bawdy house not a coalmining town. Lenie, now, is a plain, hard-working name, but at this time, you understand, I was in my prime, with high blood. I needed something more bold, more with spirit, for this ugly place. But with rich potential. Some name to keep my spirits up and attract notice. So: Eva. Eva Storm it was. Good, no? Storm on the Hill.

But to start, no storms. I lived quiet and soft, to see what was what and who was who. Jimmy, that lovely singer and teller of tales, was lost to the drink and pity, pity, all self self, for his lack of a right arm. Yet there was money in his pocket and a secret in his eye. Where from came that money if not from the colour? You would all understand, being followers of the colour yourselves, that here was a mystery I must squeeze out of that bawling bag of tears Jimmy Cork. Billy Genesis, scarred inside and out (I'll come to him later), was in on it too, I could smell that much. Meantime that sad man Jimmy moaned all day and drank with Billy and his friends all night. I had to be out! Outside in fresh air. Some new thing or go mad!

My work at Hanrattys' lasted one month. Hauling hot water and stoking someone else's fire is not my style, you understand. But they liked my Rose, I could see that, and pitied me for being with Jimmy, so looked the other way when I dropped soot on the floor or filched a potato or two.

'Oh, you poor soul,' says Totty Hanratty, sighing at me with her big blue eyes. 'Take this heel of bacon home for your pot, and some barley why don't you,' and she'd hand over kitchen scraps I'd be ashamed feeding to chickens. She was a poor fish, Totty, so I thought, fagged out with babies, two living and one in the belly. It was only kindness that I show the man of the house a lively bit of ankle for a change of diet.

'Now now,' says Tom Hanratty (a fine fat fellow with bushy brown beard and hands like plates). 'Now now; I am a family man.' But the grin splitting the bushy beard said different, so I showed a bit more of my wares out behind the lean-to, flashed him a smile or two of my own, you know? And he came to it readily enough. A 'good' man, I have found, a respected fellow who is well provided at home with food and family, is often the most hot-blooded when it comes to a bit of fun.

(And here I pause in my yarn for a moment to dig my two warm men on either side with my elbows and give them a wink, to show I appreciate them anyway, even though they are not so well provided with family and food.)

So, then, Tom Hanratty was first choice, a good meaty man. With Totty about to give birth and so pale on it, who knows he might need another wife soon enough. To be mistress of a saloon and guest house would suit my talents well, and a dally with Tom was good enough sport to persuade me to stay for a bit.

With Totty I made a mistake. Women I judge not so well. Pale she may be, and washed out, and a fine way of talking, but tough! That Totty was boot leather when it came down to it.

One night, very late, and a month into my work at Hanrattys', she comes over to the room they call the saloon. For what reason she came, who knows? Maybe bit of noise. I like to enjoy my pleasure with a cry out or two, you understand. It's hard to remember some-times, children asleep and so on. No to mention wives. Tom has me on the floor and we are in the middle of a high old time when she walks in with candle in hand.

So. Tears, I expect, and sighs. No no no. Lady T. Hanratty turns to ice. So quiet she speaks. Not to wake the precious children, no doubt.

'Tom Hanratty,' she whispers. My big Tom standing with head

down, poor fool, most hang-dog, trying to tuck in shirt-tails and whatnot. I have to smile. What I feel comes quick out on my face, it's how I am, you know, but that smile was not my best idea. Totty comes for me, big belly out in front, fingers all claws to get at my throat. They fasten there and begin to squeeze. I am a well-built woman, no? Strong like a man, but I tell you, that little woman has me pinned and gasping.

'Tom, go upstairs!' she whispers. He goes like a lamb. I made a mistake with that man — no fight at all. Like a lamb, he goes, leaving me with this cold and dangerous lunatic. Totty's eyes never leave mine to see is he going or not.

'You,' she hisses, steady and still as a snake, 'you evil woman! Oh, I have seen you rolling your big dark eyes and heaving your bosom at my poor Tom.'

Her poor Tom! He was willing enough, I would like to shout into her sharp little face, but she has my voice-box in her claw and no sound can come out, let alone breath in.

'Casting your filthy spell,' she whispers, all ice (fire is easier, you know, when it comes to a fight), 'when I am tired and heavy and not able to give my husband his needs.'

Oh, her fine talk! I was itching for a good fight but when she lets go my throat and takes up the poker, to drive me out the door like some stray dog, I can see this woman is crazy, no? Truly crazy mad. I tell you this, I was halfway across the Camp before I could draw breath easily. It was in my cold bed, Jimmy still out drinking, Rose in her box back in the cave, before natural sounds came out of this poor bruised throat.

Now. You should know that no one treats me like that without they regret it later. Her fine husband Tom was willing. I gave him a good time when the wife couldn't. Or wouldn't. Where's the harm? But I lose my job, Hanrattys' door is closed, so is their food cupboard, and Mr Hanratty turns right around to walk the other way if I even come in sight! But I will have my revenge, and plan so.

And now comes my big surprise, which lifts my spirit like a seabird catching the wind. Oh, what a fine day, just when I am feeling bad, knowing a child is on the way, no doubt Tom Hanratty's, as Jimmy is limp as a frog nineteen nights out of twenty. And in no state to provide for a child, which will have to take his name, I suppose.

So I am in poor spirits this day. Also hungry, and my chickens, like me, without feed. Rose, on the other hand, is always fed. Doors fly open to my pretty Rose — she has her head screwed on tight, that child. But selfish, my daughter, when it comes to sharing.

Well. This day I am over the other side of the Camp looking for feed for my chickens. Nothing grows up there. I am like a chicken myself, scratching the poor rock for a few greens. Over this side is one big house, among the tents and huts, belonging to the man they call Con the Brake. So I knock on this fine big door, to see if maybe the wife has scraps for my chickens. You see how low I was, begging at doors? The woman opens up. A big lady, Mrs C, with some look in her eye — not sharp, not kind, but dangerous. Something is familiar in that look.

'Well,' says Mrs C, kind enough, 'there are some cabbage stalks and peelings. Come around the back door, for my floor is polished.' That is the kind of woman she was, you see, who polishes a floor while living in a sea of mud and coal. It was a big house, as I said, with a kitchen and two, maybe three other rooms. In the kitchen, there, up at the table like lady of the house, is Rose, wouldn't you know? She nods at her own mother as if I am some stranger. Oh, it was vexing! I could have hit her.

'Sit down, Mrs Jimmy Cork,' says Mrs C, all smiles, but with this dangerous something flowing underneath to put me on edge.

'Sit down. I am Mrs C. Rasmussen, wife of Con the Brake. There is tea in the pot, and a scone too. Your Rose has left us one or two.'

The way she said her name, 'Mrs C. Rasmussen', so proud and ringing, had me thinking.

'Well,' I say, sitting to the tea and scone, 'I have a name of my own and it is Eva Storm. My arrangement with Jimmy is temporary, I hope.'

She gives me a look, very proper. 'Jimmy Cork is not the father, then?' Her eyes rest on Rose, misty and soft like a faithful dog. There is no sign of any other child in this clean kitchen. I look at her belly, but who could tell in all that swell? So she loves my Rose, I can see, for want of her own, and this may be useful.

I do not say if Jimmy Cork is the father. It is not her place to ask.

Well, she talks a little of who is who, and I am enjoying the talk. She is a woman of spirit, too, I can see, with a laugh to bounce off the log walls. I risk asking about Tom Hanratty, with a wink, and she winks back and smacks her lips like a bawdy, before the proper manners take over again. So. I am learning things. I know the Hanrattys have covered up the scandal. And I know that Mrs C is not as fancy as she might want to be.

And then the moment to lift my spirits.

There is a crashing of boots on the back porch and the sound of water being splashed about.

'My husband is home for his dinner,' says Mrs C, standing. It is an invitation to leave, no mistaking that. Rose is on her feet and out to the porch.

'Hey hey hey!' roars the big voice I know so well but thought dead. 'Wait now, little flower, I am black with coal still!' More splashing. Mrs C is caught between two hard things. She wants me to leave, wants Rose to stay. My head is buzzing, this way, that way.

So! My heart — hammer hammer. Hard to keep all this inside. Not to show, you understand.

'Well now, up you come, Rosy, Rosy tickle my fancy!' says Con the Brake. Roaring in the door, singing some song, comes the big man, my daughter laughing on his shoulder. 'Bella, guess what?' he says, then sees me. He stops, puts Rose down. Smiles. Not a flicker. Oh, this man is good!

'So, you are Mrs Jimmy Cork, I think,' he says in his thick voice and holding out his hand, like he was some king receiving a subject. 'I have met your daughter already, so you can see.'

His clear friendly look would fool a whole jury and judge, but it's him all right.

'Mrs Jimmy Cork is just leaving,' says Mrs C. 'We have already taken some tea together.'

The way she calls me Mrs Jimmy Cork brings me almost to spitting. It is harder almost than life itself not to crack her one, but then I would lose all advantage. The big woman puts one hand firmly in my back and moves me to the door.

At the door I turn back to look hard into Big Snow's eyes. 'Rose, come home now,' I say, smiling still at Big Snow. 'I see you have both taken a fancy to my daughter. No doubt we shall be seeing much of each other.'

Off we go, Rose dragging her feet, my blood singing with possibilities. Who would have thought my trump card would turn out to be Rose!

Secrets and Treasures

ROSE THOUGHT HER father was supposed to be rich. Before they came to the Hill, almost every night down at the beach her mother would tell how her father was away digging gold out of the ground and that he would be richer even than Goldie Brash who found the big nugget, and that he had a bag filled with gold. Rose imagined it in big lumps glowing like hot coal, inside a clean flour bag, swinging over her father's shoulder as he walked over hills and valleys coming to get them.

But at Denniston her father wasn't rich at all. Sometimes he went to work at the mines — 'make-work' he called it, or 'girlie-work'. Sometimes he stayed in bed all day crying or groaning while her mother shouted at him to get up, and often he ran away up to Red Minifie's saloon to drink. Two friends carried him home later. Sometimes Eva invited them in and they would all laugh and shout and stamp on the floor. Rose hid under the blankets, then, and pretended not to be there.

One night when they were all roaring at each other, crowded into the little hut, Billy Genesis tried to play hide and seek with her. He lifted a corner of her blanket and Rose could smell the drink and vomit.

'Peek-a-boo!' he shouted, and tickled her feet.

Rose wriggled away, but Billy lifted the whole blanket high into the air and then lifted Rose up close to his face, which was as lumpy as porridge.

'What about a kiss, my darling? For your Uncle Billy, then?'

Rose bit his hand, hard. And slap! Her mother's hand came sharp on that ugly face. Billy hopped around cursing bits of the Bible while Eva shrieked with laughter.

'Now, Billy Genesis, you wicked man, choose someone your own size! Though it looks like my Rose is a good match for you!'

Rose ran for her blanket and rolled up tight in it again, and hid in a crack of the cave where big people couldn't come easily.

One day when Jimmy was well and sitting at the table eating dinner with them, Rose asked about the gold. Her father looked at her a long time, then he said, 'Who told you that? Was it Billy Genesis?'

'It was her,' said Rose.

'Don't bother your father,' said Eva. 'It's all make-believe.'

But Jimmy winked at her when her mother went to the fire to serve the stew. 'I have a bag of gold, all right,' he whispered, 'and I know where to find more.'

'Don't listen to him!' said Eva in a loud voice. 'It's all gone down his gullet months ago.' But Jimmy winked at Rose again.

'Well, where is it?' she whispered, and he looked out of the window above the bed where he often stared out, and pointed with his orange beard to the dark bush.

'East,' he whispered. 'East, but close by.' But he stopped talking when her mother came to the table with their dinner.

Another time she asked if she could have some of his gold but her father said everything in life had to be earned and she would have to find her own treasure. Then he drank again from his bottle and said that one day when his arm was stronger, and if she was a very good girl, he might take her to the place where the gold was and she could dig her own gold nuggets and she could be rich too.

'When your arm is better,' said her mother, in a hard angry voice, 'and I am young and beautiful again.'

'And can Mother come too and dig up her own gold nuggets?' asked Rose.

'Only believers find gold,' said her father. 'Your mother is not a believer.'

'I believe in chickens,' said Eva sourly. 'You can depend on them.'

'I believe in gold,' said Rose.

NOW they have a door and three walls and a window around the little cave. The chimney is brick, not tin.

'A step in the right direction, Jimmy Cork,' says her mother, 'but I will want another room by the end of the year, mind, if we are to stay.'

Billy Genesis helped them, and Lord Percy, while Rose's mother laughed and shouted with them and teased them by running away with the hammer to build her chicken fence. Then the men chased her into the bushes and Jimmy chased her too.

Mostly Rose likes Lord Percy. He always wears a jacket and tie and sometimes a top hat, even when he's working on the Spinner, which hauls wood up from the gorge to the Camp. He tells her stories about trolls and princes and giants and uses long words that

Rose can't understand, but he is kind when he's sober, and at least he doesn't chase her when he's drunk. Lord Percy is very tall and thin and he grows vegetables in a little garden on the edge of the Camp. Eva gives him chicken manure and he gives them silver-beet.

But Rose hates Billy Genesis. He is her enemy. Once Rose opened the door and there was Billy. He was dressed in a black coat and a bowler hat and he had a watch chain over his stomach. His smile twisted his face in a horrible way.

'Hello, darling, give your Uncle Billy a kiss,' he said as usual.

'I don't have any uncles or aunts,' said Rose, 'and I don't want any.'

'You're too sharp for your own good,' he said, and kissed her anyway. His lips were wet and loose and the kiss went on too long. Rose wiped it off quickly.

'Jimmy, I'm off to town,' he said. 'Do you want me to — you know what?' And winked at her father. Her father frowned and told Rose to go outside and help her mother, but she only stepped outside and then looked back through the crack beside the door. She saw her father give Billy something but she couldn't see what or where it came from.

When they came to the door Rose ran around the corner and watched.

'You cheat me one penny and I'll kill you, that's flat,' said her father. He was red in the face and stamping his feet. Jimmy was always angry when Billy or Lord Percy rode down the Incline to go to town. Lord Percy told Rose how one time her father tried to ride down, but with only one arm, his left at that, and with a gammy knee, he lost his grip and fell off at the steepest part, rolling down and badly twisting his leg.

'My dear,' said Lord Percy, 'that unfortunate gentleman was within an ace of decapitation, so close was the cranium to the rail!'

Your poor father has lost his courage since that unhappy incident, and is incarcerated up here with the women and children. Needs must his friends bring him solace. And so we do.'

Rose asked about 'incarcerated' and 'cranium'. Lord Percy could always oblige with a definition that made her laugh.

After a trip to town, her father and Billy Genesis and Lord Percy were drunk every day. Sometimes she saw them sitting outside in Lord Percy's vegetable garden, laughing and throwing lumps of coal down into the gully, and sometimes they went to Red Minifie's up by the Bins and she and her mother had a quiet night until someone came banging on their door to say, 'Red Minifie says come and get Jimmy because his friends are too drunk to carry him and no one else can get near him.'

'If you can bring the message you could have brought the man,' says her mother, but she would put on her coat and go up anyway and Rose would wait in the dark house, humming songs under the blanket until her mother dragged Jimmy home and put him to bed without saying anything more. She said a lot, though, in the mornings when he wouldn't go to work. Then she would go outside and bang hard on the nails of the chicken house she was building against the cliff behind the house. Rose would hold the nails ready for her mother, or she would go up to play with Michael, or see if Mrs C. Rasmussen, in the house made of tree-trunks, needed help with her baking.

Mrs C. Rasmussen was the fattest lady Rose had known. If Rose put her head against Mrs C. Rasmussen's apron it went right in like soft cotton wool, and the big woman would laugh, wobbling her stomach, and hug the child and say she was only like that because she couldn't be bothered wearing her stays today, but not to tell anyone because proper ladies always wore stays.

'Can I look at the stays, then?' asked Rose.

Mrs Rasmussen laughed. Her laugh rolled out thick like treacle. 'Ah well, now, Rosie, my bedroom is another secret.'

The secret bedroom was pink. A handsome prince should live in it. Rose stroked the pink velvet curtains, which were softer than a cat. A cover on the bed was woven with coloured birds. Mrs C. Rasmussen's stays were inside a dark carved wardrobe. They hung there like another bony woman with long ribbons trailing down to the floor. Rose thought of her own mother, who looked thinner now, even though a baby was growing inside. Bonier even than the stays. She imagined her mother hanging beside the stays in this wardrobe, which smelt of summer flowers and other stranger things.

'Don't be frightened, Rose,' said Mrs C. Rasmussen. 'Stays won't bite you.' And she smiled and hugged the child again and asked could she keep a secret.

'I'm already keeping the stays a secret, and the bedroom a secret, and I can keep lots more,' said Rose.

So Mrs C. Rasmussen pulled back the stays and other long, coloured dresses, and showed Rose a red jacket hanging right at the back. The jacket had gold shoulders and gold cords with tassels and a silver and blue star pinned to the jacket pocket.

'Your uncle Con the Brake used to wear this,' said Mrs C. Rasmussen, and held Rose up so she could touch the gold. Rose looked at Mrs C. Rasmussen and supposed that if Con the Brake were a handsome prince in disguise, this woman might be a beautiful princess in disguise. Or the queen. When she had her stays on.

After that, Rose called in quite often and if Mrs C. Rasmussen wasn't too busy they would go into the prince's bedroom and dress up in silk scarves and hats and would dance and sing.

'Where did you learn to dance like that?' said Mrs C. Rasmussen in a sharp voice, and Rose said the ladies where her mother worked before they were at the beach taught her.

'It is not a dance for Denniston,' said Mrs C. Rasmussen, but then she laughed and said, 'Rose, Rose, we are birds of a feather and it is a good dance, for all that, and we shall dance it together in here, but it will have to be yet another secret.'

'It's a good thing I can remember a lot of things,' said Rose.

'It is,' said Mrs C. Rasmussen, and laughed and kicked her fat white legs high in the air.

One time when Rose and Mrs C. Rasmussen had a pile of glass beads and jet and amber necklaces and a tiny pair of gold earrings on the bed and they were pretending it was Aladdin's treasure in the magic cave, Rose told her friend about her father's bag of gold and how she thought it might be buried under the floorboards, but she wasn't allowed to dig down to see.

'Buried treasure!' said Mrs C. Rasmussen.

'My mother says it's a mystery where he gets the money for drink.'

'So it is, so it is, child, but I doubt Jimmy Cork has any stash of gold.'

'He could be a prince in disguise like Uncle Con the Brake.'

'Well, he could, that's true. And you his beautiful daughter. With a diamond ring.'

Mrs C. Rasmussen put a sparkling ring on Rose's thumb. The child looked at it, then closed her fingers around it. She looked up again.

'My father says I can't share his treasure, I must find my own.'

'Whispering is no use, Rose — I can't hear what you're saying.'

'I must find my own treasure.'

Mrs C. Rasmussen gathered up the necklaces and put them back in her velvet box. She gently prised open the child's hand, took off the sparkling ring, put the ring in the box and closed the lid softly.

'The ring is only glass,' she said. 'It is not treasure.' Then she smiled at Rose and hugged her with soft arms that smelled of bread. 'Listen,' she said, 'you are more of a treasure than that ring, and if your father won't share his gold at least he shares you, and that is better.'

But Rose knew only too well that a child wasn't treasure and a sparkling ring was.

ONE morning, when they have been on the Hill about a year, the sun is shining and her father has got up and stumped off along the path to his work without any argument. Her mother looks at the sun and says, 'What about a picnic?'

'Is it my birthday?' says Rose, and her mother looks at her, then looks out the window and says, 'You've got a good memory.'

Rose thinks about that other picnic on her last birthday, which was the day before they came up to Denniston. She remembers her mother screaming angry words and fighting with Gypsy Mary, who Rose liked. Gypsy Mary smoked a pipe and told strange stories. Usually her mother and Gypsy Mary laughed together and slapped each other's backs and slept in the same tent when they were not with one of the men. But this day her mother was angry about the food.

'You greedy bitch!' screamed her mother. 'That scone was a picnic for the child's birthday and you have scoffed the lot!'

'Oh yes?' shouted Gypsy. 'One scone for a child's birthday? Tell me another! For your own belly, more like, and mine is in more need! I saw Bob, who is more mine than yours any day of the week, give you a bite — and more — last night!' And spat in the sand in front of Rose's mother.

Screams and hair-pulling followed, the two women staggering to and fro. Then Rose's mother, who was the heavier, had Gypsy down on the stones beating her head against them, up and down, screeching like a wild animal with the others backing off and quieting their laughter to see such fury. Rose knew that when her mother was like this nothing could stop her, and the only thing to do was hide somewhere until it was over. She remembers seeing the blood, and Gypsy lying there without moving. She remembers the crowd of angry people waving their arms at her mother, shooing her away as if she were a stray dog.

'I don't want to go on a picnic,' she says.

'This will be different,' says her mother. 'Just you and me, Rosie. And maybe your father if we can find him.'

'Is it my birthday?'

'Near enough.'

'Can Michael come?'

'No. Don't mention Hanrattys to me.'

'Can Mrs C. Rasmussen come?'

'That's enough of questions. See if there's an egg.'

Rose goes into the back yard where the chickens are scratching in the mud. She unhooks the loop of wire and goes into the little hen house and feels in the straw of the first wooden box, but there is no egg. The red hen she calls Lady Alice is sitting in the next box and she shoos the hen off. Lady Alice clucks and walks around in circles while the child picks up two little eggs. In the fourth box one brown egg is half hidden. Rose puts Lady Alice's eggs on the ground, makes her apron into a hammock with one hand, picks up the three eggs with her other hand, puts them in the hammock and brings them inside.

'Shut the door,' says her mother, and then she sees the eggs. 'Someone is on a fuss today. They must know it's your birthday.'

Rose stands and looks at her mother.

'What now?' says her mother.

'You're smiling.'

'Well, the hens are coming in to lay and the sun is shining,' says her mother, 'and I have a secret worth three golden eggs.'

'Tell me!'

'You have your fancy friends and I have my secrets. Now, let us make some soft little pikelets. Hungry as a horse I am, and no doubt you too, madam five-year-old!' And she smiles again, so Rose thinks the picnic might be different this time and sings a make-up song about eggs and pikelets while her mother takes the frying pan and lays it on the fire. She rubs a little lard into it, then pours batter in three lovely round pools onto the smoking iron. When bubbles rise in the creamy batter she flips them over with a knife. The cooked side is brown and smooth as skin.

'Bring a fresh tea-towel, quick, quick!' says her mother, and when Rose has unfolded it her mother flips the pikelets, one two three, into the cloth, and pours three more rounds and three more until there are fifteen pikelets in the cloth.

'Where did you learn to count like that?' says her mother, and Rose says she doesn't know and then counts up to fifty-four.

'That's enough of counting, you are wearing my ears to stumps!' says her mother. 'Count yourself into your coat, or the day will be gone before any picnic is begun.'

They put the tea-towel of pikelets and a jar of jam, a knife and an apple into the basket and button their coats. Eva Storm wraps a blanket around her neck like a giant scarf, and off they go on their picnic.

They walk past the tree-trunk house but Mrs C. Rasmussen's rocking chair on the porch is empty, and they walk up past the Bins with all its clattering and thumping, and skip quickly across the railway lines in case a wagon is coming. Rose waves to Uncle Con the Brake, and Rose's mother shouts 'Cooee! Cooee!' so that all the men look at her, but Con is busy and doesn't notice. They walk up Dickson Street past Hanrattys' and Rose waves to Mrs Hanratty, who is hanging washing in the yard. Mrs Hanratty doesn't see them either.

'We are going on a picnic,' shouts Rose to Mrs Hanratty's back.

'No need to tell all the world,' says her mother.

They walk up above the skipway and watch the boxes of coal coming and going. Rose counts all the wagons full of coal going past on their way to the Bins and all the empty ones going back to the mines, the same way they are walking. She counts twenty of each, exactly equal, and tells her mother how the coal gets tipped out at the Bins and how Mr Carmichael counts all the wagons of coal and writes them all in a book and adds them all up at the bottom of the page.

'For pity's sake,' says her mother, 'give my ears a rest and enjoy the sunshine.' And Rose looks at her mother and sees she is half smiling, so tells her some more things: her names for all the hens (Annabella and Clementine and Queen Victoria and Lady Alice and the rooster, Prince Charming), and a song Mrs C. Rasmussen knows about sailing home to Ireland. Then her mother waits, looking away and standing black like a fencepost, while Rose walks behind a bush to do her business because there is no toilet anywhere.

'Will the picnic be soon?' asks Rose.

'Very soon, because this fat old body will go no further,' says her mother, puffing and blowing. 'Oh, my dear God, Rosie, this lump of a baby is a curse. I will be glad to take my own good shape again. Keep an eye sharp, now, for your father.'

Jimmy is working these days around the Banbury mine.

'Dogsbody work,' her father grumbles. 'Whatever lowly graft a one-armed man can do.' But he has promised to slip away and meet them on the plateau above the entrance for Rose's picnic. 'To tell the truth, girlie,' says Jimmy, 'the job is out of pity and I am little use anyway. They will only be glad if I am away for a bit, and they don't have to look out for me.'

Below them is the black entrance to the mine. The boxes on the moving skipway rattle in and out on their little railway lines. Here comes Jimmy Cork, scuttling up the slope, looking back to see if anyone has noticed. He is humming and smiling and nods at her in a secret way.

'Well now, birthday girl, we are making progress with our plans,' he whispers. 'I think I have found a way! But that is our little secret, eh?'

'Do you mean the gold?' whispers Rose.

Jimmy nods and winks and does a little dance.

'Someone is in a good mood,' says her mother, unwrapping the pikelets and spreading the blanket they have brought. Jimmy comes up behind her, puts his one good arm around her and gives her huge belly a good squeeze. Rose's mother shrieks, but it is really a laugh. Jimmy beats on the lump of the baby like a drum and sings:

> Bright fine gold,
> Bright fine gold.
> One a pecker two a pecker,
> Bright fine gold.

Quick as a flash, he snatches a pikelet and stuffs it in his mouth. Rose and her mother shout and chase him around the rocks and lumpy moss, all of them laughing and shouting, until Jimmy is caught and marched back to the blanket.

'There are five each and you have only four left,' says Rose, pulling her father's beard until the tears roll down his face.

'Oho! And so I have bred a mathematical genius then,' says Jimmy. 'Well, it is no surprise, given her father's intelligence, and if you have half your mother's looks you will take the world by storm!'

It is the best time Rose can remember.

'Jimmy, you will not lose your job, now, stealing away like this?' says Rose's mother, and Jimmy laughs.

'See now, Angel, this job is only a stop-gap till we find our feet, which may be sooner rather than later. My job today,' and he spits on the ground, 'is to wander around like some poor lost soul with a lamp, testing the air. The inspector has complained of the air once more and the manager is trying to fob him off with a full-time, one-armed air tester. He knows he should cut another air shaft but he's too mean to waste the money. Oh yes, the miners laugh to see me wander around. And grumble if I get in their way. Those sour-faced Scobies! Twice already they have made it damned clear they are better off without me. Well, let them laugh. I know a thing or two.' Here Jimmy winks at Rose. 'Jesus, I hate those stuck-up English miners and their opinionated sons.'

'Jimmy, Jimmy,' says Rose's mother, 'do not spoil a good day with your moaning. You have a job and it is the child's birthday.'

'And the hens have started laying,' says Rose, 'and I found three eggs — two from Lady Alice and one from Queen Victoria — and we have made these fifteen pikelets in the frying pan and so here we are on a picnic!'

He father laughs. 'What a torrent! Quick, let us stop her mouth with a pikelet before we are drowned in words.'

Her mother and her father are both hungry so they eat five pikelets each, and all the jam and a quarter of an apple each, and her mother gives the last quarter to Rose's father.

He wipes his orange beard with his hand, then rubs his hand on the grass.

'Those were the best pikelets I've ever tasted.'

'What's put you in such a good mood?' says Rose's mother.

'Well, those pikelets, naturally,' says Jimmy, but he winks at Rose.

Rose's mother shifts to find a more comfortable place. 'Lack of drink more like,' she says.

'Ah, don't start now, it is the child's birthday.' Jimmy sighs, and Rose thinks that perhaps the picnic is going to end badly after all.

'Rosie, Rosie,' says Jimmy, 'what a life we've landed you in.'

Her mother says nothing, but looks away.

Then Jimmy puts one finger into a small pocket in his waistcoat and hooks out a tiny bag made of leather, with a string to pull it shut.

'Hold out your hand,' he says, and Rose holds it out. He pulls open the drawstring and shakes a little warm thing into her palm. It is flat like a piece of paper and red-gold like the yolk of an egg. It is heavy for such a small thing and its edges are smooth as if it were a drop of water splashed on the ground and then gone solid.

'Is it gold?' she says.

'It is. Happy birthday, girlie.'

'Is it for me?'

'Why not?'

'Jimmy,' says her mother.

Her father says, 'There is no need to look like that, it is the only piece I have, which I carry for luck. She might as well have it, though she will need more than one flake of the colour to see her through this world.'

Rose closes her hand around the warm gold and looks at her mother.

'Jimmy Cork!' says her mother, flinging her arms wide and beginning to shout. 'I know you, you would not give away your last flake. You are hiding something from me, and Jesus spare you if I find you are cheating on me!'

'Cheating?' says Jimmy, 'Who is cheating who? Tell me that! I have sharp enough eyes and ears for what they are saying. And where is your evidence, woman? Do you see me a rich man? Calm down, for God's sake, or they will hear in the mine and think it is a cave-in. I have given a small piece of treasure to my daughter, who is dying for some. And anyway it is only a few pennyweight.'

Rose asks her mother if she can keep the gold and her mother looks away out over the flat land and the little humpy bushes with sun shining on the leaves, and she folds her hands in her lap where she is sitting on the rug and says nothing.

'Can I keep it?' asks Rose again.

'Keep it, keep it,' shouts her mother. 'And we will see about the rest later — count on it, Jimmy!'

Jimmy winks and smiles at Rose, and she hugs him, and kisses the bristly beard.

'Ah now, Angel,' says Jimmy, 'This fresh air puts me in the mood, and why not when the world is smiling? Rosie, my little girlie, go down to the mine entrance and watch the boxes come out, while I talk to your mother.'

'Can I have the bag too?'

Her father gives her the little bag and she drops her first treasure into it. Rose pulls the string tight and slips the loop over her wrist. She tucks the bag with the gold flake glowing inside into the palm of her hand and holds tight.

'Go on, off you go,' says her mother, so Rose runs over to the tunnel entrance with the bag soft like a little mouse in her hand.

The tunnel is dark and exciting like one of Con the Brake's stories. Big logs of wood make a square opening as if for a giant's house, but there is no door. Train rails go right into the mine, into the dark, and two heavy chains are rattling along above the rails, coming and going and never stopping. Rose hears a rumble and stands back to watch an empty wagon, pulled by the chain, disappear into the mine. Then there is another rumble from inside the mine and she looks in, but it is dark. A grey shape is coming and she screams and laughs as the full one comes out all by itself, heaped with shining black coal, out into the sunlight, and away it goes, rolling steady and proud towards the Bins.

Rose watches while two more full boxes roll out from the darkness, and then she climbs up so she can see her mother and father. They are lying down in the sun. She wants to go back and jump in one of the empty boxes, ride it way into the mine, but her mother calls her.

Her mother is standing up now, dusting her coat down and doing up the buttons. She folds the tea-towel and puts it in the basket and Rose knows the picnic is over.

'Say goodbye to your father,' says her mother. 'We will go home and cook something nice for his tea.' Rose climbs the rock that her father is leaning on and shouts to show how tall she is, then jumps off onto the rug.

'Will I have a birthday cake for my tea, like Michael?' she asks.

'For pity's sake, isn't pikelets enough?' But her mother is smiling. 'We'll see what those hens have been up to.'

'See you later, girlie,' says Jimmy. 'Have you got that treasure safe now?'

He stays to smoke a pipe in the sun before going down to the mine and they walk away. When Rose looks back he is still there with a thin white line of smoke above his head and when she looks back again she can't see him.

'That gold is worth something,' says her mother, after they have been walking some time. 'Give it to me and I'll keep it safe.'

But Rose shows her mother how the string is around her wrist and the bag snug in her hand.

'Well, don't let your father see where you keep it,' says her mother, and Rose says she won't.

They walk along over the flat bony land, past bare rock and low bushes lying flat so the wind won't blow them out of the thin soil, and all the time the rope-road is rumbling just below them with the wagons, empty or full, going back and forth, a little faster than they are walking but not much.

Then the rope-road stops. Rose knows it only stops when terrible things happen in the mine. She tells her mother some of the terrible things.

'What a chatter!' says her mother. 'Wherever do you hear these things?'

Rose laughs and tells her mother about all the houses in Denniston and who lives where and other things and her mother, who is walking slowly now and limping a little, says nothing. Rose puts the hand that is not holding the gold into her mother's rough, dry hand.

'This is my best birthday so far,' she says.

Her mother lets Rose's hand rest where it is. Her snort is half laugh, half cry. 'The choice is not overwhelming,' she says.

Rose's best day so far. Jimmy Cork's worst. Evangeline Strauss, alias Eva Storm, alias Angel, considers all days to have rich potential, which is perhaps just as well.

Con the Brake Tells Rose a Story

'LISTEN, THEN,' SAYS Con the Brake. 'What happened with Jimmy from County Cork was this.

'He was there almost from the start. Just turned up one day when we were cutting scrub for the Incline. I myself had arrived only a week. There was a quite a gang of us, mostly Maoris from the pa, you know? Big fellas who could swing an axe almost as good as me. You'd think they'd make good miners, eh? But no, underground on a cold plateau is not their idea of a sensible life.'

'You are telling Rose about her father,' says Bella, 'not the entire history of the Incline.'

'I'm giving the flavour, woman. Every good story must have the taste in the mouth, you know? Well, here we are swinging our axes in the sun when this scarecrow walks down-river out of the bush. God knows how long he been up there, you know? Prospecting, of course, like most of us. Out of luck and hungry, nothing in his swag but a blanket and a billy. Shouts to the Maoris in their own tongue, rolling it out, and they answering and laughing and slapping young Jimmy on the shoulder like they was best mates. That was your daddy, Rose, in those days. A true adventurer.

'Well, he sits with us at smoko. Draws on a pipe as if it were a drowning man's first breath of air. Says he ran out of everything a week ago. Been living on black tea with no sugar. But there he was, lively as a flea on a sunny morning. Whistles some cheerful ditty that has us all grinning. Who knows where he really come from — he's no more Irish than me by his voice, but he says County Cork and God help the man asks questions up here.

'So the boss give him a job and he sets to, ready enough when there is food in his belly, you know? And cheerful. Had a girl further south, or so he said. A raging beauty to hear Jimmy talk, with hair brighter than the sun. That would be your mother, Rose, he was describing. A Venus she was, in Jimmy's version.'

Con clears his throat and lands the gob, sizzle! in the fire. He seems to lose his drift.

'Go on, man!' says Bella, tapping the chair, click click, with her knitting needles. 'So the woman was a raging beauty, we have got that point.'

'Jimmy said it, not me.'

'So you say. And?'

'Well, Jimmy says he's going to make his fortune and take them both back to Ireland. Or sometimes it was Australia. Jimmy was a dreamer.

'You'd never think it now, but in those days Jimmy Cork would tell a good yarn — had some wild ones from the goldfields further south. He'd been up the Hokitika and the Totara but always seemed to follow a duffer, always too late for the paying gold, you know?

The fever was in him, though — his eyes would shine just talking about the colour — and I knew he'd walk off the job as soon as he had enough cash to buy a bit of tucker.

'Well, so it was. One fine morning we see him splashing up river again, full swag over his shoulder, new shovel tied atop, whistling good as the birds. He reckon he could smell gold up there, though we always told him coal's the pay-dirt here, man; this is black country. Mind you, gold was here, Rose. God knows we'd all looked for the colour enough times on our day off, you know, and the odd bitty would shine up at us from the stream. Enough to keep you looking; not enough to pay bills.

'Well, he's gone only couple weeks, maybe less. This time he comes out, his eyes are dark and the man is coiled tight as a spring. Oho! I think, this man has found the colour — you could read it on him a mile off — but he say not one word. All the men joke him, tease, you know: "Show us the true stuff, man or have you got a bag of fool's gold, eh?" But that Jimmy say nothing. He's a changed fellow, you know — silent. He gets back to work and he cuts scrub like the devil, earns the bonus every week. We all reckon Jimmy hit it big up-river and is earning the cash to stake a claim. Set up his own mine, maybe.

'Well, it stands to reason he won't tell us nosy bastards; we'd be up there like a shot ourselves.

'So anyway, we work. We have the Incline almost ready to go. Company manager shouting every day to start her up. Banbury Mine, she's already producing good coal, see. But it all stuck up on the Hill, no way to get down. The men are bringing the coal out in sacks, piling them up, waiting for the engineers to give the all-clear on the Incline. One more week and the accident might not happen. Your father's accident. Poor bugger.'

'You have a child in the room,' says Mrs Rasmussen.

'Rose hears worse up here, woman, she must learn our ways. Well now. He works too hard, you see, Rose, loses his sharp mind, I guess. One minute he's helping to shove a heavy sleeper in place, the next he's gone — foot must've slipped. Head over heel he goes, down the steepest part, with the sleeper rolling down after him. By God, it was a terrible sight, that heavy timber rolling down, faster and faster. Of course it catches Jimmy just short of the trestle bridge, just where Colin Grover get killed, you know, same spot almost.

'So that's how his arm got the way it is. We come flying down the Incline, lucky someone else doesn't fall. You can see, when we lift the sleeper off, that man is never going to lift no timber again. If he live at all. One leg is bent back, make you sick to look at. His right arm the bone shows through, sharp as glass and the blood pumping. Jimmy Cork was lucky a train was at the railhead. Or unlucky, some would say. Better perhaps if he had gone.'

'Conrad!' says Mrs Rasmussen, reminding him who his audience is.

'Sorry, Rose, but you know how it is. Well, they take him down to Westport and we think that's the last we see of him. The Hill is no place for a one-arm man with a crook leg, you'd have to be mad. But then Jimmy was mad, that's the truth of it. Next we hear that he's alive and learning to walk again, with a crutch. And that he's desperate keen to get back on the Hill.'

'Why?' says Rose. 'Why did he want to come here again?'

'Well, sweetheart, it's hard to say . . . Denniston can get into your blood.'

'Denniston!' snorts Mrs C. Rasmussen. 'Only thing in that man's blood is alcohol. And the gold. He came here to be near his gold, man!'

'True, woman, true. This woman, Rose, can see a man's heart laid out like a map. He came to be near his gold. What I reckon, now, is this. That man maybe he find good pay-gold in some high place — rocky, you know? There's no way, you see, he can get to it without two good arms and good strong legs. Up over the rocks and bluffs. No way. You see the way that man walk? Good enough straight along, but when he drinks that old bent knee gives on Jimmy. I see it many times.'

'That's just drunk, man,' says Mrs C. 'Drink turning the joint to water.'

'It is not. I saw him sober, fall from tripping on a bitty rock in the path. He go down like a sack. Get up quick, embarrassed. That bent knee got no strength, I reckon.'

'Well, you would be the expert on drunk and sober.'

'I would, woman. So. Jimmy is stuck, can't get to his gold. If it's there at all in any quantity, which I doubt. A nugget or two maybe, but a mine? I doubt.'

'Was I born then?' asks Rose.

'Let me see now, '79. Yes, Rose, you would be two or three.'

'Well, where was I?'

'A good question, which you will have to ask your mother, for none of us at Denniston knows the answer.'

'You were down Hokitika way, with your mother,' says Bella Rasmussen, but shakes her head when Con raises his eyebrows. 'Finish your story, man. It's time this little one was in bed.'

'I am trying, goodness knows. The Company man — not Mr McConnochie, Rose, Mr Dickson, it was then, a decent man — he say to Eddie, "Give the poor fellow a job if he can get up the Incline. Something to put bread in his mouth. The Company owes him." You'd wish all bosses were like that eh?

'So he come back. It was the same day, exactly, I brought Mrs Rasmussen here up to the Hill. Two weeks I been off work, travelling south to find where she got to . . .'

'Conrad Rasmussen, that is not a story for Rose.'

'Well, it is a happier one, which you will hear another day, Rose. It is entirely proper for your ears and why not? But this is Jimmy's story, your father's story. True.'

'And I will tell it,' says Mrs Rasmussen, 'before the child falls asleep. We brought him up the Incline, Rose, between us — no easy job. It was a silent ride, I remember. Even then he cast a shadow. But you couldn't help feeling pity. Lost his good right arm. Perhaps he thought, then, that one day his leg would carry him properly. Hanrattys' offered the poor fellow a bed but he would take no help. Asked for the little tent over by the cave at the Camp. Wanted to be on his own, he said.'

'But he is a changed man, Rose,' says Con the Brake. 'Where are the songs now? The whistling like a bird? The stories? All gone. The man is like a black well where the water is stagnant and sour. The pain, maybe, or the frustration has changed the man. If the gold is so important to him, why don't he share the knowledge? Willy Huff was a good friend of Jimmy's. Willy could have partnered him. The fellow that got blown down into the gully, you know . . .'

'Conrad!'

'Yes, yes, woman. How can I tell a story without the background? I tell you, Rose, gold may be a colour to melt your heart on a summer's day, but it can turn a man blacker than a storm at sea. And so it was with Jimmy Cork. He just want to sit all day, his eyes watching, watching up-river. Bitter, he is, that luck has turned against him. So withered inside, you know, he can't talk to a friend or ask for help.

'So that's why your father take to the drink. Ease the pain. The arm pain and the lost fortune.'

'But what about Scobies?' says Rose.

There is a silence while Con the Brake looks into the fire and Mrs C. Rasmussen takes up an iron poker, wrought with a sailing ship on the handle, and stirs the red coals to bring them to life.

'Ah well,' says Con the Brake at last, 'I wasn't there, sweetheart.'

'Did my father kill a Scobie?'

'It was an accident. So I hear.'

'But why, then?'

'Why what, sweetheart?'

'If it was an accident, why do they shout at us?'

'Well now,' rumbles Con the Brake, looking to his wife for help. 'Those English miners are careful men, Rose. They don't believe in accidents.'

Rose thinks about this. 'Why not?'

Mrs C. Rasmussen sighs. 'Now that is the end of your story, Rose. This man will walk you over to your home.'

Rose trots out into the dark readily enough, one small hand engulfed in Con's warm paw. Bella Rasmussen's heart breaks, though, to see her go.

The Miners' Curse

WHAT HAPPENED, ON that day of the picnic, as every mother's son and every father's daughter on the Hill knows but none will tell Rose, is this.

Underground, miners work as pairs. It's always the case. Josiah Scobie and his brother Arnold are a pair. He and Arnold have always worked as mates since boys. Mary Scobie doesn't like it.

'If there's an accident you could lose two in the family,' she says.

'Or save both,' is Josiah's opinion. 'We know to an inch where the other is and how the seam is cracking. I trust him.'

The other brother, Frank, not so fussy about his mate, changes from time to time for variety.

'I'll end up knowing more jokes than me brothers. And meeting a few more sisters maybe!' he laughs. Frank is the youngest of the brothers, and sunny natured where the others are serious. Frank can whistle to make you think a forest full of birds is on your doorstep, which brings tears to some eyes, up here on the Hill, where no bird sings. And he's a good musician, like most of the Scobies.

The day of the accident he's working with stocky Peter Fogarty — not family but a good English miner. You'd never catch one of the English miners choosing one of the 'volunteers' as mate. Frank and Peter are joking about girls, or the lack of them, and laying plans to ride down the Incline next Saturday to see who might have arrived in Waimang. Frank is twenty-eight, a full ten years younger than his brother Josiah, but he can hew as fast, despite the chatter, and is known as a top miner. Each pair is working on a separate pillar of good hard coal, a distance apart but close enough to run for help if needed. There is a certain feeling of competition in the air as to which will get their pillar down first.

To understand the accident it is necessary to picture the mine. Imagine, then, a thick slab of coal lying between layers of stone, as a wedge of meat lies between slices of bread in a sandwich. But in the case of the coal at Denniston the slab is vast — spread wider than a town and thicker than the height of a man, sometimes two men. This great slab of coal must be got out cleanly, without collapsing the rock roof in on the miners.

So first you drive a bord — a tunnel about ten foot wide — to be your haulage line. In you go through the coal, extracting as you go, and putting up timber sets, one each side of the tunnel as props, and one across the top to support the roof. When you have gone a chain in, you cut across at right angles for a chain and then drive another bord in from outside. That's your air supply. The flow of air is crucial in mining; you must have multiple shafts so fresh air can be drawn through.

So. Now you go back to the main haulage line and extend it another chain, take another right-angle cut, then extend your air

shaft to meet it. On you go, extending your two parallel shafts —
one for haulage, one for air — cutting a cross-shaft every chain. As
you go deeper in, you hang sacking curtains — brattices — over the
entrances to your earlier cross-shafts, to block the air flow. This way,
you drag the air further into the mine with you. Big blocks of coal,
a chain square, remain between your bords. These are called pillars.
Which is apt. They hold up the mighty weight of the rock roof, of
the whole land above, which no puny timber sets could do.

And so you go, more bords to north and south, more cross-
shafts east and west, honeycombing your way through the vast seam
of coal until a plan of it looks like New York city — or, if you like,
Westport itself, which is laid out square and neat with hardly a bent
road to soften the landscape.

At the time of the accident Banbury mine is all tunnelled
through, and the men are now working back from the outer edges,
in towards the haulage line, extracting the chain-square pillars of
coal. Think of digging out two pretty large houses of solid coal.
That would be your 'pillar'. Many, many boxes of coal will be
extracted from one pillar. This day both pairs of miners are in a
good rhythm, sending boxes up regularly. Both pairs want to be the
first to move on to a new pillar.

Samuel, Josiah's eldest son, sixteen tomorrow, is down in this
section too, trucking for both pairs.

'Heigh ho,' he calls. 'Hup hup!' Though there is no need at all.
Noggin the horse knows what to do with no word said, let alone any
human to say one. Noggin would go back and forth all day from
face to haulage line, trustworthy as a miner's mate.

Down comes Samuel through the mine with Noggin pulling a
string of empties. Josiah leans on his shovel and smiles. Everyone
smiles to see Samuel. He is not sunny natured like his Uncle Frank,
nor thick-set like his father. Willowy and lithe, rather — pale

skinned as a girl, and dreamy. Mary Scobie, his mother, would never admit to favourites among her six sons but the others notice an extra light in her eye when she watches Samuel. Sam is the one who will put her slippers by the range to warm, or fetch the clothes off the line when the rain comes.

Samuel loves to work with the horses.

'Look at Noggin!' he shouts now to his dad. 'He knows it's Saturday! He can smell fresh air and sunlight; I swear he knows! See him snort?'

Josiah laughs. 'We all know it's Saturday and Noggin picks it from us, perhaps. Come on, lad, get on with it! We need some space here.'

Samuel unhooks the string of boxes and rolls four to Josiah and Arnold, the other four over to Frank and Peter Fogarty. Noggin plods back up the line without waiting for his master to tell him. He waits at the correct distance, while Samuel hooks the waiting full boxes together. Seven boxes. Arnold is just topping off the eighth. His big round banjo shovel slaps a last good slab aboard. He reaches for one of his tokens, hooks it on the box to show this coal should be tallied as his, and gives Samuel the nod. Arnold is not a talker.

'Another load and we'll stop for our bite,' says Josiah to his son. 'Come down to the lay-by and we'll have it together. Where are the lads?'

His next two boys, David and Mathew, fifteen and thirteen, are clippies, clipping the boxes onto the endless chain that will take them off to the Bins.

'Two sections away,' says Samuel, who always knows where his brothers are. 'Shall I fetch them?'

'Nay nay, lad, they are old enough to fend for themselves. You worry like a mother.'

Samuel grins. 'And who has taught me to worry, eh? Who has

said a miner looks out for his mate first, last and every second in between?'

'Ah well, true, but your brothers are clippies in another section, and you must trust that section to keep an eye on the young 'uns. Your responsibility is here with your horse, and the men in your own section. Now get on out of here — your horse is halfway to the haulage already.'

As Samuel sets off after Noggin he sees a wavering light approaching.

'Someone coming!' he yells back. 'Are you waiting for the underviewer to fire your shot?'

The fellow with one arm comes past with a cheery-enough nod. He has hooked his lamp crookedly to his cap. Samuel can see the gleam of warm oil running down his nose.

'Shall I fix that for you?' he offers, but Jimmy Cork is in a hurry. Samuel tries again. 'I'd head out if I were you. The men won't welcome you.'

'Ah well, so what?' says Jimmy and keeps going.

Samuel waits for his dad's explosion.

'Bloody hell, man!' shouts Josiah, 'Didn't I tell you last time this is no place for bloody volunteers? You are a danger to us all.'

Jimmy Cork holds up his air tester. 'Hold your hair on, Mister. I am only doing my job.'

His cheeky grin enrages Josiah. 'You have tested the air once already down here. It is bad, we all know that, and you are using up precious yards of it sniffing around. I will have a word to Eddie about this.'

Jimmy backs off. Talk of the mine manager seems to fluster him. 'I'm going, I'm going,' he says. 'Now, tell me, are there more air shafts down this way?'

'Go back up above and look at your map and get out of our

hair. This section will close today, God willing, and I want no stranger to nursemaid when it comes down. Off with you!'

But Samuel, enjoying the scene from up the line, sees that Jimmy heads deeper in, towards Frank and Peter.

Later, when Samuel comes down the dark tunnel with the next string of empties, he finds Josiah and Arnold standing still, listening. The horse cocks his ears too, then tosses his head, and paws the ground.

'See that?' says Josiah to his son. 'Noggin knows it's on its way. Listen, lad.'

Samuel hasn't experienced a close before but has heard his dad talk about them often enough. When most of this pillar of coal has been extracted, the rock roof above will collapse to fill the gap. The whole landscape above settles. As the miners are working their way through the pillars, the mine is collapsing in behind them. It's important this happens, otherwise the weight of all that rock swings over above the next pillar and is a danger to the men. Samuel looks up. Above him the top-coal is creaking like the timbers of a ship in a storm. A small lump drops down and Sam jumps in alarm. Josiah smiles.

'You are right to be on edge, lad, but we have a few minutes yet. First the roof coal will come down, then we will see. Sometimes there is time to box up some of it, other times the roof comes down very soon. We'd best walk up the line a bit. Run now and tell Frank and Peter our close is on its way and they should be ready in case theirs goes with it.'

Sam looks for his horse but Noggin is already away up the mine.

'Noggin thinks it's coming soon,' he says, smiling, but nervous too. 'I bet he's right!'

Quick on his feet, he runs down to the next section.

'Coal's creaking up Dad's way. He says to shift out.'

Frank whistles. 'Ah well, looks like the ancient ones have beaten us to it, Peter. No sign of a close here, though.' Just then, a couple of lumps fall from the roof with a clatter. Frank tilts his head so the flame of his lamp shines upwards. As they watch, a crack opens up in the shining coal with a sound like a pistol shot. Sam jumps. He is not easy underground without his good steady Noggin, who reminds him of the living world outside.

'Off we go, then,' says Frank, 'but I'm guessing we'll hold here for a while.'

Suddenly he stops. 'Damn. Where is that one-arm man?'

'He was here a minute ago,' says Peter. 'Ferreting around in a strange way. I reckon he's just through that brattice.'

'Nip through quick, Sam, while we pick up our tools,' says Frank. 'Give him a yell, the silly idiot. Don't waste time, though. If he's more than two chain away come straight back.'

Samuel wants to run for the surface but the others are calm enough, taking time to pick up their tools and their powder cans. He runs the next chain, turns left and through the brattice. His lamp seems to make no impression on the dark in here.

'Hey!' he yells. 'Anyone here?' Above him the coal groans and creaks. Several lumps come down. He feels for the wall and it seems to shift under his hand. A thin trickle of stones and sand pours like a waterfall just in front of his nose. Suddenly Samuel is very frightened.

'Hey!' he yells again, but it is more in fear than warning. He turns to run back. But which way? The noise has disoriented him. In his panic he runs deeper in.

Frank and Peter hear the coal shift.

'Bloody hell, it's coming down,' shouts Peter. 'Where's that brother of yours?'

But Frank is already running down the shaft and through the brattice. As he reaches the junction the top-coal comes down with a roar. The black tide rolls towards him across the floor. His feet are trapped. Frank knows he must stay upright but is desperate for Samuel.

'Sam! Sam!' he shouts above the roar of the coal all around him. He is in total darkness. His lamp has been extinguished by the rush of air. He hears a thin wail, and then everything is engulfed in the roar of the close. The sandstone roof gives way to the ancient force of gravity. Roof and floor become one and the land in this section is solid again.

The fall is not above Frank but just behind him. His upper body is tossed like a rag doll as the blast of air roars past him. But his legs are already held: he is powerless to move. His mouth fills with dust. He cannot see the rubble but feels it rolling up over his trapped legs, up past his chest. The pressure is intolerable.

Frank gives a last despairing shout. 'Sa-mu-el!' He thinks this will be his last living word. But the fall is spent, and Frank's head is still above the pile. He is entombed, immobile but upright, up to his neck in a dead-weight of sandstone. No part of his body can move even an inch. To drag even a mouthful of the dusty air into his lungs takes an immense effort.

Frank listens: a trickle of sand still falling, a stone rolling down the pile to settle somewhere in the darkness. No other sounds. The close has settled, but will the men be able to find him? And Samuel? In the dark Frank can only guess at the extent of the fall. Surely he is at the edge of it to be left like this?

He hears feet running and voices calling.

'Frank!'

'Frankie!'

'Samuel! Oh God, Sam! Sam!'

There are lights approaching and Frank's heart gives a lurch of relief. He tries to call out but his overworked lungs can produce only a tiny squeak. He fixes his eyes on the three little pools of light and prays to God.

Josiah stops. His chest is heaving. 'Tom, Arnold, quiet! We must listen.'

In the silence Frank manages a whimper. Josiah's lamp immediately points in the right direction. He walks forward, but gingerly, then stops about three good strides from Frank. He has reached the edge of the pile. He is straining to see. Frank manages to shift his head an inch. Josiah looks straight into the eyes of his brother. His own eyes widen in disbelief to see the head sitting like St John the Baptist's on a platter of brown sandstone. Frank is crying silently. Each slow breath rasps and whoops like a child with diphtheria.

'Sam?' asks Josiah, but Frank can only let the tears fall.

'Well,' says Josiah, his voice cracking, 'we'll have you out in no time, with the good Lord's help. You have here three champions with the banjo. Take heart, brother.'

The three men work at the pile with their shovels. Josiah would like to tear at the rock like a demon but he keeps his head. If the rock pile shifts again it could engulf what is left of Frank. Others have arrived now, and John Davies helps with the shovelling, but four is all there is room for, working at the pile. The others ram timber props to either side of the cleared gap to keep the rubble from rolling back in, but the sandstone is loose and it rolls back anyway. Big Andy Fellows takes over from Peter and makes good progress. Josiah's middle sons, Mathew and David, are further back, holding hands like the children they are, and crying. No one thinks to send them above ground.

All the time Frank's breathing is weakening. His mouth is a black hole, his eyes terrified as he hauls at the air.

'Hold on, Frank, my bonny, we are closing on you,' grunts Josiah. But all can see there is much yet ahead of them.

'Is there a lad here?' shouts Josiah. His own Mathew and David, tear-streaked and shaking, come forward.

'Are you willing?' says Josiah to Mathew, the youngest, who is small and thin as a stick.

'Aye, Dad.' But he's frightened enough.

'We will hoist you onto the pile. Lie flat, not to disturb, and see if you can clear a little space around his neck and shoulders to breathe.'

'I'll try.'

'Good lad. Gentle as a lamb now.'

David wails like a baby to see his brother hoisted into the dark. Someone puts a grimy arm around his shoulder but David shrugs it off. He curls up on the wet ground, arms over his head until it is all over.

Mathew lies spread-eagled on the pile of loose stone. His own head is close to his Uncle Frank's. Gently he pulls away stone after stone. Uncle Frank doesn't seem to notice.

'Oo . . . oo . . . oo . . .' His uncle's breaths moan like a far-distant owl in the night.

'The shovels are nearly here,' whispers Mathew, his little boy's fingers working away in the dark.

'Oo . . . oo . . . o . . .'

'Uncle! Keep breathing. Please, don't stop now!' Mathew touches his uncle's dusty head as gently as he would a baby's. The head jerks suddenly but takes no breath.

'Dad! Daddy!'

Josiah hears his son scream and knows they are too late. Leaving all caution he tears at the rubble with his bare hands, scrabbling up to Frank's silent head. He passes his screaming son down to waiting hands below. He kisses Frank on each cheek, closes the staring eyes and prays.

'The Lord be with thee. Go in peace into eternal life, both thee and our dearly beloved Samuel . . .' On he prays, his voice echoing in the dark, while the miners touch their smoking caps in reverence for a lost brother.

Josiah will not pray for the one-armed man.

Prayers turn to curses later that night when it is reported that Jimmy Cork has been found, alive and (unforgivably) cheerful, drinking at Red Minifie's, unaware of any accident, so he says. It is also reported that no mine manager gave him permission to check for clean air. His job was to supervise the new clippies, see they came to no harm. Jimmy's story is that he was taking extra caution over the air on his own initiative. No one believes him. Prospecting for gold in Company time is more likely, they mutter. Somehow Jimmy had wandered into an air shaft and come out above ground safely, while the two Scobies were trapped, looking for him.

'Well, yes,' said Jimmy to the crowd of silent miners who came down from Burnett's Face next day to confront him, 'I felt something — the ground shift, and a rumble. But I was out then — in the sun. An earthquake, I thought.'

And as the miners came closer, menacing: 'Look, my friends . . .,' (Josiah spat on the ground before him) '. . . you can't blame a fellow for worrying about the air you breathe. I am sorry about the accident, but how was I to know . . .'

Josiah stabbed a finger at him. 'Accident! Murder, more like. Don't you insult us with your wild excuses!'

Jimmy took a step back and his bad knee gave way. He fell awkwardly but not a man, not even the manager, put out a hand to help him up.

Josiah, his face set like stone, eyes boring holes, pronounced the curse. 'God's wrath be called down on you! You and all your kind. We have no wish ever to set eyes upon you, in this world or the next.' He turned to Eddie Carmichael. 'If this man comes within a chain of Banbury or of any other mine on this whole hill every miner here will walk off the job.' The men rumbled assent. 'Moreover,' said Josiah, 'if he comes down to Burnett's Face at all we will find it hard to muster any Christian charity, and will more likely do the man in.'

More nods. Without another word the men left, leaving a white-faced Jimmy struggling upright, and an angry mine manager watching him.

They say Eddie pleaded with Jimmy to leave that night; offered him and his family assistance on the Incline to get them down safely. When he refused, Eddie fired him. There would be no further work, said Eddie, not now or in the future. Jimmy must have been mad or worse, they said, to stay. But stay he did, in his hut at the corner of the Camp, with few friends and many enemies. With Eva, and with Rose.

School of Six

MARY SCOBIE BROUGHT up the idea of the school, which was not surprising. The Scobies were organisers, every one of them.

'Born stirrers more like,' Mr McConnochie had grumbled on more than one occasion, but held his peace now, because they were born miners too.

Totty was pleased to stop work for a moment, and intrigued. She knew there were women up at Burnett's Face; Tom, building houses for the immigrants, had brought the news. But this was the first time in six months one had paid a formal visit.

'Come in, come in,' she says, wondering whether to put the visitor in the boarders' parlour or the kitchen where it is warm.

The stout woman, leaning heavily on her stick, makes the decision for her. 'I won't come past the kitchen, Mrs Hanratty, my skirt is a good six inches in mud. Do you mind if my Brennan comes in too?'

And there at the gate stands a sturdy little fellow in trousers a few sizes too big, mud on his knees, his hands, in his hair even. He looks down — perhaps he's crying.

'He would not take notice of where his feet were carrying him and fell twice, in the thickest mud, wouldn't you know it?' The woman sighs bleakly as she looks at the muddy boy. 'I have told him to stay at the gate till I ask permission to bring in such a rascal. But there. I am not much cleaner and have stayed upright all the way. It is more than time the Company put in a road or two.' Her flat voice rises a peg or two, then fades into silence. She is exhausted. And some other darkness lies behind the black eyes, the tightly corseted exterior.

'Please come in, both of you,' says Totty. 'We will wash off the worst of your boy's mud in a moment.'

In the warm kitchen the two women make the formal introductions.

'I am Mrs Josiah Scobie from Burnett's Face. Please call me Mary.'

Burnett's Face is the settlement further in on the plateau, close to the new mines being opened up. Fifty or so miners live there now. It is a two-mile walk and one not often made for purely social reasons.

Totty nods. She understands now, the darkness that has entered with the woman. 'My husband, Mr Tom Hanratty, has spoken of you. Of your tragedy.'

'Aye.'

'I am sorry.'

'Thank you. It is the will of the Lord.' The bleakness in Mary Scobie's voice belies her words.

'I should have paid a visit.'

'Well, it is not easy. We have our lives to lead.'

'Yes.' Totty looks down, not knowing what to say to this flinty woman. The loss of a brother-in-law and a son soon after arriving at so alien a place as Denniston would surely have broken most women. 'Perhaps,' she says after a pause, 'my husband built your home?'

'No, my dear. Scobies build their own homes, but I have seen your husband and know him to be a good tradesman.'

There is something a little patronising about this. Tom, after all, owns the only six-roomed building at Denniston, and will soon build a second boarding house. But Totty is too tired today to take umbrage. She puts tea on the table, groans with pleasure at taking the weight off her feet.

Mary Scobie looks at her with a practised eye. 'About two more months?'

'Yes. Two exactly.'

'Will you have it up here?'

'I will. Mrs C will help, as she did with Michael and Elizabeth.'

There is a silence as the two sip their tea. Michael and Brennan circle each other like puppies. Then Michael bolts into the hallway and Brennan follows. Soon they are banging up and down the corridor with whoops and Totty has to call them not to wake the baby.

'I heard you had six boys and all in the mine,' says Totty, back in the kitchen. 'Tom didn't speak about the little one.'

Mary takes a scone. It's yesterday's, warmed in the oven. 'Well, and that is the reason for this visit. I would like Brennan to have schooling. There are two more children arrived last week, up near us, nine and ten years old. With your Michael that makes four. Also,' Mary Scobie takes a breath as if preparing for some battle, 'I intend to take the twins out of the mine for a year's school-work.

To take their Certificate. Six pupils is enough for a school, they say.'

Totty flushes, not sure how to put it. 'There is another little one. Rose. She could do with the schooling.'

Mary looks her dead in the eye. 'The child at the Camp?'

'Yes.'

'Jimmy Cork's ?'

'Well, she lives there, but who can say . . .'

'No.'

'Mrs Scobie . . .' This time Totty is the one preparing for battle.

'No, my dear, not in a school with my boys.' The older woman's face is granite. 'It would not work.'

'The child did not choose her father.'

'The father should leave this place, not settle his blood here for schooling.'

'Well,' Totty smiles in spite of herself, 'Rose will likely send herself to school, and no one will have the heart to turn her away. Wait till you see her, Mary.'

'Not I nor any other Scobie will wish to set eyes on her. There will be trouble.'

For a moment the only sound is the boys' boots on the floor-boards. Then Mary Scobie, straight-backed at the table but unseeing, starts speaking. It is as if a small crack has opened, just enough for the words to edge out. The words are bitter, the voice bleak as winter.

'What kind of a godforsaken place is this where you cannot bury your dead? My eldest son, Samuel, and his uncle, Frank, both of them dead in a day and I can visit the graveside of neither. What kind of a settlement can we build here without our dead? Without a churchyard? This is devil's country. Iron-hard rock, black sky, and no shred of honest soil to bury the dead. My son is lying where he fell, who can say exactly where. His body not laid out; crumpled under a mountain of rock like some animal. Who can pray — who can commune with the dead — at the mouth of a clattering mine?'

'I'm sorry,' says Totty. She pats the older woman's hand but the gesture goes unnoticed.

'And what if our babies die? Which they will, of course.' Mary Scobie is deep inside herself, oblivious now, surely, of her hostess's condition. 'Will we have to put them on a coal wagon and watch them descend away and away for ever? Could you live through that and remain in your right mind? Could you?'

'Please . . .' murmurs Totty.

'The Incline,' Mary Scobie spits the words, 'is not fit transport for a human being. Nor a coffin. I will never travel it.'

Totty has heard of the funeral. Two days after the deaths Mary Scobie had stood in the rain at the Burnett's Face entrance to Banbury Mine while her husband, the boys and the other miners had sombrely placed Frank's coffin onto a coal box, guided it through the same mine that killed him, then loaded the body onto a coal wagon and ridden down the Incline with it, roaring down the rails, the dead out of reach forever: out by rail, past Conn's Creek, past Koranui Mine, all the way to Waimangaroa, where there was consecrated soil deep enough for a grave. Mary, with Granny Binney beside her for company, had stood like stone, they said. Had not moved while the coffin descended both sections of Incline. She had stood on after the faint shriek of the train whistle far below signalled the next stage of the funeral cortege. At last, with Granny Binney guiding her, she had returned in silence to the tiny empty house. All the men were praying at a distant churchyard and would not return until next day. Mary had ignored her silent younger children, refused to organise or attend any funeral supper; had sat through the night in front of a cold cup of tea while Granny Binney put the lads to bed.

In Totty's kitchen Mary Scobie takes a breath. Totty can almost see the crack in this woman's flinty exterior closing. But there it is — a weakness, a hairline fracture, which will open again, Totty suspects, and worse next time. A worry. You need to be rock solid to survive on the Hill.

But for now Mary Scobie is back in control.

'I am determined, my dear, that the boys — the younger ones — will have the tools to escape this dreadful place.'

Totty frowns. 'Dreadful is a strong word. This is my home.'

'Not mine.' The words are spat out. 'Never.'

Mary Scobie rolls on, inexorable as an approaching storm. Space for a schoolroom must be considered. Hanrattys' is the only place with a spare room big enough. And the teacher. Totty is the only person, according to Mary's inquiries, who has the Standard Six Certificate.

'The coming baby is a hurdle, my dear, but the need is great. Will you take it on?'

Totty will not be bullied. 'I simply cannot do it, Mrs Scobie. Tom is out all day building houses. I have the boarders to cook and wash for, and, God willing, three children.' She sighs. 'You have noticed the scones are yesterday's.'

'I have. And have done the same.' Mary nods with the solid understanding of another overworked mother. She pats Totty's hand and the younger woman finds herself in tears, seduced by exhaustion and the rare soft pleasure of a woman's company.

'I'm sorry . . . I'm sorry . . . but you are welcome to the room.'

'And we will find the teacher to fill it. We must. There is no other way on the Hill. I will come up with a plan, never fear.'

In the end it was Totty who thought of asking Mrs C. Rasmussen. That ample lady shook with pleasure at being asked, not at all deterred by her total lack of formal education.

'A teacher! Well, I suppose I could manage. I would have to confer with Mr Rasmussen, of course.'

'Of course,' said Totty soberly, though she could imagine the scene if Con the Brake was anything less than wildly encouraging.

Mrs C's confident smile slipped for a moment. 'The Chapel parents — they would accept me?'

'Mrs C, everyone loves you.'

'Love, yes; but respect?'

'If they don't now, they will learn to.'

Mary Scobie, practical woman, had immediately seen the good sense of the suggestion, and was prepared to put aside religious scruples for the time being. She herself, though unschooled, was literate enough, and respected Mrs C. Rasmussen's knowledge, even if she had her suspicions about where the knowledge was acquired. In fact it was she who suggested, with a surprising snort of laughter, that they hoodwink the officials.

'We will apply for the licence in Totty's name. She has the Certificate. Who is to know? Can you imagine that School Board in Nelson sending someone up here to inspect? Never!'

Mrs C. Rasmussen sat up straighter. 'My qualifications may not be formal, Mrs Scobie, but they will stand in their own right. I do not need to hide behind Totty.'

Totty laughed. 'Oh, Mrs C, you could run me into the ground on any subject in the curriculum, but we need our allocation of slates and chalk and blackboards. If the silly twits in Nelson want a Certificate, let's give them one!'

In the four years since Con had brought her to the Hill, Mrs C had done everything a good pillar of the community should, except, sadly, produce children. The offer of a post as schoolmistress was to her a final proof of respectability and more precious than a six-ounce gold nugget.

'Thank you, Totty, I will accept,' she said, sitting straight and formal on her chair. She smoothed back a strand of her heavy brown hair with a finger in whose plump folds gleamed the wedding ring placed there by Con the Brake and no preacher. At last she felt secure enough to add, 'Please call me Bella.'

So Mrs C. Rasmussen, alias Mrs Dorothy Hanratty, became the first teacher of the tiny school in Hanrattys' spare guest-room. Indeed she was an inspired choice, for she read and wrote fluently, knew more songs and stories than anyone in the world, and had travelled to Australia more than once, according to Con the Brake. What's more, Mrs C could add up a column of figures, especially if it was money, faster than the mine manager.

On the first day of school the Scobie twins hitched a ride on a couple of boxes coming out of the mine, rode down to Denniston, jumped off near Hanrattys' and arrived with their identical faces black as thunder — and not only with soot. Schooling was well below the dignity of this pair of experienced miners, who were Scobies to boot. Brennan, too scared to ride the skips, or unwilling to ignore his mother's absolute veto on the practice, walked through the mud beside the skipway — dangerous enough in itself, as everyone in Burnett's Face grumbled. He walked with Jackie and Donnie O'Shea, — 'Catholic, but never mind, Brennan,' his dad said. 'The O'Sheas are good miners.' Brennan smiled at the thought of spending this day and all the next days with Michael Hanratty, the gold-coloured boy with six rooms inside his house.

In Hanrattys' back room Mrs Rasmussen wrote their names firmly in her new register. She sat them at desks hammered together the previous night by Tom Hanratty and still smelling of sawdust and oil. In twos they sat: the twins at the back, then the O'Sheas, with the young ones at the front.

There is an empty desk on the other side of Michael.

'Who is this for?' whispers Brennan, awed by the newness of it all.

'Rose,' says Michael, smiling in excitement and not one whit awed. 'She's my friend too.'

There is a knock on the door.

'Come in!' calls Mrs Rasmussen, glowing, in her own school-room.

Rose, small and tightly contained, steps into the room. For a moment she stands by the door, her mass of fair curls boiling in all directions. Hardly breathing, she turns to face the door, closes it slowly and stands there, her thin little back shielding her from the six pairs of male eyes. She seems unable to turn around.

'Good morning, Rose,' says Mrs Rasmussen quietly, and Rose comes away from the door, her too-bright smile firmly in place. The boys wait in silence as Rose stands in front of the teacher. She smoothes her pinafore, good clean flour-bag, sewn by Mrs C herself, and waits too.

Mrs Rasmussen clears her throat. This must be done right. She is aware the child has had to face open enmity many times since the accident. Goodness only knew why the mother had not left the Camp. Surely any existence would be preferable to living under Jimmy Cork's reputation.

Rosser Scobie, jumping to his feet, is the first to find words.

'Is this his girl? Killer Jimmy's daughter?'

The other twin stands too. His voice tries to imitate a man's but comes out in a boy's squeak, which would be funny if the face were less rigid. 'From County Cork?' It is an accusation.

Tiny Rose turns to face the boys. 'No, I am not,' she says in her clear accurate voice, and waits for the next onslaught.

'This is Rose,' says Mrs Rasmussen firmly. 'Rose.' And smiles at the tense child. 'When we are at school we all need a second name to come and go with. Shall we say Rose of Tralee?' She walks to the back of the room where the miners' sons are still standing with their fists balled at their sides. 'Tralee. Which is not in County Cork but an altogether gentler part of Ireland.'

Mrs Rasmussen has no idea where Tralee is, though she loves the song. The shadow of a saucy smile, long subdued, pulls at her cheek and she remembers smoky saloons, appreciative customers, a younger, beribboned Bella, in lace petticoats, singing to the diggers in shanty-towns up and down the Coast. The smile broadens.

'Rose of Tralee,' she repeats. 'Now, sit down everyone, and I will give you your tasks.'

Rose of Tralee, pink as her name, trots over to her desk. She sits on the little bench and runs her hands over the fresh wood.

'Rose of Tralee,' she says, trying it out.

Michael, not a miner's son and shielded by Totty from their dramas, smiles at Rose.

'This is my other friend, Brennan,' he whispers.

Brennan, dark browed and black eyed, stares hard at Rose, but when the curls bounce and the blue eyes crinkle he forgets he is a Scobie and smiles back.

Playmate and Pariah

ROSE OF TRALEE never once missed a day's school that anyone could remember. Sometimes she would arrive late; her mother spent most of the night wrestling Jimmy Cork to bed, so was not one to wake her daughter, lay out clean clothes and see there was a warm breakfast inside her. Besides, no one at Jimmy's shack had a clock or pocket watch of any sort. So until Rose learned to time her life by her mother's roosters and the Powerhouse whistle, she might arrive at Hanrattys' back door, the usual smile in place, to find Brennan and Michael halfway through their alphabet.

On other days Totty would find her at the door a good hour early.

'I haven't had my breakfast, Mrs Hanratty,' she would say in a straightforward way, 'I couldn't find any at our home.' And would walk straight in to take her place at the kitchen table with a delighted Michael.

That was a remarkable thing about Rose: she never learned to cringe or whine; never in all those years became defensive. Goodness knows, she had reason. People on the Hill were free with their opinions, and made no bones about what they thought of Jimmy Cork and his wild, mad wife. But Rose was born, according to Mrs C, with a sunny nature, which was the greatest gift anyone could have given her, under the circumstances.

Rose and Brennan and Michael were the only children of their age on the whole plateau. Women were arriving now, of course. Babies would be born. But those three were like the spearhead of a new generation. The twins and the O'Shea boys were little men, marking time until they could go down the mine. Rose and Brennan and Michael were everyone's hope for Denniston, for a proper town. For schools and a hospital and churches and sports teams. The dreams of many centred on those three children. Circumstances, accidental but in the end too potent to be ignored, threw those three children together, tied their lives into a knot which, in the end, bred disaster. In these early days, though, their antics brought only a smile.

Everyone knew them. Everyone at Denniston town, that is. After school the three would go shouting and chasing down to the Brake Head, where Con the Brake would greet them with a roar and a cracking grin and let them try their strength on the heavy iron of the brake-wheel.

Eddie Carmichael would call them up to his office to test their addition on his coal tallies, and if they got it right he might find a piece of chocolate or an apple.

The men at the Bins would shout and wave and warn them to keep a safe distance, and the hook-men would give them rides running the empties down to the Bins.

Michael is the leader. His coppery thatch of hair, a legacy from his mother, flops into blue sparky eyes. Taller and faster than the other two, knobby knees pounding up and down, he marches along the street, leading his army of two.

'Halt!' he cries, and the two followers try to stand solemn and upright in the mud like proper soldiers. Michael's eyes blaze. Games are real for him.

Rose looks sideways at Brennan. The dark little boy is almost as small as Rose but much solider. His hair is cut bristly and short; his clothes, always hand-me-downs, are always too big for him. He frowns, trying to look the proper soldier, and Rose bursts into giggles. Rose, though oldest of the trio, is smallest. A stranger would think her delicate as glass, her mop of fair curls almost too massive for the thin neck to bear. But there's energy in her, like a coiled spring. Both boys adore her.

Rose giggles again. Brennan loses control too and they laugh and pull even more serious soldier-faces.

'Atten-tion!' yells Michael, red in the face. Brennan attempts to obey but slips in the mud and only just stays upright. His arms windmill. Rose shrieks with laughter and gives him her hand.

Michael flourishes his toy gun, shaped by his carpenter father, marches up to Brennan and strikes him. The blow is more than play-acting. Brennan stops in the middle of his pantomime. When he frowns it's like a blind coming down.

'That's not fair. I'm going home,' he announces, and turns to stump up the hill.

'About turn!' orders Michael, to no effect. He stamps his foot and shouts again, 'About *turn!*'

Rose dances back and forth between them. 'You can be leader, Brennan . . . can't he, Michael?'

Brennan says nothing. Plods up towards the skipway. Rose runs after him. She is always desperate to keep the games alive. 'Going

116

home' is not an attractive option for her.

'I'll give you a penny,' pleads Rose.

'I said *about turn!*' Michael is standing his ground, further down the road, his thin legs planted in the mud, the bullying stance an imitation of a man's.

'I'll give you two pennies.'

Brennan stops. He is crying. Though he looks tough as a boot, Brennan cries easily, earning him taunts at school and from his older brothers. Rose suddenly reaches out a small hand and rubs it over his wiry hair as if stroking a dog. Brennan pulls away but the corners of his mouth twitch at this surprising offering.

'You haven't got two pennies,' he sniffs, wiping his nose on his sleeve.

'I have, and a gold nugget.'

'You're daft. Like your mam. Show me your gold then.'

'It's down at the Camp. It's hidden.'

Michael can't bear to see them talking together up the road. He marches up, left, right, left, comes to a smart attention. But is undermined by the mention of money.

'Well, where is it hidden?' he asks.

'Somewhere secret. Near our place.'

Brennan says nothing. One of his hands reaches up slyly to rub his own hair, relive the feel of Rose's fingers. Since his brother's death, embraces of any kind have been rare in his family.

'That's not fair!' storms Michael. They all know that Jimmy Cork's place is out of bounds. The far end of the Camp, the rough men's quarters, and especially Jimmy's place, are not for women and children, except for Rose's mother, and Rose herself.

Rose raises her voice. It is high and clear with an edge to it, but not pleading.

'We can go there now. He'll be asleep. We can go a secret way.'

But even the hint of secret gold is not enough to tempt the boys. Two places the three of them never play together are near Jimmy Cork's and up at Burnett's Face. Michael can go to the miners' settlement, and does sometimes, with Brennan. Rose tried only once, soon after school started.

She had plodded up the skipway, stepping over sleepers. Because it was Sunday the ropes, usually clattering, usually endlessly jerking towards the Bins or back to the mines, were lying lifeless. Michael was inside with a cold and everyone else on the Hill was busy doing Sunday things. Rose remembered the hymn-singing the day the English miners arrived. Mrs Rasmussen said their singing at Chapel service was a wonder, especially now the Welshmen had arrived. She said it brought a lump to her throat, and Rose wanted to feel a lump in her throat too. So she walked the two miles up to Burnett's Face on her own.

But in that settlement Chapel was over, and so was the Catholic service. Rose's timing was out, as usual. Families on their way home to the Sunday meal picked their way through the mud, the mist condensing in a silver sheen on the black of their Sunday best.

Rose, not in any kind of Sunday best, her smock and hands muddy, her curls in a tangle, stands alone on a sleeper, smiling her bright, paper-thin smile. She looks for a familiar face, sees Brennan and walks up to him, bob bob bob in that way of hers, stiff-legged, making all of her — clothes, arms, hair — bounce.

'Is the singing over, Brennan? I came to hear the singing.' Her high voice carries.

Brennan looks at her, desperate for this not to happen. Desperate to hide Rose. But he is with his family, in his Sunday suit. His dad would wallop him if he ran off. He lowers his bullety head, says nothing as he tramps past her. Rose hesitates, but only for a minute. Where someone so tiny has learned this spirit, this tenacity is a mystery. She runs to catch up. Bob bob bob.

'Shall I come and play with you, Brennan? Can we ask your mother for something to eat?'

Mathew and David Scobie, Brennan's big brothers turn back at the unfamiliar sound of chatter. Walking back from Chapel is usually a sober procession. They nudge the twins.

'Is that killer Jimmy's girl?'

The twins nod. The big boys jerk their heads at the twins, motioning them to turn back. All four turn to confront the little girl in her flour-bag smock. Silently they surround her. The twins stand a little to the side, half wanting to join in, half respecting Rose from their school bond. Brennan looks at the ground but stands by her.

The boys don't move. Their stillness is more terrifying than anything else they could do, for Rose is used to shouted taunts. She looks wide-eyed from boy to boy, waiting for something to happen. They are as daunting as a coalface in their shiny black suits. For minutes, it seems, they stand. Josiah and Mary Scobie have turned to see what their family are up to. At a distance they, too, stand now, waiting. Everyone stands still, as if for a photograph, but there is menace at the heart of this scene.

Rose's cheeks are bright red. Great tears stand in her eyes. She will not look down — or is unable to. Like a cornered rabbit she faces the Scobies until Brennan, shaking and tearful himself, takes her arm.

'She is Rose of Tralee,' he says.

Silence.

'Of Tralee, not Cork!'

David clears his throat and spits like a man.

Brennan swallows. Hardly moving, he takes a pinch of Rose's cardigan in his fingers and turns her. With a small push that is worse than anything else to Rose, he starts her walking back along the skipway. He doesn't come with her but watches for a while, and when she turns, once, he moves his hand — a tiny wave. Rose returns it wildly.

In this way Rose learned it was better not to go near the miners' settlement of Burnett's Face.

Evangeline Strauss/
Eva Storm

WELL, NOW, MY friends in the firelight, try to picture how it was for me. Shacked up with a man who is cursed. Who has gone to pieces even more, if you can believe this is possible, since the accident in the mine. Me, being innocent, they connect with the accident. True, I was up near the mine that day, but did a harmless picnic cause any accident? Could a little playing in the grass with your man hurt anyone? Of course not, but those bloody miners have so little humanity as a lump of their own dirty coal. Suddenly I am invisible. Even Billy Genesis for a while prefers not to see me. In case he lose his Company job, no?

Jimmy is superstitious, you see. As if he were truly an Irishman. That wrath of God called down burns in his mind. When he drinks it is worse; he can feel the hellfire licking at his feet, and he shouts at me to quench the flames, poor sod. He can hear the dead boy screaming in the mine, he says, which spooks me too because the mine is just above us, in the cliffs above, and I too can feel the dead spirit trapped and thirsting for revenge. This makes me shout and scream at Jimmy, who has brought all this upon us. This was not a happy time, you understand.

One night Jimmy is worse than usual. He is crying and moaning, I am probably screaming, and suddenly he hits me hard with a balled fist to knock me down, which surprises us both. Poor Jimmy had his many faults but he was not a violent man. Weak, rather, built for a soft life in a city, if the gold fever had not trapped his soul. So the blow sobered him a minute, me large with child and breathless for once, lying on the floor.

'Jesus, Angel,' he says, 'look at us both. This mess cannot be mended here. We'll give up. Leave the damned Hill.'

This does not suit my plans at all. But the man is in the depths, and such men, I tell you, will often let out secrets. So I hold my peace.

'What?' say I, pretending scorn. 'Leave your precious gold mine begging for a new owner?'

'Ah, leave it, Angel, leave it. I am a broken man.'

'The gold was a myth, so?'

Jimmy sighs. Head down, hands hanging, sighing, sighing.

I cannot stand a man who is down; they are so vexing and weak. Suddenly I am more mad than I can remember. This man who was one time so good fun and laughter, and so clever with his answers and his politics, is sitting silent in the cold hut, me with him. It is true I should feel sorry but I am not made that way. I need a strong man with a spark in his eye. A Big Snow or a Tom Hanratty. I am built for happy times, I admit it, and a glad man to share the happiness. Not this silly Jimmy Cork. Maybe I reach for the poker and clip him a little about the ear. And shout more than a bit. Rose, I remember, jumped at me. She had a soft spot for this Jimmy Cork. That man would sometimes put on the charm for her, tell her stories, when he never would bother for me.

So. He lies there. On the bed, quiet. A bit of blood, maybe, around his head. Soon, then, he starts to talk. Quiet, so I must lean in to hear.

It is the story of his discovery. In a slow voice he tells me how he explored, years ago, when he had two good arms and two strong legs, up the Waimang to where it branches, and then took the true left branch, where it bends back and descends from the plateau. Here and there he found a little colour, but no great find.

About halfway up, he says, was a ledge with some growth, scarcely wide enough even for one footfall. Some of the broken rock was different — a lighter colour than the sandstone — so he followed the ledge, tapping rocks with his little hammer to break them open. A little way along he looked up and saw far above him a small waterfall, not more than a trickle, coming off the plateau. The slide of water came down the sheer cliff and ended in a rocky bowl, which had formed in Jimmy's little ledge at a place where there was room for a man to sit and admire the view. Jimmy did just that. He was watching the stain of water as it spilled again from the bowl and runs far down into the gully, lost in the scrub and bush. His eyes caught a gleam he knew so well, just balanced near the edge of the lip. Sure enough, it was the colour, and a nice piece. He tells me — but I doubt it is the truth — that the piece he gave to Rose is that first nugget.

Well, my friends, so far what is new? A little colour on a high ledge makes no fortune, as you would all bear personal witness to. But listen, now!

Jimmy speaks on, in this tired voice, like he has no reason to draw the next breath. I am very hard pressed to stay still and listen.

Naturally Jimmy looked in the little rock bowl for more. Small stones covered the floor of the bowl and when he pushed them aside, that was when his heart began to beat in his throat. For there, trapped in the bowl for the taking, was a true carpet of the colour! Many tiny grains and also many larger pieces: good colour. Each handful he scooped was more gold than stone. In less than half an hour he had his leather pouch full and weighing heavy with hope on a thong around his neck. The rocky bowl was cleaned out but where, thought Jimmy — and me too by now of course — where was the source? Jimmy looked up to mark the spot where the water-fall spilled over. Surely there must be a seam up there to produce such a rich find?

'Where, where?' I cry to Jimmy. 'Oh, you wretched man to keep it secret so long! I can surely climb where you cannot go!'

Jimmy groans. 'It is all Company land. We may not stake a claim.' He looks at me then with his dead eyes. 'It's too late, Angel. If the motherlode truly exists it cannot be reached now. A while ago I thought . . . There were signs . . . but now it is cursed and there is no hope.'

That weak sick man speaks not one word more. Concerning the source, the gold, the direction even — not one. Oh, I try! That night I wash his blood with warm water, feed him a good soup, try a little fancy play, you know? As a woman can? Nothing. Next day and all days after that he is like a walking dead. Everywhere I search for his stash, even though he said it was all spent, but I don't trust him. Would you? A man who keeps such a secret from his own woman and the child he considers to be his?

I am almost mad with the worry. You can imagine. Jimmy is no more interested in life on the Hill. Says he will take Eddie's offer of help down the Incline, but I must come too, and Rose. I shout that I will kill myself if he makes me leave the Hill, and kill Rose too. Then in all this worry the baby is born, which is lucky. For a while at least I cannot go anywhere. It is another girl, small and ugly. Looking much like Tom Hanratty.

So. Do you listen still? Not sleeping over my tale?

Now comes a time of difficulty. Nothing can be done, no search attempted or plans laid, if there is no food. We all know this. Without a roof and a bite, dreams have no life. Time and again, my friends, I have dreamed grand futures, set out proudly on them, to see them wither while I spend my poor energy searching out food and shelter. Oh, what I would have been if riches came my way! Even now. My blood carries, I know it, the print of greatness. Always I have fought tooth and claw to give that greatness its life. One chance only, I needed. A bag of gold, as Jimmy had, I would not have trickled out in drink.

But food was needed. First, naturally, I tried Tom Hanratty. The father.

Behind their guest house I found him, sawing on a plank, mercifully on his own. No time for play and sweet talk. That fiery Totty might come around the corner.

'See for yourself that this is your child, Tom,' I say, 'and all the world will know it if I am not paid a weekly amount to feed it, with a little left over for its mother.'

A reasonable request. But Tom growls. His eyes go red and his big hands clamp on my shoulders like the jaws of dogs. I notice, though, that he takes a glance at the baby, so tiny and clearly weak.

'You have caused me enough trouble,' says he, his bushy beard bristling at me, 'And I will have nothing more to do with you. The child is Jimmy's.'

'It is yours,' say I.

'Who will take your word over mine? Eh? Leave this town, woman. You are not welcome. You and Jimmy both.'

He turned back to his sawing. If I had not been low from the birthing there might have been more said, but a weakness overtook me. I admit to you that tears flowed, a rare thing for me. Tears may achieve results for some, who are gentle-natured and sweet-faced, but I have noticed that in a woman of spirit such as myself, tears breed only embarrassment or even contempt. So I turned away.

Next morning the child was dead. Coughing in the night, blue in the morning, dead between one breath and the next. Jimmy wrapped her in a scrap of canvas and carried her, weeping, to Billy Genesis, who rode with her, down the Incline and out to the unmarked children's grave at Waimangaroa.

Ah well, it was for the best, perhaps, with the father so stony-hearted. Big Snow, called Con the Brake up here, was in any case a more likely bet.

But it was hard, I tell you, to start again. The birth and the unfriendly atmosphere, not to mention hunger, had brought me lower than I can remember. Almost I gave in. Almost left the Hill as Jimmy now wished, for a another life — more soft, more warm, down below, in which case this story would maybe end now and we would all get some sleep.

But I ran into Con that very day, as the little baby's body travelled down the Incline, and the kindness that big man showed me, his warm hand on my sleeve, gave me the strength to go on. That man remembered the good times when our two souls fitted together like hand and glove; I could see it in his eyes. Maybe he missed the free life. My tired blood stirred again and I longed to slide a cold hand inside his shirt to feel the hot skin. Instead I smiled a sad smile, but with some teasing in it, and thanked him nicely for his kind thoughts. Soon, very soon, would be the time to claim this man — back from that woman who was not really his wife, and who gave him no child.

Bella's Mission

IN THOSE DAYS — '82, '83 — there were three separate communities on the plateau: the settlement at the top of the Incline around the Brake Head; the Camp, just below it, perched on a natural rock shelf; and Burnett's Face, the miners' village, a couple of miles over the plateau closer to the mines.

The Brake Head was the natural centre, with its growing collection of businesses and its great ugly sprawling corrugated iron collection of sheds, offices and machinery known as the Bins. By now there were four boarding houses at Denniston (two of them owned by the Hanrattys), a saddler, a forge, two fiercely competitive stores (the Company one and the miners' co-op), a barber, an ironmonger and, just opened, J. Dimcock's drapery. Tom Hanratty employed two carpenters in those days, and would knock up anything from cradles to coffins. Billy Genesis, when he was sober, one day in three on average, operated the forge, though his three missing fingers and livid, knotted scar from ear to sweaty breast-bone were hardly reassuring testimony to his skill. Once a month or thereabouts Doctor Ulysses from Waimangaroa rode up the Incline and sat in a Company office at the Bins. Mostly he cut hair and trimmed beards, though; people at Denniston tended to be healthy or dead, nothing much in between.

Denniston town, at the Brake Head, was raw and rough but you could sense, gathering among the haphazard, muddy streets and tracks; among the dogged, entrepreneurial individuals who decided of their own volition to live there, a sense of order — a solid core, a kernel that would in time put down roots and bear the branches and fruit, however stunted in this barren soil, of a decent, if unique community.

The Camp was another matter. No order here at all. Shacks and huts, some of them still half canvas, sprouted like mushrooms. The only businesses were Red Minifie's Billiard Saloon and another makeshift bar, even more questionable. There were no roads at the Camp, just a track down to it and then winding paths between dwellings, which faced in all directions according to the whim of the wanderers who built them. People came and went at the Camp. Took a job shovelling at the Bins or maintaining the Incline, or carting timber, whatever was on offer, then drifted away in search of a warmer climate, an easier job, a new experience. Camp people were drifters and explorers: ex-gold-diggers, some of them; others escaping a debt grown too large or a crime too noticeable. Men arrived at the Camp with brand-new names or no names at all, until their mates allocated something suitable. Billy Genesis, for example, who could recite the whole of Genesis word for word, and his friend Lord Percy, who spoke with a plum in his mouth and could tell you the name of the second cousin of the Prince of Wales's uncle. They say Billy and Lord P met in prison in Australia, but that could only be an educated guess. No one ever mentioned the past at the Camp: its one unshakeable rule.

Con the Brake and Mrs C. Rasmussen were undisputed leaders at the Camp. Their solid house, built by Con from raw logs and plastered inside with Denniston mud, stood out like a beacon in the shifting huddle of shacks and canvas. Wanderers at the Camp gravitated to Con's fireside like driftwood moving inshore on the tide. They sang there and told stories; they ate Mrs Rasmussen's raisin scones, and looked into the coals, dreaming of other times that might never be told.

No one ever drifted towards Jimmy Cork's hut. It squatted under the cliff on the far corner of the Camp, surrounded by ramshackle fences to keep in the chooks. When Rose returned from school her only welcome was a rush of chickens with muddy undercarriages and red eyes, looking for scraps.

Burnett's Face, the third community on the plateau, was roadless too then, unless you counted the rope-road, which carried the miners' boxes of coal all the way from the mine entrances at Burnett's Face out to the Bins. The Company built the first batch of houses in two straight lines either side of the rope-road so they could bring the timber and the corrugated iron in on the empty boxes. Immigrant miners from the Midlands and Wales built their own houses the same way, placing their tiny dwellings side by side, like bricks on a wall along the narrow valley floor. Only a few, such as the Scobies, spread out sideways, taking advantage of a rise or a distant view, so there was little sense, then, of a township. One would come, though. These people were from generations of colliers back Home, who expected their children and grandchildren to go underground. Oh yes, a township would develop here, decent and God-fearing. No billiard saloon or liquor-licensed pub for Burnett's

Face if the Chapel miners could help it. Already a tiny chapel stood, still unpainted, on one side of the skipway, and a larger Catholic church on the other, though only its front was wooden; the sides and rear were common old corrugated iron. Churches first. Soon Burnett's Face miners would want their own school and their own post office. Burnett's Face people considered themselves a different breed from the motley lot at the Bins and the Camp. More civilised; certainly more trustworthy. Burnett's Face people were professional miners, bred from professionals.

Bella Rasmussen, who had met with all sorts in her colourful past, recognised the seeds of division in these three communities. She glowed with a mission to unite them, a mission that included, though she hardly admitted this even to herself, an aching desire to have Rose accepted by the miners, welcomed everywhere, as were the two boys, Michael and Brennan. She was planning an event.

Stories about Rose
of Tralee

PLENTY OF PEOPLE claimed to have understood Rose. Con the
Brake and Mrs C. Rasmussen in particular, naturally, but they were
by no means the only ones. Theories about her were worked up over
a beer at Red Minifie's, the men arguing about her background and
potential as if she were prize bloodstock, not a small girl. Stories
about Rose were swapped around firesides or over a cup of tea and
a scone. Just about every step Rose took was observed, retold,
commented on and embroidered, until it was hard sometimes to
distinguish the reality of the child from the folklore.

At Denniston, of course, everyone was known, more or less.
But with Rose it was different. She was on the loose so much,
knocking on the back doors of houses, with a smile as if she'd been
invited. She became regarded as common property — an intriguing,
unclaimed extra. You could welcome Rose in if you felt like it, listen

to her chatter, pump her for dreadful new stories from home, then send her off to that same home or to somewhere else, with a clear conscience. All care and no responsibility.

No one denied her charm and good looks. Even at six years old. Rose had those tight blonde curls that made you want to bounce the palm of your hand on them. Totty Hanratty wasn't the only woman who had popped Rose into a hot bath and scrubbed at the knotty, coal-streaked hair just for the pleasure of seeing those curls come out full of light and springy again.

And her skin. Grown men dreamed about it. Pale cream and flawless, not the scruffy, scabby, nondescript stuff proper children flaunted in front of their elders. Rose, freshly washed, had a pink and white delicacy, a dimpled sweetness that melted hearts and encouraged rumours of a mysterious parentage totally unconnected to Jimmy Cork or Rose's mother.

Wise or discerning people noticed and discussed a fragility, brittle as glass, behind that wide, winning smile, that perky chatter. She might come into your house or office with a cheerful announcement: 'Hello Mr Carmichael, here I am!' or 'It's me, Rose of Tralee! Can Michael play?' But if the response was less than welcoming the facade crumpled. Rose would stand, transfixed by even a slight rejection, the famous smile first setting like rock, then bleeding to death in front of your eyes. She would simply wait, looking down, not crying or throwing a tantrum, just waiting there until someone rescued her with a kind word or a biscuit. As if the light went out on her world for a while, and she had not found a way of turning it on again herself.

This response unnerved Denniston people. They learned to welcome Rose properly, to avoid crossing her, even when things disappeared. Little bright things — a glass marble, a blue medicine bottle, a teaspoon, things you would rather have but could do without — those were the things that disappeared sometimes, after Rose had paid a visit. No one could prove she took money. Sometimes the bright thing reappeared after a few days, sometimes not. People didn't mention the losses, though — not to Rose or to each other — not until much later. Later, much later, Rose's thieving became a favourite topic of conversation, but at this time there was a kind of collective will to protect Rose, or maybe to avoid facing her stone-wall act.

Everyone had a favourite story to tell about her. Old Huff McGregor came in to the men's quarters once after late shift. He felt his way in the dark past the row of sleeping, snoring workers. His hands, reaching for his own bunk, came down on something soft and squirming. Huff thinks it's some animal come in for the warmth and lets out a great scream that wakes the whole bunkroom.

'By Christ, you could hear the uproar clear up to the Bins!' says Huff. 'Men shouting and flailing around in the black dark. We had a full-scale war in there for a minute, till Straw Nugget gets a candle lit and we see who it is. Little Rose of Tralee! Kneeling up on my bunk ready to run if she could tell where to. Jesus, you'd think the child would choose a safer harbour on a stormy night. She was a tempting sight for starving men, all right, golden curls standing on end in fright, eyes like an owl's in the candlelight.

'But the men wouldn't touch her. Not even Straw or Brando. Not Rose. She's like a mascot down at the Camp, you know.'

'So what did you do, then?' asks Red Minifie, leaning over to fill Huff's glass. Red knows the story, but it's a good one and some newcomers in the saloon should learn about Rose.

'I don't do nothing. Just tuck her down at the end of my bunk and climb in the top end, keeping well away from the girlie. I'm none too clean after eight hours at the Bins. There's a bit of a mumble goes around the hut. You know? A good sound, I mean.

The men sort of like the idea that Rose chose their rough draughty old place to hide out in. So Straw Nugget blows out the candle and we go back to our snoring.'

'And in the morning?' prompts Red Minifie.

'Well then, in the morning Rose is still there, curled up under the blanket like a puppy. Sweet and warm. I'm pretending to be asleep still. Late shift, you know? But I'm watching the early shift leave, just in case. Every single one of those buggers comes past my bunk, and most of them reach out towards my Rose. They never touch her, mind you, but you can tell the cracked, grimy old fingers are itching to wrap around those golden curls, or stroke the downy skin . . .'

'Get on with it, Huff,' Red growls, giving him the eye.

'Keep your hair on, man. You know this is a clean story. So. It gets a bit lighter then, and Rose, who's slept through all the men's boots clumping on wood boards, opens her eyes. I'm watching through half-closed eyes. Don't want to startle her. To tell the truth I'm hoping she'll settle down again. But she sits straight up, not even noticing I'm there. Out comes the grin. No one can turn it on like Rose of Tralee.

'What I hadn't noticed in the dark, see, was the gifts. Rose's end of the bunk looks like Christmas morning. There's a carved ship and some other wooden thing, a piece of coal shaped into a face, a square of chocolate. A little book, even — could have been a Bible. Someone put down a crust of bread, only thing he could find. Rose is surrounded by little offerings. Far as I know no one discussed this. Probably every damn man thought his was the only gift sneaked there. I have to shut my eyes for a bit to keep the tears in.

'When I open them Rose and her treasure have gone, light as a cat, and the hut is just a cold old men's quarters again.'

Lord Percy's story was darker. One Sunday he worked his way

down to Jimmy Cork's end of the Camp looking for small rocks. Borrowed Con the Brake's barrow for the purpose. Lord Percy believed you could grow vegetables on the Camp if you put up a windbreak, though it seemed the rock wall was Lord Percy's passion, rather than the few scruffy silver-beet plants that survived. Well, he was down near the Corks' chicken yard and heard a bit of a to-do. Rose's mother was chasing a mad chook around the yard.

'Hard to say which was madder, fowl or fiend, haw, haw!' Lord P would say.

Rose stood pressed against the fence, looking rather white around the gills. Her mother grabbed the frantic flapping thing by the legs and brought it over to Rose. She would have been only five at the time, not much bigger than the chook and clearly frightened by the squawking and pecking.

While Lord Percy watched, the mother held the chicken towards Rose, shouting at her to grab the silly thing and give her mother a hand for once. Rose shook her head and drew back further. The mother, in a wild fury, swung the bird, clipping Rose on the head with it. Rose, crying, but more quietly than the bird, took the feathery lump as her mother instructed, pinning the wings, and trying as best she could to hold the darting head over the chopping block.

'The weapon descended,' Lord Percy would say, his long arms demonstrating the act with lurid embellishment, 'in a decapitation worthy of the most skilled of executioners, and resulting in a spectacular sanguinary display.'

The head flew into the yard, blood spurted from the neck, and Rose, screaming, dropped her headless friend into the mud.

You'd think that would be the end of it. Bad enough to force a little tot to help in such a gory activity. But no, Rose's mother had to teach her daughter better. Without a word, she retrieved the running, headless thing, blood still gouting, and forced Rose to hold it properly, wings pinned again, until the blood stopped and the twitching was over. Rose stood there in the mud, white and trembling, blood all down her smock, until the mother, with a curt little nod that could have meant approval, took the chicken and clumped over to Jimmy's hut, leaving Rose crying in the yard, and Lord Percy's patrician heart melting.

'Naturally, I wished to comfort the little damsel in distress, but the mother, in one of her moods, is not to be crossed, as I have experienced to my discomfort on more than one occasion. It is not a matter for self-congratulation that I turned my half-filled barrow and headed for home sweet home. What could one do?'

Billy Genesis will never tell his story. He was drunk at the time. The mixture of excitement and shame — what he remembers of it — he relives only in his mind.

The miners up at Burnett's Face have only the one story about Rose. The day she and her mother brought a picnic to Banbury mine, and were surely an influence on Jimmy Cork's actions that day.

A Confrontation
of Madams

BELLA RASMUSSEN OFTEN lies awake in her pink velvet bedroom listening to the curses and screams clearly audible, even in bad weather, erupting from Jimmy's place. Sometimes it is only the heavy sleeping arm of her husband, Con the Brake, that keeps her from climbing out of bed, walking across the Camp in her nightgown and snatching Rose from that warring cabin, carrying her home snuggled against Bella's loving, yearning bosom, to a warm bed where the child would be sung to sleep properly and cherished like any little girl deserves.

Since the Scobie accident Jimmy Cork has been without work. Like everyone else, Bella expected the family to pack their bundle, ride the Incline down to the other world and disappear for good. But Jimmy sits stubbornly on. Con the Brake says it's his gold, but what use is some phantom goldmine to a cripple outcast like

Jimmy? No one would help him now, even if he asked, which he won't.

It's a mystery how they manage. Rose's mother keeps her chickens, of course. Every Saturday afternoon Rose knocks on doors around Denniston with a basket of fresh eggs at a penny for two, but that is not going to keep a family of three fed and clothed. Let alone Jimmy's liquor. Con says he must have a nugget or two stashed away, but if he does, someone else must cash it, as neither Jimmy nor Rose's mother have left Denniston.

So they stay on, quarantined, in the far corner of the Camp. Jimmy rarely leaves the cabin. He is not so welcome in the saloon now, and where else would he go? Their presence is like a sore in the community. A festering that never heals. Even the baby's death fails to thaw the chilly disapproval. Rose, coming and going, is a reminder that they are still there. Bella in her sprawling cabin at the Camp can hear, on still nights, the words slicing and tearing, on and on, inside the Cork cabin. It is the parents' only form of communication. And Rose is marooned there.

Once, when Bella is cooking a good soup for Con's dinner, with dumplings as he loves, she suddenly can't bear it. She moves the pot to the side of the stove with one hand, unties her apron strings with the other, reaches for the coat hanging on the back door and, with no other thought in her head than Rose, purposeful as a fired cannon-ball, she tramps over frozen mud the several chains to Jimmy's.

There's no point knocking. Bella pushes open the door and fills the doorway, waiting for someone to notice. The whole of Rose's life lashes at Bella's eyes, strong and painful as a blow from Jimmy's fist. Along the ceiling ridge of the one-room hut, sooty washing droops from a string. Over the open fire a blackened pot steams. Goodness knows how washing would dry, let alone what it was doing to Rose's lungs. The child sits on a tiny corner bunk, back in a cave-like depression in the raw rock. She doesn't see Bella, or is ashamed to notice, how would you know? A piece of something bright turns in her hands, back and forth, over and over, stroking and fingering. She is singing as she turns, very quietly; Bella can't hear the words.

A heel of bread and three tin cups stand on a rough plank table.

Near the fire, on a larger bed, Jimmy Cork sprawls, trying to fight off the woman who drags at him fiercely. Jimmy, hoarse from the whiskey, shouts and rages; the woman's voice cuts like a knife. Neither notices Bella.

'Give off! I'm not hungry, woman!'

'You will eat at the table like a proper man!'

'No one here's a proper man. Shove off, whore woman!'

'You will take food at the table!' Rose's mother screams, and hauls back to strike Jimmy.

When she sees Bella.

Suddenly her whole manner changes. Cracked and dirty fingers smooth down her apron as if it were fine worsted. The face snaps shut, black brows squared above coal-hard eyes. The spine straightens. There is no doubt that this is a confrontation. Rose's mother snarls like an animal at Mrs Rasmussen, who stands, stunned, at the door, forgetting what she has come for.

Good evening, *Mrs C. Rasmussen*,' says Rose's mother, spitting the title out word by word. 'I did not hear you knock.'

Bella takes a deep breath. She can be formidable too. 'There was little point in knocking, *Mrs James from County Cork*. I have come out of concern for the child.'

'Oh? So? And how can you worry your head about my child? You, who have no understanding of such matters?'

Bella blanches at this low blow, but rallies.

'A child in distress is everyone's concern, Mrs Cork. No child should be subjected to such language and hostility.'

'Ah!' shouts Eva. 'Keep your fancy lectures to the classroom. This is raw life down this end of the Camp, and Rose is part of it.'

Bella stands firm. 'All the Camp can hear your battling. It is no better than a brawl in a whore-house.'

'Well, you would know, you old madam,' screams Eva. 'One will recognise another, you should take care how you cast mud.'

'You are a poor deluded soul.' Bella's words drop like stones, but her heart beats in fear now. Even so, she cannot resist another cast for Rose. 'Perhaps Rose would be better off at our house for the night. To leave you free to care for your husband.'

But even as she speaks Bella knows she has made a mistake. She had pictured this differently. In her version Rose would cry out with relief at her entrance, come running to bury her little face in Bella's warm skirts. The mother and father would be too depraved or too drunk to notice as Bella led the girl gently into the night.

In the real version, though, Rose sits through the exchange, cross-legged and unmoving on her bunk. She has seen Bella but has not come running. She has smiled — a tight secret greeting; not at all the sort a rescuing angel needs.

Eva sees the uncertain smile between the two and knows she has the upper hand.

'Say good evening to your teacher, Rose,' says Mrs James from County Cork. The sudden dignity, taut as stretched elastic, and malevolent, is deeply unsettling to Bella.

'Good evening, Mrs Rasmussen,' whispers Rose. She will not look again at her teacher, but stares down at the bright thing in her hand, turning and turning.

Bella feels the blood spread up over her bosom to set her face glowing. For a moment she feels she will be stuck in this doorway forever.

'Well then,' she says finally, 'if the child does not require assistance I will take my leave.'

Rose's mother nods. As she lays a hand to the door to close Bella out of their life, she speaks. Bella is terrified by the dark triumph in the woman's eyes.

'Rose's home,' shouts Mrs Jimmy Cork, 'and her parents may not be what you, Madam Lah-di-dah, choose, but she is mine, not yours. You cannot take my daughter off like some bag of flour. No, you cannot! So. If your man cannot make you a baby, leave mine alone!'

Jimmy, like Rose, has not moved through all this exchange. Now he stirs and growls on his bed, a volcano preparing for its next eruption. Mrs James from County Cork closes the door.

As Bella clumps back across the Camp under stars, her tears are such a mixture of emotions she cannot sort them out at all.

A Concert is Planned

THE CONCERT SEEMED a good idea at the time. Bella Rasmussen had been planning it for weeks. Her theory was that the communities on the Hill needed a focus to bind them, and that focus had to be her tiny but representative school. She was right, of course, but you can't hammer human nature into a mould unless it's ready, and as it turned out Denniston just wasn't ready to be a tightly knit cosy little community.

The classroom at the back of Hanrattys' is now bursting with the addition of two new children from the Welsh miners' contingent. On this morning, March 18th 1883, Mrs C. Rasmussen's cheeks are as pink as the little flowers she has embroidered on the yoke of her teacher's smock.

'Children,' she announces, 'we are to have an inspection from the Department. An Inspector is coming especially all the way

143

from Nelson. We must make a good impression.'

'Well, I better stay at home then,' says scruffy Tonto Jowett, and the rest of them snigger.

'Maybe you should, Tonto,' says Mrs Rasmussen, which stops him in his tracks. At Denniston, no one would be seen dead missing an official visit, they are so rare.

'What will he inspect, Mrs Rasmussen?' asks Michael, ready as always to leap into a new project, polish up whatever is dull, and shine. 'Will he hear our Tables?'

'He will. And our Rivers of England. And our Capitals of the World.'

'Not Spelling?' asks Brennan, hoping against hope.

'Spelling,' says Mrs Rasmussen firmly, but adds, seeing Brennan's worried face, 'He will not fail the whole school if you get a word or two wrong, Brennan. And we will sing him a song to welcome him.'

The nightmare of the correct ordering of letters fades from Brennan's face. He beams. If there is to be singing, Brennan will be asked to sing solo. His chunky little body produces a voice as open and clear as the summer sky. He would sing all day, and most would stop to listen.

'We could sing "Rose of Tralee",' says Rose of Tralee.

'We could indeed,' says Mrs Rasmussen, trying not to notice the fresh bruise under Rose's eye, and her tangled unwashed hair. 'And Rose could sing solo. Wouldn't that charm any Inspector from Nelson now?'

Bella Rasmussen ignores for the moment Brennan's black brows descending; Rose needs something to live for.

But the miners' children have other ideas. Rosser Scobie wants 'Bread of Heaven' with the older boys doing the bass part. Dylan Rees thinks 'All Through the Night' would be more suitable.

'I can do verse two of that one,' offers Brennan, still hoping for a solo.

Mrs Rasmussen smiles at the enthusiasm. 'Well, children, this is an occasion. It would seem that a bracket is called for. And if my husband is not on duty, he may accompany us on the accordion.'

There is general excitement over this. Con the Brake's accordion brings out the best in everyone.

'But can he play "Bread of Heaven"?' asks Andrew Scobie. The twins are determined to sing the bass part, which they have just learned at Chapel.

Brennan's hand goes up. 'My father can play "Bread of Heaven" on the cornet. And our brother can do tenor horn.'

'And Uncle Arnold . . .'

'No, he can't.'

'He can. He has a trombone under his bed.'

'And David . . .'

'No, Dad says he's not good enough yet.'

'But he can do "Bread of Heaven", can't he, Rosser?'

'Anyone can do "Bread of Heaven".'

'Not David — he can't,' says Rosser Scobie.

'Not David,' agrees young Brennan, and the Scobies are quiet for a moment.

'Well now,' says Mrs Rasmussen into the silence, 'I did not know Denniston had a brass band in its midst. I believe an entire concert may be called for, not a single bracket. We will invite the Inspector to stay the night. What do you say, children, to an Entertainment! We will surprise him, shall we, and the whole of Denniston, and raise funds for the new school?'

Everyone pays homage to this shining idea.

'Will you sing too, Mrs Rasmussen?' asks Michael Hanratty, who has heard her rich, swooping voice rise from the parlour late at night as he lies in his bed upstairs. He can never catch the words but her songs throb with feelings so powerful that the boy can hardly bear it. He finds himself moaning and thrashing under the blankets until the voice sobs and sinks its way to the end.

'Well, Michael, we shall see,' says pink Bella Rasmussen, itching to kick up her heels and dance a step or two to show the children what she can do, but mindful of her new position in society.

'And another thing,' she adds. 'While the Inspector is here, Mrs Hanratty will be your teacher.'

'Why?' asks Rose. Her favourite word.

'It is a secret. A game. She will be teacher, and I will be her assistant.'

UP the plateau at Scobies' the twins and Brennan are jumping around their father like a pack of eager puppies.

'She wants a brass band, Dad, for the concert.'

'She wants "Bread of Heaven".'

'Does she now?' says Josiah Scobie.

'She wants an Item of our Choice, too.'

'David's not ready,' says Josiah, ruffling fifteen-year-old David's wiry hair. David is now first boy in the family.

'It's three or four weeks away, Dad.'

'Chapel is one thing,' says Mary Scobie, 'but to play in a concert, in the town, is another.'

The boys wait. They know what this is about and look to their father. Josiah sighs and nods to his wife. They are seated at their own table in their own home, built by the Scobie men and boys, and there is good food in front of them.

'We cannot stay up in Burnett's Face here forever, Mother,' says Josiah. 'The twins and young Brennan here have made the move, and we must too. Denniston should be one community. We have a need to stand together.'

Mary's plate is barely touched. She has grown thinner. The steady warmth that used to draw people to her has faded. She clasps her head as if she would tear out the thoughts in it.

'I know you are right, Josiah. I know it with my head. The heart is another matter. But you must get a band together and play for them. I will come if I can.'

The boys still wait. Josiah pushes himself up from the table, walks with a heavy tread around to Mary's end. He puts one rough hand on her shoulder. The boys have never seen him so gentle with her.

'You will find the strength, with the Lord's help.'

He looks at the boys with a grin that is like fresh sea air entering the house.

'Well, lads, we will make up a band, shall we? A brass band to make all at Denniston proud, eh?'

The boys grin back, hardly daring to break the moment as their father plans.

'Samuel Rees plays the tenor horn like Uncle Arnold, so I hear, and another of the Welsh miners is a bandsman, though what instrument I have not learned.'

'Cornet, Dad, so Taffy McDavitt says, but he has no instrument.'

'Oho, cornet! Is he good, do you hear?'

'Can't touch you, Dad,' says Mathew stoutly, though he has no idea in fact.

'We must see what we can organise, then. The Company might be persuaded to assist with an instrument or two, though there is little time.' He turns to the younger ones. 'Is there anyone else down at the Bins plays an instrument that you've heard?'

'Con the Brake plays accordion,' says young Brennan.

The older boys are scornful and Josiah laughs. 'That's not a proper instrument, lad; what son of a bandsman would even suggest such a thing? Accordion!'

The small papery sound is Mary. Her first laugh.

'And will you sing solo?' she asks Brennan.

The twins look sharply at Brennan, but even he knows this is not the moment to discuss the matter.

'Yes,' he says to his mother.

He doesn't say that Mrs Rasmussen is teaching him and Rose to sing 'Rose of Tralee' as a duet, and that she would like Josiah to accompany them on solo cornet.

Facing the Music

'THEY NEVER COME to the school,' pleads Brennan Scobie. 'They won't be there, Mum; I know they won't.'

'Leave your mother,' says Josiah Scobie. 'It is her choice. Now, come in the bedroom, lad, and let me hear your scales.'

Mary Scobie looks out her tiny kitchen window and up to the bleak mountains, which seem to press down on the little settlement. In the distance a heavy fog crawls down the slopes of black hills, softening and rounding the ridges. Soon all the Hill will be engulfed, silenced, deadened. She sighs. The landscape fits her mood — or perhaps augments it. Since the deaths, a lassitude that she cannot control has crept through her bones. Mary recognises the signs, has warned other miners' wives against it, knows that living with the possibility of sudden death must be accepted, but somehow cannot help this endless, slow sinking of the spirit. Back in England she had been the strong one, the Chapel wife who had used her faith and good sense to haul other despairing wives to the surface again. No one, it seems, can do the same for her.

She stands, now, at the window, her hands scrubbing and scrubbing at the same potato, waiting for the advancing fog.

In the bedroom, brassy arpeggios slide up and down. Young Brennan will be as good as his dad one day; there is music in his bones, no doubt about it. Mary dreams of another future for her youngest son. Not a mining life but one above ground, where the boy goes to work in clean clothes and returns unscathed. Where he walks down a sunny main road to a sunny office, and looks out all day at trees and other green things. Mary remembers the picnics in the bush when Scobies' gang was scrub-cutting. The softness of the air, the spread of it all. She would be ashamed to mention, in this house, that she misses that time, but there is the truth of it.

Now Brennan is singing and his father is accompanying on cornet. The instrument is muted, allowing the boy's clear voice to float above.

That made me love Mary, the Rose of Tralee, sings Brennan, and his mother, Mary Scobie (not Tralee), cries into the sink.

It is not possible to go to the concert.

'A brass band is all very well,' grumbles Con the Brake, 'but too stiff for an evening entertainment. Who can dance, you know, to a brass band?'

'Who's talking dancing? This is a formal occasion.'

'Mrs C. Rasmussen, you are taking respectable too far. A bit of a clap and a stamp — you expect it if you pay money. Who can sing a good song along with a brass band, you know?'

Bella Rasmussen closes her lovely pink velvet curtains. Her secret bedroom indulgence, which no one on the Hill, except her husband

Con and Rose of Tralee, have seen. In the parlour she has hung proper and serviceable cream cotton duck, 7 $1/2$ d. a yard and easy to wash. She raises heavy white arms and turns her back to Con, inviting him to unlace her stays. He attacks the armour with relish, the rough fingers surprisingly nimble among laces and frills. A seaman can untangle any knot.

But even in this excitement he has not forgotten the argument. 'We will need a bit more spice in your entertainment or the men will go away disappointed.'

'This is not a billiard-room occasion, man; there will be women and children. And the Inspector.'

'The Inspector, I'll lay odds, will enjoy a lively tune like any proper person. I am not talking bawdy, Bella.'

Bella turns in his arms and strokes her giant's curly chest. It is rare for him to call her by name. It reminds him of how they met.

'Tell me, then,' she says, 'what you have in mind and be quick about it, man. It is cold standing here in my skin.'

'An accordion band,' says Con the Brake. He swings his laughing wife into a step or two of the polka. 'Squinty Tim has one, and Billy Genesis can pick out a good enough tune when he's sober. And Tom Hanratty used to drum down in the Westport brass band. I want to grab him before Josiah Scobie finds out.'

Bella laughs out loud. 'Oho, now we hear it. A competition. Get into bed, man. You are worse than my pupils.'

A little later Con rumbles into her neck, 'They look down on us, you know, those Chapel miners. Think we are nobody much from nowhere. They should realise.'

'Well then, gather your band,' says Bella, softer now, 'and we will finish with a lighter bracket. But do not expect me to entertain. I will be in an official capacity. And no dancing.'

'Ah, come on now . . .'

'No dancing. It will get out of hand.'

'Out of hand is good. Kick up your heels, woman!'

'You are teasing me.'

'Ah, my Bella, Bella.' He kisses her gently, hums a tune, his fingers accompanying on the broad expanse of her bosom. 'We will show them anyway. You will see. Every Chapel foot will be tapping in spite of itself.'

Just before Con crashes into sleep, Bella slips in the news she has been holding back for months, fearing another loss.

'Conrad, I am with child again.'

Con the Brake says nothing. Bella thinks she has missed the moment; he is asleep. But slowly the big man's arms close around her. He rocks his beloved wife and they cling together like two lost children.

The Entertainment

'MY ASSISTANT, MRS C. Rasmussen, will announce the items,' says Totty, trying not to grin. Deceiving this pompous little Inspector is adding spice to the whole evening.

All day the children have been on their best behaviour: sitting up straight, answering as best they could the Inspector's curly questions. Totty has stood up at the front like a teacher, while Mrs C. Rasmussen has kept order from the back. Once, under cover of a cough, Mrs C managed to pass the answer to Rosser Scobie, who piped up, wide-eyed and innocent. The Inspector did not see through the game, although any mother would sense immediately that something was up; the held-back laughter in their faces has been transparent.

Now Totty, in fine cream taffeta sent by her mother from Westport, sits next to the Inspector in the front row at the Volunteer

Brigade Hall, which is still unfinished but at least closed in, and the only hall on the Hill big enough to hold a sizeable slice of the Denniston population.

Tom, who has built himself a cart and commandeered a pit pony to pull it, has driven around the community collecting chairs. Latecomers will have to stand.

Bella's hopes for a united community are not quite realised. A dark, respectable and silent phalanx of Burnett's Face miners and their families fill one side of the hall. The rest chat and laugh on the other side, displaying odd quirks of behaviour and clothing: Lord P's scarlet cravat, Con the Brake's outrageous waistcoat (embroidered by Bella), Totty's finery, Old Huff McGregor's huge braying laugh. It's like two families at a wedding. But there's goodwill in the air, for the sake of the children. No hint of how the evening will end.

The Inspector, dead centre in the front row, sits on a fine carver from Hanrattys' dining room. All day he has been fidgety. Trying, no doubt, to regain his dignity, lost somewhere halfway up the Incline. He had appeared over the brow, crouched inside the wagon and clinging desperately to young George Abernethy, who does maintenance on the Incline. Eight interested and experienced Denniston children, though strictly on their best behaviour, could not quite disguise their scorn. Riding the Incline was part of life.

However, a good meal of corned beef and a steamed raisin pudding seem to have smoothed his ruffled feathers somewhat. Tom, sitting on his other side, engages him on the subject of government funding for school buildings. Totty hands him a programme, hand-written by the older children, in a very creditable script, though this Inspector would not notice. He has been mean with praise all day. Tom Hanratty, stiff with pride, points out to the Inspector the amazing fact that his six-year-old son has written a poem, and will read it himself:

A MUSICAL ENTERTAINMENT
In Honour of the School Inspector
and
To Raise Funds for the New School

~ Programme ~
God Save the Queen
1. 'Bread of Heaven' sung by pupils of Denniston School
and accompanied by the Denniston Miners' Brass Band
2. A Speech of Welcome by Mr T. Hanratty, chairman
of the School Building Fundraising Committee
3. 'The Boy Stood on the Burning Deck' recited
by Andrew and Rosser Scobie
4. 'Richmond' by T. Haweis, performed
by the Denniston Miners' Brass Band
5. 'Sunrise' An original Poem, written and recited
by Michael Hanratty
6. A Sailor's Hornpipe, performed by
the Boys of Denniston School and accompanied
by Mr C. Rasmussen on Accordion
7. 'Rose of Tralee' sung by Brennan Scobie and Rose of
Tralee, accompanied by Josiah Scobie on Cornet
SUPPER
8. A Selection of Shanties and Folk Songs, performed by
the Denniston Rovers' Accordion Band. Recitations from
the floor invited.
DONATIONS HOWEVER SMALL WELCOME

On a makeshift platform the eight pupils of Denniston school
are lining up. All are in white shirts. Rose wears a white smock — a
surprise, as neither Totty nor Mrs Rasmussen has had any response

to their efforts to include Rose's mother in this event. To the left of the stage seven men of the Denniston Miners' Brass Band, three of them Scobies, are seated importantly. Each wears a miner's cap to which Mary Scobie has sewn a brass button. Outside the lugubrious moans of a tuba can be heard. The eighth bandsman, young David Scobie, is nervously warming up his dead uncle's instrument.

The hall is overflowing. Eddie Carmichael has allowed the skipway to operate an hour after closing so the families further up the plateau can ride it into town. Going back will be another matter.

Mary Scobie is not here. She has never ridden the skipway and has even less reason now. But unknown to her family, who consider her appearance a lost cause, she is plodding steadily through the dark towards Denniston. Brennan, in his excitement, has left behind the little waistcoat he is to wear for 'Rose of Tralee' and Mary is bringing it to him.

Rose is the only girl on stage. It is a mystery, the way people up here have sons. Perhaps the women's bodies know. Totty makes good daughters, of course — two so far — but then she's not bred to mining. Now five years a citizen of Denniston, Totty has become a handsome woman, forthright as ever but steadier. Everyone says she and Tom will go far. From the comfort of Westport, Totty's parents have never let up the pressure on her and Tom to leave the plateau and return to 'civilisation'. Mrs McGuire, habitually unwell, writes yearning letters to her daughter. Rufus McGuire feels insulted and in some uneasy way threatened that his pretty daughter should choose to consort with the rough trade on Denniston rather than adorn the family home.

Perhaps it is that Totty's independence needs to be challenged and sharpened by a place like Denniston; perhaps it is her good solid Tom who keeps her so contented. There is no doubt anyway that Totty loves this difficult, damp, back-breaking, isolated life.

Five years ago Bella Rasmussen, noticing soft white hands and delicate bones, gave her three months at the most, and is pleased now to admit how wrong she was.

Apart from little Elizabeth and Sarah Hanratty, Rose is the only other girl at Denniston. Not a single one up at Burnett's Face. It makes you wonder, Bella has been heard to say darkly when Burnett's Face women are not around.

Rose is as excited as the boys. She hops from one foot to the other, chatting to Michael and Brennan, while Mrs Rasmussen has a word with the band.

'I trust we will start on time,' says the Inspector, fiddling with his fob watch. 'Punctuality is a trait that cannot be learned too soon.'

This constipated little outsider can't see what a milestone for Denniston the concert is. Totty says, with a painful smile, 'I expect we are about to begin. Here comes the final member of the band.'

David Scobie, his lips swollen and red from practising these last weeks, takes his place beside his brother. He sits up straight and proud as his father has taught him, though the great precious tuba almost obliterates him from view.

The concert begins. Even the men are moved by 'Bread of Heaven'. The fervour in the children's faces and the way the Scobie twins lower their heads and frown like men to roar out their 'Ever more!' have the audience stamping and whistling at the end, with no care at all that this is a hymn. Men outnumber women four to one in the hall, but over on the miners' side are at least five new women, pale and thin from the journey out. The community is forming.

Tom gives a good-natured speech, joking with the miners, to free up the money in their pockets. The miners respond with a bit of good-natured heckling. The Inspector is invited to say a few words. He fiddles with his watch again, clears his throat, and then abruptly declines. A low growl, like a distant roll of thunder, sounds in the room. Any visitor here is expected to perform. Mrs C. Rasmussen quickly announces the next item.

Michael's poem, 'Sunrise', is a hit. Totty is in tears; she can't hold them back. What gives her son this bright confidence? His fair hair, falling finely over a high forehead, shines in the lamplight — he is like a sunrise himself.

'Very creditable,' says the Inspector through pursed lips as if he is judging a slice of lemon pie. Tom and Totty take no notice. They are too busy gathering, like a bouquet, the generous praises of local friends. The evening is going well.

But at item seven, 'Rose of Tralee', tension in the hall is palpable. An invisible but chilly wall separates Burnett's Face people from Camp and Brake Head. Rose and Brennan, County Cork and Scobie, step forward to stand side by side. They can feel that the silence is different. Animation drains from their two faces. It is as if two flowers — one fair, one dark — are fading, drooping before the stony wall of colliers' eyes.

The Inspector clears his throat. He has no idea.

Totty shifts on her chair, willing the music to start. It is clear the duet has been a mistake; Bella's instincts have been wrong this time. Bella, too caught up with Rose, has misread the mood of the people. Their readiness to forget.

Then Brennan's solemn face opens into a wide grin. He is looking to the back of the room. There is a stir as something is passed forward, hand to hand, over the crowded heads. Mrs Rasmussen, smiling broadly herself now, retrieves the waistcoat and helps Brennan into it. The audience laughs and claps to see the boy strut. The ice is broken.

'Rose of Tralee and Brennan Scobie,' announces Bella Rasmussen in a firm voice, 'with Josiah Scobie on the cornet.'

Rose smiles. It is a straightforward, hopeful offering. With a rustle as soft as leaves, the audience accepts it.

The song wavers into life. Rose's voice is true but thin as paper. Josiah is hardly breathing into his cornet but still he drowns her. Mrs Rasmussen frowns at Rose; touches plump hands to her own taffeta-clad diaphragm. Rose nods, her eyes round and clear as marbles. She takes a deep breath.

She was lovely and fair as the rose of the summer, she sings,
But it was not her beauty alone that won me.

Brennan joins in under her, stronger to match Rose's growing confidence. Josiah's cornet notes curl around the voices, a simple, beautiful thread binding them.

Oh no, 'twas the truth in her eyes ever shining
That made me love Mary, the Rose of Tralee.

The audience is entranced. Rose looks steadily at a far corner of the hall. Totty glances quickly in the direction. Can the mother be here after all? But she sees only the crowd of latecomers standing along the wall.

At the end of the song Rose and Brennan turn to each other as Mrs Rasmussen has taught them. Brennan pecks Rose on the cheek.

Every heart in the hall melts. An encore is demanded, but Bella, unwilling to jeopardise her triumph, announces supper.

The Inspector helps himself generously to scones and fruitcake. Josiah bales him up in a corner. The miner's flat nasal voice can be heard above the chatter.

'It is buildings we need, Mr Sinclair, not bureaucracy. It is stupidity to expect our children to travel to Waimangaroa. In two years the school population will have trebled up here, man. Give us a building now!'

Josiah already has a reputation as a crusader. There will be a

Miners' Union soon, no matter what the Company or Eddie Carmichael have to say about it, and Josiah will be at the forefront, you could put money on it.

Finally the Inspector breaks free and slips away to his bed at Hanrattys'.

'Good riddance!' roars Con the Brake. He has been drinking from some secret source. 'Now we'll have a bit of real music! Move back the chairs!'

'Conrad!' says Bella, but the men are already heaving chairs. There is a great rubbing of hands and stamping of feet.

Totty looks for Mary Scobie. There she is, sitting quiet and pale by the door, ready to slip out at any moment. Some have tried to speak with her but now have drifted away. In this crowded, rowdy hall she is surrounded by a small empty space. Misery and bad luck are contagious.

Totty sits down beside her. She is shocked to see how far Mary Scobie has slipped. Surely a miner's wife must be hardened to death?

'I'm glad you came,' she says. 'The Scobies were a great contribution to the concert. You must be proud.'

'Yes,' says Mary. She looks ahead and slightly down, focusing on a patch of bare floor.

'Your twins are doing well at school now. After a reluctant start. They will get their Certificate.'

Mary's bleak eyes look up for a moment. 'Good.'

Totty wades on. 'Brennan and Rose sang beautifully.'

'Yes. They are a brave pair.'

'Rose has much to be brave over. I hope you do not hold it against her?'

Totty has pushed too far. Mary Scobie rises slowly, like an old woman.

'Well,' she says, finally, 'I do not wish to hold it against her.' She sighs. 'It is time for me to go.'

'At least wait for the music . . .'

'The walk home is long, Mrs Hanratty. And work to be done in the morning.'

'Mrs Scobie,' says Totty. She has a strong instinct to rescue this drowning woman. 'I would be grateful if you could spare some time in the next day or two to look at my youngest. She is not well. Perhaps your experience might throw some light.'

This is not a complete fiction. Sarah has been flushed and feverish for two days.

Mary is only half caught. 'Not well in what way?'

'I fear it is her throat.'

Mary sighs again but there is a little animation, perhaps, in the formal smile.

'It is hard on the little ones up here,' she says. 'I will come tomorrow if the weather permits.'

She drifts into the doorway. Totty is relieved to see that Josiah is watching. He moves out quickly to take her arm.

Con the Brake is watching too.

'Josiah Scobie, man!' he shouts. 'I have sat through your Chapel music. Enjoyable too, in its way. Have the courage to stay for a band of a different sort!' The accordion in his hands opens; a long, singing, sighing upbeat. Con's head leans back, teasing the audience, prolonging the moment until all are listening. Josiah and Mary stop in the doorway. Squinty Tim and Billy Genesis unfold their accordions too, enriching the upbeat; Tom Hanratty hastily reaches for his drumsticks. Then Con's head snaps sideways and the rollicking wash of a hornpipe fills the hall.

An agonised shout from someone in the audience. 'Wait, Con! Wait, man, while I get my pipe!' Everyone laughs as old Slim

Bulliboy makes a dash for the door, but Con the Brake is away now and the music will not wait for forgotten instruments or miners' lungs or Chapel scruples. Feet cannot stand still against this.

The children heel and toe, showing the grown-ups how it goes. Bella Rasmussen, her propriety flown out the window at the first note, lifts her skirts and capers like a girl. Totty Hanratty joins her, matching as best she can the complicated prancing steps.

'Oh, Bella!' she gasps. 'Oh, Bella, it is like a dream!'

Bella is away. This is a side of Mrs C. Rasmussen few have seen. She roars out the tune, beckoning with one plump hand to those still standing around the edges, inviting the men to join in. When the band changes to a polka she draws a laughing Eddie Carmichael into the centre and the two of them gallop with a will to the shouts and claps of the whole room.

Josiah and Mary Scobie are still standing in the doorway, but both are smiling now to see their boys stamping and hopping with the best. Josiah turns to his wife; offers her his arm. It is a tentative gesture, prepared for rejection. Mary lowers her head slowly, a much younger woman's movement; a shy acceptance of a first advance. She takes her grave husband's hand and they dance privately, with no great style but with an intimacy that is noticed and approved by many in this room. The Scobies are respected in all Denniston, and their wound has left a public scab.

Young Michael Hanratty is dancing with Rose. Their two golden heads bounce and toss together. There's no sign of Jimmy Cork or Rose's mother. A good thing for the peace of the evening, but more than one voice has muttered in outrage that such a girl should be out alone, relying on the goodwill of the community to walk her to the so-called safety of home. What kind of mother can leave a six-year-old to fend for herself? In this hard place?

Totty, tired herself now, sighs and tries again to collar her whirling, screaming son. He slips away.

The youngest Scobie is on his own. The adults have all congratulated him and now he has no one to dance with. Looking like a little man in his waistcoat, he pulls on his mother's sleeve.

'It's my turn,' he whines, 'Tell Michael it's my turn.' Every line in his dark, sleepy face droops.

'Your turn for what?' asks his mother.

'My turn for Rose.'

'Your turn for bed,' says his father.

'But I haven't danced with Rose!'

Mary smiles at her dear, dark son. 'Time enough for that later, my boy. We have a long walk home.' She slips on young Brennan's coat, gives Josiah the word to collect up the rest of the boys, and steps into the night. Brennan, desperate to stay and compete for Rose's attention, protests every step of the way.

Totty hooks a finger into her over-excited son's collar and looks around for Rose. She's gone already. Perhaps someone else from the Camp has walked her down. With a nod and a wave to her Tom, who's just getting up a head of steam on drums, she marches Michael back home.

An hour later a good number of Burnett's Face men and most of the Denniston and Camp folk are still enjoying the music. A bottle or two is passed around. The men pull up chairs in a circle around the accordions and call for songs. In a pause, Bella, flushed and plump as a partridge, calls for the donation box.

'Come on, lads! A last round of the box. Squeeze out your pennies. This is the future of Denniston we're looking at tonight!'

IN a way she was right, though it wasn't the future she hoped for. The box, which should have been tucked under Tom Hanratty's drum, had disappeared. Money and box: both gone.

163

Tempers, frayed by drink and too much good behaviour, now erupted. Totty, wiping a feverish child's brow two streets away, heard the ruckus. Burnett's Face blamed Brake Head, everyone blamed Camp. Before Bella could appeal for reason, fists were up and Tom's drum trampled. Con hooked up his accordion fast, then joined the fray with a roar, defending the murky honour of the Camp.

Billy Genesis and his friend Lord Percy dashed a raging Arnold Scobie against the wall until the raw iron rang; the O'Sheas slogged it out with Old Huff and the men from the quarters — even Tom Hanratty, angered at the destruction of his new drum — whacked Red Minifie, who'd come up late for the dancing, over the head with it. In their hearts everyone knew it had to be some drifter from the Camp; the bad reputation of the Camp was sealed that night. But even Camp people possessed a pride of sorts; no way would they accept blame until guilt was proven. It was a great roaring fight, one of the best, with nothing to break it up but exhaustion. The nearest police were way down at sea level, in Waimangaroa.

Bella Rasmussen, head down, protective arms around the baby inside her, rammed her way to the door and trudged home to bed. No point searching for the money until the fight died a natural death. She had plenty of grim ideas about who might be low enough to pinch school donations and would knock on a few doors in the morning.

No one suspected Rose might have anything to do with it. Not for a minute. In fact after that night Rose was accepted by all at Denniston, above and below ground, as a true citizen of the Hill. She continued to live with her parents, but the miners managed to divorce Rose from them.

Jimmy Cork and Rose's mother could never be forgiven.

Eva at the Concert

I WAS THERE. They will all point the finger: say I am a mother without care. But I was there and Rose knew it. All day she was on, nag nag: other mothers would be there, what pretty thing could she wear, as if we were lords and ladies. The child thought I could just walk into that hall and the sun would come out. She was sharp enough, my Rose, but what does she know? Nothing. What child understands the scorn and contempt a small town can heap upon one person if they choose?

Listen. Let them screw up their sour little faces and sharpen their eyes like pencils to stab at me, but in the singing I was with Rose. I myself was a singer, who could bring a lump to tough old throats and a tickle to tired feet. I know the benefits a lively song and a throbbing voice can bring to a woman. Rose had her good voice from me, no doubt about it, and I wished to encourage it.

(And here I might laugh and wink at my friends around the fire, and admit — well, all right, motherhood is not my strongest suit, but understand that I am not a complete ogre. Rose wished me to go to that concert; it shows something, no?)

Also another plan in my mind — a possibility to meet Con, for I was desperate.

To see my face in the scrap of mirror nearly finished the evening right there. Oh, how I had come down! Thin face, lines appearing nose to chin, hair that was once so alive now hanging like some dead animal. Now, Eva, I tell myself, you are a woman of spirit, please remember! No tears.

I wash my face, tie back the dead hair and pinch the poor white cheeks to bring a little blood there. My best black coat brushed down and good black hat hide many bad points. Ha! I say to myself to build the courage, Ha! Big Snow or Con the Brake, whoever, watch out, for here comes Angel to claim you.

And this is no lie: sick and hungry though I was, spat on by all, and at my lowest, my power over that man rose, fire in the blood, to swell my lips and soften my eyes, to turn an unwilling man powerless. Oh, that night I was good, my friends, believe me!

Yes, I heard Rose sing her song — a true voice like her mother, with the power to pull the tears. A smile she gave me, just for her mother. She could be a good girl if she tried. But then I was out of the door quicker than a shadow when the audience began to stir. Who knows what scene would explode if those miners saw me, and public scenes were not my plan that night.

Outside was cold. Even in my coat the chill bit. I waited under the shelter of a piece of iron from where I could see the back door to the hall. My breath, coming out of my so-cold body, hardly made steam in the air, but I waited still.

In the end he came out. I knew my Big Snow. He would need to take a nip or two of liquor while he played accordion, and would have a bottle outside, count on it. And so it was. I heard the music ringing loud through the iron sides of the hall. Then a pause, and out comes the man himself, and alone. My lucky night: the bottle was hid almost at my feet! That man jumped one mile high to feel my touch.

The surprise is in my favour. Before he has time to think of good behaviour I am warming my hands in some private places and his body is leaping to meet me. The cold, the secrecy, the liquor glinting in the bottle at our feet, all powerful persuaders.

'Angel, Angel,' groans he, 'leave me, I beg you; I am a married man.' But all the time he leans in and pants aloud — great clouds of steam from this hot man. Oh, how my heart sang to feel him. Ten years younger I felt, and in my prime again.

At last he pulls away. Swigs at his bottle to put some space into events.

'Angel, I cannot do this,' he says.

I laugh. 'It would appear you already have, my sweetheart.'

'No no, you have caught me unawares.'

'Unawares shows up your true heart,' say I, 'which tells you we are twin spirits. These cold people on the Hill are not like you and me.'

In the dark his blues eyes are as black as mine, and shadowy. I cannot read them. 'Angel,' says he, 'the past is one thing. Now I am with Bella. Do not dare to come between us.'

'Bella is the one who comes between! I have the prior claim. And your daughter to care for!'

Perhaps I am shouting a little. Con pushes me hard to the wall, stops my mouth with his big warm hand. 'Listen well,' he whispers. 'I will do what I can for the child, not because I am the father — you would choose what father suits you best — but out of a care for the poor soul.'

I would have shouted that he should only look at her to see his own face reflected, but his hand forced me still. And his whole body. His desire was great, I tell you, even in his anger. We were made for each other, two sides of one penny.

'And hear this,' whispers Con, fierce as a furnace, me smiling beneath his hand. 'If Bella hears one word, one single drifting rumour — I mean this, Angel — of you or of Rose, you know, with me, there will likely be a broken body found down in the gully, which will not be mine.'

So. This is good news. A man who talks threats and secrets is a man who wishes the secrets to continue. I give Con a nod and a wink, take a good swig from his bottle and let him return to his music.

Rose at the Concert

ROSE STEPS ONTO the platform and looks over the heads of all the people, as Mrs Rasmussen has taught her. All the white faces are turned to her. She sees Brennan's big brothers who scared her up at Burnett's Face. She sees the man who spat on the floor of the Company store when her mother was buying flour and told her she had a nerve showing her face. On his side of the hall all the faces are hard and stony, like a wall with no way through and no way over.

Rose makes a little cough to see if her voice is still there. She can see right to the back of the hall but her mother isn't there. Then the door opens and Rose thinks this will be her mother coming in late so no one spits at her, but it is Brennan's mother with his waistcoat. Rose wants the door to open and her mother come in with a waistcoat for her but it doesn't.

Then Mrs Rasmussen smiles and raises her hands and Brennan's dad plays the introduction and she has to sing. Not much of her voice is there and Rose wants to stop and cough but she can't because she will get left behind. Mrs Rasmussen is nodding and nodding to her and lifting her hands to mean sing louder and Rose thinks she might be going to cry.

Then the door at the back opens again and her mother comes in so quietly she is like a shadow. She is wearing her good black coat and her good black hat and she turns her back to shut the door gently, then turns back again and looks over all the heads to see Rose. Her mother signals shhh, with a finger to her mouth, and nods once at her. Rose smiles to show she's noticed, then takes a big breath like Mrs Rasmussen has said, and her voice comes back.

When Brennan's dad comes in again with his cornet and she and Brennan are singing different tunes together all the people shift a bit in their seats and their faces are not stony any more and Rose sings louder because Brennan is loud and they hold hands like Mrs Rasmussen said and Rose thinks this is better even than her birthday.

At the end of the song Rose looks again at her mother and her mother wags her head and grins to show she has heard it all, and then she slips out quietly while everyone is clapping and cheering.

Brennan looks at her with his black eyes. His hair is smoothed flat on his head in a funny way and his face is wide open.

'We were good,' he says, and she says yes they were.

'My mother came to hear after all,' he says, grinning, and Rose says her mother came too.

'No she didn't,' says Brennan.

'Yes she did,' says Rose.

'Well, where is she then?'

'Gone home.'

'I never saw her,' says Brennan.

'Well she was here,' says Rose.

'If my uncle and my brothers saw her they might bash her up.'

'That's why she went home.'

'I never even saw her.'

'Well, she was here anyway,' says Rose, and runs away to find some supper.

After supper she has a turn at handing around the money box. It is smooth wood with a shiny catch and a slot in the top for people to put money in, and Rose thinks it is beautiful. She walks around the room shaking it and holding it in front of people. Some of them say, 'I've already given, dear,' and Mr Carmichael says, 'Well, one more for you, eh, Rose of Tralee?'

She takes the box over to her uncle Con the Brake, who is sitting with his accordion shining and winking on his knee. She shakes the box in front of him and the accordion groans as he closes it and hooks it up. Then with his free hand he fishes in his waistcoat pocket just like her father did when he gave her the gold. He takes out a tiny case and flips open the lid and takes out a round gold coin, holds it up for her to see.

'Do you know what that is, Rose?'

'A half guinea,' she says.

'Well, someone is teaching you well at school.'

'No, we only do pounds shillings and pence at school.'

'Not guineas?'

'Only the big boys. Mr Dimcock showed me a half guinea,' says Rose, and tells him about Mrs Hanratty buying four yards of watered silk at 1/3d. a yard and paying for it with a half guinea, and how Mr Dimcock had to go into his house behind the shop to get the change from his supply in the wardrobe because his shop till did not have enough in it.

Her uncle Con the Brake laughs and drops the half guinea into the box and says, 'You are a fount of information on all subjects, Rose, but you had best be spare with that piece.'

'Why?'

But Uncle Con laughs again. 'Explanations will have to wait, my sweetheart, because it is time to kick some life into this party, you know?'

He unhooks the accordion and throws back his head and the accordion sings a long, moaning note. He stamps his foot and moves his fingers. The music jumps out into the room and everyone starts dancing.

After the Scobies have taken Brennan home and Michael has gone with Mrs Hanratty, Rose looks to see if any of the Camp people are leaving so she can walk with them. But they are all singing and dancing still. Then her Uncle Con starts a new tune she has never heard and Mrs Rasmussen starts dancing their secret way, and Rose yawns and thinks she might lie down until Mrs Rasmussen is going home. She crawls under the legs of her Uncle Con the Brake's chair and finds a safe place behind the band. She looks out between the legs of the chair listening to the music humming down through the chair, and watching the legs and feet of people stamping on the floor.

Then she sees the money box, snuggled between Con's feet.

She strokes its silky sides and runs her finger round and round the tiny catch. Her eyes close as she lies there, stroking the box and listening to the laughing and the music. Then she thinks about her piece of gold in its soft bag and her other pieces of treasure that she has found, and how they could fit into this box and be buried like proper treasure.

When Con goes outside for a bit, she slides the box towards her until it is tucked against her body, then she kneels on all fours. She just fits under the chair. With one hand she lifts the box, but slowly so the money doesn't make any noise. The box tucks nicely under her white smock and Rose holds it there with one arm. With the other arm and two knees she crawls backwards under the whole row of chairs. It is hard. Some chairs are empty and some have people on them and they are all different shapes, but Rose pretends she is a silent cat and crawls on until she has reached the door. She backs out from under the last chair and turns quickly to open the door.

She slips outside, as quietly as her mother, shutting the music and the light and the laughing back into the hall.

Her heart is beating hard as she trots down the dark path. The box sings a soft jingling song to her.

NEXT day is a holiday from school because of the late night and because the Inspector has gone. Rose's mother goes out to dig in their garden and Rose asks her father if he is going to visit Billy Genesis.

'I am not,' he says.

'You might feel better if you went out,' says Rose.

'Ah, go to hell,' he says. 'You sound just like your mother.'

Rose plays on her bunk for a while and then she tells her father about her song the night before.

'And I suppose they all loved you,' says her father.

'Yes,' she says, 'they clapped a lot.'

He says nothing, just looks out the window up the gully to the east.

'Would you like to lie down and I could sing you to sleep?' she says and he asks what the hell has got into her and why doesn't she leave him alone and go out making friends with the whole world as per usual, so she goes back to her bunk and plays some more.

Then when her father has looked out the window without moving for a long time she goes over to the table and reaches under

173

it. She pulls out the egg basket and picks up the cloth from beside the fire and tiptoes to her bunk. Quiet as a mouse, she takes the money box from under the rug, puts it in the basket and covers it with the cloth. Then she goes to the door and puts the basket on the floor behind her while she ties up her boots, and opens the door, and in all this time her father never moves one inch. She thinks he might have died.

'I'm going to get the eggs,' she says, and still he doesn't move, but his eyes blink so she knows he is not dead.

Outside her mother sees her going to the hen house.

'I've collected the eggs,' she says.

'I'll just look again,' says Rose. She unhooks the wire of the hen-house door and goes in quickly before her mother can say any more. Inside it is dark and secret and Rose thinks this is not as good as under the floor boards but it is quite good. She shoos out Clementine and the new rooster, Aladdin, and shuts herself in. The ground looks a bit soft in one corner and she starts digging with her hands. Then she finds a stick in the straw and digs hard with that until she is angry, and when she puts the box into her hole it still sticks right up.

Rose sees that burying her treasure is not going to work anywhere up here, just like burying dead bodies. She wipes away her tears because her mother might see and she puts the box back in the basket and covers it again. She goes out into the yard and runs around the side of the house while her mother is bending down looking at something else.

There is not much room between the side of the house and the bank. Ferns lean down to tickle her. She looks for hiding places. The house is all straight boards down to the ground with no windows, just the chimney on it, thin at the top and smoking, but lower down stepping out in brick-sized steps until it is fat enough for the fireplace inside, then straight down to the ground. She looks at the bricks, then takes the box out from under the cloth and measures it against the bricks this way and that way until she is sure. She hides the box behind some ferns against the bank.

'I will make you a proper buried-treasure place soon,' she whispers. Then she takes the basket and the cloth back.

'No eggs,' she calls to her mother and her mother says nothing, just goes on digging.

Inside she takes down her coat — a proper coat that Michael Hanratty grew out of — and tells her father she's going up to the Bins. Her father says nothing too.

She walks past her mother.

'Where are you off to now?' She says.

'The Bins,' says Rose.

'Don't make a nuisance of yourself, then. And make sure you are back for your tea.'

At the Bins Rose skips over the rails and past the huge shed where coal is rattling down into the wagons, but today she doesn't visit anyone. She runs to the great pile of old railway iron and coal-slack, broken timber and just plain rubbish, all falling away down into the gully.

'Watch your step there, young Rose of Tralee,' says a man she doesn't know. 'That's no place for a little singer to be playing.'

'I'm looking for something,' she says.

'What would you find there that a girl would want?'

'A piece of wire.'

'For a handle is it?'

'Yes.'

'Well now, I think I can help you.' The man goes into the workshop and comes out with a piece of wire, which he is curving into a handle shape.

'I don't need it curved,' says Rose.

'Suit yourself, sweetheart,' he says, and bends it straight again.

She says thank you and skips back over the rails and down the track to the Camp. Mrs Rasmussen is on the porch of the tree-trunk house and calls to her that there is fresh gingerbread just out of the oven, so Rose stops to eat some.

'There was a fight at the hall after you left,' says Mrs Rasmussen, and tells Rose about the stolen money and how the Burnett's Face people thought the Camp people had stolen it, and how Mr Hanratty's drum got broken and her uncle Con the Brake had a black eye.

'And a sore head, though not from punching,' she says. 'And I myself am not the best, but it was a grand night for all that.'

'Will they still build the new school?' asks Rose.

'They will have to because there are five new children wanting to start.'

Rose asks if she can have another piece of gingerbread, and then she says she has to take the wire to her mother for a handle.

'Off you go then, little nightingale,' says Mrs Rasmussen. 'And keep your eye out for that money box in all your travels.'

'I will,' says Rose, and skips down to the Cork end, but wide, through the scrub to the back of the house so her mother and father don't see her.

The mortar between the bricks is soft — nearly as soft as sand; much softer than the ground. Rose smiles and works away with her wire and thinks about the song last night and her mother and all her friends listening to her.

Soon the brick will move out easily. Rose looks into the hollow. Her eyes widen. She looks again. Softly she reaches to grasp the next brick. It comes out without any working. There in this new hollow is a small leather bag tied tightly with a thong. Rose take it out and

176

opens the bag. She breathes out in excitement. 'Treasure!'

In the palm of her hand lie ten small flakes of gold like her own one that her father gave her, and some golden grainy dust. Rose wets the end of one finger and touches it to the dust. She puts the finger in her mouth and tastes the cold grains. They have no taste at all. Carefully she spits them back into the bag.

For a while she looks at the flakes. They are her father's. This is what her mother screams about. Rose had imagined a big sack full of golden lumps, but still, this is gold and she has found it as her father told her she must.

'You must find your own treasure,' he had said.

Rose knows this doesn't quite count, but still . . . She picks out five flakes, two big and three small, and leaves five small ones in the bag. She ties the bag up and puts it back behind the two bricks. Then she makes another hollow in a different place, down low and around the corner where a big person couldn't fit easily, and hides her little box with all its new treasure there, behind the brick.

That night, when they are eating their tea, her father says, 'We have a mouse.'

'We have not,' says her mother.

'There has been a mouse gnawing all day down by the chimney.'

'There is not enough food in the house to tempt a mouse,' says her mother.

'It is the warmth,' says her father.

'It is your imagination,' says her mother, and he says, 'Ah, go to hell.'

Rose can feel the giggles coming up. 'We could set a trap for the mouse,' she says.

'A mouse is no laughing matter,' says her mother, but she is smiling too. 'Eat your tea. There is food on the table for once and no thanks to your father.'

AT school next morning Mrs Rasmussen puts on her spectacles and marks the register, and then before she gives them their tasks she says, 'Children, I have something serious to tell you. The money that we all worked so hard to earn, which has been given by the people of Denniston for the new school, even though they had little to spare; that money which may not have been large in amount, yet was a sign of goodwill between the communities of Denniston — our money has been stolen!'

Mrs Rasmussen pauses for effect and everyone goes 'Oooh' in a long sigh, although they have all heard the news already.

'Now, children,' says Mrs Rasmussen, and she looks at them with a very sad face, 'stealing is a bad thing, and here on Denniston we do not like stealing. Indeed, in all the world no one likes a thief. I want you all to think very hard about that money box. And about that money, which belongs to the people of Denniston. I am going to ask each and every one of you whether you know something about the stealing of the money. And I want each one of you to look into my eyes as you reply and I will know if you are not telling the truth. If anyone knows about this theft, it will be far better to ease your conscience and speak out now. You will feel much better inside yourself that you have told. Now. Rosser Scobie?'

Rose hears Rosser answer, 'No, Mrs Rasmussen,' in his croaky voice. She wants to turn and see if he is looking into her eyes but no one else is turning so she sits still, facing Mrs Rasmussen.

'Andrew Scobie?'

'No, Mrs Rasmussen.'

'Tonto Jowett?'

Rose hears scruffy Tonto shift in his desk and giggle and Mrs Rasmussen rises and takes a step forward until she is standing nearly on top of Rose and Michael and Brennan. She is very frightening.

'Tonto Jowett, this is no laughing matter. Stand up.'

Rose hears his bench tip back and his boots move on the floor, and everyone else is still, waiting for Tonto to speak.

'Did you take the money, Tonto?'

'No, Mrs Rasmussen.'

'Do you know who did?'

'No, Mrs Rasmussen. But my father said he saw Con the Brake leave the hall, and when he came back . . .'

'We are not concerned with what your father saw. Sit down. Donnie O'Shea?'

'No, Mrs Rasmussen.'

'Jackie O'Shea?'

'No, Mrs Rasmussen.'

Now Mrs Rasmussen is up to the front row. Rose can feel Brennan shaking. She looks sideways quickly and sees that Brennan's face is red and there are tears in his eyes. She looks down at her hands and sees mortar dust in her fingernails. She hides her hands in her apron pocket.

'Michael Hanratty?' says Mrs Rasmussen.

Rose keeps her head down and looks just with her eyes, not moving her head, to see Michael raise his head and stare straight at the teacher.

Michael speaks in a very loud, proud voice. 'No, Mrs Rasmussen.'

'Rose of Tralee?'

Rose takes a breath as if she is going to sing. Everyone waits in silence. Rose lifts her head just like Michael and looks straight at Mrs Rasmussen's eyes.

'No, Mrs Rasmussen,' she says.

Mrs Rasmussen looks deep into her eyes, right down inside her, and Rose smiles a little and keeps looking. Mrs Rasmussen smiles back, a very small private smile, and nods.

'Brennan Scobie?' she says.

Rose feels something warm go right through her like a mouthful of hot sweet tea, and she sits quietly thinking about what has just happened, and how grown-ups don't know everything, and how she feels better, not worse, now that her treasure is still safe in its little hole in the chimney.

Then she hears the silence. Brennan hasn't answered yet. His head is still down and his face is very red. He tries to say something but all he makes is a croak. Mrs Rasmussen is frowning and all the children look at Brennan.

'Brennan?' she says again. Then suddenly he coughs and is nearly sick and out of his mouth pops his cat's-eye marble. It lands on the floor and rolls under Mrs Rasmussen's skirts. Brennan is coughing and coughing and Mrs Rasmussen comes and pats his back.

'I don't know about the money,' he gasps between coughs. 'I just swallowed my marble.' And all the class laughs.

'Look at me, Brennan Scobie! Did you take the money?'

'I did never! I was scared you would think it was me. That's why I swallowed my marble . . .'

The class laughs again and so does Mrs Rasmussen. Everyone forgets about the stolen money and they get on with their tasks.

PERHAPS if Bella Rasmussen had discovered the truth, or Rose had admitted it, the child's life may have taken a different turn. On more than one front. That is a matter of conjecture and for gossip, much later in her life.

Denniston 1884–85

The Track

ONE WET AND windy January morning, scruffy Tonto Jowett fell between the rails on the rope-road, became entangled in the ropes and was run over before his horrified friends could drag him clear. He died while his helpless mother beat her hands against her apron and moaned as loud as Tonto, for a doctor.

They held a service for him at the chapel in Burnett's Face. Then began the heartbreak of taking his little coffin off the plateau. Mrs Jowett became hysterical at the thought of Tonto's body travelling to the Brake Head on the same rope-road as killed him, so Tommy Jowett hoisted his son's coffin on his shoulder and set off on foot, with the funeral procession in single file behind him. Every so often Josiah Scobie moved up to take the weight until Tommy gave the nod that he was ready to carry his dead son again.

They had to walk the rope-road though: no other way out from

Burnett's Face. The miners and their wives, faces stony, plodded on as the skips rumbled past, inches from the good cloth of their Sunday suits. Feeling was running pretty high against the Company by the time they reached the top of the Incline.

The Incline was the last straw. Mrs Jowett, like Mary Scobie, could never face riding the wagons down. Tonto was her only son, her only child. Mary Scobie, deep in her own grief, held the howling woman as the men loaded the coffin on the funeral wagon, clean and empty for this purpose, and climbed aboard with it. Strong in her desperation, Mrs Jowett broke free as the wagon started on down. Con the Brake found his arm gripped by the shrieking woman.

'Don't let him go! Stop! Stop it!'

For a moment Con lost his grip and the funeral party in the wagon gathered speed. Goodness knows how many more were heading for the graveyard if Con hadn't fought the wagon back under control and Mary dragged the wild woman away.

Now four women on the plateau, all miners' wives, had dead in the ground down at Waimangaroa, and none had ever visited the graves.

Back up from the burial, Josiah Scobie leads a grim-faced group of miners up the clanging iron steps, open to wind and rain, to Eddie Carmichael's office, high in the sprawling hulk of the Bins. Five women from Burnett's Face, equally silent, wait, out of the rain, in the schoolroom at the back of Hanrattys'. Totty brings them tea and cake but there is no small talk. Iron determination hangs in the air, solid enough to choke any thought of conversation.

'The men are taking up a matter or two with Mr Carmichael,' says Mary Scobie, and that's all Totty can get out of any of them.

In Eddie's office Josiah's words are reasonable but his eyes bore holes. Here is the first sign of what is to come. This man is a preacher, an orator, one who can persuade others to follow him. Josiah Scobie will be famous; he has a future in the organising of labour, like his compatriot Richard Seddon. They are West Coasters now, but bred from generations of hard conditions in English mines. This is the first time, though, here in Eddie's office, two thousand feet up at Denniston, that Josiah Scobie has used his formidable power outside the pulpit. Saviour or Satan, take your pick: you could say this is where the man acquires a taste for power and politics.

'We can take no more of it, Eddie,' he says, 'and will not. You can see how it is.'

'Josiah,' says Eddie, all reason himself, 'I sympathise with your problems, of course I do, they're mine too. But what can we do? I can't change the landscape.'

'We say you can. Or the Company can. We need a road up here, through your devilish landscape. We cannot live a proper life cut off like this. Young Tonto Jowett might have survived if we could have fetched the doctor up.'

'The Incline . . .'

The miners growl and Josiah raises his voice a notch. 'Oh, we know the Incline is the jewel in the Company's crown, and the Eighth Wonder of the Engineering World, but it runs only half the time these days, as you well know. Nor our women won't ride it, most of them. We must have a road.'

Eddie Carmichael spreads his hands. 'A road, Josiah: think of the cost of it!'

'Think of the cost of lives lost for the lack of a doctor.'

'You might as well know, men, that the Company is not in good shape. Orders are sparse. We lost a ship on the bar down at Westport last week. Australia is sending coal cheaper than we can mine it.'

'Aye, you have your problems, Eddie, and what does that mean?

185

The man at the bottom cops it. You don't need to tell us it's hard times. Which of us has worked more than three days in six these last weeks? But we will have that road. We must have it. Or you'll find the lot of us walking off the job.'

Eddie Carmichael places his hands on the desk; stands up slowly. He's shorter than Josiah, but thick-set, an experienced miner too, and respected, not like the Company bosses down in Westport. He eyes Josiah squarely.

'You lot gave your word, Josiah. Your friend Lomas promised in front of the Company manager. No unions. Are you going back on it, then?'

'I am not. Who said union? I'm stating a fact, man. If conditions don't improve the men will leave.' Josiah smiles briefly. 'You should hear our women on the subject.'

The solid knot of men, black in their Sunday suits, growl agreement. Eddie sighs.

'It's a lost cause, boys. The cost of a road . . . No, don't even dream of that. Perhaps I can persuade the workshop to modify a wagon. Put in seats for the women.'

Josiah interrupts. 'Can't you see, man? It's our independence is the issue. Not one of us can get off the Hill without the Company says so. Nor anyone up. Company has enough control over our lives without this too. We need our own way up and down.'

'Tell him about my plan,' says Colin Cargill, the youngest in the group but a bright lad, bound for promotion and knows it.

'Aye, aye, all in good time.' Josiah dislikes any challenge to his control of the meeting. But it's clear to all of them that their fall-back position is needed.

Josiah takes a step forward. His thighs, inside their good worsted, press against Eddie's desk. He leans forward and stubs a forefinger once, twice on the wood. 'Well then, Eddie,' he says, 'what about a compromise? Young Colin here reckons we could cut a track up from the railhead, up the gully and zigzagging back to come out just below the Camp.'

'You must be joking,' says Eddie.

'Colin's scrambled up it. So has Tommy Jowett. They reckon it can be done.'

'Mr Jowett?' Eddie addresses him formally out of respect for his bereavement.

'Aye, sir, it's possible. There's a bit of a shelf some of the way; you'd have to pick at the rest. And use a shot or two at the bends.'

'That cliff's hard as granite.'

'It *is* granite, sir, but we've dug through worse. Being on the face there's cracks to get the point of a pick in.'

Eddie still frowns. Can't imagine a track up that sheer cliff. But he's already been surprised at what these English miners can achieve.

'You'd do it yourselves?' he asks, shrewd now, knowing bargaining is on the way.

Josiah squares up to him. 'This is only a compromise, mind — we couldn't cut a path more than three or four feet wide. A narrow bridle track for a sure-footed pony or a fit man. It won't please our women. Not much better than the Incline for them.'

'Get on with it, man,' says Eddie.

'We'll do it,' says Josiah, 'on our lay-off days, and Company will pay us hewing rate.'

'Now, now, Josiah. The Company lays you off because it can't afford to pay you. No orders coming in.'

'Then we're wasting your time, Eddie, and you'll lose your English miners. Come on, men.'

Eight pairs of muddy boots turn and make for the door. Eddie calls them back.

'Wait, man, wait. I can never get you hewing rate, you know

that. What if I could persuade the Company to pay you four shillings a day?'

'We're grown men!' says Josiah. 'Not thirteen-year-old boys. It'll take more than a boy's shoulders to cut a track up here!'

'I'm on your side,' says Eddie, 'but I can't see Mr McConnochie going past four. Can you? Not in these hard times. He's threatening to sell out as it is. I'll try him on five, though. How's that?'

'In writing,' growls Josiah. The men clear their throats to show assent. They'd all settle for four on their off days and Eddie knows it.

Eddie and Josiah shake on the agreement.

IN the end the best Eddie could get them was three and sixpence, paid out of a government grant, and even that was limited to four workers a day.

Sometimes, though, there were at least a dozen men picking away at the sheer rock. To be able to come and go without the Company say-so was a prize they'd work without any wages for. They were pleased enough with Josiah's bargaining, though, and put the money they earned towards the Miners' Relief Fund so they could all share in it.

Three or four days a week you could hear picks ringing in the gully as the two gangs — one from the railhead, one from the Camp — worked their way towards each other. At first the work progressed quickly, the lower gang following the natural shelf and the upper lot finding the rock shattered and easy to break. The men joked and hallooed to hear their voices echo off the sheer cliffs above the river. They sat on their narrow shelf to eat their bread and corned beef, and watched birds fly into trees that somehow managed to find foothold where men could not. A new feeling, this, and a good one, to be using the hewing skills to tame their wild landscape; to make it serve them for a change. A bridle track down off this great plateau — now that was something!

Mary Scobie was pleased at the thought, too, until she came down one day and saw for herself. It was a Saturday in late summer, everyone remembered that date — February 9th 1884. All hands laid off for lack of orders, not even the Incline running. A sweltering day, the sun relentless in a white-hot sky. Burnett's Face people came down to the Brake Head for the day, made a picnic of it, with the men taking shifts working on the track and the rest spreading blankets on the rocky outcrop at the top of the Incline. Just to look at the distant blue of the sea cooled you off.

Mary left the twins and Brennan playing around the rails of the Incline and walked down to the Camp and the start of the track. This time next year, maybe, she'd be walking down it, and riding the train out to the sea. Her hands tugged at the hot black cloth of her dress. Strands of wet hair lay plastered down her cheeks. Just picking her way down the stony path between Incline and Camp left her breathless. Up here at Denniston it was either a tight shroud of mist or a sun too close for comfort. Please God the men finished the track soon. She knew several miners' wives down in Waimangaroa but had not seen them in eighteen months. Mary imagined a gentle sea breeze, saw herself visiting, staying a night maybe, putting flowers on Frank's grave and walking ankle deep in that wide blue sea.

That was the dream. Mary Scobie set her feet on the raw unfinished slash in the rock that marked the start of the track, and knew the reality. This way out would be for fit men and young women. She, who had borne seven children, whose insides sagged in painful ways and whose legs were gnarled with varicose veins, was never going to make the journey down, let alone up. This whole much-vaunted exercise would not change her life one whit. For a terrible moment her head spun. The sheer cliffs with their clinging scrubby trees pulled like a magnet. Blinded by the darkness of it all, Mary turned and fought her way step by step back over the Camp. Her body felt pulled towards the ground as if the force of gravity had suddenly trebled. Bella Rasmussen, sunning her proud belly on her own porch, saw the toiling woman and called out.

'Come in! Come in, Mary. What is it, my dear?'

But Mary Scobie walked on past, one foot in front of the other. She walked up through Denniston, leaving children and picnic without a thought, walked on over the silent rope-road, her swollen legs aching, the dark cloth of her good dress drawing the sun's heat into her baking skin. She turned from the rope-road and climbed through scented, stunted bog-pine and manuka up towards the Scobie house, which faced away from mine, away from sea, up towards the grim inland mountains. Mary saw nothing — nothing but her own future. She opened the door, closed it behind her, sank down on a small embroidered chair — her mother's, which they had brought with them from England. Hour after hour she sat, still as a stone, facing the wall of her dark front room.

BACK at the Incline the twins and Brennan have not missed their mother. All the schoolchildren are there, shrieking and laughing, competing to dream up new, daring ways of riding the Incline. No wagons rumble down today; the children are free to invent their own transport. Rosser Scobie has carried an old worn shovel all the way from home. He sits on the shovel and leans forward to grab the handle sticking up between his legs. His brother Andrew gives him a push and down he flies, rattling and bumping between the rails, the metal of the shovel screaming and striking sparks on the gravel. Rosser screams too and rolls off, clutching his behind. The metal is too hot. Hoots of laughter as Rosser climbs back up, grinning and slapping the seat of his pants as if dousing flames. Andrew has an idea. A wet sack on the shovel blade will do the trick. This time Rosser shoots down a good distance before overbalancing and rolling sideways. Everyone wants a turn.

Michael Hanratty arrives with a new contraption. His dad has helped him build a wooden bogie — like a trolley but with two parallel pieces of timber nailed underneath instead of wheels. These slot over the metal rails of the Incline.

'Watch me!' Michael always demands attention, and usually gets it.

He sits, important, on the flat top of the bogie, feet on the cross-piece, hands on a guide rope, though how he can guide the thing is not clear — the bogie will follow the rails willy-nilly.

The children stand in a circle around Michael. Rosser and Andrew are memorising the construction. This looks much better than a shovel. Dylan Rees is doubtful.

'It's too steep, Michael. You'll never make it. You'll break your arm.' Dylan has broken his arm more than once and has learned caution.

'I'm not scared,' says Michael. 'Watch, Rose!'

'I'm watching,' says Rose.

'Watch, Bren!'

Brennan Scobie looks at his feet.

'Gives us a shove, Bren! Are you all ready?' Michael's voice is high and edgy.

Brennan still looks away so the twins give Michael a shove, harder than necessary. The bogie leaps forward, runs a few feet and stops. The twins laugh.

'Your boards are pinching the rail,' says Dylan. 'They're too tight, Michael, see?'

'No they're not,' shouts Michael over his shoulder. He kicks with his heels and jerks his body. The bogie, poised on the brow of the steepest plunge, edges forward, then sticks again.

'Ha ha,' says Rosser Scobie.

'Kick again, Michael!' says Rose.

Michael kicks again and the bogie moves sedately downwards.

'Told you!' shouts Michael, but the words turn into a yell as boy and bogie shoot suddenly down out of sight.

The children run to the edge: nothing but air and distant sea in front of them. Forty feet below Michael is still going, leaning back, pulling on his rope as if it were a brake, almost standing upright on the cross-piece it is so steep.

'Michael!' shouts Rose.

'He's going to be killed!' says Dylan Rees.

'Let go!' screams Brennan. 'Let go, Michael!' As if he could hear.

As they watch, the bogie sticks again, but Michael's rocketing body keeps going. The children above watch in silence as he somersaults into the air and lands sideways in a patch of scrub.

'Get Dad, quick!' says Brennan to his brothers, but before anyone can move, Michael's tiny figure climbs out of the bush. He stands, braced against the slope, both fists raised like a triumphant boxer.

'Yaaaaa!'

'I'm going to make one like that, only bigger,' says Rosser.

'I'm not,' says Dylan Rees.

'Come on, Rose,' says Brennan. 'He'll be ages climbing back up. Let's go and look at the track.'

'All right,' says Rose.

192

Charring and Scarring

THEY SAY THE fire must have started about then. While Michael limped back up, more bruised than he would let on; while Brennan and Rose explored the first section of the track; while Josiah Scobie's gang down in the gully were packing up for the day, and Tommy Jowett's gang, above, were laying a final charge; while Totty up at Hanrattys' bounced the baby's pram with one hand and stirred Irish stew with the other, and Mary Scobie, two miles away, sat facing the wall in a dark room.

No one knew how it started. Sparks from the boys riding the shovel, maybe, or from the powder charges, though the men always maintained they were well above where the fire first took hold. Josiah Scobie believed it was the sun on a bottle thrown into the bush by some drunk at the Camp. He preached a great sermon next Sunday on the dire consequences of drink and how evil earns its just deserts.

Billy Genesis knew it was the devil, sending him advance notice that he'd be the next sinner to be fried, right here on earth as well as later in hell.

Bella Rasmussen saw the first wisps. Sitting with her feet up in the sun, back to the log wall of their home, she rocked back and forth and sang to the child in her belly. She hummed one of Con's lonely sea songs — cool, smelling of salt and ice, a good one for a hot afternoon. She smiled to feel a breeze rising, coming from below, from the sea. There would be a wind tonight, the sooner the better. Something else came with the breeze. A whiff of smoke, always a good smell to Bella, reminding her of campfires and stories. But she knew also the dangers on this high plateau, where tanks were the only source of water, so she heaved to her feet and walked out to locate the source. This was not the heavy bitter coal smell of a cooking stove but the sweet tang of burning wood. On the Hill no one burned wood without careful thought. It was too precious.

She walked, not alarmed yet, down their stone path, out through the gate and over the barren rutted earth of the Camp to the point where the clearing stopped and dark trees and scrub crawled up over the edge. Through a break in the scrub she saw a fine blue line snaking up, wavering now as the breeze freshened, thickening as she watched. Walking faster now, she found the slash in bare rock that marked the beginning of the track. Brennan and Rose were on their knees poking at something.

'There's a fire in the bush, Brennan. Run and get Mr Rasmussen. You'll find him up at the Bins.'

'Come on, Rose!' says Brennan, running already.

'I want Rose here with me,' says Bella, not quite sure why, and sends the boy on his way.

Bella and Rose shout down to the gangs on the track.

'Fire!' sings Rose. It is a game to her.

'Fire!' shouts Bella Rasmussen. 'To your left! Towards the Incline!'

They hear the message shouted down from worker to worker, ringing against the stone walls.

'They will soon have it out,' says Bella, holding tight to Rose's hand. 'It has not taken hold.'

But the wind, an enemy today, rises and veers. It blows on a dull red heart that otherwise might have smouldered and died. Little yellow flames reach up tall and then taller, fingering through summer leaf litter that, for once, is dry. Soon the fire is burning on two fronts, jumping from bush to cracking bush. The twiggy, delicate manuka, white with flower, is gobbled by flames greedy for its oily leaves. Sweating men do what they can, bashing with sacks, but the slope defeats them. They cannot get to the centre.

'Get back to the Camp!' shouts Josiah. 'We must protect the Bins!'

The miners retreat to the Camp and stand in a line, looking down to see where the fire will arrive. They are tense but excited. The moment before a sporting event: Men versus Fire.

'Michael!' says Rose, remembering. She lets go Mrs Rasmussen's hand and runs back up the path to the top of the Incline. Michael is there, safe, still puffing from his last mad scramble, sitting between the rails with Brennan beside him.

'Does it hurt?' says Brennan, touching one of Michael's impressive bruises.

'Yes,' says Michael proudly. 'Did you see me go, Rose?'

'The fire's coming,' says Rose. 'It might burn the Bins.'

All three look over to the massive collection of sheds and offices. That would be a sight.

'It might burn your house, then,' says Brennan.

'No it won't,' says Rose, but she starts walking back. The boys follow.

The Camp is dark with smoke now. Con the Brake is rampaging through the thick air brandishing a sack. His wild excitement adds to the confusion. Bella directs the Camp people, handing them wet sacks or sending them to fill tins of water from their own water tanks. No one can see where the attack will come from.

'Here! Here!' shouts Con. 'Over by the men's quarters!'

'That is only smoke, man,' says Bella. 'Look in front of your nose! It will come through at Lord Percy's!'

'Mrs C. Rasmussen!' roars Con the Brake. 'Get up to Hanrattys' this moment! This is no place for you!'

'And leave you in charge? Your child will need a home, let me remind you! The fire, man!'

Gangly Lord Percy, hair and eyes wild, windmills through the smoke.

'My garden!' he screams. 'My cabbages! The fire is coming through!'

'To Lord Percy's!' shouts Con the Brake, rallying the troops. 'Josiah! Bring your gang over here!'

But Josiah and the English miners are running up the slope towards the Bins. Josiah has seen the way the fire is moving, driven by the wind. There are now two tongues of flames, two fronts to fight. One has reached the Camp and will be driven across it, towards the Cork end, where, please God, the sheer rock wall will halt it. The other is pincering from the south, from the other side of the Incline. A finger of fire has separated from the main thrust and climbed through the thinner scrub beside the Incline. It will bypass the Camp and drive around to threaten the Bins, where the great conglomeration of sheds and stacks of coal invite disaster. Already it is racing up through scrub, drawing a wide curve of leaping orange flame.

'To the Bins, to the Bins!' shouts Josiah. Saving the Camp is not their battle. In a tight group the miners run up to the Bins. Their boots crunch through loose coal.

'A hose, a hose, in God's name surely there is something!' shouts Josiah, but they can find nothing. The best they can do is to fill empty kerosene cans from the tap on the side of the big Bins water tank and to dampen sacks. Their preparations seem pitiful in the face of the crackling flames that are now creeping onto the plateau, but the miners stand fast, solid as fenceposts, waiting to see where fire will strike.

Below at the Camp people are screaming and running. Someone calls up for help but the miners are looking in another direction.

'There is only one house down there worth saving,' says Josiah, 'and that can be rebuilt. The Bins is our livelihood. It goes, our jobs go.'

'True,' says Eddie Carmichael, mine manager. 'I appreciate this, lads.'

Josiah smiles. 'We are doing this for ourselves, Eddie, not the Company.'

Eddie points. 'Here it comes! This way, this way!'

'By God, Jimmy Cork's must be burning!' shouts Tommy Jowett. 'Can you hear those chickens?'

'Aye,' says Josiah.

'It's coming around this side!' shouts Arnold Scobie, and the men start running. 'It will take hold!'

'It will not,' says Josiah. An order.

Five of the men stand shoulder to shoulder, flailing together, slapping the wet sacks again and again like angry parents where the sparks are running. The Scobies, in line, hand tins of water forward. Josiah flings the water, high and wide, to spatter over the wooden shacks at the back of the Bins. Back go the empty tins. No one speaks. Eyes and shoulders concentrate on the rhythm, on carefully passing a full tin down the line and tossing the empty one back again, fingertip to fingertip like a ball.

A corner of one of the sheds catches. Josiah flings again and again.

'Listen to those cranks down at the Camp,' he growls to his brother Arnold. 'They should be up here with us, not shouting and screaming over their few bits and pieces.'

Arnold nods.

A window shatters in the heat and flames pour out.

'Dear God,' says Josiah, 'we'll have to go inside, men. Bring the sacks.'

'Let it go, Josiah,' says Tommy. 'We can't save it. Once it gets to the coal . . .'

'We'll give it one more go. Watch your step, though!'

Josiah kicks open the door and sends an arc of water shimmering into the flame. The men charge in, sacks bashing and flailing, charge out again for breath. Another spray of water, another charge. The flames falter. A sheet of yellow flame dies as quickly as it had risen, and the men cheer. If only the tank water holds out they may just win.

At the Camp it's another matter. Lord Percy's hut and garden are charcoal. So are the men's quarters. The wind blows erratically along the ledge of the Camp — sometimes this way, sometimes that — driving the fire before it. Where the dwellings are close together, nothing can stop the advance of the flames. All the tents and half-canvas shacks have blossomed into flame, one by one, like a row of great flowers opening in the heat. Here and there are bare spaces where no one has built. Small groups of people gather in these spaces, to see where the flames will attack next.

Con the Brake's house is under threat. Everyone is dashing and beating. The water has run out. Tom Hanratty has come to lend a hand, and here is Totty, her dress sooty, baby Sarah wailing on her hip, Elizabeth at her side. She's desperate to find her son.

'Michael!' she calls into the roiling smoke. 'Michael!'

Michael runs full tilt out of blackness, coughing and screaming. He doesn't notice his parents, but finds Con and pulls desperately at his arm.

'Rose's house is burning!'

'Get on home, Mickey. This is no place for you.'

'Rose's house!'

Con the Brake pushes the boy away.

'Jimmy Cork's inside! And Rose's mother is gone mad!'

Con is caught. For a moment he stands quite still in all the mayhem. 'Rose?' he shouts. 'Rose? Is she safe?'

'I can't see her,' wails Michael. His face is a mask of soot and tears. 'I can't see her!'

Con flails with one hand, shouts over his shoulder with the other, 'Oh God, Oh God. Tom! Tom Hanratty! These people need a leader.' To Bella he shouts, 'Rose is in danger. Tom'll take over here.'

Bella's great cry is half anguish to see her man disappear into the smoke, half outrage that he should leave his own house and wife for another's.

'Michael!' shouts Totty, 'Come up here! *Michael!*'

But the boy has run back into the smoke towards the Corks' end.

Tom has arrived, stout and reassuring, with an armful of sacks. 'Go back with the girls!' he shouts to Totty over the crackle and pop of exploding wood. 'I'll see to things here.'

'Michael!' wails Totty. Tom turns her gently and pushes her in the direction of the path. 'Con is seeing to the children. Off with you.'

Tom is already running back into the smoke. Little Elizabeth Hanratty, clinging to her mother's hand, screams to see him go.

On a Sunday; Con the Brake might sit in church, thinking about his misdeeds and hearing the preacher preach hellfire and damnation, and he might imagine, sitting there, promising never to do it again — how fearful those fires of hell would be and how dreadful the screams of the damned. Well, nothing he could imagine, not even with the preacher fanning the spectacle with his fiery words — nothing could be dreamed up worse than the Cork corner of the Camp, the day of the fire of '84.

The chickens, what's left of them, are mad with fear. Rose's mother had always clipped their wing-feathers to stop them straying. They flap madly a few feet in the air and flop back to run on scrabbling feet round and round against the paling fence, then back the other way, necks stretched, beaks wide open, cackling like mad witches. The rooster, red eye glaring, red wattles shaking with rage, screams damnation louder than any visiting evangelist. On and on he crows, and the flames build higher.

The hut is a sheet of fire. Against the yellow and red, Rose's mother is a dancing black dervish, whirling a blanket high above her head. Her mouth is open but the sound is drowned. The mad silhouette dashes again and again against the flames. On stage it could be a dance of great wild beauty but this is real. The blanket is only fanning the fire.

Con sees a writhing on the ground a little to one side. It's the two boys, Michael and Brennan, holding Rose down. She is a good match for the two of them. Con sees her fling them both off and run at the burning hut as if towards water. The boys and the man run after her. Rose's mother, whirling the blanket, capers on, unheeding.

For one moment Rose disappears into the flames. The boys rear back in despair. Con, roaring like a bull, charges the yellow curtain, scoops the girl with one arm, and brings her out before the boys can take breath to scream. Rose's yellow curls are on fire and so is her smock. Con snatches the blanket from the mad woman, rolls Rose and holds her tight. The girl is silent now, but struggles grimly. Both boys are howling to see the blanketed lump that is Rose. Con holds her, fighting the thrashing limbs.

'Rose, Rose, little sweetheart,' he sobs. 'Lie still, little one. Oh Jesus, lie still!' He fears she will damage her burnt skin.

Rose's mother has left the fire now and is clawing at Con's back.

'So! You come at last, and see what a disaster! All I have is burning in there!'

Con shrugs off the mad woman. 'And Jimmy?' he grunts.

'Jimmy, yes Jimmy! All! All! All what you have done! See how it turns out!'

Con turns away. If Jimmy is inside, he's done for. If not, why is he not here when help is needed?

At last Rose stops jerking. Con lifts the blanketed bundle. Gently he separates the folds so she can see out. One side of her face is yellow and red like the fire, the skin folding and drooping away from the flesh.

'Rose, Rose, be still,' whispers Con the Brake. 'Your father is dead. He cannot be saved. But your mother is here.'

Rose turns her head away. Silent tears run down. Goodness knows what other damage may be wrapped inside the blanket. Only her poor face is visible. Con remembers her arrival at Denniston, wrapped in a tarpaulin parcel, with the hole cut for her face. He turns to Eva, who capers and flails still, shouting curses.

'Angel! For God's sake listen! Your house and husband may be burned but your daughter is alive and in need, if you care.'

'My daughter! My daughter!' screams Eva. 'And you? Is it not yours too? Take her, then.' She picks up a clod and throws it, like an angry child, at Con. She reaches down for another. Brennan and Michael stop their howling and gape to see her mad antics.

Con turns away, sheltering Rose from the onslaught.

'I will take Rose to a safe place,' he says. The mother continues her barrage as Con, walking soft as a cat, heads back across the Camp. The boys, silent now, cling to his coattails, one each side. Behind him Con hears Eva screaming on. Curses or laments you couldn't tell.

The hut has caved in and the fire is dying but Rose's mother will not leave the burning husk or Jimmy's body inside it. Young Brennan, looking back, sees Rose's mother snatch a charred pole from the wreckage and poke the embers as if she's fishing in a red sea. Sparks shoot up. Eva screams and dances like a dervish.

At the Camp and the Bins there is more smoke now than fire. A skeleton of building is exposed towards the front of the Bins but the main bulk is safe. Josiah's gang have isolated a small pile of smoking coal, shovelling it to one side where it may safely burn itself out. Half the shacks at the Camp are smouldering ruins, sheets of iron and charred beams sticking up at crazy angles out of the ashes. Con's great log cabin still stands, though one corner is charred. The Camp people stand near it in the smoking air, as if gathering around a hearth for comfort.

'Jimmy Cork is gone,' says Con the Brake to Tom. 'The mother is still there — mad, you know, but unharmed.'

Suddenly rain falls: steady, cleansing, roaring rain. The people groan with pleasure.

Bella Rasmussen, the apron over her huge belly black with soot, comes out from the house with a kettle of tea. She sees Rose lying in Con's arms.

'Rose!' shouts Bella.

'She is burned but not in danger. I am taking her to Totty. You have enough here,' says Con. He has difficulty looking Bella in the eye.

Bella reaches out to touch Rose but stops and draws breath at the sight of her face. It is streaming with rain, the skin floating downwards off a flaring cheek.

'Oh, Rose,' says Bella, 'my Rose of Tralee.' She beats her fists against her apron. 'Take her up quickly to your place, Tom. It is chaos here. Tell Totty to bathe the face all night with a soft flannel cloth in a solution of carbonate of soda. I will come in the morning.' Tom takes the still bundle from the big brake-man and walks into the sheeting rain. Michael and Brennan follow behind like dogs, but Bella calls Brennan back.

'Where's your Dad, then?'

Con growls, 'They are all up at the Bins, all the miners, saving Company property while people's houses burn.'

'The Company is your livelihood too, man,' says Bella.

Con glares. 'Down here it is lives, not livelihood. Which is more important?'

'Good God, husband, you would start up an argument on your way to hell! Where's that Brennan?'

'Here,' says Brennan.

'Ask your father if he would send a message to Granny Binney to come in the morning if she can make the trip. Her ointments are needed for Rose's face.'

'Aye,' says Brennan.

'Well, go on then, boy. Your father will be frantic.'

'What about Rose?'

'Rose will live, but her face will be less scarred for Granny's curing.'

'But where will she live?'

'We will see to that, Brennan. Rose will never lack for a roof.'

'What about her mother then?'

'Go on, off you go, this is no time for conversation! You are worse than Mr Rasmussen.'

Brennan stands. 'But . . .' he says.

Bella Rasmussen looks at the boy. Brennan stares at the ground. The stubborn line of his brow is set, his hair plastered, stocky legs rooted.

'Brennan,' says Bella more gently, 'you did well, you and Michael, to look after Rose. Now leave it to others.'

She takes him by the shoulders, turns him to face the Bins and pushes between the square little shoulders. He starts walking.

Bella picks up her kettle of tea. 'Come in, come in then,' she says to the waiting homeless. 'Though I'll have no soot tramped in on my clean boards. Leave your boots in the rain. And Billy?'

Billy Genesis is cheering himself up with a swig or two. He looks at Mrs C. Rasmussen over the rim of his tin mug.

'Billy Genesis. Your friend is burned, his body still lying and his widow in need of assistance. You are a good distance away from your next drink, my fellow. Drag Lord Percy away from his charred cabbages and see to it!'

Billy's eyes are thoughtful. 'Mrs C, you are quite right. I will see to it.'

'And I,' says Con the Brake, draining his hot sweet tea and clapping Billy Genesis on the shoulder, 'will see to *you*!' Con propels the stumbling man out of the yard and over smoking ashes towards what was the Cork end of the Camp.

Who Killed Jimmy?

EVERYONE HAD A different theory about how Jimmy Cork died. He was burned — no doubt about that. But why he didn't get out of the hut was open to debate. Jimmy might have been uncertain on his pins, but even a lame man can move in an emergency. There was warning enough. Even drunk, Jimmy could crawl. Billy Genesis reckoned Jimmy had been on Straw Nugget's sly-grog and that his breath ignited, boom! from the first spark; that he burned from the inside out, as it were.

Some believed he had a horde of gold hidden under the floorboards and that the boozy bugger wouldn't leave it. How else did he get the money for drink? And where was the horde now? More than a few were seen heading for the Cork end with a pick and shovel.

Bella thought Rose's mother could've clocked Jimmy so hard

over the head in one of their endless battles that he was too dizzy to crawl free, and that Rose's mother was gone crazy with guilt. Who but a crazy woman would go and live with Billy Genesis? Worse than crazy when you consider she had a daughter.

Tom Hanratty said it was suicide. He said Jimmy Cork would never have the backbone to take his own life squarely, but that he would take the opportunity, when it was in front of his nose, to give up.

For once, Con the Brake had no theory at all.

The truth never came out, as far as anyone told.

Rose's mother stayed sitting in the ashes all that night and half the next day, looking like a charred stump herself she was so still. Finally she let Billy and Lord P haul her upright and went home with them, all three in the one hut until Lord Percy rebuilt.

The funeral was unusual, even for Denniston. Rose's mother, who hadn't said a word up to now, came up rock solid when coffins and the graveyard down in Waimang were mentioned. Jimmy's body wasn't going to some distant graveyard and that was that. She gathered brush and some of the scattered charred timber from the fire. She built a new fire over Jimmy's body right there where the house had been — wouldn't let a soul touch him. The smoke rose thick and acrid because of the rain and the chickens and because of Jimmy himself. A black funeral pyre. Most of the Camp were standing there, at a distance, behind Rose's mother, who stood alone.

Con the Brake dug Billy Genesis in the ribs and told him to make use of his one accomplishment, so Billy cleared his throat and said in his queer grating voice:

"'And Joseph went up to bury his father: and with him went up all the servants of Pharaoh, the elders of his house, and all the elders of the land of Egypt.

"'And all the house of Joseph and his brethren and his father's house: only their little ones and their flocks and herds they left in the land of Goshen.

"'And there went up with him both chariots and horsemen: and it was a very great company.

"'And they came to the threshing-floor of Atad, which is beyond Jordan, and there they mourned with a great and a very sore lamentation: and he made a mourning for his father seven days.'"

Then Con the Brake told Billy that would do, so he stopped.

When the ashes were cool Eva Storm scraped around in them for Jimmy's bones, and for other things, who knows? She found the bones at least, put them in a clean flour sack, tied it tight with twine and gave it to Billy Genesis. She told him to throw the bones as far as he could into the gully, in the direction Jimmy always looked when thinking of his gold. Billy drew back from the sack as if it contained snakes or a wild dog, which people noted and whispered about. Was it guilt? In the end it was Con who grasped the neck of the sack in one huge paw, swung it once, twice, around his head and then let go.

He and Eva watched it rise, twisting against the sky, due east, and then plummet, like a shot bird, down into the great trees far below.

Then Eva went up to claim Rose, who had all this time been lying and moaning in one of Hanrattys' guest-rooms, her face smeared with carron oil and then floured as Granny Binney had instructed.

Eva Storm

THE FIRE? POOR Jimmy's death? No no, my friends: you will not draw me on that. Call it Act of God and move on. Up there on the Hill, theories were plentiful, facts sparse. After the fine sport of invention had palled, no one much cared about the truth, Jimmy being who he was. So say he died. Of burning.

Consider the ones left alive. Consider my true bad luck. Not Jimmy's death so much, which could only be a blessing, but the timing of it. That fat bag of flour, Bella (who called herself Rasmussen), was finally got pregnant to my Con, and both of them oily with the joy of it all. Six months earlier and I wager you my man would surely have walked off that black plateau with me on his arm. There was a moment, I tell you!

Consider also the gold. My bad luck kept its grip. All day and night I scraped and scratched around that burned hut, but Jimmy had the last laugh there. In my bones I could feel his stash whispering to me, but where? Where? Nowhere that my tired eyes could seek out.

So. No money, no house, no chickens. And for the moment, no Con. My only and single asset is Conrad's daughter, Rose, who is good now and then as a lever with Con for a bit of food.

Now. It will do no good to look sideways at me and throw hands in the air over Billy Genesis. A woman in such a situation has no choice. None. If no good man is on offer then take a bad one. Or two. Billy Genesis at any rate was a small step up on poor Jimmy, or so I thought. One: he had a job. Two: his spirits were higher. Three: I will not mention in mixed company but my drift is clear, no? Against the man, an entire book: ugly, bad-tempered and free with his fists, a drunkard, breath to knock you down at ten paces, and wandering eyes when it came to the girl. To be true, more than wandering eyes, but what could I do? What choice did I have? I could shout, take a poker to the man, but could I change the man's nature? I could not. Well, Rose had to learn some day the way of the world. Sooner or later, given her start in life, she had to learn to get along, and she was sharp enough to learn quickly. It was painful for a mother, yes, but in those days what was not painful? So no wagging fingers and long faces please, or my story finishes right here.

That scarred blacksmith Billy beats no bush but comes to a point smartly, which I like about him.

'Woman,' he says, the day after the fire, standing over me, his feet planted in rubble and me filthy from scratching in the embers, 'I know what you are after. You lust after Jimmy's gold, it is writ like the finger of God in your face, and I have the same lust.' Here he winks and digs me with his beefy elbow. 'And a lust or two of another variety! What say we pool our knowledge and see what profit might come of it?'

'What do you know, then?' say I.

'Aha. I am not so foolish as to spurt out a valuable commodity without some payment in return.'

He taps his fat nose as if he is some sage, which he most surely is not. But he has the air of a man who knows something, so I stand up from the ashes and prepare to do business.

'Well and I know a secret or two with gold at the heart,' say I. 'So what is in mind here?'

'In mind is you in my bed and keeping house for me.'

'House? What house? You live in a pigsty.'

'I will set to and build it better. The Company will help with materials. A blacksmith is not so easy to come by.'

'And?'

'And I will feed you and your child. And we will seek Jimmy's gold source.'

'Equal shares?'

'Well, now.' Billy looks shifty. 'Equal is man's talk. And I am feeding two mouths, both female. Equal will depend.'

'On what? Spit out the terms, Billy. I am no tender baby here, but tougher than you and smarter.'

'On favours, and how pleasing they are.'

Well, how am I to know the favours include Rose? And if I knew, was there another choice?

So we shake hands like men and Billy quotes from the Bible something about 'cleaving' and 'knowing' and plenty of 'unto's and in Billy's poor sick mind I am now bound to him.

One piece of business first though, before the new regime. The business was Jimmy's remains. Oh those church ladies and proper gents up there put on faces sharper than knives when I refused to send the body down the Incline. What body? A charred and stinking mess, poor Jimmy was. Better to finish the job. There's plenty of countries where they burn their dead right out in the open so everyone can see that the right body is going up in flames. Plenty, no? But these people ran their lives in straight lines carved deep and unbending like wheel-ruts. No change possible. They brought Mr Carmichael down to talk to me.

'Mrs Jimmy Cork,' says he, always polite when death is around, 'we must take the body down for a proper burial.'

'Oh,' says I, 'Jimmy's proper now, is he, now he's dead?'

'You are upset,' says he, but he will not approach close, as if I am a wild beast to be wary of.

I tell you, I am suddenly sick of the lot of them. Tired and bone-sick. 'Go about your little ways and leave me to mine!' I scream. They will not dare to come close, or do not care enough to make the effort. I light my little funeral bier and the body smokes and stinks. My man Con stands nearby. He understands. It is he who throws the bones far, away and off the plateau, and my heart is eased to see them fly.

At the time, my friends, I am not in the mood for speeches, you understand, with my own luck so low. I give you a word now, for Jimmy Cork: Jimmy was a loser and a weak man, but we had some good moments. If dice had fallen another way he would have been someone of note in this country, be sure of that, the way he talked and knew of history and governments and the workings of the mind. Jimmy was a dreamer whose bad luck, you might say, was that he found the motherlode. Found and lost it. The dreaming of it suited him better, do you see? The shining hope, before he found the real colour. No? We all know it. The practical side, when the dream turned real, was too much for him, poor sod.

So, then, that was Jimmy. My story continues. And a sorry chapter it is, so I'll make it short. Who can argue with dice? Your luck runs crossways, you move on and prepare for the next roll. In this, Rose features.

My daughter has been sharp, which is good, but has tricked her mother, which makes me spit with rage. For Billy Genesis has told me a thing or two.

After the throwing of the bones he takes me by the arm, rough, but claiming me. He has seen my look towards the big man Con.

'Now,' says he, 'one: your pretty daughter is a thief.'

'Oho,' says I, sharpish. 'It takes one to know one.'

'Two: she has found Jimmy's stash.'

That set me back. Rose being only seven years old.

'Three: I have found *her* stash and hid it safely.'

That my own daughter should have such secrets from her mother! I wait in silence for a four, but Billy has done. He hauls me away from the gawking funeral crowd to the little overhang of rock that was once part of Jimmy's hut. A sheet of iron forms a porch of sorts, a pile of charred debris a windbreak to the north. I don't like it. Too close to uncomfortable matters. But this, he says in his new master's voice, is to be our home until he has rebuilt.

Billy grins at me with his good eye and comes up close. Phaw! That man's breath! Hot he is, which I have known before, but with it something nasty now: a new edge to the set of his mouth; a heat that is more rage than desire; his blacksmith's hands clenching me, all cruel strength, not even one tot of loving. This man thinks he owns me, and the very idea pumps him up like his own forge fire.

'Now!' he says. 'Now, then.'

He takes me with a brutishness lacking any style at all. A thing I detest. Where is the advantage for the woman? (Any man sitting around this fire who harbours ambitions take note.)

Well, it is over quickly at least, and Billy is for a while a quieter man. We discuss gold. I tell him of Jimmy's first discovery and of his belief that the source outcropped on the cliff close to one of Banbury mine's air shafts, but that the fall-in had blocked his passage. Billy's eyes gleam. He has access to the mine for shoeing the horses and could maybe scout a different route through the maze of tunnels.

To be honest, I think him a fool. The source will likely be embedded in quartz or rock and require proper mining. What hope is there of carrying on a noisy operation within earshot of an army of belligerent English miners?

'None!' I say to this dolt. 'You are as mazy as Jimmy.' Which earns me a clout on the ear. Just let me get back my strength, I think, and we'll see. But for the time I divert the man to thinking on Jimmy's existing stash and the possibility of retrieving more from the same place.

'The Lord giveth and the Lord taketh away,' intones Billy. 'Meaning the stash is spent all but a few pennyweight. Rose took half and left half and neither would keep a man in drink more than a month. But,' says he, with a thoughtful look in my direction, 'I will climb to this place you talk of and take in the lie of the land for myself. Why in the name of fortune Jimmy didn't take me there earlier to be his arms and legs I cannot fathom.'

Well, friends, we can all guess why. I can read betrayal all over the man's face myself. No doubt Jimmy Cork, who was no fool, whatever his other faults, could read the same signs. Already I am making plans. This Billy Genesis will not do for long.

Now. Soon it is time to collect my Rose, who is up at Hanrattys' like a little lady, her good looks spoiled by the flames that killed Jimmy. Maybe a lesson to her.

A Lone Chimney

ROSE LIES ALONE in a dark room. She looks straight up at the ceiling, trying not to move. Her face hurts. If she moves it hurts more. When she cries the tears coming out of one eye run back into her ear in a warm line but the tear from the other eye makes a line of fire across her cheek and she screams.

Mrs Hanratty comes into the room and looks down at her. Her white nightgown and the candle make her look like a ghost.

'It hurts,' says Rose. 'My face is hot.'

Mrs Hanratty gives her something to drink, pouring it into her mouth from a little jug so Rose doesn't have to move her head. The jug is white and on it is painted a little pig with green trousers and a red scarf, and the pig is playing the bagpipes.

'The candle is too hot,' she says. Mrs Hanratty has put it down on the table by her bed.

'Poor Rose,' says Mrs Hanratty. 'Poor Rose. The drink will help you to sleep.'

A baby starts crying in another room and Mrs Hanratty and the candle go out again.

Rose tries not to think about her house burning and her father burning and her mother dashing against the fire with the blanket. She doesn't want the tears to burn her face again. She thinks of the words of all the songs she knows and she counts to one hundred and then she starts on the Rivers of England. Then she thinks about her treasure in the chimney, and in her head she names all the things and the money and the gold inside the treasure box.

In the morning Mrs Rasmussen comes to see her. Mrs Rasmussen has a bandage on her hand. She and Mrs Hanratty look down at her, their faces one each side of the bed, but it hurts to move even her eyes so she looks straight up and sees them both in a fuzzy way.

'The flour is not right,' says Mrs Rasmussen.

'Granny Binney sent carron oil and said to flour over it,' says Mrs Hanratty.

'The burn is not ready for that,' says Mrs Rasmussen.

'Granny Binney said . . .'

'Granny Binney is a fount of knowledge, no doubt, but she has not seen the child.'

'What do you think, then?' says Mrs Hanratty.

'A clean cloth, soaked in boiled, cooled water with bicarbonate of soda.'

'She was more comfortable with that, certainly, in the beginning,' says Mrs Hanratty.

'Well, let us return to that.'

'And we will not mention it to Granny Binney . . .'

'We will not,' says Mrs Rasmussen. 'I am as frightened of that old crow as everyone else.'

Soon Mrs Rasmussen is bathing her face gently with cool water and then she lays the cloth over her face and sits quietly beside the bed.

'Now my head is cold,' says Rose, and Mrs Rasmussen smiles a sad smile and says that half her hair is burnt away and she will be feeling the draught. She goes out of the room and soon she comes back with a soft white bonnet and tucks it with gentle fingers over Rose's head.

'What happened to your hand?' says Rose.

'It is burned, like everything else at the Camp.'

'Is my house burned right up?'

'To the ground. I believe one corner of the chicken house still stands but I have not been over to see.'

'Is my father dead?'

'He is.'

'Where is my mother?'

'She is seeing to your father.'

'But he's dead.'

'She is seeing to his body.'

Rose cries out as Mrs Rasmussen lifts the cloth by two corners, dips it in the cool water and lays it on her face again. A baby is crying too, and Rose hears footsteps on the stairs going into the baby's room. Mrs Hanratty sings to the baby and the crying stops. Then she hears faster boots in the corridor and through the cloth she sees a shadowy Michael running into the room. The noise hurts her face.

'Don't bother Rose now,' says Mrs Rasmussen.

'I can't see her face,' says Michael.

'No,' says Mrs Rasmussen.

'Can you lift up the cloth so I can see?'

'Certainly not,' says Mrs Rasmussen.

'Will she be all right?'

Rose wants to hear this answer too.

'The burn is not too deep,' says Mrs Rasmussen, and she laughs. 'She will still be our Rose of Tralee. When her hair grows. And her eyebrow.'

'Will I have a scar like Billy Genesis?' asks Rose.

'I certainly hope not,' says Mrs Rasmussen in a sharp voice. 'Not with all the care and attention you are getting. Your face will be dark and scabby for a while, and then red for a while, and then there might be a white patch, but not much.'

Michael kicks his feet around and asks when can he see under the cloth. Mrs Rasmussen clears her throat loudly. 'Michael,' she says in her school-teacher voice, 'you are making too much noise altogether. Go out to play.'

After Mrs Rasmussen has gone Rose lies still under the cloth, thinking about Michael. Mrs Rasmussen doesn't like him much. Most grown-ups like Brennan better. Sometimes Michael makes her laugh, and he thinks up good games, but Rose likes Brennan better too, most of the time.

Then she listens to the noises in the house. She hears Elizabeth and Michael shouting at each other, and then Mrs Hanratty shouting at them both to go out and play. She hears one of the boarders clumping down the hall, then he tiptoes past her door, then he clumps along again. The baby cries again and Mrs Hanratty comes running down the hall. Soon she comes into Rose's room with the baby and lays the baby on the bed on Rose's good side.

'Hold her there while I wet the cloth again.' The baby smells of sweet milk. Mrs Hanratty arranges the cloth so she can see out with one eye.

'How is that now?' she asks, and Rose says her face is not so hot.

'You are a brave little girl,' says Mrs Hanratty. 'My Michael would never lie so good and still.'

'I like listening,' says Rose.

'There is certainly plenty in this bedlam to listen to,' says Mrs Hanratty.

Rose touches the baby softly. Her finger is gripped tightly by the tiny fist. Rose wants to hold the baby forever. Mrs Hanratty says that might not be a good idea and takes the baby out again.

Later Rose hears the bell ring for tea in the boarders' dining room. Footsteps go down the hall: a humming woman whose little boots click and two men going along together in a rumble of boots. She can hear talking and laughing in the dining room and at one time a great shout of laughter going up into the air like an explosion, and then for a long time little bursts of giggles as if bits of the explosion are falling down to earth again. She can hear Michael and Elizabeth's voices laughing, and Rose smiles a little too. Her face is not so stiff.

Then Mr Hanratty comes in and stands looking down at her. The smell of pipe smoke comes in with him. He is in his shirtsleeves and his waistcoat is stretched tight across his stomach. His gold watch chain curves from buttonhole to pocket like a smile. His curly brown hair and bushy beard shake from side to side for a bit.

'Dear, dear me,' he says. 'Poor little mite.' And shakes his head some more.

Then he takes a breath and says, 'And how is our littlest boarder feeling?'

'They forgot to bring me my tea,' says Rose. Mr Hanratty laughs.

'Those are the most welcome words we have heard from you these three days,' he says.

218

'Have I been here three days?'

'You have.'

Rose thinks about three days. Three day-times and three night-times.

'Am I going to live here now?' she asks.

'We will worry about that later,' says Mr Hanratty, and pats her toe where it makes a little hill under the blanket.

'Is my mother sick too?'

Mr Hanratty clears his throat with a kind of growl. The hair around his mouth bunches and twists like a tiny forest in a storm.

'Well now,' he says. 'Food for the little lady. Mrs Hanratty will be delighted to take your order.' He pats the bed again, but gently so it doesn't bounce, and goes out. Rose likes the way he walks, tramp tramp as if he is stepping in mud and is afraid of slipping. His back is solid like a tree and his stomach points the way.

Michael's slippers run down the hall. His are the fastest of all the footsteps in the house. Rose has counted nine different footsteps. He runs in.

'Mother is bringing some soup,' he says, and comes close to the bed. 'Can I see under the cloth now?'

'No, it hurts.'

'Is your eye still there?'

'I think so.'

'Is your ear?'

'Yes.'

'You might be ugly,' says Michael.

'I know,' says Rose, and thinks about being ugly.

'There isn't any blood,' says Michael. 'The cloth is clean.'

'I know,' says Rose.

'Or pus.'

Rose feels a tear in her good eye. She doesn't say anything.

'So I don't think you will be all that ugly,' says Michael. 'And if you are you can still be my friend.'

Rose lies still. The tear rolls down.

Mrs Hanratty comes into the room with a bowl of soup and a smile, but frowns when she sees Rose.

'Michael Hanratty, have you been upsetting Rose?'

'No,' says Michael. 'Anyway, I'm going to give her my lucky rabbit's paw.' And he runs out. Rose hears him next door crashing drawers open and shut.

'That boy!' says Mrs Hanratty, and she puts the soup down while she lifts the cloth. Michael comes running in again but he stops still when he sees Rose's face and his eyes and his mouth open wide. Mrs Hanratty starts spooning soup into her mouth and it is meaty and creamy and the best thing Rose has ever tasted. Michael tiptoes to her other side with a solemn face and puts something soft and furry into her hand.

'You can have it to keep,' he says, and watches without saying anything while she eats all the soup. Rose wants the cloth back so he can't see her.

'You'll be up in no time,' says Mrs Hanratty, 'if you eat like that.' She soaks the cloth and arranges it, and tells Michael to come out now and leave Rose to sleep. Michael's solemn face comes close to Rose.

'Your eye is still there,' he whispers, and he goes out with his mother.

IN the morning she hears her mother's voice downstairs. Her words are short and strong and they stick out of Mrs Hanratty's running words like rocks in a fast creek. Mrs Hanratty's voice goes higher and Rose thinks she might be angry.

Rose looks at the cloth in its basin by the bed. She doesn't need it all the time now but anyway she squeezes it out and lies down and puts it on her face. She doesn't want her mother to see. The talking has stopped and her mother comes up the stairs very slowly. Rose lies still.

Her mother comes into the room. With one eye Rose looks at the tangled hair. Her mother's good coat is muddy and her face is bruised. She stands away from the bed, just looking at Rose.

'Are you all right?' she says.

'Yes.'

Her mother lifts the cloth to look under, then puts it back without saying anything.

'Your father's dead,' she says.

'I know.'

'And is buried.'

'Where?'

'In the gully,' says her mother.

'East?' says Rose. Her mother looks at her and then sits down slowly on the chair by the bed.

'East,' she says. 'Yes.' And slowly she lowers her bruised, tangled head onto the bed and cries out loud. The sound is like something wild, not human at all. She bashes her fist again and again on the clean coverlet. Rose howls.

Mrs Hanratty is at the door.

'Leave us alone,' screams her mother and Mrs Hanratty goes. After a while they both stop.

'You forgot to do your hair,' says Rose. Her voice comes out in hiccups. Her mother slowly takes two pins from her pocket and puts them in her mouth. She twists the dirty hair behind her head as if she would tear it out, and stabs the two pins any old where into the mess.

'Is that better, madam?' says her mother in a sharp voice.

'Yes.' Rose likes the sharp voice better than the howling. She wants to ask her mother to clean the mud off her good coat but she decides to wait till later. Her mother says that she has come to collect her, but that Mrs Hanratty wants her to stay for two more days until she is better.

'Will I be ugly now?' says Rose.

'You are not a pretty sight at present,' says her mother, 'but that will change when your hair grows back. I doubt you will ever be ugly.'

'Will my hair grow back soon?'

'Yes, yes, yes!' says her mother, and throws her arms about as if she's angry.

Rose decides to keep the rest of the questions for later. She feels better, though. Her mother usually tells the truth.

Her mother picks at her nails. Rose looks out the window. The questions come out anyway.

'Where will we live?' says Rose.

'Well . . .' says her mother. And then nothing more.

'Is our house burned right down?'

'It is.'

'All of it?'

'Yes, all of it.'

'Even the chimney?'

Rose shrinks back as her mother jumps to her feet. 'What use is a chimney standing lonely in a black field of charcoal? What use, Rose? Eh?'

'We could build a new house around the chimney.'

'Yes? Around the chimney? Who is the carpenter of you and me?'

'You built the chicken house.'

'Don't talk to me of chickens!' shouts her mother, 'Not

chimneys either. You! You!' But then she stops and sits down with her hands folded like a lady. In a little while she says, 'We are going to live with your uncle Billy Genesis.'

'He's not my uncle!' says Rose.

'Well, he has offered to take us both in, and we do not have much choice.'

'We could stay with the Rasmussens.'

'Ha!'

'Why don't you ask her?'

'That's enough of questions,' says her mother.

'I don't want to go!' wails Rose.

'Well, so. I am going and so are you.'

'I won't,' Rose cries. 'I don't want to!'

'You will!' says her mother, hands on hips. 'Enough of this, you ungrateful girl. Billy is building on a special room for you, which is more than a thief deserves.' She looks hard at Rose and says she will come back on Tuesday to collect her.

Rose pretends she hasn't heard.

ON Monday morning, when Mrs Hanratty is collecting Rose's breakfast dishes, Mrs Rasmussen's huge body fills the door. She is smiling and holding some white flowers and her cheeks are pink from climbing the stairs.

'Well, Bella!' says Mrs Hanratty, and she smiles too. 'Not long, now!'

'Any day,' says Mrs Rasmussen, and heaves her body over to the bed.

'Just smell this manuka!' she says to Rose. 'It makes your heart glad to be alive!'

'No it doesn't,' says Rose.

'She's down in the dumps today,' says Mrs Hanratty.

Rose looks at the little white flowers. She pulls two off and drops them on the floor and looks up at Mrs Rasmussen. The two women look at each other.

'She knows?' says Mrs Rasmussen.

'Her mother was here yesterday.'

'Out of the frying pan,' says Mrs Rasmussen.

Rose looks up from picking at the flowers. 'What is out of the frying pan?' she asks. Neither of the women answers, and Rose starts crying and asks why she and her mother can't stay at the tree-trunk house.

Mrs Rasmussen pats her hair and sighs. 'Well, sweetheart, I've offered to take you until your mother finds her feet, but it's not so simple . . .'

'Why can't she come too?'

Mrs Rasmussen sighs again. 'Ah well, there it is.' Then she says she must get down to the schoolroom, the children will be running riot, and gives Rose a quick kiss, not her usual hug, and goes downstairs.

'We could stay here,' says Rose. Mrs Hanratty puts the tray on the bed and sits down.

'Listen, Rose,' she says. Rose knows she is going to say no.

'We all love you, Rose, and are trying to do our best for you and your mother. Your mother is an independent woman who will go her own way. She wishes to live with Billy Genesis, who has been . . . kind . . . to her.'

Mrs Hanratty's face is not kind at all. Her eyes, which are usually warm like brown toast, look more like burnt raisins.

'Your mother,' she says, 'wishes you to live with her. Billy Genesis is willing to have you both, so that is what will happen. A child cannot choose.'

'He's not kind to *me*!' says Rose.

'Well . . . perhaps there is some good in him and perhaps he will be a better man with a woman in the house. And Rose, you can come and visit as often as you like.' But Mrs Hanratty's face is black as coal as she picks up the tray and goes out. The baby is crying again.

Rose wants to cry too so someone will come and pick her up and tuck her into a pram and wheel her away. She climbs out of bed and goes to the window, walking softly so as not to bounce her face. The nightgown, which is Elizabeth's and has little pink flowers, is too small for her. It pinches her armpits. She looks out the window and sees Brennan running across the yard from the schoolroom to the dunny. Then he runs back and looks up and sees her. He waves and she waves back. He doesn't stop and stare with his mouth open or anything, just waves.

She looks down Dickson Street. Over the roofs she can see the big chimney of the Powerhouse smoking and she thinks of her own chimney standing all alone with the ashes of the house around it and her treasure inside it. Her feet are cold on the wooden floor so she goes back to the bed, still treading softly. On the end of the bed is her slate and chalk, where Mrs Rasmussen has left it. She picks all the white flowers up from the floor and arranges them in a circle on the slate. Then she counts them. Thirty-seven.

37 she writes. And then she draws a chimney on its own, with no curl of smoke and no roof.

A Door Facing Out

ROSE LOOKS THROUGH the open door. Inside, the little room is dark. There is one window, high on the wall.

'Go in and see,' says her mother, so she steps inside, but carefully in case there are nasty surprises.

'I can't see out the window,' she says.

Her mother snorts. 'I might have known you'd find fault. Your Uncle Billy has gone to a great deal of trouble.'

'He's not my uncle.'

Rose sits on the little bed. There is a box beside it, and a chest in the corner for her clothes. On the floor a rag rug in colours of mud and coal. She looks down at the rug. Billy Genesis is watching from the doorway.

'Well, say thank you,' says her mother. 'There's not many little girls have their own room specially built for them.'

'Thank you,' she says without looking up.

'Don't I get a kiss?' he says in a funny way: too loud.

'Billy Genesis, don't start that,' says her mother, raising her hand to him. Billy catches the arm and twists it back. 'The mother will have to do, then,' he laughs, and kisses her hard in full view of passers-by.

'The door goes the wrong way,' says Rose.

'Speak up, child,' says her mother, and then she says to Billy Genesis, 'I don't know what's got into her; you usually can't stop the chatter.'

'It's all the change,' says Billy. 'But she'd better get used to it quick.'

'The door,' says Rose in a louder voice. 'It goes outside. Anybody might come in.' She looks hard at Billy Genesis.

'Oh for heaven's sake,' says her mother.

'My room isn't joined properly to yours.'

'I don't know what you're going on about,' says her mother. 'Of course it is.'

'Look, madam,' says Billy Genesis. He goes out her door and puts his big red hand on the other door and pushes it open into the main part of the house, to show how easy it is to get there.

Rose looks at her mother. 'Why don't you sleep here with me?' she says.

Her mother looks away out the door. 'I'll be next door with your uncle Billy.'

'He's not my uncle.'

'We'll have no more of this!' shouts her mother. 'We're lucky to have a roof over our heads.' Her voice is edgy and rough. Rose knows her mother wants to hit her, but won't because she is so ugly and burned.

'Now, come next door when you have done sulking,' says

her mother, 'and we'll have our tea.'

Rose goes to the door and shuts it hard. It nearly catches her mother's skirt. She goes back to sit on the bed. Something about her mother is different. She doesn't like the different thing. She wants to be back in their messy little house at the Cork end of the Camp. This room is too empty. It's like a little prison. She thinks about the princess in Rumpelstiltskin, locked alone in the attic until she had spun all the straw to gold, and she thinks about the poor little princess in the tower. She goes to the corner and drags the chest across the floor. This floor has proper floorboards. You could hide treasure under them. She pushes the chest until it is under the window and then she climbs up and looks out.

She can see right across the Camp. She sees Mrs Rasmussen's shadow in the window of the log house. Mrs Rasmussen is lighting a lamp; Rose sees her turn to pull the curtains and her black lumpy stomach is all edged with orange. Rose sees, in the distance, past the charred ruins of the men's quarters and the tents of the new people, a single black chimney standing on its own.

She remembers about tea and gets down from the window, but leaves the chest where it is.

In the night Billy Genesis comes into her room and does things to her. He says she is a lovely girl and a pretty girl but he hurts her.

Rose shuts her eyes and thinks about her treasure.

Next morning she gets up quickly before Billy Genesis or her mother are awake. She thinks about school and she thinks about her ugly face. She wants to go and get her treasure but she is afraid. The chimney is waiting, like a birthday present, but also like a dark man. The dark man picture is stronger so she decides to get her treasure another day.

She walks into Hanrattys' yard and looks up at the window of the room where she used to be. No one is at the window. She knocks on the door. Mrs Hanratty has floury hands and a pink face.

'Hello, my chicken,' she says. 'Have you forgotten about the new school-house?'

'No,' says Rose. 'Can Michael walk with me?'

'He can indeed,' says Mrs Hanratty, 'and show you the way. Now, where is that boy?'

She gives Rose a piece of warm bread to eat while she shouts upstairs for Michael to get a move on. Michael comes and fidgets around while his mother buttons him into his coat and puts on his gloves. Michael is looking at her.

'Stop staring,' says Rose. 'It's rude.'

'It's not,' says Michael.

'Yes it is.'

'Boys are allowed to stare at girls,' says Michael.

'Who says?'

'I just know.'

Michael stares at her.

'The scar's still there,' he says.

'I know,' she says.

Michael comes up close. Rose stands still while he reaches out one finger and touches her face.

'Does it hurt?' he says.

'No.'

'Does it hurt there?'

'No.'

He taps harder. 'Does it hurt now?'

'Don't,' she says.

Mrs Hanratty takes Michael's shoulder and shakes him. 'Michael Hanratty, you cruel little boy!' she says. 'Look what you've done now! Poor Rose.'

Mrs Hanratty smiles at Rose and wipes away her tears. 'Boys!' she says.

Michael is still staring at her. 'I was just testing,' he says. 'I won't let anyone else hurt you.'

Rose says nothing.

'I'll bash up anyone who hurts you,' he says.

Rose looks out the window.

'Or stares at you,' says Michael.

'All right,' she says.

'Go on, off to school the pair of you,' says Mrs Hanratty, and she whispers to Rose, 'Don't take any notice of that boy. He's a natural ghoul. Your scar hardly shows at all.'

'What's a ghoul?' says Rose, but Mrs Hanratty has run upstairs because someone is screaming.

The new school-house has two rooms: one for the big children and one for them. There is a new teacher, Mr Stringer. He has to run from room to room looking after them all because Mrs Rasmussen is away until her new baby is born.

Mr Stringer is tall and thin, with no moustache or beard. His hair sticks out this way and that like an old broom. He keeps patting and smoothing it but it stays stormy. He moves his legs back and forth when he talks, as if he wants to go to the dunny. One of his boots squeaks.

'Hello, Rose,' he says, 'I am Mr Stringer.' He puts his hand on her shoulder and turns her to the class. She wants to run away.

'We must welcome Rose back,' says Mr Stringer. 'Some of you are new and have not heard about Rose. Her house was burned down and she herself was burned trying to rescue her father. Rose is a hero.'

Rose smiles at the class but not all of them smile back.

'Come and sit with me,' says Brennan.

'She's sitting with me,' says Michael.

'Not only a hero,' says Mr Stringer, 'but a popular companion, I see. At the moment, however, we have more than enough desks in the junior room, so each pupil will occupy a double desk. Spread out, children! Work, not talk, is the rule.'

He wags his head like a jack-in-the-box, but a smiling one, and runs back next door in his squeaky boot. The children all giggle.

Brennan leans over. 'He's funny, but he's nice,' he says. 'He teaches us good things.'

Then Brennan starts copying his sentence without saying anything about her face.

One day, after Rose has been back at school for a while, Brennan and Michael come down to the Camp after school to see her new room. They lie under her bed and pretend they are British soldiers at the Crimea and the Russians are waiting outside to kill them. Then Michael stands on the wooden chest and jumps right across her room onto the bed, and Brennan does too, and Rose nearly gets there, so the boys move the chest closer because she is a girl.

'You're lucky to have a room of your own,' says Michael. 'I have to share with Elizabeth.' He screws up his face.

'*I* have to share with Rosser and Andrew and David,' says Brennan.

'Why doesn't your mother stop us making a noise?' says Michael.

'I don't know where she is.'

'Well, you're twice lucky then. My mother's always there.'

Then the boys start fighting because Michael says Rose got well from his mother's nursing and Brennan says Rose got well from Granny Binney's medicine and no one down at Denniston knows much, and Michael says the miners at Burnett's Face are stuck up.

'And your father drinks,' says Brennan.

'So does yours,' says Michael.

'I mean the demon drink,' says Brennan.

'Who cares about Chapel wowsers?' says Michael.

'Who cares about Catholic drunkards?' says Brennan.

'Anyhow, my father's not a drunkard, he just sells drink.'

'That's worse.'

'Is not.'

'It's tempting the weak.'

Then they both stop and look at her because her father was a real drunkard and weak, and he's dead, and now her mother is living with another drunkard.

'Your mother is living in sin,' whispers Michael.

Rose says nothing.

'Your mother will go to hell,' he says, 'and burn in eternal damnation.' He screams and dances around the room as if flames are burning him.

'But Rose will be all right,' says Brennan.

Michael goes on dancing and Brennan laughs at him.

Rose screams very loudly and the boys stop still to look at her. Another scream comes out of her mouth before she can stop it. She tries to dance like Michael, whirling and screaming.

'Billy Genesis!' she screams. 'Billy Genesis! Billy Genesis!'

The boys watch her. Then they join in, laughing and screaming: 'Billy Genesis!'

Rose whacks the bed with both fists and the boys join in too. 'Billy Genesis! Billy Genesis!' Laughing and whacking.

'Billy Genesis is uglier than a toad,' says Michael and makes a horrible face. Rose screams with laughter.

'Billy Genesis does hot farts,' says Brennan. 'Billy lights his furnace with his farts!'

The three of them roll around on the floor.

'Billy Genesis still wets the bed!' shrieks Rose, and the boys laugh and shout and do rude things with their willies.

Then they all lie still on the bed.

'Let's find something to eat,' says Rose, and they all go over to Mrs Rasmussen's.

Clouds Thicken

THAT YEAR, 1884, was short on celebrations, long as a hungry child's reach on misery. Far as anyone can remember the only two good things in 1884 were the opening of the Track and the birth of Bella's baby, and both those events carried their cloud.

After the fire the Company built a new men's quarters twice as big, and began filling it with any labour that might be recruited in Westport. There was the occasional fit young adventurer among them, who fancied that a spartan life at Denniston would somehow stiffen the sinews for the Game of Life ahead, but on the whole these men were dregs: past their prime physically, unable for one deplorable reason or another to hold down good work elsewhere, and now desperate enough to come to the cold and windswept coalfields of the plateau.

Josiah Scobie, with a deputation from Burnett's Face, was down knocking on the mine manager's door more than once. In one week there were three accidents, one of them nearly fatal, and all, according to Josiah, the fault of sloppy work habits and untrained men.

Eddie said the Company had promised a new recruitment drive in England next year.

'Next year will be several lives too late!' stormed Josiah, squaring his shoulders and setting his feet apart in the boxer's stance that became his trademark later, on the hustings. 'Eddie, you must not send this riff-raff down the mine! It is not in anyone's interests.'

Eddie Carmichael was a great man for reason and compromise; the only one who could take on Josiah and once in a while come out a point or two ahead.

'Look, Josiah,' he said on this occasion, 'what say the Company puts you on to train the new men? We'll pay you the deputy's rate, and you take them for a week before they go down on their own. Eh?'

'I couldn't train these men if you gave me a year. Two years. They are not miners and never will be. The Company should be ashamed putting good workers at risk.'

The miners standing behind Josiah nodded and rubbed their hands and stamped their feet in Eddie's cold office, like corralled horses waiting to be let out into a more familiar landscape.

'They are not exactly queuing up to come to Denniston,' said Eddie. 'There are other mines now, less isolated, less harsh . . .'

'Don't give me that whitewash, Eddie.' Josiah was getting going now. 'The Company is sitting on the best seams in the country up here. Let them pay men a bonus to work the Denniston mines and they'll get their men. And keep them.'

And so it would go on. Arguments and threats, reason and counter-reason, with no progress made. Eddie's point was that the

Company couldn't afford to recruit miners from England; that competition from Australian coal was too fierce; the Company was running at a loss. Mr McConnochie would have to sell out, and then they might all be out of a job. Josiah and his men reckoned the Company could be more competitive if they employed qualified men at proper rates and got a decent day's work from them. They had a point. Almost every day, somewhere on the plateau, part of the operation would shut down with damaged equipment or damaged men. And mostly the shutdown was attended by a knot of angry miners accusing a group of indignant Camp people, with more often than not a scuffle and a few punches thrown.

The cold and the mist did nothing to lighten moods. Anyone with two eyes could see confrontation was on the way.

Conrad VI

THOSE WHO TAKE notice of omens would scarcely be optimistic over the birth of Bella's long-awaited baby. It was only March, yet the air hung dank and chilling as midwinter and the mist so thick you could not see house to house at the Camp. Breathing was like dragging something solid into your lungs: a spongy mass spiced with coal smoke and stale ash from the January fire. Not cheerful flavours.

Yet Bella Rasmussen was cheerful and everyone on the Camp knew it. Lamplight reflecting softly onto the fog from the windows of the log house sent a message to anyone passing close enough to see that warmth and life and hope were not strangers to the Camp. Every lonely passer-by trudging off to work or coming back exhausted from late shift would smile, thinking of Mrs C. Rasmussen humming and polishing away inside that glowing house.

The expected baby was a symbol of respectability for everyone at the Camp. As if a baby could bring that motley collection, scorned and reviled for their incompetence, acceptance in the wider Denniston community. Not a hope to lay on anyone, let alone a tiny child.

And there he was, newborn and perfect, coming with no great difficulty before Con the Brake, coughing and cursing up at the Brake Head, could find someone to spell him. Finally John Gantry Senior came to the rescue and Con charged down through the blanketing fog to welcome his son.

Bella, mountainous as a queen bee and as regal, is lying on the day-bed in the central room of the log house. A fire is roaring up the chimney and Totty Hanratty, heavily pregnant herself, is in attendance. She has removed her bloodied apron, bundled it into a basket, and is now tucking back odd strands of coppery hair, smoothing down the creases in her blue smock. This is the first time Totty has acted as midwife. She cannot disguise her delight. Indeed, the triumph radiating from both women is like a blare of trumpets.

Con's woven Swedish rug, an heirloom, glows on the polished wood of the floor. Although it is early afternoon, every lamp in the house is lit against the gloom outside and in celebration. The news is out and several well-wishers are waiting outside, fuzzy shadows in the mist, but Bella will let no one in until Con has come.

His boots crash on the porch, one two. The door is almost unhinged as Con roars into the room, bringing fog and a trail of black footprints with him. In four strides he is over to his wife, then midway to reaching for her his hand stops. He stops altogether. Looks from his out-reached hand to his boots, back to Bella again, waiting for the tirade. Con the Brake, straight off duty, is black with soot: damp, clinging soot that streaks his hair, his face, every part of his body. He has forgotten to wash up, forgotten his home clothes, forgotten to remove his boots at the back door.

Bella and Totty roar with laughter to see his rigid dismay. All Con the Brake's desire is to hold his wife, to touch his newborn son, but here he is, caught in the spotless room, hardly daring to move. He inches his head around and moans with frustration to see his son's rosy face, eyes wide open in surprise at this colourful world he has just entered. The linen tucked around the baby is purest white; the carved wooden cradle, carved with designs from Con's own childhood, is of white kahikitea felled from the gorge below the Camp and dried three years in slabs behind the log house before Con would work it.

Still he has not moved. A black giant, marooned.

'Bella!' he moans. He has no idea what to do.

'Mr Rasmussen,' says Bella, her eyes alive with love, 'you would be wise to turn around and walk in your exact footsteps back out the door, locate, if you can, the back of the house, and wash up in the laundry, where you will find hot water in plenty.'

'My home clothes,' murmurs Con. 'My clothes are up at the Bins.'

'I have a new child to look after,' says Bella. 'A second I do not need.'

The fog-shrouded people on the porch see the door open again, a shaft of milky light, and silhouetted against it Con the Brake tiptoeing out like a ballerina. He shuts the door softly behind him and glares at the gathering crowd.

'I will clobber any man of you that sets foot in my house before I am washed up and dressed and ready to receive. Understood?'

They nod, and wait, coughing and wheezing, as Con roars around the back and flings water in the laundry.

When Totty finally opens the door, and the people of the Camp are allowed to file in with gifts and smiles, they see Conrad

Rasmussen sitting on a chair beside his wife. He is straight-backed and dignified like a prince. He wears the dark trousers of his best suit and a scarlet jacket, gold braided and gold buttoned, its high collar embroidered and embossed in whirls of silver and gold. The bundled baby rests on Conrad's knee, surrounded by all this scarlet splendour.

When everyone has arrived, even Michael Hanratty and Rose of Tralee, both agape at the fairytale jacket, Conrad unpins a silver and blue star from the pocket of his coat and lays it upon the linen wraps of his son. Then he stands slowly, holding his son out towards the ill-assorted people of the Camp.

'This is our son, Conrad the Sixth,' he says, and kisses him. He hands him down, silver decoration and all, to Bella, who is lying there in her earrings and best nightgown as if she were simply resting, not recovering from giving birth for the first time in her life, at forty-one years of age.

Then, while the people stand around, naturally a bit dazed by all this drama, Conrad asks Totty to bring all their glasses from the kitchen and he goes to another room and brings back a dusty green bottle, which he says has been awaiting this occasion for fifteen years. He pours the clear, fiery liquid into the ten glasses, which is eight more than most people possess. Toast after toast is pledged as the glasses are passed around with great sipping and laughing and choking.

Tom Hanratty, who has just arrived, smacks his lips over the fiery liquor, then smoothes his curly beard and moustache with one hand, clears his throat, and solemnly welcomes the newest citizen of Denniston, and they all cheer.

They would have stayed all night in that glowing haven but Con the Brake, back to normal in his shirtsleeves, thanks them for coming, sweeps them with outstretched arms towards the door and chases them out into the cold and the dirty, clinging damp.

Cold Feet, Hot Head

ROSE'S MOTHER IS visiting the men's quarters and Rose wants to come too.

'It's no place for children,' says her mother.

'I know some of the men,' says Rose. 'I could visit too.'

'Out, out!' shouts her mother. 'Here is sun and no washing hung yet. This is your task, madam.'

'I can't lift the sheets,' says Rose. 'And anyway the sun is gone again.'

'What has got into you these days?' says her mother. 'You're as surly as a goat.'

'Why can't I visit the men too?' says Rose.

Her mother raises her hand to strike and Rose runs away quickly.

'Put your boots on!' shouts her mother, but Rose runs quickly in her stockinged feet.

She runs over to the log house but then thinks she can't go in with her stockings muddy. Mrs Rasmussen would be cross too. She looks back. Her mother is standing outside Billy Genesis's house, shouting and waving at her. She runs around the back of the log house and past the men's quarters so no one can see her. She leans, puffing, against the back wall of the men's quarters and looks over the bare scrubby patch to where the chimney is standing. Her chimney. Perhaps today she can go there. Twice already Rose has tried, but her legs wouldn't take her.

She takes three deep breaths as if she is going to sing, but her stockinged feet are stuck like concrete in the ground. She counts to twenty. Then to fifty. At fifty her legs will go. Her mouth smiles just a bit and she starts humming to keep her legs going. Rose walks quickly and looks at the ground all the time. The chimney is frightening, like a man waiting to get her.

She doesn't look at the ashes of the house, or the ashes of the chicken coop. Her heart is banging in her chest. It is jumping up into her throat.

Behind the chimney wet ferns lean down. She squeezes past them and they dribble on her. She looks at the chimney. She wants to get her treasure and go away quickly, but everything is different. A piece of roof iron has fallen down and is covering part of the chimney. Some burnt pieces of wood are hiding the place where the treasure is. She has forgotten to bring a knife to scrape the stuff out from the bricks.

Something scary is here.

Rose tries to stop sounds coming from her mouth but they keep coming. She breathes fast, in and out, in and out, and the sounds stop.

Rose pulls away the pieces of wood and they crash down. The chimney is all different. Some bricks are lying on the ground and some bricks are hanging half off the chimney. She pulls at a brick where she thinks her treasure is. It comes away easily. The stuff between the bricks is crumbly and black. It pours down onto her stockings. Rose moans again. She drops the brick and her hands are black too.

There is no hole behind the brick.

Rose tries another place and another. Strange sounds come out of her mouth again and again. She can't stop them. The chimney is all coming apart; she can lift the bricks off anywhere. Her treasure box isn't in any of the holes.

Rose wants to scream and howl. She wants to run and stick her face in Mrs Rasmussen's soft front. She wants to run away down the Track to the railhead and right out to the sea. She looks at her black hands and her black smock and stockings. The cold is coming up through her feet.

Because of her cold feet she starts running. Her feet run back past all the houses to her own room. They run around to the back of Billy Genesis's place, to the water tank.

The water tin is heavy even with only a bit of water in it. The wire handle cuts her hand. She drags the slopping tin into her room and shuts the door. Her fingers are too cold to pull off her dirty stockings. She flaps her useless fingers in the air and tries again. Her whole body is shaking. She drags her smock over her head without undoing the buttons and drops it in the tin. Then she lifts the dripping smock and rubs at her face and hands. All the time she is thinking of her father burning to ashes inside the house and his smoke going up the chimney. The soot on her face might be him.

The door opens. She is shaking so much she can't see properly. Then she sees it is Billy Genesis standing in the doorway. He comes inside and shuts the door. She can't move away.

'Here is the little thief,' he says and winks at her. 'You have been at a certain chimney by the looks of you.' He reaches out one of his red hands to touch her bare shoulder. In his other hand he holds her treasure box.

Rose can't move.

Billy Genesis raises a finger to heaven. '"If a soul sin and commit a trespass against the Lord, and lie unto his neighbour, he shall make atonement unto the Lord with burnt offering."' He lowers his finger and touches her again.

'You're cold,' he says. 'We must do something about that, little thief.'

Looking at her all the time, he puts her treasure box on the high window ledge. Rose can't move towards it or move anywhere. Billy comes over to her and takes off her vest and her undergarments with his hot hands, and he peels off her stockings and drops them all in the tin. He dries her face with a corner of the blanket and puts his face into her hair.

'Little Rose,' he says.

Her whole body is shaking and there is a fiery lump in her throat so she can hardly breathe.

He carries her to the bed and puts a blanket over her, then he puts his hand under the blanket and rubs her all over.

'Rose, Rose,' he says in a voice thick as mud. He is breathing very fast.

There is red in her eyes. The only sound she can make is a frog's croak.

His hands pull at her shoulder, turning her over until she lies on her stomach. The pillow stuffs up her mouth. He lies on top of her and squashes her into the bed and grinds her into the mattress.

'Rose, Rose, Rose, Rose,' he moans. 'Rose Rose Rose.'

It hurts and she can't breathe. She is very hot now. Everything looks fuzzy. Her head feels too big.

Billy stands up and looks at her.

'This is the law of the burnt offering,' he says. '"Because of the burning upon the altar all night unto the morning, and the fire of the altar shall be burning in it." Leviticus Chapter Six.'

He covers her with her blanket. Then he gets her other clothes from the chest and dresses her. His hands are cold now. He tries to sit her up but she only wants to lie down.

She keeps her eyes shut but she can't stop his voice.

'That wasn't so bad, was it?' he says.

After a while he says, 'Now, Rose, this is our little secret. I will not tell everyone you are a thief and you will not tell about our game. Is that a bargain?'

She wants to ask for her treasure. She wants to say it belongs to her and she's not a thief, but her throat has closed up and her head is banging.

Billy says, 'The people here will send you away if they know you are a thief. They will call you a wicked sinner and shake their Bibles at you and drive you like a dog away from Denniston.'

Rose keeps her eyes shut and in her head she sings 'Rose of Tralee' right through. He strokes her hair and then after a while he goes away. She can't even see if he has taken the box.

Later she hears her mother bang on the wall to call her for tea. Then her mother comes in. Rose can't breathe properly. Her mother comes to the bed and puts her hand on Rose.

'Dear God,' she says, and goes out shouting and calling for help.

Rose sees flames. People are walking around in the flames. They are walking slowly. Their mouths are wide open as if they are screaming but no sound comes out. The flames don't burn them, they just walk on and on through the fire.

Once she opens her eyes and sees her mother sitting by her bed.

The light is from a candle on the table beside her. The candle is set in a tin mug and its flame is huge and swollen. The flame swells and swells until her mother's face is gobbled up by the flame and she tries to scream but only fire comes out of her mouth.

Another time she thinks Mrs Rasmussen is in the room. Mrs Rasmussen's fresh soapy smell is there and her big white apron, and some other smell that she is trying to make Rose drink. It won't go down. Then Mrs Rasmussen's cool hands with their sparkling rings suddenly change into Billy Genesis's big rough red hands. The little room is thick with hands and fat sausage fingers, all moving and waving like trees in a storm, all different colours and sizes, some small as a baby's and some giant hands with claws instead of finger-nails.

Sometimes her ears are full of shouting and roaring, the voices breaking over her like waves, each wave bigger and louder than the last. Sometimes there is no sound at all, only the wild jumbled people and colours moving silently round and round the room, crowding up to her bed until she can't breathe, and when she pushes them away her arm goes right through them and they crowd even closer.

And then, one morning, Rose wakes up. Her room is empty and quiet. By her bed is a tin mug of water. Her hand, reaching for it, is white, with blue veins like tiny rivers running over it. The water is the best thing Rose has ever tasted.

She lies quiet as a mouse. Sun is slanting in through the high window and silver dust is moving in a slow dance through the beams. She watches them for a long time. They are beautiful. The slant of sun moves down the wall and reaches the floor. Rose watches it light up one floorboard and then creep over the crack to light up another.

Her mother comes in and looks at her. Rose looks back.

'Well,' says her mother, 'this is an improvement.'

And her mother smiles.

Later Eva comes back with a bowl of soup. It is hot and salty and it stings Rose's throat, but even the stinging feels good. Her mother undresses her.

'So, so,' she says, half singing, 'you are weak like a baby. Oh, these poor thin arms!'

Rose can't remember her mother ever undressing her. Eva bundles the dirty sheet off the bed and spreads a clean one with a wide flick of her wrists, and smoothes it down. Rose sits on the chest in her fresh nightgown and watches while her mother pulls off the damp pillowcase and tucks the drooping grey pillow under her chin to fit a fresh one. She swings the pillow through the air and plumps it down onto the bed.

'What is madam gaping at then? You could catch flies.'

'You don't usually make my bed.'

'Well, I am not a complete monster, you see. We must get you well and pretty again, eh?'

'Am I ugly now?'

Rose's mother steps back and looks hard at her. She sighs. 'Well, apart from the tangled hair and crusty nose you are still pretty, but delicate. Pink cheeks and plump body is better.'

Then her mother bundles all the dirty things up inside the sheet and takes them out, and Rose walks on her wobbly legs back to bed and lies down again. Everything in the room smells of soap. The bed feels better than a palace.

Later her mother comes in again with hot tea, and Rose is sitting up.

'You are the lucky one,' she says. 'Hard times have made you tough.'

Rose opens her mouth but first no sound comes out, and then

too much. Her voice is like a rusty door hinge.

'Others have not been so fortunate,' says her mother. She walks around the room, back and forth. Rose thinks she may have a fever too.

Rose tries her voice again. 'What happened?' she croaks.

'You have had diphtheria, and are now recovering.'

'Billy Genesis made me sick.'

'Your Uncle Billy had nothing to do with it.'

'Yes he did.'

'So, enough. I can see you are better,' says her mother. After a while she says, 'Other children have been lost.'

'How?'

'You might as well know,' says her mother, 'that Mrs C. Rasmussen has lost her baby. And a Hanratty has gone, and four or five from Burnett's Face.'

'Lost where?' says Rose. Her voice is losing its creak.

'Dead,' says her mother.

'Brennan?' says Rose.

'Not Brennan.'

'Michael?'

'Not Michael. The little girl.'

'Conrad the Sixth?'

'Conrad the Sixth.' Rose doesn't like the glittery hard look in her mother's eyes when she names the dead baby.

Rose shuts her eyes and thinks of the dead children. And then she thinks that Mrs Rasmussen will be able to come back to school now and will want to play games with Rose in the secret bedroom again.

'Conrad the Sixth was too little to matter,' she says.

'You might think so,' says her mother, 'but he matters more than you think. Oh yes.' She begins her walking again, round and round the tiny room. 'Oh yes, our time is coming now, soon, and you are to play your part it this. You.'

Rose turns away from the sound.

'Also,' says her mother, in a voice that is thin as a knitting needle, 'your good friend Mrs Rasmussen thinks you are the cause of her precious son's death. We are to blame, it seems. When death occurs they look first towards us to see if any blame may stick. If your dear Mrs Rasmussen cared about her son, why did she come to visit you? She is the one who carried the disease. She. She is to blame!'

The hard words drop out of her mother's mouth one by one. They keep coming. Rose thinks her mother might be sick too.

'Billy Genesis is to blame,' says Rose. 'He started it.'

Her mother's eyes roll in a funny way. She doesn't even look anywhere near Rose. 'Billy Genesis,' says her mother in the knitting needle voice, 'has nothing to do with it. Nothing. Not with anything. Billy Genesis is of no importance now.'

A Granite Plinth

BELLA RASMUSSEN'S PROBLEM was with the survivors: the three or four children on the Hill who contracted diphtheria and then recovered. Rose was one. Of course age was on her side; you'd expect recovery in a six-year-old, but Mrs Rasmussen was blind to reason. At the Camp there were two children, Rose and her Conrad the Sixth, who contracted diphtheria in the same week. Rose, uncared for, weakened from her burns, living in conditions that were at best unsanitary, at worst downright sinful, was on her feet in a fortnight, coughing and pale but alive. Conrad the Sixth, a healthy baby, fat from his mother's plentiful and rich milk, cherished, cleaned and cuddled every hour of his short life, died two days after his first wheezing cough.

Totty and Tom Hanratty came to commiserate. Their own loss gave them a point of contact. But Mrs Rasmussen turned her head away from the sight of Totty, bereaved like her but, unlike Bella, heavy with the next child. What woman at forty-one, with a history of miscarriage, could expect further children? How could the world or God or the gods deliver such a blow?

'It is easy for you,' says Bella in a voice heavy and ugly with tears. 'You have Michael and Elizabeth still. You will have many more . . .'

Tom's usual good nature takes a dive. The bristles of his glossy beard stand out in indignation. 'Well, you are quite wrong there, Mrs C. The loss is the same, no matter how many others are left.'

'How can it be?' shrieks Mrs C. 'I have no children left!'

Tom Hanratty ploughs doggedly on. 'Our little Sarah was the sweetest-natured . . . Nothing could replace . . .'

But Totty, seeing her friend's distress, lays a hand on her husband's arm and shakes her head gently. 'Leave it, Tom, she is too upset.'

'Well, and so am I!'

'This is not a competition for the most bereaved.'

'Competition! I am trying to explain she is not alone.'

'I *am* alone!' shouts Mrs C. Rasmussen. She turns on Totty. 'And where were the medicines that might have saved his life?'

'Bella, diphtheria is difficult to cure.'

'The carbolic acid? Where?'

'Carbolic is a precaution, not a cure.'

'The spirits of camphor that you promised? Your fine family in Westport promised?'

'Bella, they are not easy to find.'

'The miners' children had camphor. You promised.'

'Miners' children died too, Bella.'

Mrs C. Rasmussen beats the air and howls. 'You promised

camphor, Totty, and did not deliver. His death is on your head!'

'Bella, I will put this pie in your kitchen,' says Totty. Her dragging steps and pale face show better than any words how she feels. 'And I will come again tomorrow if I can. You must eat.'

'How can you talk of food? I would rather die!' Mrs C. Rasmussen tears at her breasts. Damp patches of unclaimed milk spread over her smock. 'Oh! Oh! Oh!' she weeps.

Tom Hanratty, his own deep-seated grief belittled before this display of towering passion, frowns. 'I'll wait outside,' he says.

THAT night people at the Camp and up at the Brake Head heard a great clumping explosion. They felt the ground beneath them rise and settle again. Miners sat up in bed imagining coal gas igniting in some deep mine. They reached for trousers, expecting the siren that would call them to attend the cave-in, to dig their friends out of the rubble. None came. After listening in the dark to the rain pouring down outside, the cold wind slicing around the corner of the hut, the men in the men's quarters grumbled and scratched and settled down again. Someone would call them soon enough if they were needed.

Eddie Carmichael calmed Mrs Carmichael, who was inclined to nervous attacks, put on oilskins and plodded into the dark to invest-igate. Everything at the Bins was intact. He knew it wasn't the mines. An explosion at the mines would have echoed in a distant, ominous way. What Eddie had heard was the sound of a small explosion at close quarters, but he could not imagine the cause. Nothing was moving in all the sprawling tangle of sheds and railway tracks except the wind and rain, and Eddie's own cursing progress. In the end, wet and cold, he went back to bed.

A worker on early shift brought the news up from the Camp, and Eddie Carmichael, his face thunderous, stomped down to investigate. He found a group of spectators and a defiant Con the Brake.

'Where is your sense, Con?' shouts Eddie. 'You could have blown the whole place to kingdom come!'

'Well I didn't, man, so calm down,' growls Con the Brake.

'You know nothing about laying a charge!'

'That's true.'

'You put in far too much!'

'I got the job done.'

'Look at that crater!'

'I'll fill it in.'

'And who in the name of God authorised you to take powder?'

'My wife, who is the highest authority I recognise in this damn world. Leave off, Eddie. I done it wrong, you know, but who cares now? It's done.'

'Con the Brake, if you weren't such a fine brake-man, and if you hadn't just lost your son and heir, I'd fire you on the spot.'

'Well, Eddie Carmichael, you got me now. My son is buried on the Hill, so here I stay. And my wife. Till we two die. And then you can supervise the laying of a second charge.'

'Amen,' says Eddie Carmichael, and crosses himself like a good Catholic. 'Mind you,' he warns as a parting shot, 'the authorities won't like it. This is scarcely consecrated ground.' The sweep of his arm takes in the ravaged Camp, the great slagheap, the mud and desolation. But in the end he claps Con a couple of times on the shoulder and walks back up to work.

Con the Brake must have worked all through the night in that wind and rain. Behind the log house was now a wide, shallow crater, torn out of the granite. Tumbled stones, their fresh-cut grey surfaces gleaming in the watery morning sun, lay in an irregular circle around the crater. In the middle of the depression was a raised square plinth, built of granite stones, the same ones Con had blown out of the ground. The pieces interlocked cleanly: the top surface of the monument was smooth as a table. Set into that surface was a carved cradle, its wooden rockers clamped and held in place by the newly exploded, newly re-laid rocks of the plateau. The beautiful blond kahikitea of the carved and empty cradle steamed in the sun.

The people watched as Con the Brake brought out a wooden chair and set it at the lip of the crater. Then he brought out Mrs C. Rasmussen, his arm around her as if this great-hearted woman were fragile as glass. He sat her in the chair and stood beside her, one hand on the nape of her neck, both of them facing the monument to Conrad the Sixth, the only person ever buried on Denniston.

There they stayed all that day, one upright the other seated, side by side and silent, not acknowledging the people who brought small things to put on the monument or who simply stood and prayed. At sunset Con the Brake led his wife inside again. He made her eat some of Totty's pie and then led her to bed, undressed her and lay all night with his arms around her, the warm milk that should have been sustaining his son leaking over his chest and running away into the mattress.

The next day Con the Brake was back at work. No one ever saw the scarlet jacket again, nor did he ever tell its story, though clearly there was something interesting to hear about such a garment.

Bella Rasmussen took longer to recover. She shunned all company, would not answer the door, even to Totty Hanratty. With Rose she was almost demented. For weeks she couldn't bear to see her, would cry out and shoo the dismayed child away if she came skipping up the steps onto the porch. Rose would back off, puzzled, quieter and thinner than ever, but never cowed. Again and again she returned to the porch, like a once-loved dog endlessly visiting the home of a dead owner. She would creep up quietly with a few flowers or a pretty stone, something she'd found; would place the gift on the doormat and then just sit there, undetected, sometimes for hours.

The life seemed to have gone out of Rose too.

The Bottom Drawer

YOU DON'T WISH death on anyone, but in some ways the bereavements up at Burnett's Face were a relief to the Scobie family. For a few weeks Mary Scobie gave up her silent sitting in a dark room and was busy and bustling as befitted the wife of a leader of their community. When the first child, the youngest O'Shea, began fighting for breath, Granny Binney ordered a sheet soaked in carbolic to be hung in his doorway, and bade anyone who came and went in that room to wash in a light solution of carbolic. But still the disease spread. Diphtheria was common enough at Home, and you expected to lose the odd sickly baby, but here four children died in a matter of days, two of them only a few days old. That left but two children under five in the whole of Burnett's Face: a heartbreak for everyone, not to mention the parents themselves. Mary, senior woman in Burnett's Face, took her duties seriously. She visited each bereaved family, warmed them with words of good sense, fed them with her funeral cake made with brown sugar and ginger, and left them calmer, accepting that though the Lord's will is inscrutable at times, His purpose unreadable, yet a pattern would emerge in good time and all would eventually work towards the greater good.

Mary herself no longer believed this. She heard the well-worn words slide out from behind her teeth; saw the comfort they gave to weeping Elizabeth O'Shea and silly Lizzie Dowd, whose lack of common sense surely competed with the diphtheria as cause of death, and to the stunned Gormans, who lost both their children on the same day and would have to start a family all over again. Mary found pleasure of a kind in her skill, but to her the words were empty husks. Her imprisonment on the Hill, the distance from her home town, her parents, the house where she and three generations grew up — all these losses had scoured away at her faith. She no longer believed in God. In this devout community, her loss of faith could not be admitted. Mary carried it like a secret and shameful disease.

Years later, when she became a famous free-thinker and atheist, entertaining prime ministers and influential leaders in the capital, Denniston people nodded sagely and said you could see it coming in the way she behaved over Brennan and Rose, and the way she walked for miles, heaving her stiff and swollen legs from side to side, leaning on her cane of English walnut, walking alone over the contorted rocks of the plateau. Before '85, though, people only noticed that Mary Scobie grew thinner in spirit as her physical body lost bulk.

There was a night, shortly after the diphtheria epidemic, when the bare bones of her misery were laid in front of the shocked family.

The five boys and their dad walked in the door from band practice. Chatting and laughing, humming the polka (not a hymn for once) they had been playing, they discussed Uncle Arnold's new wife, fifteen years younger than him and pretty as a rose.

A month ago, as soon as Uncle Arnold had finished building his new house, he'd taken a fortnight off work, made the long journey up to Nelson — as distant and exciting to his nephews as a trip to the other side of the world — and stood at the wharf as the clipper ship *Mary Brae* berthed. Aboard her were 'thirty-seven women of good character', come to be wives of any in need of one. Uncle Arnold had spotted the one he fancied as she and the thirty-six others, flanked by grim-faced chaperones, walked demurely down the plank between rows of staring men. At the soirée that night, arranged by the shipping company, Arnold in his best suit and boots had walked straight up to her, jostling aside a red-faced lad who could barely stammer out a how-d'ye-do, and another weed of a fellow, more persistent but 'my miner's shoulders soon got the better of him!'

Throughout the room shy young women were eyeing the colonial men, looking for a gentle manner, a wealthy aspect, a sign of good breeding. According to Arnold, Janet Dickie from Whitechapel, London, took a liking to him directly, charmed by his jokes and his forthright manner. He had glossed over some of the grimmer details of life on Denniston and by the end of the evening she had agreed to his proposal of marriage.

Two days later they were married along with twelve other couples, in the Nelson Methodist chapel, Janet being easy about which religion tied the knot. They were on the road to Denniston, bumping along in the Peach Brothers' coach, by mid-afternoon, and spent their honeymoon night at Peach and Haycock's Hostelry, Murchison.

Mary herself has not yet paid a visit to the new wife, a fact that has attracted much comment.

This particular evening, the Scobie boys rattle on about Janet's easy-going ways, her laughter, her stories of teeming life on the London streets, for her father is a barrowman at Covent Garden markets.

'She's a right dolly, Mam,' says Mathew, blowing out his cheeks and rolling his eyes. 'Far too good for an old dodderer like Uncle Arnold.'

Josiah cuffs his son, but he's laughing too. The music and the new family member have all the Scobie males alight.

'She can ride too,' says David. 'She rode the pony all the way up — didn't even get off at Hickey's bend.'

'Even Dad gets off at Hickey's bend,' says bright-eyed Brennan.

'Uncle Arnold too,' says Mathew. 'He *falls* off at Hickey's bend!'

They all laugh.

'And she's riding down the Track again come Saturday, right out to Waimang to visit a friend who came out with her!'

'Uncle Arnold says she better be back by nightfall to cook his tea.'

The boys all laugh again.

Mary Scobie explodes.

'And my six able-bodied men, who should be seven, cannot get me down off Denniston in three long years!'

Josiah smiles uneasily. 'Come now, Mother, we would tie you down aboard a horse if you would let us . . .'

But Mary Scobie is away. 'It is not a matter of bundling your lumpy wife up and down a track fit only for mountain goats. It is a matter of leaving entirely. Packing up before more Scobie lives drain away into this accursed soil!'

The men and boys stand in dismayed rows, ears pinned back before her tirade.

'Look here!' she shouts. Mary stumps over to the linen press and drags at the bottom drawer. Lying in it is a row of neatly folded pyjamas in assorted sizes. The men flinch. It is surely bad luck to acknowledge their presence.

'Five pairs!' says Mary. 'Five, that have been six! What wife and mother should have to live her life with five pairs of pyjamas groaning and moaning in the bottom drawer, waiting for their corpses?'

Brennan starts crying. His mother rounds on him. 'Aye, chick, cry while you can. The twins have their pairs back in the drawer and soon enough yours will be there too if your dad has his way. And I am to sit up here, trapped, is it? My lot is to sit on the Hill while the mines, and disease, and the wretched clawing damp pick off my family one by one? What man would bring a wife and children to this?' Mary, dressed today, as every day, in black, as if ready for the next funeral, crashes down into her favourite chair and weeps.

The boys are mesmerised by the row of waiting pyjamas. They stare at the yawning drawer. Josiah's black brows pull together as if on a drawstring. He takes a chair and, using the wooden legs as a lever, closes the drawer. What man would touch his own funeral clothes?

'Go on back to bed,' he says to the shocked boys. 'Your mam is not well.'

Josiah sits frowning at the table. He rises to add coal to the fire, turns up the wick of the lamp and goes back to his waiting. Mary weeps. Josiah drums his fingers on the table. He will not comfort her.

At last Josiah sighs. 'Mary, I have work to go to in the morning.'

'Oh,' weeps Mary.

'This will not do.'

Mary is silent.

'You, better than most, understand the life of a collier.'

'Here it is different!'

'Not so different.'

'In every way! If the mine takes you, who will comfort *me*? There is no family. No old friends. I am alone here.'

'There is Janet now.'

'Janet!' Mary spits the word, 'A brash cockney girl who could be my daughter!'

Josiah says nothing for a moment. Then lays one palm flat on the table. It is a gesture of strength. He lays the other next to it. The two hands, black-haired, fingernails black-rimmed where the scrubbing brush has missed, press down into the wooden planks. Josiah is making a statement — I am a worker! These hands are my livelihood. Don't mess with me!

Mary looks at him out of her lumpy, swollen face. Her husband's hands, lying there, are almost a threat. She has never known him to threaten.

'Mary!' says Josiah. 'I need your strength now, not your weakness.'

'I do not choose . . .'

'We are organising, Mary. At last we are taking the bosses on!'

Her husband's skin is glossy with energy, the excitement of the battle. She watches him. She is outside and above all this, looking in at a small scene in a shoe-box. The little man in the shoe-box rants on about a Mutual Protection Society, rights of miners, holidays, standing firm, accepting hardship. The words emerge and disappear like bubbles.

Mary rises. She walks out the back door and into the night.

Hours later, cold and calm, she returns by the same door. Josiah is in bed. He pretends to be asleep but Mary knows he is watching her undress. She feels his uncertainty but is not moved by it. With small sure movements she pulls on a clean nightgown, folds back the covers, climbs into bed and turns her face to the wall.

'Goodnight,' she says. Her voice is clear and cool, like a girl's.

The Anvil of
Denniston

NOT MANY CLAIMED to know Mary Scobie well, but those
who did — her own boys, that indestructible crone Granny Binney,
the Reverend Godfrey Parkin who worked underground all week
and took Chapel on Sundays, a few of the older miners' wives — all
these swore Mary changed overnight as if visitors from outer space
had magically extracted the essence of that quiet, capable English
woman and poured a new personality into the waiting skin.

Granny Binney said it was the sudden lifting of a depression.
That she had seen it many times and experienced it herself at about
Mary's age.

'Oh yes, oh yes, you reach the bottom of the pit,' said Granny,
rocking in her dark corner of the Binneys' kitchen and wagging her
hairy chin back and forth in the certainty of her knowledge. 'And
then the fright of what might happen next opens a door. Overnight

the darkness clears. Light enters. Overnight. No, no, no, nothing to get excited about here. Many times I have seen it. Many times.'

The Reverend Godfrey Parkin knew it was the hand of the Lord. When people pointed out to him that Mary had turned away from the church, walked on the plateau instead of attending Chapel, he simply produced the smile that came and went over his face all day like sunlight — the result of a sunny nature — and said that the Lord moved in mysterious ways and Mary would one day realise that she was His chosen handmaid.

The boys were simply relieved that the darkness had lifted. Were both proud of and embarrassed by their newly galvanised mam. They groaned over the way their house became a railway station for visitors, for other wives, for the new school teacher, all arguing politics, arranging meetings, distributing food. But a railway station was better than a mausoleum any day of the week, and a bossy, driven mother better than a sighing one. Children never puzzle over their parents' moods, but accept whatever is handed down as best they can.

Con the Brake, who never knew Mary well but who had a theory about everything, believed it was Denniston itself that changed her.

'This place is an anvil, you know?' he said, banging the hammer of his fist down on Tom Hanratty's new bar to illustrate his point. 'All we are beaten to new shapes, new metal even, up here. Take me.'

Tom Hanratty took him up on that one. 'How in the name of Jesus can we take you, Con the Brake, when we know not one damn thing about you?'

'I am talking about Mary Scobie, man, do not divert. That woman, she come here in shape like a true English wife. Miner's wife, you know? Stoic, dependable, life laid out cradle to grave, the pattern bred in generation to generation.

'But inside, you know, is this little kernel, hard shell around it like a walnut, waiting. If she stay in England, in her home town, that hard shell never break — she is good wife, good mother, good neighbour, the pattern never change. She come to the Hill, wham!' Con pounded the bar again and Tom leapt to save toppling bottles. 'Wham! Everything different, you know? The anvil of Denniston! I seen her face when she arrive up the Incline that first day. By God, she change fast! Then blow after blow, she is beaten on that anvil. We all too. All the same, you know? Wham, wham!'

As usual, Con was carried away by his own argument. Everyone laughed as a glass, escaping Tom's reach, crashed to the floor.

'But for Mary it is no laugh, you know? She is not bred for strange and new. All her breeding is for same, generation by genera-tion, same same same. Denniston is too different. She is beaten till her spirit grows thin, thin like sheet metal, and she herself might crack, as metal does, you know? Beaten too hard, too thin. Then. Then!' Con raised his glass in triumph as if proposing a toast. 'Then that little walnut, she crack. The hard shell split, you know? At last the little kernel can grow. Behold, a new Mary Scobie!'

Jesus, Con,' said Tom, grumpy over his lost glass, 'you are as full of bullshit as you are of my good beer. You know how long a walnut tree takes to grow? Mary changed overnight.'

Con spread his arms to his audience and shook his head sadly. 'Tom Hanratty is a good barman and a better builder, but where is his soul, eh? This is Con the philosopher speaking, Tom. I am illus-trating human nature, man, not writing encyclopaedias!'

He drained his glass, grounded it on the bar, and went for the door. Since the baby's death he never left Mrs C for long. At the door he turned. Con always went for the dramatic exit.

'That anvil of Denniston lays bare we all,' he said, 'but every kernel is not so sound as Mary's.'

Tools to Bank

THREE TIMES THAT terrible winter Josiah Scobie, newly elected committeeman of the Denniston Miners' Mutual Protection Society, tramped up the iron steps to Eddie Carmichael's office with the demands of the men. Three times he came stamping back out into sleet or hail, cursing at the bland reason of the mine manager. How could a unionist make progress against such a shifting target?

The fourth visit was different. Eddie rose from his seat, wouldn't look the committee in the eye.

'Men,' he said, 'I have my orders from Westport, and they have theirs from Dunedin itself. They are brutal orders and I don't say I'm agreeing with them, but there it is. My hands are tied.'

'Well, spit it out, Eddie,' said Josiah. 'We are not strangers.'

'Your men will not be happy . . .'

'Eddie.'

'I beg you to consider the situation the Company is in.'

'What is there to consider?' growled Josiah. 'You have said not one word of substance. Get on with it, man.'

Con the Brake, at the top of the Incline, reckoned he heard Josiah's roar of fury that day. There's no doubt the men loading skips at the Bins heard it. They heard him pound the iron walls of Eddie's office until the icicles on the eaves shook clear and rang like bells on the lean-to roof below. They saw the men emerge, their angry words blowing clouds in the cold air, as if they were engine, not man, and they saw them turn back at the foot of the steps to shout up at Eddie that this was war; that the bloody owners had finally given themselves a headache worth whinging about.

By midday, deep inside the three mines of Denniston, the news was spreading. Josiah, back in the darkness of Banbury mine, stood at a crossroads where the arms of two sections bisected the rope-road. Here the roof-coal had come down cleanly. In the vague flickering light of miners' lamps the bare rock showed grey between the timber props. At Josiah's feet the rails of the rope-way gleamed faintly before disappearing east and west into the dark tunnel. In the midday break the rope-road shut down. The mine was silent except for the steady munching of the horses as they fumbled in their nose-bags, their snorting as they blew chaff away from soft nostrils.

In sweaty groups the miners ate their lunches, dimly lit by the glow of the oil lamps that hooked onto their cloth caps. Some men sat on upturned shovels, others stood, propped against the damp walls, the bread of their bacon butties the only white thing in this black world.

Josiah was still on fire. His words rang against the rock and came back eerily from the branching tunnels.

'Come in closer, lads. I want to see you. Tom! Jack! Crowd up, crowd up! Aye, bring your pony too, Rhys: it's his livelihood as well!'

The men laughed, catching his mood. They jostled and crowded, eager for the news. This dark and tunnelled world, so oppressive to outsiders, wrapped these men in security. Living underground was second nature to them and most of them entered it each day gladly, ready for the challenge. To end the day stiff and sore maybe from the shovelling but with a good tally of boxes to your name, now that was something to be proud of.

Josiah peered at the grimy, sweat-streaked faces, acknowledging each one, drawing out the moment. When he had them all listening he threw his arms out, wide and empty. 'We are rejected on all counts! And that is only half of it. One: they will not recognise our miners' holidays, which we have had by right before, and our fathers before us. If an important order falls due on our holiday, says the manager, we work!'

Josiah paused to let the growl die down. 'Two: they will not recognise the committee to be negotiators on your behalf. Nay, listen, men — they will not recognise the Society at all! Three: they cling to the right to employ unskilled miners. They care nothing for our safety!'

Josiah rammed a balled fist into his open palm, driving the points home. 'They are short-sighted bastards who care only for cash today! Forget about a dependable industry, forget about steady production. They say, "We want our profit now!"'

Josiah paused again to let the men rumble, then raised his voice a notch.

'And *that* is only half of it. Hear this! They are punishing us for being so forward. For wanting safety, and a day or two off to be with our families. From today they are *cutting* the hewing rate for skilled labour. *Cutting* our rate and lumping us with the riff-raff. Each man's box is to be riddled before it's weighed!'

'What?' shouted Rhys Blunt. 'They never would!'

Josiah jabbed his shovel into the loose floor-coal to make his point. 'Oh, they will, they will, the fools. We will be paid only on our riddled coal. Any loose stuff or slack will not count. The bosses take no account of what type of coal the mine produces.'

'Jesus,' moaned Fisty McCulloch. 'Coal down my section has been one-third slack all week. How can I get to the clean stuff without digging the soft first?'

'We'll be down to working unskilled rates!'

Josiah had to quieten his men for fear their shouts would loosen rocks and cause a cave-in.

'Aye, lads, you are right to be wild. But we must stand firm too. For it will take time and hardship to right this wrong. Are you firm?'

'Aye!' shouted the miners, 'Aye!'

Rhys Blunt's terrified pony broke his traces, dashed for the entrance, and was not sighted until three days later, when Con spotted him, belly-up and bloated at the bottom of the gully.

Josiah, triumphant as if his wife had just produced twin boys, raised his hand.

'I say it is time to take tools to bank!'

'Tools to bank!' roared the men. They left boxes where they were, shouldered picks and shovels and headed for daylight.

Up at Burnett's Face, Arnold Scobie in Ironbridge Mine and Tommy Jowett in Coalbrookdale were whipping up the same fury. By mid-afternoon all three mines were silent, a stack of picks and shovels at each entrance, the empty skips returning empty on the long loop of the rope-road, back to the Bins.

The matter of what next, and how to eat, was left to the women to solve. In particular, to Mary Scobie.

Bread on the Table

THE PROBLEM, NATURALLY, was food. The getting of it and the paying for it. There were some fifty families involved, over a hundred miners. The strikers were the English miners, the ones recruited in England, who came out qualified and expected to be treated differently, paid more than the Camp drifters who got the jitters after a few hours underground and whose shoulders never learned the rhythm of a steady day's hewing. The Burnett's Face miners knew they had a good case and believed they could win, but the wider support wasn't there in those days. In the whole colony there wasn't one properly established miners' union. English miners were beginning to organise, certainly, from Coromandel to the deep south, but this was the first strike. Where were the strike funds, the support of other workers to see them through? The pittance in the Miners' Fund would not last a week. As Mary

Scobie pointed out to Josiah when he came home that first day, eyes ablaze from the excitement of the battle.

It was all very well, said Mary, planting her feet like a man, to sit out the strike, knowing right was on your side, but the families had to eat, and no one was going to survive on the few wizened carrots and parsnips, the dwarf-sized cabbages and silver-beet they managed to wrestle out of Denniston's stony soil. A hundred and fifty stomachs needed filling three times a day, and that was going to take as much organisation as running a mine and a strike put together. Why, for pity's sake, had the men not planned a little in advance so that supplies might be laid down and a system of distribution worked out?

It was typical of this new Mary, though, that she would not waste time in unproductive railing. She organised.

Josiah Scobie tried at first to curb his wife's zeal. He tried only once.

'Mary, it is not seemly you should call the men to a meeting. Wives, surely, but the men are my business, and I will organise them.'

Mary looked at him with her newly clear eyes and spoke in a deep, surprising voice, unknown to him.

'Well, they are called and coming. You orate and I will get the work done.' She patted his arm as if he were a good old dog, and buttoned her coat.

'Well, come on then,' she said as she headed for the door. 'We need you there too, Josiah.'

She called him Josiah, not husband or my dear, or your dad. Josiah. Equal footing.

Two days after the strike began she sent Brennan to school with two notes. One was for the new teacher, Henry Stringer (from this time on Mary Scobie called everyone, man or woman, by their

Christian name, whether or not there had been a formal introduction, causing more than one man to rear back in fright or look desperately from side to side like a cornered mouse, and causing many women to draw their lips tight together in case such familiarity might be catching). The other note was for Totty Hanratty.

Her letters:

> *Dear Henry Stringer,*
>
> *You will be aware that the miners of Denniston have brought their tools to bank. Their demands are modest and justified, but the Company will not bend without a fight. You may well have to deal with animosity and rivalry between children whose families hold opposing views. I trust you will not allow victimisation of the miners' children, and will endeavour to teach your charges what are the true facts of the struggle.*
>
> *If you can possibly find a way to provide a square meal a day for the miners' children it would be a great service. There is no money we can offer in payment at present, but if the cause is won we will try to repay our debt.*
>
> *My husband, Josiah Scobie, or I would be happy to inform you of the facts of the strike. So would Brennan if you ask him; he is fully aware and a bright boy, as you will know.*
>
> *Yours faithfully,*
> *Mary Scobie*
>
>
> *Dear Totty,*
> *I have not been to Denniston to commiserate over the loss of your dear Sarah. Please forgive me. I have been living in a kind of madness, but am well now. You must*

*be desperate with grief; a daughter is so precious. I am so
sorry, my dear. Please convey my respects to Tom, too. He
is a good man.*

*Totty, we need your help. The men have brought tools
to bank, as you will have heard, with no thought about
bringing food to mouth. There would not be more than a
few spare shillings saved among the families here, I
imagine, and God knows how long our men will be out of
work.*

*You will no doubt be caught between Camp opinion
and Burnett's Face opinion, and I do not ask you to take
sides, simply to help those in need.*

*Is there any way you can persuade your suppliers to
provide, as charity, flour, sugar and a little meat for our
families? Failing that, would they provide for us on tick?
We have been good customers in the past and will be, God
willing, again.*

*I will visit when I can. I have let my legs become lazy
but will wrestle them into shape again, never fear! Is all
well? Brennan tells me your new baby will come soon. The
young ones know all the Denniston gossip. I do hope the
strike does not inflame feelings. The children will suffer.*

Please do what you can.

Yours faithfully,

Mary Scobie

*P.S. Brennan seems worried about that wretched
child Rose of Tralee. Should something be done?*

As soon as Brennan had stumped off to school, important with
his letters and his information, Mary was buttoning her coat,
leaving dishes in the sink and washing unfolded, and setting off,

forcing her ungainly legs to pump along as fast as they could towards the new home of her brother-in-law Arnold and his brassy London wife.

Arnold, driving in fenceposts in his shirt-sleeves, looked up from his sweaty labour and nodded to her. Mary had not once visited his house during her dark illness, but nothing ever surprised or moved this stolid man, whose trip to Nelson to get a wife was the one independent action of his life. Everything else, except the getting of future babies, was done in the shadow and the footsteps of his powerful brother.

Mary pauses, her face grey with the strain of the walking, 'Well, Arnold, a strike is good for getting repairs done to the house!'

If Arnold is startled to see her so jolly and familiar he doesn't show it.

'I've come for a word with Janet,' says Mary. 'Is she in?'

Arnold nods towards the house. 'Clearly,' he says. There is pride in the voice.

Indeed the whole house is ringing with Janet's song, some swooping ditty that she is embellishing with her own arrangement as if she is an opera singer, not an assisted immigrant wife stuck on a wild and lonely plateau in the distant colonies.

Mary finds her slapping dough in the kitchen. Janet is as voluble as her new husband is dour.

'Mary Scobie! I swear I thought we two would live our lives strangers. Welcome! Sit down and let us have tea. I'll just get this bread in the tin.'

Mary sits with a groan and watches while the strapping girl, cheerful as a sparrow, flours her hands again, shapes the loaf and sets it beside the coal range to rise. Janet has milky-white skin and rosy cheeks. She is not, in a strict sense, pretty — the features are coarse, the nose large — but the openness of her manner gives the impression of beauty.

'Save that flour,' says Mary, watching her young sister-in-law sweep the coated table. 'We'll need every ounce in the days to come.'

'Oh, what a lark,' chirps Janet. 'A strike! Me dad back in London would have a fit to think I got hitched to a striker. He's a loner, my old dad — every man for himself — you'd never get him to stand alongside his fellow workers. Climb on the back of 'em, more like!' She smiles at Mary's frown. 'Don't fret, love. I'll stand by the lot of you: we're family now, right? I think you're feckin' barmy to take on the bosses, but if Arnold and Josiah think it's worth a go, I'm in. Not that I'm keen on starving, mind. Will it really come to that?'

To be called love by someone twenty years younger is galling, but Mary ploughs on.

'We will not starve if we work at it. You have a friend down in Waimang?'

'I have. Two, in fact. Molly and Cherry Tartt. They married brothers.' Janet bursts into laughter. It is like showers of gold coins spinning in the air. This girl is infectious. 'They married the Dumpling boys!' she gasps. 'True! The Reverend couldn't keep a straight face when he married them and the whole Chapel was in stitches. Will you, Cherry Tartt take this man, Sid Dumpling, to be your lawful wedded husband? Oh!' The laugh breaks out again. 'I reckon Cherry only done it for the name — to give us all a good laugh. Who knows what kind of man you'll get, anyway, coming out blind? It's a lottery whatever way you look at it. Not that I'm complaining. My Arnold will do good enough, I dare say. So she's Cherry Dumpling now, which her husband says is a more suitable name for a married woman!'

Janet stops to take breath and wipe away the tears. Mary jumps in before the chatter starts up again.

'Are they sensible women?'

'Right enough.'

'And I know two down there that came out with us, though I've not seen them in two years. They'll help if they're still alive. We need a committee of women down in Waimang, Janet. To collect food, charity, on our behalf.'

'*Can* they help, though? No doubt their lives are just as much a struggle.'

'They'll help. The mines are their livelihood too. You must persuade them, Janet. The men will hump what is donated up the Track, but they'll never organise the collection properly. You must fire the women up, my dear. I'll write letters, but it's not the same as a direct appeal.'

NEXT day Janet was setting off, atop Arnold's precious pony, Duffer, a placid old plodder like his master, as easy going above ground as the mine horses were below. Arnold, uneasy about his wife's free-ranging ways, walked behind to keep an eye on her. Mary expected them back in a day or two with news of a supply line from Waimang.

Denniston itself was another matter. Mary waited two days for a reply from Totty. None came. Brennan, when questioned, avoided her eyes. On the third day Brennan claimed a sore stomach and stayed home from school. Mary, struggling back to the house mid-morning, following her daily strengthening walk, heard the clear notes of his cornet slicing through the mist and knew his problem was nothing to do with stomach pains. But he would say nothing.

'Have you talked about the strike at school?' asks Mary.

Brennan nods.

'Did you put the miners' case to them?'

Brennan nods again. 'Aye.'

'And do the teachers agree?'

'Mr Stringer does. Mrs Rasmussen doesn't come to school any more.'

'Mrs Rasmussen is from the Camp. She won't agree.'

Brennan looks out the window.

'Brennan, I can't help you if you won't say. You're not sick; that much is clear.'

'Yes I am. It still hurts.'

Brennan screws up his face and holds his stomach. After a while he peeks up at his mother. She is still watching with her head on one side. Not believing. He screws up his face again and tries a whimper.

'What about Michael and Rose?' asks Mary. 'Are they for us?'

Brennan says nothing.

'I see,' says Mary. 'Well, I'll come in with you to Denniston tomorrow, my boy, and see for myself.'

'You walk too slow,' says Brennan. 'Anyway I might still be sick.'

Which he is. Mary leaves him with his cornet and sets out for town. The rain has an icy edge to it, although it is high summer. Mary ties her scarf tight against the wind and slogs her way along the skipway. The few passing boxes, filled by non-unionists, earn a scornful glance or two, but mainly it's head down, hammering away with the legs. She shakes rain from her face, nods vigorously, stabs her stick into the muddy ground. Her lips move. Mary is arguing with the wind, driving home points with only the rumbling skips for audience.

As she nears Denniston she realises her legs are not aching. That the placing of one foot after the other is no longer heavy labour but a sharp-edged pleasure.

'Well!' says Mary to her legs. 'Well, my beauties. This is your land now and you will learn to walk on it.'

Hanrattys' guest house is larger than she remembers. A saloon has been added to one side, with a separate entrance for the drinking men, so that any lady guests will not be embarrassed. Though lady guests are rare, God knows. Mary hammers on the door and a maid opens it.

'Oho!' says Mary. 'Servants, is it? Society has come to Denniston, I see. Is your mistress in, my dear?'

'Totty's in the kitchen,' says the maid, 'drying the flour. It's got the mould with all this damp weather. Go on in.'

'Ah well,' says Mary, 'it's a comfort to know that upper-class habits have not entirely taken root.'

The maid nods cheerfully, not understanding a word but too busy to care. Mary removes her own coat, shakes out the head scarf and hangs them both to drip on the coat-stand.

In the kitchen Totty is sliding a huge meat dish, heaped with flour, into the coal range. Another stands on the top and a third waits, the flour lumpy and grey, on the kitchen table. Totty bangs the door shut, closes the damper and hangs up the oven cloth. Her face is flushed, her body swollen with the next child.

'Mary Scobie!' she says. An awkwardness hangs in the air. 'I should have replied to your letter but it is hard to find time.'

'Well, here I am!' says Mary. The booming voice sets Totty back a little. This is not the withdrawn woman she remembers.

While Totty pours tea, the women exchange details of children, bereavements, confinements, husbands' health, but Mary cannot hold back for long.

'Now, Totty, the strike.'

'Yes. The strike,' says Totty, her eyes sparking.

'Can you help us over the food? You and your husband are leaders in Denniston. Others would follow.'

'Tom,' says Totty, 'is opposed to the strike.'

'Surely not. He's a man of good sense . . .'

'And I agree with him.'

There is a silence in the kitchen as the two spirited women square up. Mary Scobie has the dark energy of a crusader, solid and implacable as a sledge-hammer, ready to drive all opposition into the ground. Totty Hanratty, large with a fourth child in six years of marriage, red-gold curls straggling from an untidy bun, is more of a blast furnace, fiery in her indignation. Totty starts in first.

'You think you're a law unto yourselves, you miners up there at Burnett's Face. Suddenly, out of the blue, there's a strike. No discussion with the rest of the community. No warning. Overnight the mines are closed. It's our livelihood too, you know!'

'All the more reason for you to back us.'

'Back what? You never even discussed the issues.'

'I am here to do just that. We have a just cause, Totty.'

'Oh, I know all about it *now*! Michael brought it back from school. That's how we glean information here. From the school-children! You huddle together up in Burnett's Face and forget we are all dependent on each other. And now you expect our charity!'

Mary drives into Totty's torrent, her voice booming. 'My dear, we must not let selfish anxieties cloud the real issue. We are fighting unfair oppression. We are fighting for recognition of the working man's rights! You would surely understand.'

'Selfish anxieties!' Totty slaps her hand down on the table and a cloud of flour leaps in the air. 'My anxieties are for my children, and for this fragile community. If there are no wages paid, who will buy supplies from G.G. Ball's? Who will buy Mr Dimcock's cloth or pay poor Mr Holyrood, who has just arrived, to cut their hair? Now that we finally have a plumber, who will employ him?'

'Listen . . .' says Mary, gathering strength like a storm.

'No, *you* listen to *me*! They will all leave, that will be the result of all this. Walk off the plateau. The miners too. And why not? Life is easier down below, at any rate. Your precious strike will be for nothing but to destroy Denniston. This town that Tom and I have shed blood and sweat to build up these last six years.'

Mary stands. Her stick rings on the wooden floor, underlining each word.

'Totty, Totty, my girl, you have it all wrong! The town will die if we do *not* strike. The miners will leave if we do *not* stand up for a decent wage and safe conditions. It is the *bosses* you should be arguing with, not the miners. The bosses have cut the hewing rate. *They* have employed unskilled men who don't know one end of a pick from the other. Your quarrel is with the bosses, Totty!'

Totty rises too, stirs the flour on the range furiously, shakes the ladle at the miner's wife who stands like a dark force in her kitchen.

'Mr McConnochie is almost bankrupt, that's what Tom says. He can't afford to pay more.'

'He can't afford *not to*, my dear. It is false economy to skimp on skilled workers and yet they make the same mistake over and over. Your precious Mr McConnochie is scuttling his own boat, the stupid man.'

'And the miners are speeding up the sinking.'

'Ah, good God, Totty!' Mary beats her own corseted side with a fist, then sits abruptly. Totty stirs flour. Somewhere upstairs a child is singing.

'You'll not win,' says Totty. 'Eddie Carmichael has gone down to Waimang and to Westport to recruit new miners.'

'He may recruit *workers*, my dear, but *miners* he will not find.'

'Are you so sure?'

'Of course I am! Working underground is a skilled job. You can't drag men off the street and expect them to hew coal. Eddie's recruits will last a week, then run away home again as soon as they are paid.'

Both women are now attacking the sour lumpy flour on the table as if it were the issue to be solved. Mary rakes lines through it with her fingers.

'This Denniston climate,' she says. 'Why do any of us want to stay?'

Totty snorts. 'I for one would not shift if you paid me. Even when the flour grows mould.'

'Ah well, Totty my dear, we may not agree . . .'

'We do not!'

'But will you stand by and see the children suffer? Could your principles not take a back seat while you give them a square meal?'

'They are without food because *your* principles won't take a back seat!' But Totty's voice is softening. 'There would be ten of them at school? Ten Burnett's Face children?'

'Aye, counting Brennan, who often has a midday meal with you anyway, as I well know, despite my sending a good buttie in his satchel!'

'Well, perhaps,' says Totty, 'as long as the men are not out too long. Mrs Dimcock might help. And Bella Rasmussen, poor soul. Feeling is high in the Camp, though. The English miners are not loved.'

'The feeling is mutual,' says Mary. Her face breaks into a creaky smile. 'I had best take my leave before we are fighting over this lumpy flour again. Thank you, my dear. You will not regret helping us.'

At the door she turns to Totty. Totty waits, one hand on the knob, unwilling to let in the elements until the very moment of exit.

'Do you know someone called Billy Genesis?' says Mary.

'Do not get me started on him,' says Totty, kicking at coal dust that has drifted under the door. ' It will be worse than the strike!'

'Brennan brings home stories. About Billy and the mother. And Rose.'

'Michael too.'

'Can something be done?'

'What could we do?'

Both women are silent for a moment. But Rose's small personal tragedy is too uncomfortable. Mary shakes her head briskly and sighs. 'We have more than enough to do, without interfering in private matters.'

'True,' says Totty, though she will not meet Mary's eye. 'True. We must all survive this strike.'

Locks and Bolts

ROSE HOLDS THE doorpost, ready to run. Inside the big workshop Billy Genesis is hitting a metal rod with a heavy hammer. His face is red and his vest sweaty. The scar down his neck bunches and jumps when he moves, like a nasty little animal clinging to his shoulder. Behind him on a high stone fireplace a coke fire is roaring, and Willie Connelly's older brother is pumping it with bellows to make it roar harder.

Billy looks up and sees her. He says something but she can't hear because of the banging. Her eyes look up and down, everywhere, but she can't see the treasure box. She's been looking for it every day. She thinks Billy Genesis might have hidden her treasure here at the Bins somewhere, maybe in his blacksmith's shed.

The Connelly boy makes a funny face at her and fools with the bellows. Billy snarls at him and hits him. Then he waves a hairy arm at Rose and shouts.

'Out! Go out! Beware of the fire of damnation!'

Rose hates the noise and the fire but she waits until he is banging hard and not watching her. She hops quickly, just two steps inside and looks around all the shelves. For a moment her heart leaps into her throat and she forgets about the noise and fire. She sees it! There it is, a corner of her box, poking out behind a pile of metal things. The wood is winking and golden in the firelight. It's waiting to be rescued. She skips outside again before Black Billy sees her looking.

Rose hops and dances around the corner. She runs up the steps to Mr Carmichael's office and knocks on the door.

'Come in, then!' he shouts in a rough voice, but when he sees it's Rose he grins and opens his arms wide. 'Why Rose, I haven't seen you smile in a month. Are you feeling better, then?'

'Yes,' says Rose.

'Well then, my little miss, how about tackling this row of dismal figures?'

Mr Carmichael gives her some numbers to add up — a long, long line in his book — and she adds them as fast as she can.

Mr Carmichael whistles. 'Hey, sweetheart, that's what I got too.'

'Is that good, then?' says Rose in her best business voice.

'The adding is excellent but the news is bad. Not enough people want coal from Denniston, and not enough miners will hew it.' But he gives her a piece of date square anyway, that Mrs Carmichael has made. Rose would have liked an apple better; Mrs Carmichael's cakes are hard.

She looks out the dirty window, down at the tangle of railway tracks. Often these days the Incline is closed but today the coal wagons are coming and going, full ones to the Incline, empty ones back. She sees John Gantry Junior running the wagons. He looks tiny from up here. While she is watching, Mr Carmichael tests her mental arithmetic.

'Fourteen take away six?' he says. 'Three days' work at six shillings a day?' And then a hard one: 'What is a hundred and sixty-nine doubled?' Then he says, 'You're a walking marvel, Rose: you are only seven years old and already better with figures than most of my men. I would employ you any day of the week.'

'I'm going to work at the mine when I'm older,' says Rose.

'If they don't close it down first and put us all out of work,' says Mr Carmichael with a heavy sigh.

Rose looks at the rows of keys hanging on hooks by the door. They all have numbers under them.

'Test me on the keys,' she says. 'What key is this office?'

'One, of course,' he laughs, and she keeps asking questions until she knows all the keys and knows that the name of Billy's shed is the forge and the key is number seventeen.

Mr Carmichael stands up and stretches. 'Well, Rose, you must run along and let me grapple with these dismal figures.'

He puts a hand out to touch her but she jumps back so he can't, and he watches all the time while she is going out the door. She can't take the key.

After tea her mother is sitting at the table, close to the lamp, studying a scrap of paper. Rose is playing with the bolt on the door. There are three metal straps, two on the door and one on the wall. A bar of black metal slides across, and the straps make sort of tunnels for the bar and hold it in place.

'For goodness sake,' says her mother, 'stop all that racket.'

'My door hasn't got a bolt,' says Rose.

'Just as well or we'd all be driven crazy with the noise.'

'Why can't I have a bolt too?'

Her mother looks up. Her eyes are frightening. 'Be grateful for what you have and shut up.' Her voice cracks as if she is going to cry.

Rose sits at the table and watches her mother for a while. Eva takes a stub of pencil and draws a line. The paper is covered in short lines crossing and criss-crossing. She looks hard at the paper and draws another mark. Suddenly she slams the pencil down.

'Ahhh!' she shouts. 'We are wasting our time!'

'Shall I draw it?' says Rose.

Her mother snatches the paper up and screws it into a ball. 'You will not, you little thief! Hiding things from your own mother! Ah!' She looks at what she's done and smoothes the paper out again. Rose has never seen her mother look frightened before.

'Rose, Rose,' she says, 'I am sick of the bloody gold. Sick of it. Who knows what curse will come down on us? That Scobie curse! To hell with it all.' She sits with her head hanging above the table like a ropey old floor-mop. Then she sighs. 'So. You and I, Rose, must move in a different direction. If we have the strength.'

Rose goes to stand by her mother. She waits, but nothing more is said. After a while, when her mother is looking safer, Rose says, 'Robbers might get in, or murderers.'

'Whatever are you on about?' says her mother.

'If I haven't got a bolt,' she says.

Her mother bangs her hand on the table and stands up. 'Ask your blasted Uncle Billy then — he makes hundreds of the things. What do I know about it?'

She goes into Billy Genesis's bedroom and puts on a pretty dress. When she sees Rose watching she says, 'For goodness sake go to bed. Can't a body dress in peace?'

Rose wants to know who her mother visits in the night. She wants to go with her but she knows her mother will only shout again if she asks questions. So she goes to her room and puts on her coat and her boots and waits until she hears her mother bang the other door. She listens as her mother's footsteps go slap slap, softer and softer on the muddy path.

She stands on her clothes-chest to look out the window. Lights are shining in other windows. It's a clear night. Rose is not afraid of the dark — she likes it, but she is afraid of Billy. She can see no one anywhere all along the Camp, only the dark shapes of the houses and the new hook-man's pony, Flora, tied to a post by the men's quarters.

She opens her door quietly, shuts it and runs around behind the great log house in case anyone is looking out. She walks up the path to the Bins, being careful not to kick stones, and trying to keep inside the shadows. Rose is good at not being seen.

The Incline is not running. The railway yards are quiet. A big empty wagon waits all alone on the rails. Rose stands in its black shadow and looks up at the Bins. The light on the wall of the Powerhouse is on. It makes a pool of yellow light on the ground, outside Red Minifie's saloon. Singing and shouts come out of Minifie's. Rose thinks Billy will be inside getting drunk. Mr Carmichael's light is on too. He often works late and sometimes Rose calls in to see him. She walks along a railway track, counting the sleepers, fifteen, and then she runs across the yard in a big circle past Minifie's. She tiptoes on the iron steps up to the office so no one at Minifie's might hear.

There is another man in Mr Carmichael's office with him. The other man is sitting in Mr Carmichael's chair and they both look angry. The other man is dressed in his good suit and he says, 'What's this? Is this one of yours, Eddie?' when he sees Rose. Mr Carmichael says he is busy tonight and she should go home.

Rose stands right by the key-board. She smiles at Mr Carmichael and says she thinks she left her shoe-bag under his desk. Mr Carmichael bends down to see and the other man looks too and she unhooks number seventeen and holds it tightly in her hand.

Mr Carmichael frowns and says the bag is not there and anyway surely a shoe-bag could wait until the morning. Rose says her mother is angry that she's lost it and Mr Carmichael nods and gives her piece of chocolate because he's sorry she has an angry mother.

The door to Billy's forge is around the other side of the Bins from Minifie's. There are no lights here at all, and no houses either. She looks at the door. It is two doors together and they are very big. The two handles are threaded by a chain and a heavy padlock hangs from the chain. Rose reaches up. She can just reach the padlock but the key won't go in. She rests her arms for a while and tries again. She feels the key slide in and then she hears the click of the padlock opening. She smiles in the dark and thinks of her treasure inside.

But the padlock is stuck in the chain. She pushes up and the padlock bumps against the chain but it won't slide out. She is too small — her hands won't reach high enough. She tries again. It's too hard. The padlock is making a noise and she can hear herself starting to make a noise too. She sits down on the cold stones to rest her arms and to make her crying stop.

In a little while she gets up and walks back around to the other side of the Bins. She tiptoes past the steps to Mr Carmichael's office and right up to the door of Minifie's. Someone is singing; it might be Uncle Con the Brake. She can't hear Billy's voice. Beside the door is a pile of wooden crates. She lifts one. If she holds it high against her stomach she can keep it off the ground. She starts running but the steps are in the way and she doesn't see them. Her leg bangs right into the iron step. It hurts and she can't stop herself crying out, but no one comes. She keeps going.

She puts the crate down under the padlock and climbs up, and this time her hands can do it easily. The padlock slides out of one side and the chain clatters through the handles and falls to the ground. Rose is glad no one is near because the sound is loud. One big door swings open a little until it hits the crate. She steps down, moves the crate back and squeezes through the door.

Inside it is thick black. She can't see anything at all. Rose waits. Then she can see a faint glow where the fire is. She walks across with her hands out in front, in case there is something in the way. Her hands touch the cold anvil and she feels her way around it. Then her hands touch a sharp-edged metal rod and she picks it up. She pokes at the glow with the rod, raking back the dull coke, and the glow is brighter. She can see a little way. The big bellows are beside the furnace. She heaves the metal tip of the bellows onto the stone ledge, and pumps with the handles like Willie Connelly's brother did. The fire glows brightly. Rose smiles and pumps again. It's fun.

She turns now and sees her treasure box. She starts to hum a little song, 'Mountains of Home', which Mrs Rasmussen taught her. She goes back to the big door, brings the crate from outside, puts it under the shelf and climbs up. She can reach her treasure! The polished wood feels silky and happy. But when she pulls at her box something falls off the shelf and crashes to the floor. Rose's heart starts pounding and she stands perched there with her hands quiet on the shelf for a minute. Her hands feel the things that are falling. Her mouth opens in a big O. The things are pieces of latch — the tunnel-shaped straps and the bars just like the one on Billy's door. She counts four straps and two bars — more than she needs, but some might break — and puts them in the pockets of her coat. They're heavy. Then she slides her treasure box off the shelf and rattles it gently. Something is inside. Her own treasure. She undoes the top button of her coat and pushes the box down inside. Her heart pumps fast against the cold, smooth wood. Now she has a sticking-out front just like Mrs Rasmussen. Rose giggles. She can't stop smiling.

Outside she shuts the doors again. The chain and the padlock are too heavy to lift together. She unhooks the padlock and heaves at the chain. It's still heavy. Climbing onto the crate is hard with all the things in her pockets and down her front. And the chain won't go through the handles. She thinks she might leave the chain on the ground but then she thinks about Billy finding out, and she tries again. Link by link the chain slides through. It doesn't want to go. Rose hates the stupid chain; she wants to scream at it.

Then she hears someone coming. The footsteps are stumbly and once the man falls against the iron side of the Bins and he curses. It's Billy Genesis. She presses against the door and holds one hand over her mouth to stop any sounds coming out. She's afraid even to climb down off the crate. She shuts her eyes, facing the doors, and waits in the dark.

Billy crashes against the wall again and this time she can hear him falling right down. He is talking to himself.

Someone else further away shouts, 'Billy, you addle-pate, that's not the way home!'

Rose hears the other man — it might be Lord Percy — bumping around and banging against the wall himself. She hears one of them being sick. She keeps her eyes shut. Her treasure box is slipping down inside and she hopes the belt of her coat will hold it.

The two men are going away. Their grumbling voices grow faint. Rose slides down the door and sits on the crate for a while. Her hands are shaking from holding the chain still. She blows on them until they are quiet. Then she climbs up again and now her hands will do everything right. It's magic. Her treasure is helping her. The padlock slides through as if it's buttered, and she can snap it shut. She rolls the crate along in front of her until it's around the corner. She runs across the yard and when she passes the great rubbish heap she throws the key into it.

Rose runs like a crab, holding on to all her things with her elbows and hands. The pieces of latch rattle in her pockets, and her treasure sings little tunes, clink clink, inside the box.

Behind Conrad the Sixth's tomb she stops and crouches. The stones are sharp and cold when she runs her hands over them. She knows there is a loose stone — she felt it last time she was sitting here. Mrs Rasmussen won't let her into the log house now, but sometimes Rose sits and talks to the dead baby, Conrad the Sixth. Mrs Rasmussen can't see her if she's behind the tomb.

Rose is tired. Her fingers are slow and cold. She pulls out the stone and wiggles another until it's loose too. She's afraid the whole pile will start to fall. Conrad the Sixth's dead little body might be in the hole. But she thinks Uncle Con the Brake would have put it in a box. She jams her treasure box in the hole she has made and stuffs little stones over it. The pile is not so smooth now but you can't see the box. Rose thinks she will come tomorrow and every day to make sure it's there and make it look smoother.

Rose stands and points all her fingers at the place where the box is hidden. She whispers a fierce curse: 'The ghost of Conrad the Sixth get you and cut you to pieces if you touch my treasure!'

She puts the pieces of latch and bolt under some other rocks in case Billy Genesis is awake when she gets home.

Rose yawns.

There's no light in Billy Genesis's house. Rose thinks he'll be asleep by now.

But when she opens the door of her room Billy is there on her bed. He wakes up when the door creaks. He smells of sick.

Heartsick

EVEN CON THE Brake was tired of arguing about the strike, it had dragged on so long. Con was against the strikers. He agreed they had a point — nobody liked to see a good working man under-valued, you know? But the way the miners conducted the strike — the dogged, bitter, disciplined way they clung to their principles — drove Con crazy. It was like the army, he said. No freedom, no fun. If they didn't like the life or the pay there were other, softer jobs down below. What bloody right, said Con, did the miners have to dictate what happened to the whole of the Hill, where his son was buried? He, Con, had chosen Denniston as his home soil, and he expected to find a bloody job here until his hands or his eyes or his heart, or all three, gave out. You know?

The coal stored at the Bins ran out in three weeks. Con lowered the last wagonful down the Incline, parked his brake-handle, and listened to the slowing beat of the Powerhouse engine as the whole plant shut down. Con hated that dying sound. The rattle and rhythm of ascending and descending wagons was in his blood now. God knows when the place would come to life again. If ever.

Walking back down to the Camp under a sky as black as his thoughts, the pungent smell of coal heavy in the air, Con sees, a little further down, a shadow separate from the dark of the high rock wall and step out as if waiting for him. Eva Storm.

Henry Stringer, the school teacher, also on the rocky path but out of sight around the bend, hears Con's angry words and her wheedling answers.

'For the love of God, woman, leave me alone. I done what I can and that's the end of it.'

'Conrad, Conrad, you are my man. We both know it.'

'You dream. Step aside.'

'Hey now, big man, feel this. I know what you like.'

Henry shrinks back against the wall as the two shadows mix and twist. Con grunts as if in pain and tears away.

'No! Jesus Maria, stay away! You are worse than a limpet.'

'Don't give me that. Come! Come here!' Eva's words vibrate in a way that has poor Henry in a sweat, let alone Con for whom they're intended. Con moans again and Henry sees Eva's long arms grapple Con into the darkness. Henry, who knows Eva's reputation, wills Con to resist, but all above him is silent now, apart from a shout or two up at the Bins. He turns to go back down when Rose's name is mentioned. Rose is his pupil. Henry listens.

'So. If not me, then your daughter. Rose needs her father.'

'You have a great skill, Angel, in finding fathers for her.'

'You are he! Take us away!'

'I will not. Bella needs me.'

'Bella!' Henry hears her spit. 'Rose needs you more. Far more.'

'Then see to her. You are the mother.'

'Billy Genesis — you know what he's like. He . . . hurts her. Worse . . .'

The noise Con makes is half cry, half snarl. A wounded wild animal could make such a noise.

'Ah Jesus, woman, you are pure bloody evil. You would use that toad Billy to bait the trap?'

'Who baits what? Come, my sweetheart. Leave this hell-hole with me and Rose and start again. It's the right way.' Her words carry more than a tinge of menace. Again Con groans in the dark. This time there is more anguish than anger, and less certainty. Henry Stringer is astonished. Con the Brake and Bella are a famous couple. He's never heard a single rumour concerning Con and Eva Storm.

Just then they all hear footsteps crossing the Camp from the top of the Track.

'Out!' growls Con as if ordering a dog. 'One word and I'll break your neck, I swear.'

Henry imagines she goes because the next thing he sees is Con himself, stamping and cursing down the path to the log house, where Bella still grieves for her baby. He turns, now, to face the little party winding uphill. The leader is that cold fish Arnold Scobie just coming over the lip of the Track. On his shoulder is a sack of flour, in his hands the reins of a pony laden with fresh vegetables. Arnold's head is down. The man is tired and puffing from the Track, but he hurries. No Burnett's Face miner wants to linger crossing the Camp or he might collect a lump of coal or an earful of abuse. There is no other way up to Burnett's Face except across the Camp and through Denniston. A gauntlet of ill-feeling.

Con the Brake is there. The silence of the pump engine roars in his ears; Eva's words claw at his heart; his wife's dumb misery lies, a sour knot, in his belly. This is the moment when Con's famous anger finally breaks loose. Great fists akimbo, he plants himself square in Arnold's slow pathway. Arnold glances up, changes direction to plod around Con. The giant shifts to block him again.

Arnold grunts. 'Will you stop us feeding our families, then?'

'I will,' shouts Con, all control lost, and lets fly. Arnold drops like a stone. Blood from his pulped nose drips onto the sack of flour. The pony stands, placid as a cow. Henry Stringer rushes forward to shift the sack — a foolhardy move with Con berserk, but good-hearted Henry is thinking of hungry children and spoiled flour. Con roars and turns to swat him back — when a screaming banshee leaps onto the brake-man's broad back, beating and biting, clinging like a limpet. Con shakes like a dog but she sticks there still.

'Jesus Maria!' shouts Con, reaching around behind. The screaming stops for a moment while teeth sink into his wrist. Con lets out a bellow.

By now a crowd has gathered to gawk at the scene. There's no way Con can escape. Even Con in his present state can't dash a woman to the ground, if this wild creature can be called a woman.

'That's my husband you have struck to the ground!' yells Janet Scobie, riding Con the Brake as if he were a bucking horse. 'Bringing food to hungry families! You feckin' bully! Look at the size of you! Shame! Shame!' She strikes again and again, her fists drumming a furious tattoo on Con's broad back.

Con is beaten. He stands now, taking the blows until the woman slides off. A young thing, sturdy and long-legged, hair tumbling out of her bun, down between wide shoulderblades. Slab of a nose. The crowd has become ugly, egging Con on, but he won't move. Bella has come out of the house to watch. Her eyes, too, are scornful.

One of the new Camp people bends to pick up the sack of

flour. Quick as a whiplash, Janet turns on him. He shrinks back.

'Carry your own food up the Track, you feckin' sod! Yer bunch of idle layabouts! We've worked for this lot, and we're taking it to Burnett's Face. Willy-nilly!' She faces them, teeth bared like a cornered dog. Arnold is on his feet now, shaking his head. He says nothing. Picks up the reins, shoulders the sack, takes his wife's arm and leads her away. The Camp people growl as they pass but let them go, because Con, who started it, stands aside.

For a moment there is silence. Everyone watches then as Mrs C. Rasmussen, bleaker than winter, turns without a word and goes back into the house. Con the Brake walks after her, as if pulled on a string. His attempts at a nod and a wink to the crowd are pitiful. The door of the log house swings open and closes behind them.

THAT night a quiet sort of depression, rank and raw as the smell of wet coal, settled on the people at the Camp as they returned to their huts and their tents and their men's quarters. Con was a great man for a fight, but who had ever seen him in an unprovoked attack? It was as if his action had removed a rule that Denniston needed, especially at a time like this.

And up at Burnett's Face, word was spreading among the miners that Con the Brake, undisputed leader of the Camp, had struck Arnold Scobie to the ground for no reason at all. From now on, any miner crossing the Camp should carry a weapon.

INSIDE the log house Bella is waiting for her husband. He removes his boots slowly, avoiding her eye; sits heavily, hands hanging between his knees. Bella has not lit the lamps yet.

'So,' says Bella, 'you have become the man who hits a peaceful fellow bringing food to his family? What next? Would you like to take a fist to me?' She spreads her soft arms as if inviting it.

Con the Brake looks at Bella. His seamed face is older, less spirited.

'Ah, Bella,' he says, and his voice has a defeated ring. 'You will not set foot outside the house to visit your friends or to teach the children but you come running to see your husband shamed.'

There is silence in the darkening room. Bella sighs.

'You are right. We must stop this.' Then she cries out. 'Ah! Ah! If only I had never borne the baby! I was happy enough before.'

'And I,' says Con, his great head hanging, 'I was happy, more than, with you, my Bella.'

'Was? Was, is it?' whispers Bella, too soft for him to hear.

It is almost dark. Con the Brake rises slowly, kneels before the great fire that never goes out, and blows it to life with long, steady breaths. Bella rises also, lights a screw of paper from the fire and touches it to the three oil lamps. Polished wood glows. The beautiful simple room warms, throbs with a steady life of its own. The Scandinavian of noble blood and the retired whore move slowly in the room, as if through water. They come together and stand, heart to heart, taking each other's weight.

'My Bella,' whispers Con. Bella is surprised to hear fear in his voice. 'Bella, what am I to do?'

She holds him.

'It will be a hard time, this strike,' says Con at last. 'We will be needed, we two.'

Bella nods against his shoulder.

'The children at school need you, Bella.'

She nods again.

Outside, not far away, they hear curses and shouts, a door banging, a woman's scream — or is it a child? Con and Bella look at each other and away again. Bella is uncomfortable, Con in anguish.

'We will start with Rose,' says Bella.

Con searches her face. All he sees is deep concern. He lets out a great sigh. 'By God, I am glad to hear you say that, woman. The child has been every day this week, at the porch door . . .'

'I know.'

'And when you send her away she sits behind the baby's tomb, singing to him.'

'You have made your point, man. I will take care of it now.'

Con takes heart to hear the bite in his wife's words.

'Hitting that man . . .' he says. 'I am not really a violent man . . .'

'Mr Rasmussen,' says Bella, 'you *are* a violent man, as we both well know, but you are half a world and half a life away from the last time you struck down a weak man . . .'

'Ah now, you cannot bring that against me. The issue was entirely different. I was severely provoked.'

'Well, so you say. This time you were not.'

Con looks down humbly. Actually he is trying to hide a great grin. He and Bella are quarrelling again. The salt has returned to life on the Hill.

'Arnold Scobie,' he says, still looking away from the fierce woman, 'is a man without joy who deserves to be shaken up once in a while . . .'

Bella takes a handful of the flesh of his cheek and twists.

'Hey, woman! But I admit I was wrong. There! It will not happen again. I swear.'

Con the Brake was a man who could ignore his problems until they presented directly in front of his nose. He and Bella went to bed that night thinking the nightmare might be fading, that life might take on a lighter shade from now on. They did not know that in the shelter of their back porch a shivering Rose of Tralee huddled, waiting until her mother returned from wherever she spent half of most nights, or Billy Genesis went back to his own bed.

A Child's Voice

PLENTY OF PEOPLE guessed what Con the Brake was up to, the day he strode over to Billy Genesis's house when Billy was out, up at the forge. Guessed, but not openly — not admitting out loud what was happening. You'd have to ask why Billy was tolerated, why things had to drag on to that terrible end. Afterwards people would shake their heads sagely and say the community was in turmoil with the strike, men off work, new workers arriving, old ones leaving. Or they'd say blacksmiths were rare beasts and Billy's skills were necessary to the community. Said with a shift of the eyes, a quick clear of the throat and a subsequent change of subject. No one liked to admit that a child's voice is always harder to hear than an adult's. That a child who speaks without her parents' backing is practically inaudible.

Even Bella and Con the Brake fudged the issue.

'She wants a bolt on her door,' says Bella, holding the iron pieces in her hand. 'She says Billy gave her the hardware.'

Con's eyes turn to ice. 'Let the man screw it on, then.'

'She says he is too busy to screw it on.'

Rose, thin and pale, dark circles under her eyes, watches them.

'I can't interfere with another man's house,' says Con. 'You know I can't.' But already his hands are hefting the iron pieces as if they are dangerous weapons.

'It's my door,' says Rose. 'Only my door, not the rest of the house.'

'She's afraid, with all the new people at the Camp,' says Bella. A sideways shift of the eyes. 'And her mother out — entertaining.'

'Billy Genesis doesn't mind if you do it,' says Rose, her eyes honest and steady.

Con tries to turn his strangled cry into a cough. 'Well then,' he says, reaching for the door, 'I'll fetch my tools.'

Rose stayed inside the log house. Watching from a window, she saw Con the Brake enter her little add-on room with its own door; saw him close the door to work on the inside of it, and watched, smiling, as he walked back.

No one could see Con the Brake, grunting with effort, drive the screws in with all his force. No one watched while he took his file and carefully filed back the slot of each screw-head so that removing the bolt would become a difficulty. No one asked, later, why, if he knew to do all that, he didn't know how to confront Billy directly.

'Thank you,' said Rose, all smiles, but she wouldn't give him a hug or sit on his knee for a story. These days Rose skipped like quicksilver when a man reached out.

'She's just growing up,' said Bella.

Eva Storm

GOLD, MY FRIENDS, is a commodity we all of us have followed for a good part of our lives. For my part I was born into it. Born in a tent with the rattle of the box and the swish of the pan in my ears. Cut my teeth on my papa's shovel. Oh, those roaring days! The search, the shout of joy, the bitter disappointment, the free spending! You know as well as me. So it will surprise you to know that at this very moment in my story all that sly and golden thrill slipped away out of my body like grog from a cracked cup. That cursed Billy Genesis was the root and source of my loss, who caused me to turn my back on any prospects of gold.

In Billy the lust for the colour was black as night. An ugly thing to see, turning all nearby a dirty shade too. Tied as I was to him, I lost all stomach for the project. With poor Jimmy Cork the lust had been all romance and dreams — stupid, yes; tiresome, yes; but not ugly. Something to lift your heart now and then on a dark night. But Billy sold his soul, I swear. And tried with all his evil strength to drag me down too.

So. Here is how it went. His plan was to use the strike, the days the mine closed, to further the search. My opinion, my sharper judgement, was not sought. I shouted at him that the area in question was closed off: a dead Scobie haunting it and a living Scobie's curse lying in wait. He laughed.

'The curse is laid on Jimmy, not me, and I am stronger than any English miner's curse.'

Fool, fool, but the man was driven. I suspect he found a few grains more in Jimmy's pool on the cliff, which kept the fires going. But he wouldn't admit such. No sharing with that black bastard. Yes, so I made a mistake, I admit. How was I to know the change that swelled like something putrid inside Billy Genesis?

Twice during the strike he had entered the mine on some pretext but the horses were not kept anywhere near the section in question, and twice Billy had found himself face to face with an irate scab who'd lost his silly way in the maze.

Now Billy seizes me by my hair and draws me close. 'Tomorrow the mine closes. You will stand guard for me while I search.'

'I will not,' says I through clenched teeth.

He knocks me flat. 'You will if I carry you.'

'Then carry me and be damned!' I shout. 'That will be a fine and secret start to your mission!'

The man was an idiot, no?

He knocks me flat again.

In the end I go, if only to prevent further beating. At this time I am working hard on Con the Brake and what man would sigh and moan over black eyes and broken teeth?

Billy leaves me at the small opening of an air shaft down to an unused part of the mine. It would be close to right above Jimmy's golden rock pool, he reckons. I did not trust Billy's reckoning one jot. He used up what small portion of brain he had memorising the Bible. Well, he squeezes in, and I hand down the lantern and the little pick. I am left alone, holding one end of a ball of string, which he will use to retrace his steps. I tell you, I would not go down that gaping maw for a sack of gold. The day is fine and clear, the wind keen, but all around I can feel darkness rise from the rocks and the twisted little bushes like the direst of storms brewing and boiling up on this very spot to teach us a lesson.

I sit there shaking. Which to fear most — the miners' curse or Billy's fists? I decide on fists, which at least are there to see and to avoid. So I tie the string to a branch shaped like a witch's claw, and run for it.

But imagine this! Three steps down over the wild plateau — no more — I hear a dreadful rumbling like the voices of all the Scobie men growling and droning. I am flung to the ground howling in fear. Under me all is heaving and swaying and gnawing very horridly. Over it all I swear I can hear the high keening cry of that young Scobie boy, entombed still, his soul restless and thirsting for blood, and another wild scream that could have been poor Jimmy in the flames. Oh, it was your worst nightmare!

A simple earthquake, you'll say. So indeed. So maybe! But why at that time, I ask you? Why that place? There are matters here beyond natural explanation. None of your narrowed rational eyes and twitching mouths will persuade me otherwise.

When the land has settled and my feet will carry me I'm up and off that weird rocky place and down to the Camp, one shoe gone and hair in a wild tangle of fright. Billy Genesis can shift for himself. Or not, for all I care.

So. All night, with Billy still not home, I sit by the fire, fearful of what ghosts might visit me if I sleep. Every moment I expect fresh quakes; a chasm opening at my feet with the hands of the dead reaching for me. Also there was Billy. If he never returned, what then? Questions would be asked. 'Where is the blacksmith?' If he *did* return he would be like to kill me for leaving him up there alone.

You can understand how unfair all this was. I who had no part in Scobie deaths was attracting the curse. I could feel it working its way through me from the inside out like a boil coming to the surface. Once that night I lost all reason and ran barefoot to the Incline thinking to ride a wagon down — to escape, leaving all behind. But I had forgot it was closed. The only way I could think to end it all was to stay outside till I froze to death, but the cold got the better of me and I returned to the stove.

Well, this was bad but you cannot get Eva Storm down entirely. My friends, I am a hard nut to crack. Am I not here around this fire, flesh still on my bones, stories aplenty in my head?

That hell-hole of a man Billy Genesis was not dead in the mine, but escaped. How, he never told. My lucky night — he came home by way of Red Minifie's so by the time he was ready to warm my cold flesh with his raw fist the drink had sapped his strength. Nothing for me but a few bruised ribs before he fell down senseless. I sat there by the stove, Billy snoring on the floor, and looked at the poor sodden fool. No more, I thought: no more of this madness.

So. In time the spirit rises: weary, damaged, but ready again to fight for a place in the world. By morning there was a plan of sorts in my mind. No more prospecting. No more motherlode. My sole drive was to separate Con the Brake from his precious Bella and to bring him down off the Hill with me to a warmer life. A difficult task, you think? Impossible when the man has a comfortable home and a good job? Well consider this. Big Snow — or Con the Brake if you like — was a lovely wild man. Oh, I fancied him more every day I set eyes on him! He loved his Bella, yes, but that slabby fellow was a rover like me. You could still smell ship's tar and sea salt and bracken from lonely highlands on the man. In his blood. He had to move or die. You would see him shake his head sometimes, lift his nose and smell the air, those blue eyes seeing nothing of the coal-damp world around him. Distant places were calling him. I knew it. I *knew* it.

The sticking point was that Con was also a decent man. No fellow with the wanderlust should ever be born decent; it will not sit with comfort on the shoulders, ha ha! So. To catch the decent man — to lead him in the direction his nose wishes to follow — my Rose is the bait. This decent man will leave his wife to protect his daughter, is my plan. Then, away and on the road, he will know where his true heart lies.

My friends, the plan worked better and more terrible than I hoped.

Holding the Line

TWO MONTHS INTO the strike Eddie Carmichael had managed to recruit forty new men — only three trained for underground, and even those had worked only tiny goldmining operations, nothing remotely resembling the underground city that spread under the Hill. Eddie started up one section of Coalbrookdale mine with the recruits, he himself acting as deputy. The coal came out in a trickle. Con and the others at the Bins had work one day in three, bringing coal down the Incline and into the waiting train below. A week after Coalbrookdale started up, four of the new men walked off, just as Mary Scobie had predicted. Their shoulders ached, their backs were ruined, working in the dark all day was unnatural, they missed their families. Eddie pleaded and raged but one by one the men hopped behind a descending wagon and left for the coast.

Down in Westport, Mr McConnochie was not displeased at the lack of miners.

'Leave it, Eddie,' he said. 'Orders are always slack in the summer. We can save money if the workforce is light. The strikers will cave in before the winter orders are rolling, mark my words.'

Eddie, grey from overwork, worn out by all the arguments, was not so optimistic.

'They are leaving already for work in other mines. You are running a fine line, Mr McConnochie.'

'I am, and that is business, Eddie. Now leave me to it.'

These days Mary Scobie, that tireless dragon, visited the Brake Head twice a week. People learned to skip quickly into a doorway or slide away down a side lane when they saw her black figure striding down from the skipway and into town. If caught, you were bailed up for a donation or a pledge of support, or even food from your own table.

On each visit she clanged up the steps to Eddie Carmichael's office and clanged down again. Goodness know what they discussed, but Eddie, poor bugger, always had a hangdog look after she left.

And the letters Mary Scobie wrote! Eddie was postmaster as well as mine manager. His chatty little sparrow of a wife, Mrs Carmichael — Ivy to her small circle of friends — sorted the letters each morning on the breakfast table. The outgoing mail went down the Incline either in the coat pocket of one of the maintenance men, who rode down the stones on their shovels, checking for debris on the rails, or in Eddie's satchel when he was summoned yet again to Westport.

'They should charge her extra,' says Ivy Carmichael, in full flight, to Mr Dimcock the draper.

'Charge who?' asks Totty, come in to inspect the new consignment of cloth.

'That Mrs Scobie. The mail she sends! You'd think *she* was running a business, not my Mr Carmichael. How much is the Welsh flannel?'

'One and threepence the yard, Mrs Carmichael.'

'Daylight robbery. And the folk she sends out to! Three times to the Premier. That old goat Larnarch, Minister of Mines, gets one every week. Several to some subversive organisation in Australia.'

Totty fingers the flannel. It is fine and warm. Mr Dimcock watches her. These days he is anxious to make a sale.

'I'll take two yards,' she says, 'and five of your best black alpaca.'

'Two won't get you anywhere, Mrs Hanratty. Take five while I have it.'

'Three, then. The new little one must be warm this winter.' She sits on the high stool sighing with pleasure to take the weight off her feet. Everyone is silent a moment, to honour the last little one, buried so recently.

Ivy takes breath again. 'She's writing to someone in Brunner mine too, down at Grey. Oh, she's a stirrer, that one.'

'Well, she believes in the cause, I suppose . . .'

'Believes in herself, I'd say. Have you noticed the change in her? Mrs Important? I'll have three of the flannel too, Mr Dimcock. When you're ready. Oh yes, Mrs Scobie would run the world single-handed if you gave her the chance. She bails up my Mr Carmichael and says the most cruel things. *And* it's all for nothing.' Ivy lowers her voice. 'Twenty letters a day go out, and not one in reply. Not one. She is all puff. I tell you, no one out there takes one blind bit of notice. They'll lose the strike, mark my words. Thank you, Mr Dimcock. Put it on my bill.'

Mr Dimcock clears his throat. 'Ah . . . Perhaps this time . . .'

His embarrassed question is stopped in its tracks by Mrs Carmichael's frown.

'My husband always pays at the end of the month,' she says. 'Good day to you, Totty.'

When she is gone and the air in the store has settled, Totty asks, 'Is it that bad?'

'It is,' says little Mr Dimcock, his hands smoothing the Welsh flannel and folding it back onto the bolt.

'Give me my bill now then,' says Totty, 'and I will see that Tom pays tonight. We must all hang on if we can.'

THREE more months passed. The Company limped on. Complaints arrived on Eddie's desk — about the quality of the coal hewed, the amount of slack and rock in it. The Miners' Society committeemen were up and down the Track like yo-yos. There was an article in the *Westport Times* about a meeting Mr Scobie addressed in Westport, and another saying he was a troublemaker, stirring up discontent in other West Coast mines.

Once the committee brought Mr H.P. Jimson, a famous unionist from Wellington, up the Track and there was a public meeting in the Volunteer Brigade Hall.

'Amalgamation is the word, lads!' shouted the important man. 'We must join with our Australian brothers. I see the Amalgamated Miners' Association spreading the world! Who could withstand us? No, my good fellows, hold firm to your principles. You are making history here! Workers throughout the colony are behind you. *I* am behind you!'

He brought no money with him, though. Josiah watched the miners trail out of the hall. They would not meet his eye. These were no longer fighting men. The rhetoric of the important man had not raised their spirits one notch. Stolid Tommy Jowett, whose section of Coalbrookdale mine was being worked by unskilled labour, stood at the back of the hall, waiting for a word.

'I'm off in the morning, Josiah,' he said. 'That's it for me.'

'Now, now, lad,' said Mr Jimson, puffing up like a blow-fish, his florid jowls shaking with conviction. 'The battle is near won — you cannot desert the ship now.'

Tommy seemed not to hear the outsider's bluster. He spoke directly to Josiah.

'I've stood by the committee, Josiah, and we had just cause, but I can no longer swim upstream. Nor my seven lads from Coalbrookdale. We'll be gone by morning. There is work at Koranui, so I hear.'

The unionist shot a stubby finger into Tommy's waistcoat. 'Now look here, man. The union has worked tirelessly on your behalf this five months. Strength in unity! Unity, man!'

Tommy ignored him. 'We had word today that the Company is evicting us, Josiah. All of us in Company houses must be out by Friday. They want the room for more bloody scab labour.'

'Ah, the devils,' growled Josiah, hanging his head like a cornered dog. 'That's a low blow.' Scobies owned their own home but most of his friends were still under Company roofs.

'We cannot hold out, Josiah. Not without a roof.'

Mary Scobie, finished in the kitchen, came stumping across the floor, her cane striking the bare boards, black bosom leading the attack.

'Tommy Jowett, you're not giving in now! You can stay with us. All the family.'

Tommy's eyes fixed to a spot a few inches from Josiah's boots. Like most of the miners he was uncomfortable with this woman who came to men's political meetings, who listened and argued instead of staying in the kitchen with the teacups.

'Thank you, Mrs Scobie, but you cannot house thirty households. They are clearing the lot. We've given it our best shot, Josiah, but we are not made of granite, like this damned plateau. We cannot survive the winter without food or shelter.'

Josiah opened his mouth to argue but Mary Scobie was ahead of him. 'Cannot you see that the Company are desperate? Why else are they evicting you, if not to break the strike? Winter means big orders. They cannot fill the orders without skilled labour. Stay, stay, Tommy, we are almost there!'

The man from Wellington cleared his throat. All the men were embarrassed. Tommy Jowett looked briefly at Josiah, turned and walked out. In the doorway he raised one hand briefly, without looking back, and was gone.

While her husband walked the guest speaker back to Hanrattys', Mary sat alone in the hall. An onlooker may have seen a neat and proper wife, waiting quietly for her husband. She sat near the back of the hall on a folding wooden chair, her feet neatly together, the heirloom necklace of black jet gleaming faintly against the black pintucks of her good bombazine. A plain steel hatpin skewered her flat black hat at a perfect horizontal, safe against all movement or weather. The black wool coat, brought from England and still as good as the day it arrived, lay folded on her knee, ready for the long walk home. But Mary's thoughts were galloping helter-skelter like pit ponies on their day above ground. She knew her forthright manner embarrassed the men; knew and cared not a jot. Perhaps an addiction had set in — a kind of drunkenness. Mary Scobie wouldn't describe it like that — in her whole life alcohol had never passed her lips — but, having tasted the joys of organising, cajoling, speaking out, of driving an issue forward against opposition, Mary Scobie would never again relinquish the pleasure. Winning the strike mattered more than any sidelong glances. A win could set Josiah (and herself) on the first step away from the Hill. But more than that: just conducting the fight against entrenched and hide-bound male opponents was a new and heady seduction. Unknown to her, temperance and suffrage, issues made to order for her delight, were waiting in the wings.

Josiah said nothing on the long walk home. He walked behind his wife, fidgeting at the pace, dying to stride out, to converse comfortably with one of the other miners. But by the time he reached Burnett's Face his irritation had disappeared, leaving only depression.

'We've lost, Mary,' he says, scraping muddy boots on the iron bar at the door and reaching for her boots that he might do the same for her. 'Most of the men are in Company houses. They will have to leave the plateau.'

Mary shakes out her coat and hangs it to dry on the door, stirs the embers in the coal range, moves the kettle to the hottest part. She crackles with energy.

'Let them go, Josiah, let them go. Koranui is close by. We need the money, God knows. They can come running back soon enough, when we win the strike.'

'Ah, win: I don't know.'

'What has happened to you, Josiah?'

'Tommy's a leader. If he goes . . . And think, Mary, those ruffians from the Camp, living in here, at Burnett's Face. There will be fights.'

'Aye, and that'll be bad for orders.'

'The community is divided enough as it is. I've been responsible for nothing but the destruction of our new town.'

'Josiah!' Mary bangs down the teapot for emphasis, and follows it with ringing teacups. 'You have not failed. You have nearly won.'

'The men are losing faith. I should not have tried so soon. We were not ready.'

'Let them wait two more weeks. No more. I know. In my bones

I know it, Josiah. The pressure of winter coal orders will win our cause. You know it too. The coal creeps out of Coalbrookdale in spoonfuls. *I* could hew faster than those fumble-fingered recruits. The Company will give way, I know it!'

Josiah sips on tea, weak and sugarless, as Mary has served it for a fortnight, in order to provide tonight's meeting with a proper supper. There are no scones or cake to comfort his growling depression.

'The committee cannot conduct a strike without the men, Mother,' he says. But something about his wife's fierceness makes him smile.

Mary crashes into a chair beside him, takes his seamed worker's hands in hers, kneading them like dough. Strength pours out of her.

'My dear.' She hasn't used an endearment in months. 'My dear, I believe you *could* conduct a strike on your own. More than that. Look at that useless what's-his-name from Wellington. If that's the workers' hope, let us despair right now.'

Josiah tries to keep a stern demeanour. 'In Wellington he has a fine reputation for results . . .'

'He could not persuade a fly to land on sugar! All the way down here he comes, rides up the Incline like Moses to the promised land, and then orates as if he's telling the women's knitting circle a new recipe!'

Josiah laughs out loud. 'Well, I must admit he was a bit daft.'

'Daft! Josiah, what good can he be doing up north? You could drive him into the ground in three sentences. You can nail an audience: have them roaring for blood or weeping for injustice, listening for an hour, forgetting to re-light their pipes. *You*, Josiah, should be up in Wellington arguing the workers' rights, not that wad of wet wool, gorging himself right now on Hanrattys' best beef!'

'I am a miner, not a politician, my dear, and not even a miner these last months.'

'Then miners must be politicians. You are needed in Parliament, Josiah!'

Mary Scobie's will hammers behind her words. The house vibrates with it. Young Brennan, woken by the sheer force of the conversation, stands unobserved in the doorway, sleepy in his nightshirt, his mother's words ringing like bells in his ears. He sees his father stand, lift his mother by her shoulders, and hold her at arm's length. His father seems puzzled by her, as if she is a strange new creature, observed for the first time. But the boy also notices that his father is rapt, hypnotised almost, taking into himself, through his connected arms, a new source of power.

The atmosphere in the kitchen is somehow disturbing, too rich; it excludes him. Brennan turns and pads back to the bedroom where he tucks in with his already stacked brothers.

He thinks of Rose, who has been more herself again these last weeks, readier to talk and play, but who came to school today with a flaming and swollen ear and a bruise all down her neck.

Skirmish in a Hell-hole

HENRY STRINGER, SUPERVISING teacher at Denniston School, was on the side of the strikers. After school closed he would walk with the miners' children back up to Burnett's Face, partly as a bodyguard, for feelings were running high, but mostly so he could sit in on meetings and expound his theories about worker solidarity, stabbing bony fingers in the air or pacing restlessly in rooms that were always too small for him. At eighteen he was over six feet tall. His bony limbs jerked as if he were a wooden marionette; his words spluttered and gurgled, half the meaning lost in his eagerness to get them out.

The miners treated this unco-ordinated bean-pole with indulgence — as an endearing but hopelessly idealistic mascot. Their children, on the other hand, had learned to love and revere him. He was on their side, not only in the matter of the strike, but in the

315

matter of children versus adults. He talked to them as if they were equals. He spoke of the world beyond Denniston as if it were a marvellous treasure chest waiting for Denniston children to unlock. He laughed and threw his arms about and ran over the plateau with high, flailing leaps as if he were a child still. Henry Stringer and the six miners' children careering home along the silent, rusting skipway was a sight few could keep a straight face over.

Brennan adored this teacher who would calmly haul off attacking children in the playground; who sprawled in Brennan's home, listening to him play the cornet, waving his arms in time, singing along in a tuneless drone; who took seriously Brennan's plan to be a builder of magnificent railway bridges and never to go underground into a dark and terrifying mine.

Mary Scobie would watch in amazement as her shy youngest son chatted and laughed with this gawky, bristle-headed young teacher. But she smiled, too, thinking of the hot, sweet, powdered-milk drink he served the children each day, a drink that he lovingly heated on the class room pot-belly stove, then passed around in four tin mugs, exhorting reluctant sippers to drink deep, making them all laugh with stories of how tall they would grow and how strongly their muscles would develop. That hot milk, often accompanied by a handful of bread to dip into it, held the balance between health and slow starvation for the children, whose parents grew more and more gaunt as the months passed.

In the early days of the strike, before Mrs C. Rasmussen returned to train the infants, Henry Stringer took especial care of Rose of Tralee. That alone ensured Brennan's adoration. Somehow Mr Stringer always looked the other way when Rose fell asleep at her desk. Bigger boys who laughed at Rose's livid scar were themselves ridiculed mercilessly by Mr Stringer. A cardigan and a woollen hat, old but clean, were quietly popped into her shoe-bag.

'Well, Rose of Tralee!' Mr Stringer would shout, spittle showering the front row. 'I will have to put you out here to be teacher, for you can figure faster than me! Is she not amazing, children?'

And Rose's poor bruised face would glow with pride.

Michael Hanratty and Brennan were in opposite camps for the strike months. Michael was a junior member of the town gang that tormented the Burnett's Face gang whenever they dared. The nuggety little miners' children were no pushover, but their numbers kept dwindling as strikers left Denniston to seek temporary work. They became adept at running for cover or forming a fierce knot, back to back, as the town gang pelted them with stones or ambushed them with wild shrieks.

The one point of contact for the two boys was Rose of Tralee. They were rivals for her love but partners in her protection. Once, the worried boys went together to Mr Stringer. He listened frowning, his jerking arms and legs still for once.

'Well, boys,' he said, 'you have done well to show your care. But there is little I can do when it is her own father beats her.'

'He's only a stepfather,' said Michael, kicking at the leg of a desk.

'It's not fair if she hasn't done anything wrong,' said Brennan, his eyes fierce under black brows and shaggy hair.

Henry Stringer smiled at the indignant pair. 'Well, my two young Galahads, I cannot interfere, but perhaps a word to the mother . . .'

'That won't do any good.' Both boys were adamant on this point. They left the classroom disillusioned.

MICHAEL and Brennan never found out that their teacher did, in the end, against all wisdom, make an effort on Rose's behalf.

That particular evening Henry Stringer downed a drink or two at Hanrattys' bar — a relatively unusual experience for the young man, and one that left him even more unco-ordinated than ever. He plunged out into a stormy night, heading for Minifie's saloon bar over at the Bins.

Inside he stops, blinking like an owl at the noisy shouts, the thick pipe smoke, the smell of stale ale and sly grog. But this young man, who has been headlong and stubborn all his short life, falters only a minute. Shaking the rain off his back like a wet dog, earning curses from those nearby, he crashes his way through the dark and crowded room until he locates the bar — a rough-sawn plank laid between two wooden barrels. Red Minifie, a red-eyed, gap-toothed apparition from hell, glowers behind the bar waiting for his order.

Henry Stringer clears his throat.

'I'm looking for Mr B. Genesis.'

'By God, you'll have to do better than that if I'm to hear a word!' roars Red. 'Listen to the lad: he has a pretty woman in his throat!'

Leaning forward across the bar, Red Minifie grabs a handful of Henry's coat, draws him close and places a wet and stinking kiss full on his lips. Henry Stringer jerks back as if shot, trips over a table behind and crashes to the floor. Everyone guffaws. Henry, scarlet with fright and embarrassment, jumps to his feet, hits his head a resounding crack on a low beam, and down he goes again, poor lad, with not a soul offering a hand of friendship.

This time he comes up mad as a meat-axe, arms flailing, voice a high-pitched scream. 'Mr Genesis! Is Mr Genesis here?'

The blacksmith, weaving drunk, pushes through the crowd. For a moment Henry's stout heart fails him. Scarred and ugly, thick as a tree trunk, shirt sleeves rolled to his elbows despite the cold, Billy Genesis is looking for a fight. He waits, fists on hips, face two inches away from Henry's. A soft growl rumbles in the room. Men are preparing for entertainment.

'Well,' says Henry, offering a hand, 'I am Mr Henry Stringer, the school teacher.'

Billy ignores the hand.

'I have some concern about your step-daughter, Rose.'

Henry speaks quietly, but when Rose is mentioned, suddenly, eerily, all sounds ebb away. The whole dark saloon-full listens.

Billy Genesis lowers his head. He is about to charge.

'I do not wish to intrude on domestic matters,' Henry is babbling now and backing away as he speaks, 'but Rose is a clever girl. I mean . . . The bruising . . . I cannot help observing that her school-work suffers. Her physical condition . . .'

Billy lashes out with one meaty arm. The drinkers murmur at the sound of flesh splitting.

'Then damn well stop observing!' screams Billy, laying in the boot. 'Keep your eyes in your books and off my Rose!' He swats Henry back down as he attempts to rise.

'"Then the Lord rained upon Sodom and upon Gomorrah brimstone and fire!"' shouts Billy Genesis, raining down blows, until others haul him off and bundle him outside to cool off in the rain.

Someone pulls the shaken and bleeding Henry Stringer to his feet. Another dusts off his cap and replaces it carefully on his head. There is respect in the gesture. No one will look him in the eye. Henry opens his mouth to ask a question, then closes it again. The sense of shame in the room, the shuffling silence, defeat him. Red Minifie opens the back door and stands by it. Henry limps through, keeping his distance.

After that night, Henry Stringer never touched liquor of any sort. Rose's plight continued to haunt him, but what could he do?

Moving On

ROSE SHUTS HER eyes tightly to remember, then opens them quickly before she falls off the chair. Two pounds of flour: that is eight cups. She lowers the cupful carefully into the big bread bowl so the flour doesn't fluff out and mess up Mrs C. Rasmussen's clean kitchen. Little moths and worms struggle in the grey flour. She pinches them up and drops them one by one into the cracked mug Mrs Rasmussen has put there for them. Now two dessertspoons of yeast. They look like brains frothing on top of the warm water.

Mrs Rasmussen comes in the back door. A slab of misty cold air comes with her. She shakes out her coat and scarf and hangs them to steam on the rack over the coal range. Her cheeks are rosy but her fingers, when she pulls her gloves from them, are white. She claps them together and laughs at their whiteness, and stamps her feet on the wooden floor.

'Oho!' she says, her eyes round with surprise. 'I am only just in time with the salt. What a busy little cook.'

The paper bag with the salt is wet so Mrs Rasmussen brings the wooden box from its place by the range and scoops the soggy white stuff into it. Rose takes two teaspoons before it goes back to dry along with the washing and the coat.

All the time little songs are running in her head, about the warm steamy kitchen and the bread and Mrs Rasmussen's big soft stomach. Her mouth can't stop smiling.

'Ah, Rosie,' says Mrs Rasmussen, bending to pick out a stray worm. 'The prices things are these days you'd wonder how the miners can afford to eat at all. Where will it all end?'

'Is Uncle Con the Brake richer than the miners?'

Mrs Rasmussen laughs in her golden-syrupy way. 'No one on the Hill is rich, Rose, and if the strike continues much longer not a single body, not even your Uncle Con, will have the price of a loaf of bread.'

Rose thinks about being rich, and her treasure hidden in Conrad the Sixth's tomb. When Mrs Rasmussen goes into the bedroom to change she looks at the big black purse on the stool by the door. Rose wants to open it. The purse is like a secret cave calling her, but also she doesn't want to go. Then her feet jump down anyway so she has to. Her fingers leave floury marks on the leather and she wipes them with her sleeve. Inside is a little purse with two sixpences, some pennies, three shillings and a florin. She takes a sixpence and a penny, closes the purse, snap! and runs back to her stool. When Mrs Rasmussen comes back Rose is rolling the dough around in the bowl, punching it and slapping, and singing a song about loaves of crusty dusty bread.

Mrs Rasmussen looks at her purse. There is still a floury spot on it. She looks at Rose but she doesn't say anything, or open her purse.

Rose feels hot. She smiles at Mrs Rasmussen and doesn't say anything either. She punches the silly dough hard. Her singing stops.

After a while they hear shouts outside. Through the window they can see two men fighting, rolling on the ground and punching. One has blood on his face. Mrs Rasmussen growls like an angry dog. She picks up the bucket of cold grey water by the back door, stamps out onto the porch and flings an icy sheet over the fighters. The watchers cheer, but not as if they care, and walk away. The two men shake themselves and stare with mean eyes at Mrs Rasmussen, but she stands there on the freezing porch, staring right back, until they walk away, one towards the men's quarters and one up the track towards Burnett's Face.

Mrs Rasmussen slams the door and sits down hard in her rocking chair.

'What are we coming to, Rose?' she says. 'Hatred is an ugly thing.'

'Do you hate those men to throw water on them?'

Mrs Rasmussen laughs. 'No, sweetheart, the hatred is theirs, between Camp and miner. Oh, it's a dangerous thing, Rose, like a spark in dry brush, and at present all Denniston is like dry brush, waiting for the spark to ignite it.'

'How can a fire catch in this misty winter?'

'Rose, Rose, I am talking metaphorically. If that miner from Burnett's Face had badly wounded the new recruit or vice-versa we would have war up here in a few short hours, and many dead or damaged. It is the same old story the world around.'

'I don't know that same old story — you never told me.'

Mrs Rasmussen smiles. 'Come and sit here by the fire. You must learn, little one, the difference between truth and lies, between give and take.' Rose squirms and looks away, but Bella continues. 'That is a lesson for you. But the same old story I talk about is that violence is evil and breeds more violence and ruins good men's lives. Take your Uncle Con the Brake, who was a great and important man in his own country. One day a single word from a friend sent him into a rage. From that sudden rage came one thoughtless blow of his fist that ended the man's life, who was his friend, and ruined his own. My Conrad had to run far away and can never, never go back to his home country, where he should be a hero and leader.'

'Why is his life ruined if he has the best house on the Camp and the best wife too?'

Mrs Rasmussen smiles but her face is sad. She hugs Rose. 'You are too sharp for your own good, my girl. But violence is still wrong. And so is stealing.' Then she adds with a small sigh, 'And I am not sure that Con thinks he has the best wife any more.'

That night Rose's mother puts hot sausage stew on the table, with potatoes and carrots, and a cup of sweet cocoa afterwards. Rose knows it is not her own birthday, and Billy Genesis has not come in for his dinner yet, so it can't be his. Rose asks if it is her mother's birthday.

'You are too sharp for your own good.'

Rose doesn't feel sharp but everyone says it. 'Why are we having a party, then?' she says.

Her mother throws her hands in the air. 'Questions, questions! Today I feel like a party is all. Eat and enjoy while you can.'

Rose eats while she can.

'And be ready to move.'

Rose stops in the middle of a mouthful. Her mother's eyes are fierce and black.

'With no fuss,' she says, 'and no outcry about fancy friends.'

While Rose tries to swallow, her mother adds, 'That madman Billy Genesis will not be coming.'

Her mother beats with a spoon on the table — a dancing rhythm.

'La la diddy la la *la*,' she sings. She tosses her wild hair and stamps her feet. Rose backs away from the table. Her mother has gone mad.

'La la diddy diddy,' sings her mother. 'Oh Rosie, Rosie, we have won the war, just see if we haven't!' She hugs and squeezes Rose. Her hands are hungry and fierce — almost as bad as Billy's.

'I don't want to go *far* away,' whispers Rose. 'Just away from Billy Genesis.'

'Well then, be happy that you have half your wish!' sings her mother. She catches Rose's hands and tries to make her dance too. 'I also will have my wish, Rosie, and you, *you*, my Rose, are my little pot of gold who makes all come true!' She plants a smacking kiss full on Rose's mouth. 'Down down dilly down the Incline, off off and away,' she sings, 'with a sailor by my side, yo ho, with a bonny man by my side.'

Rose can smell fiery drink on her mother's breath.

Questions are buzzing in her head like flies. About school and the Rasmussens and Billy Genesis and the bonny man by her side. When her mother stops singing the questions come out in a rush, like round balls, and her mother picks each question up and throws it back, not caring where it goes.

'Never you mind your pretty head about my bonny man. You will know soon enough . . .

'Billy Genesis knows nothing yet. So trap shut, please. He will kill us both if you blurt one word . . .

'I will fetch you from school at the right moment — tomorrow, the next day, maybe — and you will come quiet as a lamb, you understand?

'How can I know where we will live? On the road, on the sea — one place or another. We will see the wide world, Rosie, where sun shines and a body is free!

'School? You have learned enough of that. Now is time for a new learning . . .'

Rose can feel screaming coming up her throat so she tries to keep talking. She asks if the new bonny man is a violent man, because Mrs Rasmussen says violence is evil.

Her mother slaps the table hard. 'Mrs Rasmussen, that soft bag of dough, has her head in the sand. All men are violent, Con the Brake included, there is no escape from it. But,' she adds after gaining her breath, 'there is good and bad violence and Billy's is the bad sort.'

Suddenly the screams escape. They fill every part of Rose's head. Her arms smash at the plates and the walls and her mother. She flings around the room screaming and wailing.

'Mother of God!' screams her mother. 'The whole Camp will come running!' Her hard arms wrap around Rose and squeeze until no air is left to fill the screams.

When Rose can breathe again she says she doesn't want to live with any new uncle, or with her mother or away in a new place.

Her mother slaps her hard on her ear. 'I said we would have none of that. Be happy. Be grateful your mother makes a new life for you. Now, get off to bed and bolt your new bolt if you know what's good for you.'

Inside her room Rose pulls the bolt across and waits to hear it click. She carries the heavy iron candlestick that Billy Genesis made at the forge over to the little table. The glow makes the room look warm, even though it is freezing cold. Rose likes her own little room now. The bolt has made it safe. For a whole week there have been no visits. By the light of her candle she folds her clothes neatly to be ready for school, then she hops quickly between the cold sheets and beats her feet up and down until the bed warms up. In her head she says the twelve times table, and then the eleven. She sings both verses of Rose of Tralee. She adds up all the money in her treasure box, pounds shillings and pence, thinking of them all in their right columns.

In the end she manages to fall asleep without thinking about leaving school or leaving Denniston and Michael and Brennan and Mrs Rasmussen and everyone.

Suddenly Rose is awake. Something is crashing next door in the kitchen. It sounds like the table being thrown around. Rose pulls her knees up in the bed and hugs them. She keeps her head under the blankets but the sounds still come, thud, thud through the wall. Her mother is screaming. Billy Genesis sounds like a wild animal, swearing and growling. He's in a rage. Something else smashes. Billy howls as if he's been hurt. Rose hears a door bang and her mother's footsteps running away. For a while there is silence. Then more stumbling and crashing. Billy is throwing things at the wall.

Then everything is quiet. Rose thinks Billy might have passed out with the drink.

But then, just as she's drifting into sleep again, something jars her awake. Rose is out of bed and flying in her nightgown across to the trunk under the window. Billy Genesis is crashing against her door.

'Rosie, Rosie!' His voice is thick and blurry. The whole room shakes as he crashes. Rose stands on the trunk, trying to pull open the window. The catch is icy cold and her hand is shaking so hard she can't do it. She feels as small as a white moth beating at the window.

'Rosie! Rosie!' Billy crashes again. The bolt holds. Then nothing happens and Rose thinks she might be safe. She stands on the trunk, shivering. She is not sure what to do. Maybe Billy is waiting under the window.

There is another huge thump and a splintery sound. The whole door, and Billy with it, crash into the room. Rose can't breathe. She presses against the cold wall, trying to be flatter than paper. She can hear him blundering around, swinging his arms.

His hand touches her. It closes tightly around one ankle. Everything in the room turns red and wild. Rose falls on him, scratching and biting, kicking to free herself. She would give all her treasure to be able to reach that paler shadow of the open doorway and run away. Even if it's freezing outside. Even if it's a snow storm. She kicks again and Billy stumbles back. Rose's hand finds the cold iron of the candlestick and she swings it wildly in the dark, back and forth. It hits some part of Billy with a soft thud. Billy grunts in surprise. Rose can't see where he is. She keeps waving the candlestick back and forth but it connects only with black air. Then she hears a sound like the thud of an axe into wood. Billy has fallen and lies still. She stands there in the dark panting and trying not to scream. Cold wind blows in.

The lump that is Billy is snoring — a loud, ugly sound. Rose pulls the blankets off her bed and throws them on top of him so she can't hear the sound.

Then she runs next door into the house. No one is there but the room is full of broken things — the chair, both plates, the coal-box and the shelf. She shuts the door, bolts it and stands by the coal range until she stops shivering. She thinks about going to the log house but Mrs Rasmussen will be asleep. And she will be cross because of the evil of violence. Rose thinks about crawling into the men's quarters, but she doesn't like going there any more. So all night she sits by the coal range, wrapped in a rug, waiting for her mother to come home. Billy's heavy breathing, sawing through the wall, never stops.

Her mother doesn't come home.

As soon as it's light, Rose, holding the rug tightly around her, tiptoes to the door, unbolts it and pokes her head around the empty hole that used to be her door. Billy is still under the pile of bedclothes. His snores sound strange. They catch sometimes, then start up again with loud snort. She needs her school clothes but they are under the bedclothes too.

Rose creeps her hand under the sheet. She makes a little noise and pulls her hand back when it touches his cold body. Her hand has blood on it. Inch by inch she pulls the blanket back from his head. Rose jumps because his eyes are half open, but they're not seeing anything. A beetle is crawling on his chin. His horrible hair is dark and sticky with blood.

Rose looks at him. The beetle starts crawling down his neck.

Quickly she feels for her clothes. There is not much blood on them. She runs back to the kitchen, which is now grey with morning light, and dresses by the dying fire. Her mother is still not home.

Rose knows what to do. She runs past the log house and up the path to town. Patches of snow sit like hats on all the rocks. Her breath steams. There is no wind this morning, and the mist has gone. She is excited. This is an adventure! Mrs Hanratty waves from the water-heating fire outside. She doesn't knock on Hanrattys' door but goes straight in and up to Michael's room. Brennan is there too, which is surprising. Rose thought they were enemies now.

She tells the boys to get dressed quickly because they are needed to stop a war.

'But I haven't had breakfast yet,' says Brennan.

Michael is grinning and quickly pulls on his vest.

'It's a secret,' says Rose. She's still puffing from the running. 'I need your help or else Violence will spread like fire over Denniston!'

Brennan says, 'Can we still have breakfast after?'

'After we've fixed the Violence,' says Rose.

Mrs Hanratty calls to them as they run out but Rose says they will be back in a minute for breakfast.

Even Michael is quiet when Rose pulls the blanket away from Billy's snoring head.

Brennan moans. He edges back from the doorway. 'Have you killed him, Rose?' he whispers.

'Not quite.'

'Well, you are the violent one, Rose,' says Brennan.

Rose shouts at him. '*I am not!* Billy was violent first!'

Michael stares at Billy's head. Slowly he bends down and pokes at one half-open eye and then the other. Billy goes on snoring.

Brennan puts out his hand slowly and shakes the man's shoulder, gently, as if he is asking for attention. Billy's head rolls a little. Brennan screams and holds his hand as if it is burnt. Michael shakes Billy's other shoulder, much more roughly. The head rolls back and forth. Rose laughs — little hiccuppy yelps. Michael grins and kicks the head as it rolls, just tipping it with his toe.

Billy snorts — a long rattling sound. The children all jump back. Then the snoring stops altogether.

They watch him.

'He's dead,' says Brennan. He is trying not to cry.

Michael pushes him again with his boot, but Billy doesn't snore.

'You killed him, Rose,' says Michael.

'I did not it! It was you!' cries Rose, 'You kicked him!'

Brennan is crying hard now. 'We'll all go to hell now,' he sobs, 'and burn in the eternal fires.'

'No we won't,' says Michael. 'Not for one tip with my toe like that.' His eyes are bright and hard. 'But Rose will be punished,' he says. 'She'll probably go to prison.'

Rose wants to hit Michael but she needs him for her plan. 'We need to hide Billy,' she says, 'so war won't break out.'

They all think about this.

'No one would go to war over Billy Genesis,' says Michael, but none of them is sure.

They look at Billy. He's very big. His face is blue.

Rose keeps watch outside and the boys pull Billy by his legs. He bumps over the crashed door. No one's coming. They pull him around the side of the house, over the snowy ground, to the edge of the Camp. Then they roll him over the ledge. He rolls twice and stops against a tree. Michael says, 'Damn!' like a man and climbs down. Rose and Brennan watch while he holds onto a branch and kicks at Billy, but the body is stuck.

'Break off a branch to hide him,' says Brennan quietly.

Michael does that, and puts the branch over Billy. Now you can hardly see him.

The hardest part is propping the door up so it looks shut. Rose has spread her rug over the bloodstain on the floor.

Then they all go back to Hanrattys' for breakfast.

'I don't know what's got into you three,' says Mrs Hanratty, ladling porridge. 'You're like skittery rabbits!'

That only makes them giggle more.

DURING the morning break that day the pupils of Denniston School were throwing snowballs in the playground when Rose's mother came to the fence and called Rose. Rose shook her head and dodged behind the dunny.

'Come! Come quick!' shouted Eva as if she were calling a dog. She dropped her bag in the snow and charged into the playground. The pupils gathered together and stared as Eva dragged a screaming Rose out onto the road. Michael and Brennan wanted to call Mr Stringer but they were too frightened. Was Rose going off to prison already?

'No! I don't want to!' screamed Rose, wriggling and kicking, but her mother's grip was iron hard and the child was dragged, leaving long raking ruts in the snow, down the street and out of sight, heading towards the Track.

Eva Storm

NO ONE KNEW. Ha! Not one soul up there on the Hill had a single idea what went on under their so-pinched noses. Con the Brake was some kind of mascot to them — popular, larger than life. They loved to hear this wise man talk; he coloured their own dull lives. Which Con enjoyed — don't we all? — and played up to. Do you see? So they make a small saint out of the man and are blind to any other side.

The other side is the wanderer, the adventurer, as I have said already. In the end change and excitement and things forbidden will rule a man like Con, over love or contentment and those settled dull virtues. On the Hill they saw a man loving his Bella and his work and his friends. True; he did. But they never noticed the man who was drawn to the stirring of unwed flesh on a dark night — my flesh; who needed, like a drug, to taste all the flavours of this world, and to smell darker scents along with the light.

So. My story is ending. This story at least, for my life is full of chapters.

'Con,' I say to him one dark night under bright stars, 'now is the time for moving. We two and your daughter.'

'I love my Bella,' says Con, all the time panting and roaring at me in the cold air. Oh, there's nothing better than a hot man on a frosty night! 'And why should I move when you are here also?'

'Rose . . .'

'Rose is better off here, Angel.'

'Not with that sinner Billy Genesis prowling.'

'But I have fixed the door, woman.'

'If I leave, with Rose, you will follow, no?'

Then that lovely man would laugh and shake his head and go at me again to make me forget all. But the great ship of Con's life was unfurling sails, the signs were there. The horizon glinted in his eye again. He would come; he would come.

The matter of Billy Genesis. Who knows the full story? Roaring drunk that night he was. Me, I was perhaps also under the drink, and more than ready to provoke a fight. Bring matters to a head, no? I hoped for Con to kill him in a rage, and so make a reason to leave the Hill. Ah well, not so smart a plan. I tell you, that night was all muddy water and no good sense to it.

I know this: we fought. Some taunt he made provoked me. Before I know it I am telling Billy that Con the Brake is my true lover. That we plan to leave. Not wise, yes? But who can make a sensible speech when a bad man is raging? So. Billy shouted half the Bible and destroyed half the kitchen, but directed his anger at me rather than Con. Well, the stupid man was too drunk to know hand from foot, let alone man from woman. At one stage the iron poker was in my hand and I swung it. I fancy it connected with some part of Billy. My memory is not so clear.

In any case I woke with a black eye and a sore head in the bed of a new recruit over at the men's quarters. Bruises dark as prune juice all down one arm. My mood just as black, to think what further damage Billy Genesis may have done. To house and to my plans both. Out I stamp over fresh snow to inspect. Oh, my friends, imagine the shock to see Rose's door smashed off its hinge and inside Billy Genesis heaped on the floor, near death in a pool of blood. No sign of Rose.

So. I remember the poker and the smash of it into some part of Billy. The sound of the fight must have been heard all over the Camp. They will come for my blood, I know it. Here is their excuse to get rid of me into some distant prison unless some new story can be arranged. I leave Billy lying there, snorting like a sick horse, pack some few things in my bag and go looking for Con.

After such a night, not to mention the shock of Billy lying there, a certain exhaustion would be understandable, no? A lowering of morale? I tell you, for me that day it was the opposite. My blood sang: I could feel the spirit rising up like a lark, and a smile shine through all the bruises. Who can understand these things? That day fortune was on my side, every minute. Not one step faltered from the line my fortune drew.

My luck began at once. The Incline was running and Con the Brake was on first shift. Eva, I said to myself, a good sign yes, but this must be done quiet as a cat. The morning was bright with snow and my coat black, so care was needed. For some time I hid behind a rusty wagon, waiting till the hook-man turned away. Then like a dark shadow I slipped into Con's little shed and pressed close to the wall. Above me drums and cables moaning and grinding.

Con starts and looks around to see who might be watching. No one has noticed. He frowns and goes to speak but I lay a finger on his lips. To build his excitement I drive the tip of my tongue into his ear, in out, in out. Then, quickly to the point, I whisper into the same juicy ear.

'Billy Genesis is murdered.'

Con grunts but keeps his eye on the cables and hands on the wheels.

'Rose has killed the man. Billy lies in a bloody mess inside her room.'

'What?' For a moment Con lets go his handles and turns a raging face towards me. The cables whine as they pick up speed.

'Con!' I shout, for all will be lost if we are discovered. He calls down all manner of curses as he fights to bring his wagons back under control. Our luck holds: the hook-man is too busy to notice the rushing wagon. When he turns back it is well behaved again and out of sight over the edge.

'Listen,' say I, 'I will take Rose away now, this day, and we will wait for you in Westport.' I give him the name of a place I know. 'If you haven't joined us in four days I will lose hope and take her to the police.'

'You wouldn't,' growls Con. 'Your own daughter.'

'And yours. You will come. You will, Con. I feel it.'

Yes, my friends, I knew it. Knew the moment was right. These days not much work on the Hill. Incline closed six days in seven. Slow times are no good for the adventuring spirit. That big man needed only the excuse. Before he could raise questions or threats I had slipped out again and around the back. Oh, my feet wanted to dance! But first to find Rose.

He came. Oh, he came all right. Would I tell a story with a sad ending? I tell you this: gladly would I live again every minute of the worst times of all my life just to lie one more month in that man's arms. The dark house of my life — too many bad times to remember or count — now contains one beautiful window that looks out on a glory. Over and over I can remember that glory. What a gift, my friends! One month we had together, before he moved on. A month as sweet and full of good living as any woman could wish. Those four weeks passed as if inside the red throat of a fiery volcano: fierce, wild, every minute beautiful and dangerous as fire.

Then the salt sea won the battle for his love and I lost him.

A Bloody Victory

EVEN EDDIE CARMICHAEL didn't know the strike was over until Tommy Jowett and the Rees family and a whole bunch of old Burnett's Face miners came back up the Track with their ponies and belongings, cheering and carrying on as if it were Christmas. Eddie stood on the steps outside his office, stamping and grinning as Tommy shouted the news up to him. The miners had won! The Company had given way on all points and hired them back on full hewing rates!

'You got your holidays, then?' shouted Eddie, surprised at the capitulation.

'Aye. We got the lot!'

'No more unskilled miners, then?'

'You've said it, friend. Proper pay for proper miners. Here we are, come to claim our homes back.'

'Well, wouldn't you know I'd be the last to hear.' But Eddie was pleased, you could tell. All he wanted was to run a good clean mine, and fill the orders, which was far from the case at present.

'Josiah will fill you in,' said Tommy. 'He's on his way up with the missus.' The men all laughed, but with some pride, vying with each other to tell the story.

'Mrs Scobie could go on the stage, the story she told . . .'

'Aye, she had them howling into their handkerchiefs, eh, Tommy?'

'Children starving, women scraping moss off stones . . .'

'Then Josiah would weigh in about us never giving in while there was breath in our bodies . . .'

'Which wouldn't be long, according to Mrs Scobie.'

'And the rest of us knowing secretly we'd go back tomorrow . . .'

'We never would!'

'I heard you say just yesterday!'

'Aye, well, that was yesterday. Today we've won.'

'Thanks to the Scobies.'

'God bless them both.'

Josiah and Mary Scobie, toiling up the Track, stopping every ten minutes for Mary to catch her breath, were the toast of Burnett's Face, and of Denniston town, though those at the Camp, knowing their jobs were under threat now, were less welcoming.

'Well done, Josiah!' says Eddie when the beaming man finally comes up onto the plateau. 'You know I was on your side in my heart.'

Josiah laughs. 'Oho! Our side, is it? This is only the beginning, Eddie. We'll be face to face over the bargaining table soon enough.'

Eddie groans in mock horror, then sobers up to add a warning.

'I don't want trouble, now, Josiah. Will you watch your men with the new recruits? It's not their fault they weren't born with coal dust in their veins. Give them decent time to pack up and leave.'

Josiah nods. Mary, beside him, her face blotched scarlet from the climb, also glows with a gentler warmth.

'Go on up,' she says to her husband. ' You deal with the men. I must talk with Totty.'

'There is a prayer meeting called.'

'Say one for me, then. I can go not one step further.'

But she plants her feet steadily enough in the direction of Hanrattys'. Josiah nods to see her go. He knows what the talk will be about.

Totty pours tea in the front parlour. At first the chat is general.

'Well, and how is the outside world, then?' asks Totty. She has still not managed the trip.

'Overrated,' says Mary, kneading her aching knees. 'That gaggle of geese that call themselves society in Westport are soft as pillows. We could eat them for breakfast. And did.'

'Watch your words!' laughs Totty. 'That is my family you're talking about!'

'Well, you are worth a trainful of them, my dear.' Mary closes her eyes and groans. She will not be making that journey again in a hurry. And when she does it will be for a larger pond than Westport. Politics has entered her blood.

Totty waits until a more normal colour returns to the older woman's cheeks before she opens the topic both of them are waiting for.

'Tell me about the churchyard,' she says.

Meanwhile Josiah tramps on up to Burnett's Face. It is time for the thanksgiving.

THAT prayer meeting was where common sense and the law of the land finally gave up the ghost. After all those months of control and

339

discipline, of sticking doggedly to peaceful negotiation, it all blew up over a prayer.

Josiah was standing there, at the front of the little chapel, head bowed, and all the miners with him.

'Oh Lord,' he cried, his voice ringing like bells, 'we thank Thee, that Thou hast blest our endeavours, and brought us safely back to our homes and our families. We thank Thee that Thou hast seen fit to grant us all that we have sought, that we may now work with dignity and safety in our chosen workplace, knowing that our fellow workers are skilled to do Thy work, the hewing of coal, to bring warmth and light and power to all mankind. We thank Thee also . . .'

When a voice from the back of the chapel, no one knows who, interrupted. Two or three of Eddie's recruits must have been standing at the door listening.

'Stuck-up English bloody black-faces!' this fellow shouted.

Sixty heads snapped up out of their prayers.

'Chapel-creepers! Chatting to God like He was in your pocket! We can hew as good as you any day of the week!'

The fellow must have been drunk.

That is the end of prayers. With one mighty shout Josiah and his men roar out of the Chapel, caring not at all who they might be trampling as they go. It is like floodgates opening. House by house they sweep through Burnett's Face, herding the usurping recruits before them. No one is given time to pack, women and children are bundled away from their washing or cooking or playing and deposited outside in the needle-sharp air to fend for themselves.

They rage through Coalbrookdale mine, wrenching men from the coalface, loading them onto skips and running them off the job. The pit ponies, ears pinned back and eyes rolling at the din, refuse to pull their human loads so the miners shunt the skips themselves, a fierce relief lending weight to their shoulders. Out in the open the recruits are tipped to the ground, then driven down the skipway by the storming miners as if they were sheep.

Denniston people run to doors to see what is up. When they see the approaching boil of miners they run back inside and bolt themselves in until it is over. Michael and Brennan, wide-eyed, hang out of the upstairs window at Hanrattys'. This is war all right, just like Rose said. Downstairs Mary Scobie's outraged orders, shouted from the doorway, never reach her husband's ears. He is as lost to it as all the rest.

At the Camp, tables are turned briefly as the second shift of recruits emerge from the men's quarters to support their friends. The rout becomes a battle involving rocks and railway iron, anything that comes to hand. Bella Rasmussen tries a bucket of water but quickly realises there are far too many hot tempers for one woman to cool. She watches anxiously from the window to see if Con will join in.

Con is fighting a battle of his own at the Brake Head. Two frantic recruits, boys hardly out of childhood and desperate to escape the madness, are trying to leap aboard the loaded wagon that is about to descend.

'Stand back! Stand back, man!' roars Con, feeling the pressure of the pistons building and ready to slip the brake. The hook-man grabs both boys by their coat-tails and hauls them bodily off the wagon. He gives Con the nod and the wagon starts on down.

'Jesus Maria!' shouts Con as the boys run after it. One, then the other jumps at the moving wagon. For a moment, incredibly, both seem safe; then there is a boom like a cannon exploding. The steel cable, four inches thick, flies into the air as if it is thistledown. The boys, God rest their souls, must have dislodged the hook or broken the connecting flange. There is nothing now to stop seven tons of coal hurtling down, free of all control, until it derails or smashes over the edge at Middle Brake.

'Jump! In God's name, jump!' yells Con, but the boys, well past hearing anything, are clinging desperately to the instrument of their death. The wheels scream as they gather speed. All Con or the hook-man can do is to signal below and wait for the smash.

At the Camp the battle is dying. When Con charges down with his dreadful news he finds another death, again a young one, whose head has caved in under someone's wild swipe. Five or six others are on the ground bleeding or nursing broken bones.

Con's rage is worse than a southerly storm. 'You call yourself a Christian!' he shouts, grabbing a fistful of Josiah's coat. 'Look, man, look! You are fighting babies!' His mighty shove knocks Josiah clear off his feet. Both sides back away, wary of this dangerous giant.

'Ah Jesus, look at him.' Con kneels, moaning himself, beside a gangly lad whose arm is at a frightful angle and who is howling for his mother.

The miners stand, sheepish now, as an old fellow, grizzled hair and beard obscuring his expression, gathers up the dead lad, slings him over his shoulder like a saddle and walks away without a word. Another, a weather-beaten bushman by the look of him, stained old hat jammed on his head, blue eyes blazing, faces Josiah and the miners.

'You are welcome to your lousy jobs in your stinking mines. We are not so desperate for money that we will sell our souls to coal one more blighted day.'

The battered recruits growl in agreement.

The bushman raises a bleeding hand as if it were a badge. 'But you might perhaps do us the courtesy, *sirs*, to allow us to patch up our young lads here and gather our swags. If that's not too much to ask?'

Con and the bushman lead the howling boy away without waiting for an answer.

All that day the recruits and their families, their ponies and belongings straggled across the Camp, heading downhill. Con walked down the Track with the first batch and stationed himself at the bottom, a human gate, to hold back returning miners.

'Well then, pray a little while you wait,' he growled at the impatient miners. 'For the souls of three innocent departed lads, you know? And for the sins of your mates up top. You walk up the Track now — maybe you feel tempted to throw some pregnant woman down the gully, eh? Or a child and her doll in her arms, maybe? Over the edge so she make room for real miners, you know? You start one foot up, I knock that foot off its leg. By God, this is a sorry day for the Hill, and I, Con the Brake, will damn well see it gets no sorrier!' Oh, Con was a dark and stormy man that day, not a flicker of smile or lightness, a fact that drew some comment in the days to follow.

The miners, expecting joyous welcome, the brass band maybe, fretted and stamped at the foot of the Track, but none would pass Con the Brake in this mood. Towards evening, when they finally headed into Denniston, a couple of lads — Jock Galloway's boys — reported seeing a dead body caught against a branch just below the Camp.

Billy Genesis.

At first it was assumed that Billy Genesis was another victim of the rout. It was certainly in character for Billy to join in any fight. Then two nights later Lord Percy strode into the smoky fug of Minifie's bar shouting murder and foul deeds. He had been clearing out his friend's house and found the smashed door and the blood-stained floorboards. Anyone could see, he screamed, that Billy Genesis was not the unlucky victim of a random hot-tempered clout, but of a vile, pre-meditated murder in his own home. He omitted to declare that the bloodstain was in Rose's room.

A piece of gossip like this was just the antidote for Denniston's collective guilt over the rout. The deaths of the three boys had been officially recorded in Eddie's register as *Death by riding a runaway wagon* and *Accidental Death following a fall.* The fall was fudging it, Eddie knew, but surely everyone wanted to put the strike and the driving away of the recruits behind them now and get on with earning a living and making a profit?

The murder of Billy Genesis, though, could be investigated with relish. Cold-blooded murder: that was serious. If there was a murderer on the Hill he must be unmasked. Rose's disappearance and that of her mother were noted. Con swore they never came past at the bottom of the Track. Perhaps two other bodies were concealed in the bush below the Camp? A search of the bush revealed nothing but old rubbish, drifts of coal, rusting railway iron.

Michael Hanratty and Brennan Scobie had nothing to report about Rose's absence.

Henry Stringer the teacher was suspected. Remember the fight in the bar? He wouldn't stand a chance in a fair fight with Billy, true, but what if Billy were drunk? Or perhaps Con the Brake had lost his temper again. Con could easily have done it. That man didn't know his own strength. Theories ran wild in pubs and parlours. Con's unusual behaviour was noted — surly and bad-tempered. Opinion hardened in favour of Con as murderer. These last two days his arguments carried a razor-sharp edge that quickly deterred any opponent. Several people reported hearing bitter argument coming from the log house: not at all the usual genial word battles that all the Camp relished and repeated. The police were not called in. Denniston dealt with its own crime.

Four days after Billy's body was discovered, Camp people heard a final brawl at the log house. Bella wailed and screamed. Con, uncharacteristically muted, grumbled and swore. Next morning Con the Brake, Big Snow, Conrad Rasmussen, his head hanging low and a swag on his shoulder, disappeared down the Track. Not one word of goodbye to another soul.

Bella smoothed her apron with shaking hands, held her head high. The show of dignity could not hide her distraction. 'My husband has gone to find Rose of Tralee,' she announced. But to many, his disappearance was a clear sign of guilt.

The Bite of
Conscience

HENRY STRINGER CALLED the meeting. He sent notes to the
Hanrattys and Scobies:

> *An urgent matter has come to my attention which*
> *should be discussed in private. Could we meet at*
> *Hanrattys', Saturday afternoon next at four p.m.? Michael*
> *and Brennan should attend, but no other children, please.*
> *I have also asked Mrs C. Rasmussen to be present.*
> *It concerns Rose of Tralee.*
> *Yrs faithfully*
> *Henry Stringer, Schoolmaster*

'What's all this then?' says Mary Scobie, brisk and ready to take
charge. 'My Brennan has been drooping around the house like wet

flannel all week but I can't get a word out of him. Are the boys in trouble again?'

Bella Rasmussen eyes the others. Since news of Con's disappearance has spread, people avoid her. The empty space left by Con is never mentioned. She smoothes her purple tussore, aware that she has overdressed for the occasion. Tom Hanratty clears his throat, frowns at Michael, fiddles with his pocket watch.

The two boys are wound like springs and not speaking to each other. Michael fidgets on his chair in Hanrattys' dark front parlour. He glowers at Brennan. Brennan looks away, trying not to cry.

'Henry,' says Totty, 'you had better spit it out quickly. With all this secrecy you can see what a state we are in.'

Henry Stringer unfolds his insect legs and stands up, running bony fingers through hair freshly cut this morning by the new barber in Dickson Street. He is nervous in the company of these five, who, in one way or another, form the backbone of Denniston. He can't stand still in their presence. His chaotic feet crash into the polished brass fender; his attempt to steady the swinging fire-irons only makes matters worse.

'Now, now, lad,' says Josiah, 'we know the rumours buzzing round. About you and about . . .' He looks quickly at the silent Bella, '. . . about Con. But no one here holds truck with that nonsense. We won't bite you.' He strides to the fireplace, takes the teacher by his shoulders and holds him still as if he were straightening a picture on the wall.

'Now, sir,' says Josiah, 'you are the head teacher at Denniston, and we respect you for the care and attention you give our lads, so if something is amiss, spit it out and we will sort out the matter. This is our half-day and spare time is precious.'

Henry's shoulders receive a final encouraging slap to keep them in place, and Josiah returns to stand behind his wife.

Henry nods several times. 'Yes, yes, yes, quite, sir, quite. Well. Now.'

Michael giggles.

'The boys have some-something to tell you,' says Henry, stuttering and spitting in his eagerness to get things right, 'which they need to get off their chests, and which Brennan told me in confidence and from a troubled conscience. But look here, sirs . . . and ladies,' Henry blushes scarlet and begins to pace again, 'before we judge the boys too harshly, I suggest we examine our own part in the tragedy . . .'

'For pity's sake, Henry!' cries Mary Scobie. 'We have no idea what the tragedy is, let alone our part in it. Brennan!' This is an order. 'Stand up and speak!'

'*We* killed Billy Genesis,' says Brennan in a low voice. He sits still on the big chair, feet dangling, tears running silently down.

'We did not!' Michael is on his feet, fists balled, ready to fight the whole roomful. 'He was dead already!'

'He was alive!' howls Brennan.

'Dead!' shouts Michael at the silent adults, 'Almost. And it wasn't Rose's fault either. We were trying to stop the war!'

Henry Stringer goes to Brennan, leads him to the fire, stands behind the weeping boy, hands on his shoulders. 'Just tell the story, Brennan. It's all right. Tell the story.'

And Brennan tells it, his voice so low they have to lean forward to hear. Michael stays on his feet, twice interrupting, still defiant. The boys' story is one of simple aggression — a bullying man, a helpless girl repeatedly attacked in her own room. A lucky blow with a candlestick. Only too well can the adults fill in details that the boys' inexperience and Rose's reticence have not revealed. When the story is finished, the room is silent. There is much to think about.

'Will we go to prison?' asks Brennan at last.

'It's not fair!' shouts Michael, close to tears now himself. 'Why didn't a grown-up kill him?'

Tom clears his throat. His voice, when it finally comes through, is rough with love. 'Well now, Michael, killing, that is not right — killing is no answer. But I tell you clear, son: not you, nor Brennan, nor our Rose of Tralee has done murder. Self-defence, or accident maybe, who knows? And no one will lay a finger of blame on any one of you. No one.' He blows his nose; looks fiercely around the room.

Suddenly Bella Rasmussen lets out a wail. 'Ah, sweet Jesus, we all knew! Blame! Here it lies, right here in this barren breast!' She beats on the purple tussore until her corsets twang. 'We all knew about that vile man, yet she had to seek help from two six-year-old lads!'

Michael swells a little at this, looks his father in the eye, man to man, but Tom Hanratty purses his lips, playing the serious citizen. 'Well, as to that,' he says, smoothing his beard, 'Surely the mother should have done something. That is where responsibility lies . . . ultimately.'

'Oh Tom,' says Totty. 'Rose's mother . . .' Her voice trails away.

There is nothing any of them can think to say. Even the boys are silent. The room darkens as a spatter of hail sweeps down the street, rattling windows. They listen as the hail, moving north, clangs over the Bins and dies away.

Henry Stringer looks from face to face. He expects decisions. Mary Scobie sighs, shifts in her chair, sighs again, then takes charge.

'Well then. It is clear some form of this story must be broadcast. Con the Brake's name must be cleared. We cannot have malicious rumour running wild. So: an accident. The drunken man attacked Rose. Fell, hitting his head. Died. Rose told the boys, the boys told us. The mother moved away, taking Rose. That is the story. And when you think about it, that is the truth.'

The adults nod gravely.

Tom Hanratty pulls at his beard. 'A well-deserved accident,' he says. 'Billy Genesis was a shame to Denniston, and no loss to the world at large.'

They nod again. Henry runs fingers through his hair. He is not happy. His head wags back and forth like a puppet as he searches for words.

But it is Brennan who finds them first. 'No it's not!' he cries out, 'It's not!'

Michael understands. 'Not all the story!' he says. 'What about Rose?'

'Rose!' shouts Brennan, fired up now, made bold since the threat of prison has passed. 'Rose!'

The two boys face the surprised adults like a pair of puppies suddenly turned nasty.

'Rose's mother made her leave!'

'She wanted to stay with us!'

'She wanted to stay!'

'It's not fair!'

'Rose was afraid!'

'You have to find her!'

Finally their teacher, half boy, half man, weighs in on the children's side. Stumbling against the furniture as he paces, pulling words from the air with bony fingers, showering his elders with sprays of spit, he delivers his oration.

'Surely! Surely we all are responsible. We took Rose into our homes. We . . . I . . . we all, didn't we? Hardly a household where she hadn't eaten. Taken shelter. How many times have I heard it — heard people say — Michael and Brennan and *Rose* — first three children of Denniston? She belongs here. Here! She is Rose of *Denniston*, not of some mythical Tralee.'

The boys cheer their Mr Stringer, though the parents seem less impressed. Henry charges on through the furniture.

'We cannot give Rose hope and then take it away! A good pupil. The best. Sorry boys, but you must face it: Rose, on a good day, can outclass you both. What will happen to her down there? We know; we can guess! A sorry end, a slow drift to hell. Who can support that poor lost mother down there? Who? For that matter, who supported her up here? No, no, she must be found, returned to Denniston. Surely you all can see this?'

Henry Stringer stops abruptly in the centre of the ring of chairs, turns slowly on his heel, hands spread in appeal. The boys hardly dare to breathe. The others sigh, shift a little, look into the fire.

Totty rises to refill cups of tea. 'What I *can* do,' she says slowly, 'Is write to my father . . . see if we can trace her . . . them both.'

Bella nods. 'I have contacts too,' she smiles, 'in a rather different walk of life. I also will write.'

'It is agreed, then,' booms Mary Scobie, as if wrapping up an unruly meeting, 'that we will try to keep contact with the child, remind her that she has friends — a gift parcel from time to time . . .'

'That's no good!' shouts Brennan at his mother, and would have struck her if Josiah had not taken his arm quickly, pulled him to the back of the room.

'Brennan!' says Josiah. 'Where are your manners, lad? Enough! Rose cannot be taken from the mother . . .'

'Why not?'

'. . . nor the mother from the child, nor the mother from the man she chooses to live with.'

'Why *not*? Rose doesn't want her mother!'

Mary Scobie rises. 'It is time we went. Thank you, Totty, thank you, Tom. The boys are understandably upset. But we will pursue the matter. Brennan, fetch your boots.'

Bella is slower to leave, less sure of answers. She walks down to the Camp, where the population is back to thirty again and life is quieter. Already the sky, the rocks, the buildings are merging in different shades of shadow. Halfway down the path she stops to look below to the outline of their sprawling log house. Behind it Conrad the Sixth's tomb stands square, the rock surfaces gleaming faintly in the last of the light. Bella's tears flow.

'Ah Con, Con, you foolish man,' she whispers, but her heavy heart aches even more for Rose, whom they have all abandoned.

A fist of wind sends her on her way again. At her back the Incline and the railway yards have been shut down since noon; the only sound a sheet of loose iron rattling on its nails with each gust. Her dark shadow enters the log house. But tonight there is a little purpose to her slow movements as she bends to unlace her own boots. Inside, she lights one lamp, fetches paper and begins to write.

The Search

'Glenmorgan'
Westport.
July 20th 1885
Dearest Dorothy,

Well, at last I have some news for you about the child, poor wee mite, though it is perhaps news you would rather not hear.

Mrs Thomas Throne, perhaps you remember her, President of our Society of Charitable Ladies, has been doing Good Work among the Fallen Women and has heard of a child called Rose whose mother, it seems, is living a Questionable Life down in the wharf area. There are a great many labourers come to help build the new wharf and break-water and I fear they have brought an *unsavoury entourage with them. Just yesterday five men were found drinking on the job and were summarily dismissed. Your father was most upset about it. Shantyism and sly-grogging are aspects of life we thought Westport had left behind.*

The child has excited some attention as she is evidently a clever soul, and the men like to bet on her ability to add up figures or some such story. It all sounds Most Unsuitable to me; the child is merely a side-show, a performing monkey, put to work, perhaps by her mother, who can tell? Mrs Throne has tried to remove her to our Home for Destitute Children, but somehow she or her mother have eluded us.

For the last week there have been no sightings. Mrs Throne's informant reports that a thick-set labourer was down at the wharf asking after the mother and child. We believe all three may have moved on south. Hokitika, of course, is where such people usually end up.

Our Society will continue to inquire, my dear, and already I have sent the details to our Hokitika Branch, a very Active Group, and much needed, alas.

Oh Dorothy, I cannot tell you how thrilled I am that you are planning a Visit in the Summer, with the little ones and your husband! The news has quite perked me up and I have not had to take my drops for a whole week. I am planning a Musical Evening in your honour and a special Children's Garden Party for the children! Let us pray for fine weather, though what is the use, rain is bound to win out. Contingency plans will be laid, never fear.

Well, dear, I will write if further news about Rose is

to hand. What a poor wee battler! Love to Michael, Elizabeth and Nelson, and my warm regards to your husband.

> *Your affectionate and smiling*
> *Mother*

Education Department Inspectorate,
Nelson District
Dear Mrs Scobie,
Our Department does not keep records of all those enrolled in schools within our area. I advise you to apply directly to schools for information about pupils. Enclosed is a list of schools in the West Coast area, and their addresses.

I do indeed remember the child, Rose, who sang at your school concert, and was, if I recall rightly, unusually precocious with figures.

> *Yours sincerely,*
> *C. Sinclair*
> *District Inspector of Schools*

Hope Primary School:
> *Dear Mrs Scobie,*
> *There is no Rose enrolled at our school.*

Greymouth District Primary School:
> *Dear Mrs Scobie,*
> *We have a Rose Perlham, 10 years old, whose father is a railway worker. No other Rose, but I will make inquiries in the area. Good luck in your search.*

St Theresa's Primary School, Greymouth:

Dear Mrs Scobie,

We do not divulge, without clear reason, the names of our pupils. However I can tell you that we have no Roses.

Kumara Primary School:

Dear Mrs Scobie,

I wish, indeed, that a Rose or any other child had enrolled here recently. Our roll is one short and we are in fear of closure. Try Hokitika Primary. Their roll changes like the tide.

Blackball Primary School:

Dear Mrs Scobie,

We have a Rose Blatt whom I would hand over with pleasure. She has five siblings who are all equally troublesome. Come, please, and collect the whole Blatt tribe!

Hokitika Primary School:

Dear Mrs Scobie,

Rose of Tralee is surely a pseudonym. Perhaps she is travelling under another name? Another song perhaps? In other words, madam, you are searching blind, for a needle in a haystack. I cannot assist.

'The Paladium'
Gibsons Quay
Hokitika
Dear Bella,
Well, what a turn-up! The girls and I all thought you was long gone to Australia or worse, the dogs more like,

ha ha! And here you are up the coast and a respectable woman, to boot. Good on you, Bella, we all wish you the best, though Denniston sounds like a right old dump. I've had diggers down here has been mining on Denniston, couldn't stand more than a day of the foul weather they said. Well anyway, a good man is worth a storm or two I dare say!

Florrie says to tell you she has lost ten pounds weight and can now fit the beaded dress you left her, and Liz wants you to know that her little Annie you were so fond of is now dancing with us! How times fly. My ankles are not what they were, sad to say, don't talk about weight with me! So I am mainly on the business side these days and doing nicely, thank you, though I suppose we must accept that the good old days are well and truly gone. Such is life!

Now. Your Rose. We have kept a sharp eye out with no success until yesterday when Florrie comes in with a story of a pretty little girl, fits your description, singing down on Gibsons Quay. No mother in sight, says Flo, but this tot was sharp enough herself at taking around the hat after. Then slipped away into the crowd, like a silverfish in a box of handkerchiefs, before Flo could get to her.

Anyway I had a bit of business down that way today, don't ask what sort, ha ha! So I keep a weather eye open and there she is, voice like an angel, singing 'Mountains of Home', just like you did, Bell. I knew right away she was your one.

Well, I nosed around a bit without putting the wind up child or mother. I have my connections in all sections of society, as you well know, my dear! Any road, they are

357

new in town, living rough down by the wharves among the shanties. Some giant of a feller the mother's living with is working the boats and she likewise but in cabins rather than holds if you get my drift. Slag end of the market. Florrie says the feller looks the spit of Big Snow, remember that one was keen on you back in the old days and died off Gibsons Quay? The child runs wild so they say, no schooling, and very wary of human company. No one can get near to her.

Well, Bella, Mrs C. Rasmussen I should say, that's the long and short of it. I advise against making contact with the child, it will only end in grief, but if you must, send me a letter and I'll try to put it in her hand, or the mother's, though be quick about it, my guess is they are drifters. At any rate the authorities won't let them stay long, we are becoming a respectable town now, so they say, though in my experience the respectable ones like a bit of spice just as much as the drifters and diggers. And can pay better, to boot!

All the best, my dear. I hope you have not become so respectable that you have forgotten how to sing and 'show yer ankle'. You were always top of the bill!

All the girls send hugs and kisses.

Your friend ever,

Ida

The Log House
The Camp,
Denniston
Dear Ida,
How I long to write a good gossipy letter, but this is in

haste to catch the coal-train out. Ida, Ida, please run and put the enclosed note into the hand of the man on the wharf you say looks like Big Snow. Oh, if only I could get down from here I would do it myself. Ida, if you love me at all, pick up your skirts and run with my note this very minute. I will explain later.

Thank you, my dear.

In haste,

Bella Rasmussen [Mrs]

Bella's note:

My dear Conrad,

You are a good man at heart, I know it, but that wicked, guileful woman has trapped you. Leave her and bring Rose back, I beg you. It is the right thing. We will care for her together. Con, Con, think of the child, think of me, your wife, and come back. We can mend what has been broken. My harsh and bitter words were spoken out of a jealousy which is now spent. Come back.

Your loving wife,

Bella Rasmussen

'The Palladium'

Gibsons Quay

Hokitika

Dear Bella,

Oh, what a mess, I knew grief would come of it — your letter has come too late.

They are gone, Bella, vanished, just like I said they would. Mr Cream, you remember him, Bella, one of yours, says he thinks the feller got a job on the S.S. Star of the

South, *bound for Dunedin, then Australia. No sign of mother or your Rose, they could be anywhere. I have sent word to Lizzie, she is in Dunedin now, in case they are headed that way, but it is a long shot.*

You cannot change what is meant, Bella. I see it in my girls often. They get daft and sentimental over every child comes their way, as if they were pets to be taken in and fed. Best try to forget, is my advice, and count your present blessings.

Your friend,

Ida

P.S. I return your note. Was that really Big Snow then, alive after all? You are a dark horse, Bella!

The Denniston Rose

WHEN JANET SCOBIE set out to look for her, Rose had been gone two months. Two weeks later Janet returned empty handed, but by then she had spread the story to everyone on the West Coast, give or take the odd bushed hunter or prospector. Well-bred charity ladies and tough old miners all knew her name and were mobilised to search for her. A heart-rending little song about Rose was often sung in the parlours of Westport, and a more ribald one around campfires. 'The Denniston Rose' she was, in the song, not Rose of Tralee any more:

> Oh, there's plenty of English Roses
> And there's Mary, the Rose of Tralee
> But the Denniston Rose was a Coaster —
> Wild and thorny and free.

She arrived on the Hill in a blizzard
No more than a tiny nipper
As tough as a boot our Rosie was
And as pretty as a slipper.

She was trickier than Donnelly;
Light-fingered too, they say
She'd winkle a shillun' out of your purse
While she bade you a sweet 'Good day'.

She killed a man with her own bare hands,
She started a miners' riot,
Then ran off to Hokitika
When she fancied a change of diet.

A law unto herself was Rose,
She came and went at will,
From north to south she travelled the Coast
But her heart was on the Hill.

Oh there's plenty of English Roses
And there's Mary, the Rose of Tralee
But the Denniston Rose was one of us
It's the Denniston Rose for me.

Railwaymen were on the lookout, and mine managers, store-keepers and farmers. The story, expanding with each telling, of the brave little girl who fought off a brutal attack, bringing down her giant assailant, appealed to rough Coaster hearts. Perhaps the story became so embroidered that no one recognised the real Rose. After the Hokitika report there was not one sighting. The

Denniston Rose became a myth.

Yet somehow the real Rose of Tralee, that tough little survivor, scarcely seven years old, found her way up through Greymouth and Westport, to Waimangaroa, through the gorge to Conn's Creek, up on the coal train to the railhead, without one single adult noticing.

Later it turned out several children saw and helped her.

'She sat with us in the playground at lunchtime.'

'Me and my brother let her sleep in Dad's barn.'

'She said it was a secret.'

'She said she had treasure.'

'She said she was Rose of Tralee . . . but it was the Denniston Rose all right.'

Rose trusted people her own age.

And the mother? Rose said she lost her mother, which officials took to mean the mother abandoned her. More likely, said Denniston people, Rose abandoned the mother. Said it with pride. No one on the Hill was going to question *that* sort of behaviour. Who at Denniston hadn't abandoned family at some stage or another? Rose, smarter than most, simply did it earlier. Rose was vintage Denniston material, they reckoned: born to live on the plateau and return to her mother town like a homing pigeon. Look at the way that little tiger came back!

THE sky bristled with stars that night, over a sharp new moon. Night shift were at it hammer and tongs, running wagons to and fro, brake-man and hook-man sending them down every four minutes, yard lit with the big new electric lamps.

Yet she still managed to slip in unnoticed! Con the Brake might have seen her if he'd been there. Con might have noticed a small curled and darker shadow in the bottom of an ascending wagon; might have sensed a pair of eyes peering over the rim as the hook-man uncoupled her and ran her down over the rails towards the Bins. Rose herself would surely have jumped out with a smile and a shout if Con had been there.

Or would she? Rose was always a mystery.

At any rate, no one noticed her arrival. Con was who knows where, still searching for Rose (or so Bella said). Mary Scobie, peering in poor lamplight, was sealing up the next batch of letters, some asking after Rose but more angled towards political matters. Totty and Tom Hanratty laughed with their guests in the parlour as a travelling salesman gave a humorous recitation. Michael, sent to bed for fidgeting, teased his sister by pretending to be the ghost of Billy Genesis. Up at Burnett's Face, Josiah and his boys, at band practice, blared out 'Lead Kindly Light' in Uncle Arnold's front room, Brennan taking cornet solo, while Eddie Carmichael, alone in his high office, added up long lines of rather pleasing figures, which Rose would have understood and enjoyed.

DOWN at the Camp, Bella Rasmussen is washing face and hands in preparation for an early, lonely bed. She recognises the cold lump in her stomach, the sour taste in her mouth as despair. Con has been gone too long. No word, no message. Her life has shrunk, closing in around her shoulders like a shroud. She looks out the little back window but the eyes are dull, disinterested. Then she frowns. Something is moving in the back yard. Too large for dog and too small for man. The thing is scrabbling behind Conrad the Sixth's tomb. She seizes the broom, flings open the door and shouts.

'Shoo! Get away! Off!'

The scrabbling stops. The dark shape slides from view. Something about the quick movement stops Bella in her tracks. Her heart thumps hugely, blocking breath and speech. Gently, not daring to trust eyes or instinct, she lowers the broom, prays for another sign. Someone is there. No ghost, no animal, but a small person who is waiting too. Who also waits for a sign.

Above them, the Incline rattles on through the night.

'Rose?' Bella whispers at last.

Rose stands. In her hands is a scratched wooden box. 'I can pay for my board,' she says in her tight clear voice, older, much older than any child's should be.

HISTORICAL NOTE

Readers may be interested in the real dates and events surrounding the period of this novel:

1879 October 24th declared a public holiday in Westport for the opening of the Denniston Incline.

1881 First women and children arrive on the Hill. Some will not go down again for twenty years.

The drive through Banbury Mine to Burnett's face is completed. Some 50,531 tons of coal produced.

First school opens, run by Miss Mary Elliot, mine manager's daughter.

Thirty colliers, recruited from England, arrive, via the Incline, at Denniston.

1883 New school built.

1884 The Track — a bridle path up to the plateau — opens.

John Lomas arrives on the Hill.

1884 September: Denniston Miners' Protection Society launched. John Lomas president.

1884 December: First miners' strike in New Zealand begins, led by John Lomas.

1885 March: Company sends eviction notices to thirty-one collier families. Many go to work at Koranui mine and support those at Denniston.

1885 June: Company capitulates. Returning miners drive scab labour off the Hill.

John Lomas was the real leader of the first miners' strike in New Zealand, at Denniston. Like the imaginary Josiah Scobie, he was a Methodist lay preacher, a collier and a unionist from England. He and his party of recruited English colliers were temporarily stranded in Nelson because the Westport Coal Company feared an outbreak of unionism. However, apart from these similarities, all personal and family details of Josiah Scobie are fictional.